Last of the Third
By John Lindholm

All the best,

To my family... Thank you for encouraging me to write.

1

June 8, 2013 - 2:03 AM

Shawn McMaster stood in the dairy section of Fresh Mart, choking the handle of his shopping cart with both hands. He inched the cart forward, then back. Forward, then back. Feet frozen in place. The florescent lights, high above pulsed, their buzz growing in Shawn's ears, as if a fleet of vacuum cleaners was attacking from above.

Aisle 6 would be the best escape route. What could Larry Last possibly want in Aisle 6 of a supermarket at two o'clock in the morning? Cake mix, frosting, peanut butter? In fact, why would Larry be in this supermarket at all, at any time of day, two hours from his home in Quail?

And yes, it was Larry Last, his grandfather's best friend and regular customer at McMaster's Restaurant. The way Larry gawked at Shawn's eyes, as if he had never seen brown eyes before. There was no question in Shawn's mind that Larry had recognized him, even though they hadn't seen each other in almost four years.

Nobody from Quail had seen Shawn in all that time. That was his game plan, and it was undefeated so far. At least until seven or eight minutes ago, when Shawn walked into the dusky front end of the supermarket, ball cap drawn low over his face. A face covered by his blond beard, scraggly from years of growth. Hands stuffed into the pockets of his jeans. Shoulders rolled forward. Six-foot-two curled down to five-foot-eleven.

Scott, the overnight clerk, was in there somewhere. He had packed up Shawn's weekly order, which he had just signed for in the dairy refrigerator. Scott had Shawn's credit card information. Scott had Shawn's confidence that he would not reveal his whereabouts. Who would he tell, anyway?

But the way Larry looked in his eyes. Shawn was spotted. Shawn was found. Shawn was sure Larry would head back to Quail and first thing in the morning, he would sprint into McMaster's Restaurant and tell Shawn's mom and dad that he had found their son. Shawn had to escape the supermarket, and return to the safety of his apartment, his comfortable couch, his reliable laptop and effortless email job. He didn't want to cross paths with Larry again.

Shawn breathed in two lungs worth of cold, milky, air then burned down the back aisle of the store. Toward Aisle 6. He pushed the groceries like a busboy pushing a cart of dirty dishes, tearing across the polished floor with a volatile mix of care and speed.

At Aisle 11, he slowed to peruse a freezer of Philadelphia Phillies Graham Slam Ice Cream.

"Just get out of here. What the hell is wrong with you?" He resumed, hustling along the back of the store, peeking to the right at the opening of each aisle. Was Larry down there? No. Where was Larry? Who knows?

Aisle 6. Finally. Shawn stopped short of the back entrance to Aisle 6, the nose of the cart poking out, like a child playing hide-and-seek; checking to see if it was safe to run to the home base. The aisle was empty. Clear all the way to the front. Even from the end of the aisle, from the back of the store, Shawn could see the registers, the front windows, and the front door. He started forward, careful not to make a sound.

He made it half-way to the front of the store when a voice found his ears. It chilled the sweat on his back.

"Hi, Shawn."

Slow as a second hand on a clock, Shawn turned to see who had spoken.

"Oh, hi, Scott," nodding his head to the cart, "thanks."

"No problem. How about those---"

But Shawn had already resumed racing for the front of the store. For the parking lot. His car. Safety.

But when he turned back, he nudged a jar of peanut butter, which was a hair too close to the edge of the shelf. The jar plummeted. Shawn saw exactly where it was going to hit the hard, linoleum floor. He imagined the sound of breaking glass, setting off fireworks and confetti worthy of the appearance of the store's millionth customer.

Or the reappearance of a scared twenty-two-year-old man.

Shawn pushed the cart with his left hand and lunged for the jar of peanut butter with his right hand, meeting the jar an inch above the spot on the floor where he knew it would hit. A shoestring catch, preserving the silence, protecting Shawn's secrecy.

He replaced the jar. No stop at the front opening of the aisle. From there, he could see his car in the parking lot. He could ignore anybody on either side of him. Blow right past them, pretending not to hear.

Through register lane nine. Passed the automatic door, and out into the parking lot. He tossed the groceries into the trunk, then drove toward the main road. Looked in the mirror. Nobody.

Shawn drove east on Farmview Road. Every so often, a store or a restaurant, ranch homes with long driveways and large front yards. He lowered the front windows and the early June air rushed in. Still cool, but the moist warmth of the coming summer tickled his beard, rustled the hair above his ear, eased a smile onto his face. Shawn breathed deeply, sucking June eighth deep into his lungs, then blowing it out. The whiz of the air and the loud croak of tree frogs soothed his racing mind. The stars bright, glinting flecks in the navy, overnight sky. There was no moonlight to guide his way. As he drove home, he thought of his couch, the familiar gray glow of his laptop screen, the soothing yellow light of his desk lamp.

2

Larry Schneider plopped into the front seat of his car, tossing down a plastic bag containing a half gallon of strawberry ice cream and a twenty-four count box of plastic spoons. He tried to insert the key into the ignition with his right hand, while fumbling to remove the box of spoons from the bag with his left.

Crap, he had forgotten the peanut butter. Oh well, toast and jelly for breakfast tomorrow. Or, he could run out first thing in the morning to the Eden Market in Quail which would be open at six. Or sometime next week. Whenever. Or never.

He removed a spoon from the box, then slid the business end of it into his mouth so he could use both hands to operate the tub of ice cream. As he rested the frosted container on his lap, his mind wandered to what he just saw.

A ghost. It must have been a ghost. Or maybe the people of Quail-- the people who called him Larry Last-- were right. He had gone crazy. With one hand on the body of the container, and the other ready to remove the lid, Larry tried to make sense of the last fifteen minutes.

He had been watching a minor league baseball game, a game that had taken eighteen innings to declare a winner, a few minutes before two in the morning. The walk-off home run was still on his mind, but more prominent in his memory was the taste of the strawberry ice cream cone he devoured. Sure, the doctor had said less sweets, more fruits and vegetables. But Larry didn't care anymore. What was the use? And hell, don't people argue whether a strawberry is a fruit or a vegetable anyway?

Eden Market in Quail was long closed, as was McMaster's Restaurant, so the twenty-four-hour Fresh Mart, minutes from the ballpark, was the only option. Larry

4

had shuffled in and crossed paths with what appeared to be a young man who had an unkempt beard and hair to match, both light brown or even blond. The hair was hidden by a baseball cap, as were the young man's eyes, until he lifted his head and the two late night shoppers made eye contact. It couldn't be true, and the only way to make sense of it was to call it a ghost, because the young man had the eyes of DJ McMaster, Larry's long time best friend. The eyes were large and white as baseballs, scared like a child who is convinced there is a monster under the bed, like DJ's were the last time Larry had seen him. The night DJ died.

But that was years ago. The tenth anniversary of DJ's death was less than two months away, as was the deadline of the mission DJ had given him that night. "I tried to save... the property... Muldoon knows," DJ had said, "never tell a soul what you are doing." DJ sent Larry on a nine year and ten-month scavenger hunt. Larry, the only person with the cryptic, garbled clues, and a torn piece of paper. After almost ten years of looking, Larry had turned up nothing.

Larry shoveled a spoonful of ice cream into his mouth, and turned on the radio. It was on the Phillies' station, but their game was long over. Overnight talk radio was on instead. A woman with a voice softer than whipped cream was talking about forgiveness and mindfulness.

More ice cream... Was it a ghost? Or a young man? Or both. With DJ's eyes? Another spoonful. Larry's bloated gut ached, and he wished it would explode and end it all. No more guilt about the McMaster property, or how he had treated his estranged wife, Cynthia.

Larry opened the windows and was caressed by the early morning air. He drifted into a lactic, sweet, semi-sleep trance.

The most difficult person to forgive is yourself; you are with that person all the time.

5

Larry raised his eyelids, but they were heavier than geometry textbooks. They slammed shut.

Accept and respect yourself; don't deny your screw ups, accept them, and move on.

He squirmed in his seat, the container of ice cream sliding down his thigh. His grip on the spoon loosened, and it skidded between the driver's seat and console, leaving behind a smear of pink ice cream. Larry's head tipped onto his right shoulder, his snore echoing in the empty parking lot.

To forgive is to set a prisoner free and discover that prisoner was you. Remember what the Buddha said, 'To understand everything is to forgive everything.' Forgive yourself, love yourself, and enjoy each and every moment of the rest of your life.

Larry slept for forty-five minutes until it hit him, with such force that it woke him from his late night snack coma, his knees, raising the half gallon of ice cream so high that it coated three inches of the steering wheel in pink. It wasn't a ghost with DJ's eyes. Or any young man. But it was a young man... with DJ's eyes.

Even though he had a terrible stomach ache, Larry felt more positive than he had in ages. Not miserable, almost happy. Free. And after years and years of guilt and sadness and searching, maybe things were looking up. Larry had finally found something: DJ McMaster's grandson, Shawn.

3

June 28, 2001 - 5:59 PM

Billy McMaster walked out of the dugout and toward home plate carrying a bat and a bucket of baseballs with his right hand and a Styrofoam cup of Diet Coke with his left. Shawn looked at his father from center field, fiddling with his glove, amazed at his dad's strength. Shawn could barely pick up that bucket of balls with both hands.

Ready to hit, Billy pointed up at the flag with the barrel of the bat. Shawn looked up to the top of the hill, above the dugout on the first base side, above the bleachers, even above the restaurant, and noted that the flag was hanging limp, like a dish towel on his mom's shoulder. He nodded at his father, ready to go. Billy told his son to always check the wind, especially as an outfielder. And certainly at McMaster's Field, which sat down in a bowl below the parking lot and McMaster's Restaurant. "It may feel calm down on the field, but who knows what's going on up in the sky," Billy had told him.

Billy launched the first fly ball toward Shawn, an easy one. Shawn had to travel two steps to his right and one back to catch it. Shawn stood in place for eight or ten seconds before the ball fell into his glove, his bare, throwing hand next to the glove, just in case.

"One hand! Just your glove hand," Billy called out to Shawn. Every other coach Shawn had ever played for telling him to use two hands whenever possible. But Shawn knew his father was smarter than those three guys put together. Shawn waved to tell his dad that he got the message. "You need that other hand, for balance, or to brace your fall."

Billy peppered fly balls, line drives, even some ground balls to Shawn in center field. Shawn made the correct decision on each ball. He arrived at the landing spot of the fly balls with seconds to spare. He caught every line drive that was possible, backing off or circling around the line drives he knew he couldn't catch, instead scooping them up on one or two bounces.

Shawn trotted in toward Billy after he had fielded two entire buckets of balls. Billy leaned on the bat with his right hand, his left leg crossed over his right. He almost had a smile on his face. "You've got a gift for that, son."

"For what?"

"Playing the outfield."

Shawn smiled, not feeling gifted. The ball gets hit, you run to where it is going, you catch it. Easy. Mom's ability to bake pies, dad's knack for flipping pancakes. Those were gifts.

"So tell me, do you see yourself playing baseball all the way through high school?"

"Yeah."

"College? Or straight to the pros?"

"Hmhmm," mumbled Shawn, looking over Billy's shoulder, up toward the restaurant, at his friends, Dusty and Chuck, who had just appeared out of the parking lot.

A full smile appeared on Billy's face. It felt, to Shawn, like school, the face the teacher gave him when he answered a question correctly.

"I think you can do it. You have this… life, and this gift. You should appreciate it, use it the best you can." The smile was gone from Billy's face.

Shawn nodded his head, but his full attention was with his buddies. They were waving at him, urging him to join them. It was Thursday evening, after all.

Billy continued talking, saying something about the big leagues, something about excellent fielding, something about working on hitting. Then, "Are you listening to me?"

"Yup, hitting. Work on hitting."

8

More words… Larry's going to be around more, batting practice, best ten-year-old outfielder in the county…

Billy was not done talking, but Shawn was done listening. He wanted one thing, to join his friends at the top of the bleachers, and head inside for ice cream pie.

"… And I'm really going to have to push you to get there. Are you ok with that?"

Shawn reestablished eye contact. "Absolutely. I'm going to head in, ok?"

"Let's go peewee, I'm starving!" called Dusty, lifting up his t-shirt, rubbing his bare belly.

Shawn charged up the bleacher steps above the first base dugout, taking two at a time.

"Here he comes, Dusty, the best outfielder in the state of Pennsylvania," said Chuck, speaking into his thumb as if it were a microphone. "Two steps at a time. Can you say… advanced?"

Dusty, also into his thumb, "There's nothing like this kid, Chuck. Look at how high he gets his knees. Look at the muscles in his chin. Look at how stupid his pants are. Truly one of a kind."

"Oh, shut up," said Shawn.

The three boys hustled into McMaster's Restaurant. They rushed back to the kitchen, where Shawn's mom, Greta, was waiting. The boys didn't even notice the two cute girls from school smiling at them. Tradition was tradition.

"Here you go, guys. Enjoy," said Greta, pointing to three empty pie crusts. Last summer, one overnight baking bonanza had left Greta with too many pie crusts. The three friends found them the next day, and did what any boys with access to a diner-style restaurant's supply of ice cream and fixings would do.

Shawn shouldered through the swinging kitchen door, careful not to damage or-- don't even think it-- drop

9

the pie crust on the ground. Dusty and Chuck followed. They each grabbed an ice cream scooper, dipped it in hot water, and filled their crusts with ice cream. Then, they topped them with personally crafted combinations of chocolate sauce, hot fudge, caramel sauce, peanut butter sauce, whipped cream, wet nuts, sprinkles and cherries.

They sat in a booth in the back corner of the restaurant, still not noticing the smiling girls, or any of the other patrons in the crowded restaurant.

Dusty motioned toward Shawn's pie with his spoon, "Your ice cream looks like Nancy Wilson!"

Chuck and Shawn examined Shawn's ice cream pie with wrinkled foreheads. Then simultaneously, recognition and understanding washed over their faces. Chuck also added a huge smile. Shawn blushed. Nancy was the first girl in class to... develop.

Chuck turned his long ice cream spoon into an announcer's microphone, doing his best radio voice, "Most definitely, Dusty. Two mounds of whipped cream, each topped with a cherry. A work of art."

The boys laughed and laughed. Then one of the smiling girls passed on the way to the restroom, and they laughed some more.

This was dinner, every Thursday evening for the boys, since that first ice cream pie night last summer. That night, Dusty had declared ice cream pie dinner every Thursday night for the rest of time.

Chuck had seconded the motion, stating, "Sounds like a plan."

Shawn said nothing, but nodded in agreement.

4

June 8, 2013 - 2:47 AM

Shawn hopped two steps at a time with the last of the groceries, nudging open the door of his apartment, which sat atop his employer's garage. He placed the last two shopping bags next to the other three on the table in the kitchenette. He dropped into a chair at the table and leaned back, his chest rising and falling.

So many times over the last four years, especially in the first year after he had disappeared, Shawn thought he had seen somebody from home, that somebody from Quail had found him. Every guy in a white t-shirt behind a counter was his dad. His mom's face appeared on the body of any woman in a Chunky Soup commercial. Dusty and Chuck showed up in pictures of ballplayers on ESPN.com and in fantasy baseball magazines. And every single young woman with red hair…

Shawn turned to the picture on the counter in the kitchen. The picture was in a frame, but the edges were worn and bent. A diagonal crease separated the upper right one-third of the picture from the rest. But the subject of the senior school picture was plain to see. Even through four years of handling and sunlight, the colors of the young woman popped. Strawberry blonde hair, more red than gold, but enough glistening highlights to turn heads. Eyes bluer than a thousand spring mornings. And more freckles than even a lover could count. Shawn thought he saw his girlfriend CeCe everywhere, but the red hair was never gold enough. The blue was never deep enough. And he didn't deserve for it to be her.

Shawn placed the container of 2% milk in the refrigerator, followed by two bottles of Coke. Six apples in the crisper, two bunches of bananas on the counter. The pasta went in the cabinet with the roll of paper towels and a small container of paper plates. The bags emptied quickly, and like the pile of Saturday early mornings that had come before, all the groceries found their place. Once a month, Scott would add some toiletries and other items that Shawn needed less frequently. Overnight pick up. Limited exposure, little chance of making new acquaintances, less chance of seeing somebody from his old life. It was a good system. It worked for Shawn.

He opened the sliding door and stepped onto the balcony on the back of his apartment. Shawn had spent hours and hours out there, both during the day and night. Nobody could see him there. The houses in the distance were blocked by a thicket of trees. Between the trees and Shawn's apartment was a creek that he would listen to with eyes closed. Mostly at night. Thinking. Between those trees and the houses was a baseball field.

"What the hell is wrong with you?" Shawn asked aloud, interrupting his line of thought. The plan didn't work that well tonight. "Larry Last looked you dead in the eye." Shawn had managed to stay hidden all this time. Four years. The amount of time he spent in high school. The amount of time he would have spent in college. Instead, he spent it here, on this balcony, in the apartment, or in the woods near the creek. Now what?

There was so much that he missed back in Quail. The warmth in his mom's hands as she grabbed his cheeks. Or the smell of her apple pie baking in the oven all hours of the day and night. His dad flipping pancakes while complaining about, well, just about anything. Even one of his lectures on the importance of balance in the batter's box. The sound of the breakfast crowd downstairs at the restaurant, waking him from sleep. The sight of a line drive off his bat, back through the middle for a base hit. Turning a double or a triple into an out by tracking a long fly ball. The penetrating power of CeCe's eyes, melting through all of Shawn's words, moods, clothes, strengths and fears, uncovering the real him.

Was any of that available to Shawn anymore? How could it be? How could it be after what he did? People don't forgive that kind of stuff. Not townspeople. Not even girlfriends or families. They rip pictures off walls. Burning them, or making them into dart boards. They, as a practice, don't use their names. It becomes part of the lore of a community. Utter the name "Shawn McMaster" within the Borough limits of Quail and lose your hot water for the entire winter. Or your family's pool pass for the summer.

Shawn imagined walking back into the restaurant after all these years. The conversational hum of dinner would halt. Forks and knives silenced. Cups tabled. Eyes on Shawn, then the male of each family would make eye contact and nod. They would kiss their children on the forehead, slip away from the table. Then close in. When they had Shawn down, his power bar barely visible, his avatar fading, blinking, CeCe would blast through the door and plunge her sword (which she had named Disappointment, or Sadness, or I've Moved On) right through the middle of his chest. Game over.

But this system *worked*. Sleep through the day, work at night, or the opposite. Two bottles of Coke, six apples per week. Free rent, just answer emails. A life of anonymity. Venture into the public to pick up groceries once a week. At two in the morning. Simple. Sure, there was a little glitch this time. But what other options were there?

Go back to Quail, back *home*. Go back to the restaurant, back to CeCe. Play baseball again. Such a strange feeling, longing to get back on the baseball field, to swing a bat, to catch a fly ball; but at the same time, those very thoughts made him sick to his stomach. What to do…

Shawn looked up to the overnight sky for a hint, a clue, an answer. But the moonless, silent sky simply stared back.

5

June 8, 2013 - 9:57 AM

Larry Last walked along the outfield fence of McMaster Field, peering in toward home plate. The away team was finishing their pre-game warm ups: ground balls to the infielders. A Teener League game was scheduled for ten in the morning, like every Saturday morning for the entire season. After a quick breakfast, Larry would venture down to the field, to poke around in the crowd, to wait for something, anything, to happen. He had the pre-game meeting, and two and a half innings before he was expected.

Larry passed behind the first base dugout and climbed the steps through the bleachers toward the restaurant. Several groups of fans waited for the game to start. One family decided, whether their team won or lost, that they would stay for lunch at McMaster's Restaurant. The husband of an elderly couple sitting behind them leaned forward, placed his hands on the outside shoulder of both the husband and wife of that family, and, nodding toward his wife, said they've been doing that on Saturday afternoons during the spring and summer for as long as they could remember.

Larry reached the top of the steps, stopped, and turned back toward the field. The sun warmed his face and burned his eyes, causing them to close. The smell of newly mown grass, baseball dirt, pancakes, and coffee arrested his attention. The chirping of birds, the cheering of teens, and the clapping of fans stroked his ears. In the distance, the hum of a lawn mower. Late spring warmth embraced his entire body. His shoulders relaxed, his hands opened. That moment was perfect.

Then, he remembered why he was here, and what he was planning on doing, and the deadline that was barreling forward like a spring storm. His eyes shot open, and the sun, again, stung his eyes. He turned, and continued on his way.

Larry shielded the right side of his face from the sun as he walked in the front door of the restaurant. Cool air greeted him; as well as the sounds of breakfast, the clinking of silverware against plates and coffee mugs, in one booth; a discussion about the final out in the Twilight game from the night before. At a table close by, plans for the summer being laid out by a mother, father and two bouncing elementary school-aged children, and at their normal booth by the side window, Dusty and Chuck fumbling for their spoons as soon as they saw Larry walk in.

"Stepping in," said Chuck into his spoon "is Larry Last. I can only imagine what it will be this morning."

Larry dropped onto his stool at the counter, turned and looked at the guys. Shook his head, forced a smile, then looked for Greta.

"I've been handed this..." said Dusty, into his own spoon, coffee trickling down the handle toward his fist, "For, get this, the *entire* Teener League season, Larry has had either three pancakes and two sausage links or scrambled eggs, bacon, and toast."

"Rye, Dusty?"

"Sourdough, Chuck."

"I've been hearing word of a tendency toward pancakes, sausage, and coffee on odd numbered, sunny Saturdays," said Chuck.

"Always coffee. Half and half. One pink packet."

"That's why you're the best color guy in the business."

"I'll take that as a high compliment, coming from an excellent man of color," said Dusty.

Greta hustled over. "What can I get you, Larry?" she asked, smiling, as she wiped the counter.

16

"Veggie omelet," Larry said, looking over his shoulder at the guys, lips pursed, eyebrows raised. "And coffee, cream, and sweetener."

By the way, saw your long lost son last night.

No.... You'll never guess who I ran into last night. Dusty's shoulders dropped. Chuck's spoon hit the table, but then, he looked at Dusty and said, "Coffee."

"Always coffee," said Dusty. The two toasted with their own coffee cups.

Larry could hear Billy's voice in the kitchen, louder when the door swung open as the waitresses kicked through. Billy always sounded like he had just been told that he had two inches of water in his basement, or that not only did he need new tires, but brakes as well.

Greta walked passed, raising her eyebrows and tipping her head toward the kitchen, toward the ray of sunshine in the sweaty white t-shirt who was finishing up Larry's breakfast. As she pushed through the swinging door, without looking up, she tapped the frame of a picture that was hanging on the wall. It was about as wide as an eight by ten, but not as long, cut out of a newspaper from sometime in two-thousand-eight. It had yellowed. The identity of the young outfielder would be difficult to make out if it weren't for the caption below, "Outfielder Shawn McMaster proudly shows the ball after a diving, game-ending catch."

To the right of that, with its top in perfect alignment, was a listing of the First Team All-League baseball players from the spring season of two-thousand-nine. Listed among two other outfielders was Shawn McMaster, Quail HS, highlighted in bright yellow. Below that, with its right side aligned with the picture above, and its bottom aligned with the picture to the left, was a four by six color photographs of Shawn and Billy, in matching McMaster's Restaurant twilight league uniforms. Billy, smiling, has his left hand on the small of Shawn's back.

Shawn, laughing, has his right hand on Billy's shoulder. The picture was taken before Shawn's one and only appearance in The Final Exam.

The kitchen door flew open, and out came an omelet trailed by Greta, who trailed a waitress carrying a tray above her head loaded with four full breakfast platters and sides. Her ability to deliver meals in this manner had become a featured attraction at McMaster's Restaurant. Patrons would over-order so they could see her fly out of the kitchen looking like the Statue of Liberty. Upon arrival at the table, she would lower her arm to the front of her body, waist high, pivoting her hand so her fingers were pointing toward her customers. Her left hand would deliver all the meals.

"CeCe," Larry said, with a nod of his head as she passed by.

"La-Ree" she replied, giving his name the same cadence as hers. She weaved to the other side of the restaurant hoisting her tray.

"Vegas has the line at seventeen and a half forkfuls," said Chuck.

"Taking the under," said Dusty, "our boy just has that look today."

Larry, ignoring the noise to his left, started in on his omelet. A boy approached the counter to Larry's right, and asked Greta for two scoops of strawberry ice cream in a cup. Larry looked over at the boy, "a little early for ice cream, isn't it?" he said with a grin.

"Early for ice cream or late for breakfast?" said Chuck.

"Time check, Chuck."

"Ten-o-nine."

"It is appropriate to order ice cream after 10:02 AM, and it's always appropriate to order breakfast," said Dusty.

"The ruling on the field... stands!" said Chuck.

CeCe, returning from her delivery, waved Greta off and reached for the ice cream scooper. The boy's mother, standing right behind him, tapped him on the shoulder and pointed her chin at CeCe.

"Oh... and 'Shawn McMaster'," said the boy.

Larry stopped his eleventh forkful mid-flight, and looked at the boy. Then CeCe. Then Greta, then around the restaurant.

Speaking of Shawn... ran into him, well, at least his eyes, at 2 o'clock this morning.

Larry still wasn't sure he saw what he thought he saw.

"Free scoop," said Greta, looking up from the counter she was wiping.

CeCe closed her eyes, longer than a blink, but not by much. Then, she opened them and dug into a tub of ice cream. She dug out a scoop of vanilla, then shook her head and flung it into a trash can. Then, she grabbed another ice cream scooper and leaned over the tub of strawberry, and dug in.

Larry had watched CeCe scoop ice cream a million times, but he could never get over how angry her face looked as she did it. And the muscles in her arms, flexing. Firing. Then, as soon as she was done, before the scooper could reach the bottom of the bucket of warm water, the smile on her face would return, and she would hand the ice cream to the customer. Today was no different. The boy told his mother that this was his favorite ice cream place as they walked toward the door.

"That's so stupid," said Billy, rumbling through the swinging door, meeting eyes with Greta, but only for a second.

"Alice thought it would be a good idea, to keep Shawn's name in the restaurant. Utter 'Shawn McMaster' and get a free scoop of ice cream."

"Your sister is a dummy."

"I suppose," said Greta, "but --"

19

"But nothing, Shawn can put his name in this restaurant by walking right through that door whenever he wants. You get letters from him, you know he's ok."

Larry looked on. *I know he's ok. At least I think I do.... Am I ok?*

Greta squeezed CeCe's shoulder on her way past, then stopped by her husband. "He's sort of a living legend, at least on this property. For these people. And you know darn well that we need a hero right about now."

"He's not --" Billy said, stopping himself. His face relaxed, the wrinkles around his eyes disappeared. "OK," OK."

Larry washed his last bit of egg down with his last mouthful of coffee. He spun around and squinted his eyes, scrutinizing the scoreboard. Top of the third, still a few minutes.

Dusty bounced his spoon on the lime green Formica table. "How many?"

"I didn't count; you were supposed to count."

"I'm the color guy, I don't count."

"I do play-by-play."

"Who the hell counts?"

"We all count," said Chuck, his voice softening. "We're all children of the Lord."

"Oh God."

"Exactly."

It was time. Larry looked at Greta. Billy had retreated to the kitchen.

I saw Shawn last night, he was taller, and he had a long beard, and DJ's eyes!

Larry turned out the door. He called himself a wimp, among other things. Two outs in the top of the third. He walked over toward the flagpole, and looked at the three plaques in the mulch. The one farthest to the right was DJ's. He leaned in for a closer look, resting his hand on the electrical box. Or what DJ had called the fuse box. It was really neither. It was simply a weather proof storage container for the old scoreboard operating system. It hadn't been used in years, except for folks to lean on. The lock on it had become a little rusted, which dripped on DJ's plaque. Larry knelt down and wiped it off.

Below, the third out was recorded and the teams began to switch places. Larry looked down at the field, at the scoreboard, at DJ's plaque and the other two, then back at the restaurant. He stood up and marched back in. Greta was standing at a table just inside the door.

Larry opened his mouth, but nothing came out. Greta looked at the table, she was wiping, at the dishes she was clearing, at Larry, and back at the table again. Larry stared at her, mouth agape.

"Yes?" asked Greta, then paused. "Larry?"

"Tell Billy... Tell Billy, um," Larry said. He looked out the window, then back at Greta. "Tell Billy the omelet was good."

Greta studied Larry, "OK."

Larry flew out the door, again called himself all the names he called himself before, and headed for the bleacher steps. As he walked, he could see the housing developments, Muldoon's developments, on both sides of the McMaster property. House, after house, after house; deck, after deck, after deck; lawn, after lawn, after lawn. But in the middle, right in front of him, a ballgame. And right behind him, a family restaurant.

He grabbed the railing as he reached the top of the steps, bracing his first step. He descended two more steps, sliding his hand down the sun-warmed railing, then stopped. He looked around and called out, "Last of the third!"

6

May 2, 2008 - 10:43 PM

"Seriously? On YouTube?" asked Shawn.

"I'm telling you, it's there," said Chuck, hands on his computer keyboard, eyes on the screen.

"I can't believe it."

"Bro, you ran three miles to make that catch. My mom said she overheard a bunch of people talking about it… at the barber," said Dusty.

"Really?" asked Chuck. "Your mom goes to a barber?"

"Beauty salon, whatever. The point is, you're like a cult hero or something. Captain Quail!"

"Please," said Shawn, looking over Chuck's shoulder. He made the catch that everybody is talking about, but he had never seen it himself, at least not in the third person.

"Here it is," said Chuck. "I'm going to download it and send it in to ESPN. They put stuff like this on all the time."

Shawn shook his head. ESPN wouldn't show this. Some high school kid catching a fly ball in left field. Very deep left field, but still. "Just press play."

The camera was behind the first base dugout, up on a small hill. Not at McMaster Field, but at Quail High School. The clip started with the pitcher on the right hand side of the screen, the batter on the left. The pitch is thrown and everybody oohs and wows when the batter clobbers the pitch. The camera turns to focus on left field. Shawn pivots to the right and takes off. There is an outfield fence that starts in right field, and extends to center field, but then turns to hug the back of Quail High School. Shawn is

22

sprinting through a left field that turns into the right field on the softball field.

The camera was far enough away that the ball could be seen flying through the air toward the softball field and Shawn tracing a ruler-straight path to where he thinks the ball will land. Somebody near the camera says, "That's a home run. He can *walk* around the bases. It's going to be on the softball field."

Shawn is closing in on the right fielder, her back turned. Shawn whizzes past her, maybe taking half a step to his right to avoid her. Three sprinting strides later, Shawn reaches up and stabs the ball out of the air, then tumbles to the ground right behind the second baseman on the softball field.

Exclamations erupt around the camera. "What?" "No way!" "I've never seen anything like that!" The camera zooms in on Shawn, who is running back toward the infield, carrying the ball in his bare hand. He has a small grin on his face. He tosses the ball to the field umpire.

Dusty and Chuck looked at each other, saying nothing. Shawn stared at the screen. Then Dusty, eyes wide, grabbed Chuck's arm and said, "send it to ESPN."

7

June 10, 2013 - 9:31 AM

He sliced the banana right down the middle, long ways, like he was fixing to carve out two canoes. But the knife didn't scoop out the insides, it spread peanut butter along both halves of the fruit. A bowl of cereal, Rice Crispies, with 2% milk. And a huge glass of water. This was Shawn's breakfast. Every day.

Now, breakfast would sometimes be at seven or eight AM, with the rest of the world. Or four-thirty in the morning, or eleven forty-five AM, or two in the afternoon. Whenever Shawn woke up. It didn't matter, the emails would always be there. The only rule was that he had to answer them within 24 hours of receipt. No problem. Thanks for ordering your software electronically. Use the link below to download your update, or respond to this email to order a physical copy. Automatic. Free room and board, *and* a salary for doing that. Like stealing second base when the pitcher was in the windup.

Shawn balanced the cereal bowl and plate with the banana halves in one hand, and carried the glass of water in the other as he approached the kitchenette table. One of the peanut butter banana boats rolled over as he placed his breakfast down, leaving some peanut butter on the table.

"What the hell is wrong with you?" Shawn said aloud, raising and lowering his shoulders with a puff of air through his nose. He shook his head as he picked up the banana with his fingertips and placed it back on his plate as if he were topping a house of cards with the final level.

Shawn reached over toward the window and pulled back the blinds far enough to see into the backyard. Some of the darkness leaked out of his apartment and visible was the kitchen with its empty sink and cleaned counter tops, unstained stove top; refrigerator door, free of pictures, tests, Christmas cards, shopping lists or fingerprints.

As he ate breakfast, Shawn looked out the window, past the trees, beyond the brook, at the baseball field. He could only see a sliver. Part of the earthy infield dirt, some of the green outfield grass. Then, he saw Larry Last, his aging face and his eyes. Those eyes peering right into his. Shawn shook his head and walked his empty bowl, plate and glass to the dishwasher.

Answer some emails, push-ups and crunches, a shower, then the rest of the emails. Shawn sat down at his small desk in the corner of the living room and opened his laptop. Entered the password, and the light from his home screen lit up the rest of the living room. Couch with two pillows in either end. Coffee table with one book: a picture history of the covered bridges of Pennsylvania. No drink coasters, no water stains. No newspaper from three days ago, or even yesterday, or this morning. A television, off, with two remote controls sitting right below it on the entertainment center. No dust, no red mailer from Netflix leaning up against the side of the TV. No tipped over pizza box holding a week old slice. Vacuum tracks were visible on the carpet.

Shawn opened his email. Stacey from the Detroit office. 'Our laptops are saying we need version 2.6.4....' He read the email, looking past it, through his computer screen, like he was trying to see one of those magic pictures from when he was a kid. The kind where if you looked at it just right, the picture jumped off the page. But the email turned into Larry's face, then his mom's. Then CeCe's. Shawn clicked send, rubbed his eyes, and went to his sent folder to see if he had sent Stacey the correct information. Somehow he did, and the same for eight other emails.

Then, Shawn dropped onto the floor of his bedroom and started his push-ups. One hundred and fifty today. His six-foot two-inch frame flat like a diving board, pulsing up and down. Still in great shape, strong and lean. His arms, back, and core tiring as he pumped, fighting images of Larry, his mom, his dad, and CeCe. Blinking them from his mind.

Shawn rolled over, onto his back, and repeatedly picked his shoulders up off the floor and put them back down. Over and over, until his core burned, until his abs cramped up. On the ceiling, a mental video of his last at bat rolled. Shawn turned his head to the side, squeezing his eyes shut, refusing to look. He wiggled his head, grinding his hair into the carpet.

Shawn allowed the summer, midday sun into the bathroom through horizontal blinds as he stripped for his shower. The warm water pelted his back as he stood there. Shawn dried himself in the shower and stepped out onto the rug in the middle of the bathroom floor. He replaced the towel on the rack, smoothed it so it would dry evenly.

Thirty-two emails, twenty-nine from before, three since he had been in the shower. *Thank you :)* from Stacey in Detroit. More laptops in need of 2.6.4. Afternoon sun through the sliver in the blinds, yellowing the kitchen and staining the television screen. Shawn walked to the window and looked out past the trees and beyond the brook to the baseball field. He looked at the sliver of infield and outfield and felt a knot in his stomach.

"What the hell is wrong with you?" he said.

Shawn sat down at the table in the kitchenette, his hair and beard still moist from his shower. He ached to sit in the restaurant, eat a burger with the guys, drink coffee with mom, talk baseball with dad. Even hitting. And to hold CeCe's hand, to touch her smooth face-- riddled with freckles-- once again. To jog out to left field, turn in toward home plate, and hope for a batted ball. He longed for it all.

He longed for it to be four years ago, the way it used to be, before his last game. But that wasn't possible. Nothing that happened over the last four years was reversible. Nothing. Not a single thing Shawn could do about it.

But he could keep the blinds drawn. He could send emails. Watch baseball on TV. Do push-ups and crunches. He could do sprints in the back yard in the muggy summer night. He couldn't go back to 2009. This current plan would have to do. It had been. Sure, there was a glitch, but he was still here. Nobody had come to find him. Nobody had found his apartment. Larry had stumbled across him, but nothing had changed.

Shawn stood and walked toward his laptop. He would stick to his plan. It was safe. For everybody. He hadn't hurt anybody in almost four years. He flipped the screen up, clicked on the password box and typed *celine9easter*.

8

April 28, 2006 - 4:32 PM
Billy McMaster's son stepped into the left handed batter's box, a number "9" dominating the back of his jersey. *"Let's go Shawn"* and *"Go get 'em nines"* called from mouths in the dugout. Some from the crowd. Billy didn't say anything, didn't hear anything either. But he did notice that Shawn was a little too far away from the plate. Billy removed his hands from his pockets and rubbed them together in front of his chest. He took a more athletic stance with his feet as he focused all his attention on his son up to bat.

The first pitch was up high, ball one. "Ok, ok," said Billy, under his breath. Some fans around Billy yelled *Good eye! Good eye, Shawn!*

The next pitch was a fastball down the middle. Shawn hit a high, foul pop up behind the third base dugout, out of play.

Billy paced. Stuffed his hands back in his pocket. Pulled them out again. *Step to the pitcher, Shawn. Like we worked on. Like you did in the batting cage.* The next pitch was a curve-ball that rode too far inside. Shawn skipped out-of-the-way. Ball two.

Shawn stepped out of the box and turned toward his dugout, and squinting against the sinking spring sun, looked at Billy for just a moment. Billy nodded his head, forcing his hands back into his pockets. A couple words of advice to Shawn would be very helpful right now. Just a reminder of what they worked on. He was hitting the ball so well in the batting cage, stepping straight toward the machine. He could do it here too. Shawn was a remarkable fielder, and he could be a tremendous hitter also. *Shawn, do what we worked on. Don't waste your gift.* But Billy

28

thought of Greta's advice: Just watch, just cheer for the boy.

The next pitch was a fastball, a little up, but right down the middle. Shawn strode, stepping his front foot, his right foot, toward the second baseman, and swung. The timing was right, but he missed. Billy couldn't resist. He had to help, he knew how good Shawn could be. He had to say something, a quick reminder. That's all. It would help. Billy knew it would help.

"Stride straight, Shawn! Straight!"

Shawn's shoulders tensed as his father's words bounced off his back. Then, he stepped back into the box, allowing his shoulders to drop. *Two-two count, Shawn. You know he's coming for you. He's doesn't want to go to a full count.*

The next pitch was another fastball, this one on the inside half of the plate. Shawn didn't swing. After the ump called strike three, he dropped his head, turned, and walked back to the dugout.

9

June 13, 2013 - 8:03 PM

He turned off the lights in his bedroom. Closed the blinds as well. It felt like the right thing to do, given what was about to happen. He had seen younger folks in a movie do it in several different positions, none of which looked comfortable. Well, *they* looked comfortable, but Larry certainly wouldn't be, legs contorted, bent in ways they shouldn't bend. He had heard of places people go to do this type of thing, but he would try this all by himself first. And on his back, definitely on his back. He was old, on his way out really, and this was new. But for some reason Larry had gotten into his head that he needed to do this. To enjoy his last years. Months. Days.

He breathed in. Held it for a three count—because five felt too long---then blew out. In, out. In, out. Larry listened to his breathing. He counted his breaths. And after forty-five seconds, Larry's mind cleared.

Dark. Empty. Silent. Like an early evening nap, deep in winter.

Then, at exhale number seventeen, a poster that was hung on the back of the door in the men's faculty bathroom at Quail High School, where Larry taught math for thirty-six years, interrupted his meditation.

"Beauty is truth, truth is beauty." Yates. Or was it Keats?

Didn't matter. Larry was out of bed, out of his bedroom, out of his house and in his car before he stopped to think exactly what he was doing, and how he was going to do it. Regardless, he would tell Greta and Billy, together, or separately if he had to, that he was almost certain he saw their son at two in the morning at a grocery store.

Mostly dessert eaters at the McMaster's Restaurant at this time of night. Ice cream, pie, and coffee. A couple of tables of college-aged kids, home for summer break, catching up with high school friends, enjoying a late dinner. Some regulars too.

Larry slipped past Dusty and Chuck, avoided eye contact, waited for the verbal assault on the way he walked, or the shoes that he was wearing, or what he had for dinner, or what kind of beer had caused that belly, or when was the last time he lay with a member of the opposite sex. "Or the same sex," Dusty would occasionally say. "I'm ok with that," Chuck would reply. "Why wouldn't I be?" Dusty would ask.

But they didn't notice him that night. They let Larry make it to the counter with all quadrants of his self-esteem intact. Dusty and Chuck were in the middle of an argument. The only people they treated worse than Larry, were each other.

"Eight team play-off system. It's that simple, dope," said Chuck.

"OK, butt-breath, so the regular season is meaningless? Great plan."

"It's meaningful. More meaningful than ever…"

As best he could, Larry blocked Chuck and Dusty from his mind. One of them actually had a college degree, he couldn't remember which. Difficult to tell. They both worked at the local flooring concern, which was also where they worked in high school. They started in the back, hauling boxes of laminate hardwood flooring and such, but had made their way to the sales floor. Rather good at it, Larry had to admit.

Focus. Task at hand. This moment. Larry turned his attention to the kitchen door. Greta or Billy, or both, would come swinging through at any moment. Truth. Just tell the truth and go from there.

But what if Greta, upon hearing that her one and only son had been located, latched onto Larry's shirt and sobbed. Or what if Billy, cloaked in a sweaty white t-shirt,

31

asked Larry "why didn't you tell us sooner?" bashing his head into the counter with each passing syllable. And Christ, CeCe over there. From the other side of the restaurant, she could get quite a head of steam. She was built like a linebacker, or a strong safety at the least. She could potentially knock him off his stool, onto the floor, spine severed from the rest of him like a cocktail shrimp.

Stop. Refocus. Smell the coffee, hear the forks on plates, feel the smooth, clean counter top. Greta pushed through the swinging door, drying her dry hands on a towel.

"The usual?" she asked, without looking at Larry. She reached for a coffee mug.

"Yes, I would like that," Larry said. Bees bounced around in his mouth, forcing at his lips, but he kept his mouth shut.

Greta slid the coffee cup in front of him. Tiny pitcher of milk and one pink packet. Larry opened his mouth again, but only "thanks" snuck out. Greta zipped back into the kitchen, and Billy snuck out through the swinging door. Larry was lost in his coffee, and didn't see him.

"Gonna stick your face into that?"

Larry snapped awake, looked at Billy, then considered that option. Second, maybe even third degree burns to his face. Straight to the hospital, unable to speak. Unable to broach the topic of Shawn. When Billy and Greta came to visit, with his face wrapped in gauze, Larry could tell them. How angry could you get at a mummy?

Be present. "No, but I am going to enjoy every last drop of it."

Billy squinted, turning his head so his right eye was pointed at Larry. Billy looked at him as if he were trying to figure out if Larry had gotten a haircut, or new glasses, or burned his cheeks with the coffee. "OK, old man, you do that." Billy filled a glass with diet soda.

Larry lifted his coffee cup, and opened his mouth. But neither the rim of the coffee cup, nor the creamy brown liquid sloshing around inside the cup went in. "I saw Shawn last night."

"What did you say to me?" said Billy, with both hands on the counter in front of Larry, leaning in.

"Last night, in a supermarket out by Deerfield, I think I saw Shawn," said Larry, sitting erect on his stool.

"You saw him, or you think you saw him?"

"I—"

"Because there is a huge difference." Billy did not lean back, and a bead of sweat ran from his hairline, across his temple, and down toward his jawbone.

"It was about two in the morning---"

"Geez, Larry, two in the morning. I'm supposed to believe that you saw Shawn at two in the morning, in a supermarket, two hours away from here?"

Larry peered into his cup. The coffee was the color of light brown hair. "His hair was long, he had a beard, and he was wearing a baseball cap pulled low."

"My word, Larry. That could be anybody," Billy said, leaning in. Then, with less volume, but more feeling, "And for the love of God, don't let Greta hear any of this crazy crap." Billy backed away, leaning on the counter in front of the soda machine. "She still expects Shawn to come waltzing in here one day."

"Shawn? Who expects Shawn to come waltzing in here," said Greta, who had just stepped out of the kitchen. She held a dish towel in her hands. "Me?"

Billy crossed his arms and looked at the floor. Larry twirled a spoon in circles, creating a whirlpool in his coffee cup. Now what? Greta needed to-- deserved to-- know what Larry saw. He could tell her exactly what he had told Billy. She would believe him. Instead, he said nothing and looked at Billy, watching for his next move.

"Go ahead, tell her what you told me," said Billy, his elbow wedged on his belly, his hand propped under his chin.

Greta looked at Larry. The expression on her face bounced between hope and fear, excitement and doubt. He had no choice. "I think I saw Shawn last night." Larry told Greta about the supermarket and the beard and everything else. Greta's expression settled on doubt, laced with more than a pinch of disappointment, like a poker player who needed a particular card to finish a straight, but was sure he wouldn't get it.

"But it wasn't any of that that made me think it was Shawn. This person was bigger than Shawn, more muscular."

Billy and Greta stared at Larry. They said nothing, they didn't interrupt, they didn't move. Just stared at Larry.

"It was his eyes. At first I thought…" Larry stopped, laughed, played with his coffee.

"What, Larry, thought what?" said Greta.

"At first I thought it was DJ's eyes. I thought it was DJ. A young DJ. Which, of course, is ridiculous."

Billy and Greta looked at each other, then walked toward Larry. Both of their faces had softened. Their hips touched as they stood in front of him. It was no secret amongst the three of them, or anybody else close to the McMaster's, that Shawn had DJ's eyes.

Billy put his arm around Greta's waist, then turned to her and said, "Holy crap, Larry found Shawn, who would have---"

A loud clang behind them attracted all of their attention. CeCe's eyes darted between the three of their faces, her mouth hanging wide open. An ice cream scoop lay on the floor at her feet.

34

10

June 14, 2013 - 5:21 AM

Greta watched as CeCe stretched and reached to lower the blinds on the front window of the restaurant. The sun would be rising over the left field before long, blinding anybody facing that direction. CeCe's white skirt crept up her toned thighs as she moved. Not an ounce of fat. Greta's legs used to be slender, but now time had added layers to her hips and thighs. And she was sure her butt never looked anywhere close to as good as CeCe's.

"Sit. Eat," Greta said, pointing at oatmeal topped with sliced peaches and a large glass of orange juice. It was CeCe's favorite breakfast. Greta wanted to make sure CeCe was all right. She could still see the look on CeCe's face from the night before, when Larry gave his news. The wide eyes of shock, and a smile of relief. But finally, a curled mouth of concern. Greta knew Shawn's disappearance was especially hard on CeCe. They had become so close, boyfriend and girlfriend, but also best friends. They had just left for college together. CeCe hadn't told her, but Greta knew that CeCe had bounced around for the past four years. She had seen her with this guy and that, but never any one of them for very long. There was more to the story, but Greta had never found out what, and was afraid to ask.

CeCe slid into the booth in front of her breakfast. Ordinarily Greta would wipe down the already immaculate tables, one last time before unlocking the front door, and CeCe would yell across the empty restaurant to her, telling her what she had done the night before, or where she was headed after work, or what she was doing that weekend. Greta kept tabs on how CeCe was doing. The talks were helpful for Greta as well. Keeping close to CeCe was a happy reminder of Shawn.

But today, Greta dropped onto the bench seat across from CeCe. This conversation shouldn't be shouted across the restaurant, even an empty one. "I didn't see that coming. Did you?" Greta asked, kneading a dishtowel in her hands.

"No, not at all. I mean, Larry. Larry Last. I never expected that *he* would be the one to find Shawn, youknowwhatImean?"

"I suppose, but don't count out old Larry. Despite what people think, his marble isn't empty yet."

The corners of CeCe's mouth curled upward, and she dunked a peach under the surface of the oatmeal. A few rays of sunlight slipped past the blinds and made an orange streak on the floor. The sound of plates and metal utensils rattled around in the kitchen. The scent of brewed coffee filled the restaurant.

Greta gazed upon CeCe's face as CeCe stared over her shoulder. What colors. The orangey freckles on milky skin, hair a strawberry blonde that couldn't be found in the beauty aisle, and eyes so blue that even the Lord himself must be impressed with his own handiwork. But not even that layer of natural makeup could cover up the emptiness that CeCe was hiding. Greta knew she had tried to fill the void, but nothing, nobody, could replace Shawn. Greta leaned in, her ribs pressed against the table. "You ok?"

"Just a little tired."

"Celine Easter, you know what I am asking you."

CeCe leaned against the seat back and looked at her oatmeal, looked at the table, looked at her nails, and didn't look at Greta. Until Greta reached across and grabbed her hands. CeCe's eyes filled with tears as they looked in Greta's.

"I miss him too. So much," said Greta.

"It's like... he became a fable, or a legend, or something. Every now and then somebody would see the pictures," CeCe pointed at the wall behind the counter, "and tell a story about a catch Shawn made, or how fast he was. It's almost like a remembrance... of him, not really

36

him. Like freakin' Santa Claus, youknowwhatImean?"
CeCe laughed through her tears.

"I do," said Greta, but she was lying. Greta remembered everything about Shawn, like she had seen him that very morning. CeCe and Shawn were in love, she knew that, but she was Shawn's *mother*. That connection could never be compromised. Hat or no hat, beard or no beard, Greta remembered him. No, *knew* him. "So what now?"

"I don't know, I mean, I need time. To think. Four years is a long time. What if he's forgotten me?"

"CeCe, *please*," said Greta, shaking her head.

"What if there is someone else?"

Greta lowered her voice. "One time, shortly before you guys left for college, Shawn told me, 'CeCe is the one, mom. She's the only one who gets me.'" At the time, that felt like a kick in the stomach, but Greta had learned that her connection to Shawn was unquestioned. Shawn was talking about people out in the big, scary world.

"That was a long time ago. We're twenty-two now," CeCe said, inspecting a peach as if she were at a crime scene looking for fingerprints. "I have so many questions. So many things to think about. To figure out. Time," CeCe said, watching oatmeal drop from her spoon back into the bowl. "I need time."

Greta closed her eyes and shook her head. She slid out of the booth and stood over CeCe. "Tonight," Greta said, "I am going to see him."

11

CeCe almost pulled a muscle in her neck as she jerked her head backwards. Greta was going to see Shawn. Tonight. She watched Greta walk to the front of the restaurant and unlock the door. Five-thirty, time to open. CeCe started to shovel the oatmeal into her mouth.

"Take your time," Greta said with a smile. A your-new-boyfriend-just-walked-into-the-hallway kind of smile. There was always tension, or some sort of secret, or *something*, that Billy and Greta kept between them. They weren't angry with each other. In fact, each office session of discussion, file searching, and drawer slamming ended with Billy and Greta hugging, or holding hands. Or Greta kissing Billy on the forehead, then scurrying out to the dining area, leaving Billy in the back to cool off, catch his breath, and wipe the sweat off his forehead.

CeCe balanced her empty juice glass in her empty bowl and headed toward the kitchen, checking her phone with her other hand. Nothing. Who the heck would text her at five in the morning? Shawn used to, to ask if she had combed her hair yet, or if she was having milk with her cereal. But she knew he was checking in, psyching himself up for a day of school, making sure she would be there to help him through. Greta's mention of Shawn must have sent her back in time, triggering her check-your-phone reflex.

Greta was standing by the dishwasher. "Thank you, dear," she said, as CeCe handed her the dirty dishes.

"Are you sure it's a good idea?"

"You practically licked the bowl clean, but we still need to wash it," said Greta, avoiding CeCe's glance.

CeCe grabbed Greta's arm above the elbow. "You know what I mean."

38

"I do know what you mean. And I do think it's a good idea. Shawn needs to come home, and if I have to go get him, then that's the way it will have to be, I suppose."

"Do you even know where to go?"

"Right where Larry said he was, right when Larry said he was there."

"What if it's not him, or if he's not there?"

"Then, I'll do some early morning grocery shopping." Greta took both of CeCe's shoulders in her hands. "Billy would never admit it, but we need Shawn back here. I need him back here. He's my son. This has gone on long enough, don't you think?"

There was a purpose in Greta's eyes that CeCe hadn't seen for a long time. Even if she disagreed with Greta, even if she thought seeing Shawn after all this time might hurt more than help, there was no way she could say that now. "Yes, it has."

"We can play 'what-if' roulette all day long if you like, but sometimes you just have to take the cow by the horns," Greta said with a wink, then scurried out of the kitchen, drying her hands on her apron.

CeCe leaned against the counter, closed her eyes and breathed in the scent of warm peach pie that Greta had, no doubt, been baking since the early hours of the morning. They were lined up next to the grill, on top of the oven, and anywhere else there was room.

Billy emerged from the stairwell that connected the McMaster's living quarters upstairs to the kitchen of the restaurant downstairs. He looked at all the pies and shook his head. Then, he grabbed an apron, and as he tied it around his back, said, "Find room for all these damn pies. Throw away any that are left from yesterday."

"You got it, Mr. M," CeCe said to Billy's back as he headed out of the swinging door. She headed over to the counter next to the grill, and balanced as many pies on her left hand and arm as she could.

12

June 14, 2013 - 8:32 AM

Albert Muldoon stopped halfway up the stairs to the McMaster's Restaurant and looked over the ball field. While it was the location of several triumphs, netting him many trophies, he was hoping to win the biggest trophy of all today: the property itself. He pulled a crisply folded handkerchief from his pocket and wiped the sweat from his forehead; in the process, stretching damp gray hair toward his temple. He tucked the handkerchief in his shirt pocket and smoothed his tie from top to bottom.

Houses and a mega-store replacing a ball field and restaurant property. That's what Muldoon saw as he looked down below. Far off to the left was one of his housing developments, meandering ways and sweeping lanes, lined with houses like a necklace of pearls dropped on the Pennsylvania countryside. Houses with well-manicured lawns and beds re-planted and re-mulched each spring. Houses with families on the go, with minivans, with busy schedules, with only minutes to wolf down dinner, but always with time to say goodnight, to say I love you; knowing that tomorrow, they would wake up and face another day together.

Far off to the right was another of Muldoon's housing developments. Townhouses with single-car garages, common lawns and gardens maintained by the Association, and an enormous gazebo in the middle with its own, permanent gas grill for any and all to use. Birthdays, holidays, any day. Happy, affordable, family living close to the farming country of central Pennsylvania.

Two successful, profitable housing developments, severed by the McMaster's property, which held its ground in between like the strong man fighting two challengers at a mid-summer county fair. Muldoon shaded his eyes as he looked over the field, from dugout to dugout, left field to right. The sun, watching over center field, stung his eyes and made him sweat under his shirt. He turned and hustled up the stairs, north of 70 years old, but still light on his feet. *Today is the day*, he thought, as he pulled open the front door of the restaurant, cool air finding all the gaps in his shirt. They couldn't possibly turn down this offer.

"Well, good morning, Greta," Muldoon said with a smile, sliding onto a counter seat.

"Al," said Greta, making eye contact only for a second, continuing to wipe the already-clean counter top.

"I'll have a cup of coffee and a conversation with your husband."

The kitchen door swung open and Billy came hustling out, a ring of sweat around the neck of his t-shirt, darkening half of the McMaster's Restaurant logo on his chest. "Coffee's on the menu, I'm not."

"I just want to talk, Billy."

"We have nothing to talk about."

"I think we do."

Billy leaned most of his body weight on his crossed forearms, on the counter top directly in front of Muldoon. "I'm not selling," Billy whispered through his teeth, only loud enough for Muldoon to hear.

"Do you understand how much money I am offering you? Enough to take care of generations and generations of McMasters," Muldoon said, palms up and hands extended in front of him, just below Billy's face. It was no exaggeration.

Billy stood up and motioned to the patrons in the restaurant. "The people of Quail have loved this place for a hundred years, and will for a hundred more." His voice trailed off on the last few words, and Greta, rubbing Billy's arm, took over.

"Al, we appreciate the offer, we really do," Greta said, "but we simply aren't interested." She waved her arm out in front of her. "We're baseball and restaurant folks, I suppose," she continued, pointing to the pictures behind the cash register.

Muldoon crept forward on his chair, leaning toward the McMasters on both elbows. "OK, this is my final offer. Same dollar figure as before, but also 2% of all future profits on the land." He slapped the breast of his jacket, "I have the paperwork right here, sign it and the money and 2% are yours. Forever, nobody will ever able to take it away from you." This offer made Muldoon nervous, that 2% would gnaw on his profits. But the McMaster property would be his. Sometimes there were prices one had to pay.

Greta filled a small glass with orange juice, handed it to CeCe, then looked at Billy. Billy was leaning against the back counter, arms crossed tightly on his chest, a single stream of sweat creeping from his hairline toward his cheek. He locked eyes with Greta for, what to Muldoon seemed, an eternity. Muldoon forgot the question for a moment, forgot the property and the houses and the mega-store and the money. Instead, he watched the McMasters, who only looked at each other for a second, two at the most. In their gaze, he saw an unspoken understanding, commitment, and love. The bedrock of a happy family. The McMasters nodded at each other, tiny but decisive, and they both looked at Muldoon.

Muldoon woke from his dream as Billy extended his hand. The restaurant noises left Muldoon's ears and everybody, but Billy and Greta left his eyes. It was as if they were alone on the hilltop, the restaurant gone, the ball field gone, bulldozers moving in as Muldoon pulled the papers and pen from his jacket's inner pocket. Billy took the papers, but instead got a pen from CeCe. He smoothed the papers in front of Muldoon, which caught a drop of his sweat. Billy flipped through them, stopping only long enough to read a sentence or two on each page.

Greta watched her husband as she dried a coffee cup with a dish towel. CeCe hadn't been around for the conversation, but she peered over Greta's shoulder, looking at the stack of papers on the counter. Billy dropped the pen toward the last page of the packet. The veins in his hand flared as he pushed the pen across the document. The enormous N and O almost ripping the paper as he carved them, sliding the document back toward Muldoon.

The smile on Muldoon's face evaporated like that of a hitter whose screaming line drive was just stabbed by the pitcher. "I don't know what else I can do for you people, I gave you a chance." His words were quiet, only CeCe and the McMasters could hear them, but suddenly everybody in the restaurant took notice of his presence. He leaned across the counter toward the McMasters, all but on his tippy toes. "I don't care what I have to do, I'll get this property from you, and I'll bulldoze this restaurant and pour the damn concrete on the pitcher's mound myself!"

Muldoon stormed out the front door and turned a hard left toward the side of the building. He flipped through his keys and found the one he was looking for as he descended the stairs along the side of McMaster's restaurant. He inserted the key in the deadbolt on the door that said "Winner's Locker Room" in fading red paint. He ripped passed all the lockers and threw himself into the chair behind the desk at the back end of the room, rattling the pictures and a key hanging on the wall behind him.

Muldoon thought about Billy and Greta, the love they shared, enduring through two unthinkable losses, the latest being Shawn's disappearance. Then, he thought of his own parents, who suffered an untimely death, which turned out to be a blessing and a relief. His family life had always been a mess, which contrasted with the all-American

43

lifestyle of the McMasters, and built up a healthy jealously, laced with shards of hatred.

Muldoon put his feet up on the desk. His desk. Well, not technically, but he yearned to make the desk his. The whole McMaster property. The restaurant and the ball field, which he would then demolish, and put up the crowning jewel of his property chain, Muldoon Manor. Eight estate homes on eight sprawling pieces of land. On top of the hill, but hidden from the Manor by giant Blue Spruce pine trees (transplanted from Canada), would be Al's Everything Shop. Kmart, Walmart, Target, all rolled into one. But better. The convenience of modern family living, happy modern family living.

Muldoon knew Billy would never accept any offer for the McMaster property, not after he turned down that sweetheart deal today. But he would wrestle it from Billy somehow. Perhaps a trip to see District Justice Cahill was in order? Maybe he could leverage the McMasters out. Maybe Billy and Greta had forgotten to pay their taxes, their trash bill, or forgotten to cross a "t" or dot an "i."

One thing was for sure, The Muldoons would beat McMaster's over-matched team for the 10th year in a row. At the very least, he could hold on to the winner's locker room for one more year.

13

Shawn scampered through the drizzle, through the mostly empty parking lot toward the automatic door of the supermarket. Clouds overhead, but to the west it was clearing, some stars riding a dry breeze. There was his car, two cars owned by Scott and whoever else was working the overnight shift, and maybe one other car around the corner. Shawn couldn't tell as he shielded his face from the mist.

He stopped inside the door to dry his feet on the rug. Shawn had slipped on the linoleum floor of his elementary school one day after recess. The grass was wet from an overnight rain. Shoes slick with grass clippings and water. His feet flew out from under him as he sped into the hallway. His classmates hovered over, laughing, as he tried to catch his breath. Shawn swore that would never happen again.

No classmates here, though. Or shoppers. Nobody to the left or to the right or in front of him. Shawn combed his scraggly beard with his fingers as he planned his route. Aisle 6 again. Why not? Shawn would bury his head in his cell phone and walk to the back of the store, sign the receipt, then double back down Aisle 6 and out. No problem. What could go wrong?

Everything could go wrong. Larry could be back, or maybe his entire 4th grade class, shopping for baking needs, or sugar free pancake syrup, or evaporated milk, or whatever else is in Aisle 6. Shawn looked down. He was still standing on the rug just beyond the automatic door, which was still open. "What the hell is wrong with you?" Shawn said, a little louder than he had intended. *There's nobody here*, he thought. He pulled out his cell phone and started walking. He slid sideways through a display of flowers with tiny American flags buried in the soil, red, white and blue Mylar balloons, cakes with patriotic icing,

45

one with frosting designed like exploding fireworks. Shawn negotiated the area as if he designed that section of the store, didn't rub up against a plant, didn't knock over a flag, didn't jostle a cake, and didn't notice any of it because his eyes were on the rest of the store. Watching the end of each aisle, peering back at the automatic door, checking the checkout aisles. He even looked at the ceiling once, then giggled.

Aisle 2, Aisle 3. Past each end cap, two-for-one salad dressing, marshmallows, chocolate bars, graham crackers, sports drink for eighty-eight cents per bottle. Aisle 4. Shawn peered down each aisle, empty except for a vision of Larry, or a long lost elementary school classmate, or a home plate umpire, or Paul Jackson, the last pitcher he ever faced as a hitter.

Shawn shook his head as if here were trying to clear the screen of an etch a sketch, then focused on his phone. Weather, check the weather. Clearing, sunny and warm tomorrow. Maybe a sprint through the woods tonight. Or maybe a talk with his imaginary friend from second grade. Shawn had taken a step past Aisle 6 when he looked up from his phone. He stopped and scanned the store from one end to the other. All the way to the dairy aisle, and back to produce. To the automatic door. Nobody. Even Scott was nowhere to be found. Shawn looked at his phone. Five after two.

Aisle 6 was empty. Shawn glided toward the back of the store toward a person back by the meats. He rubbed his thumb up and down the front of his cell phone as he walked, eyeballing the Phillies' box score from earlier that evening; Shawn's eyes were pulled off Jimmy Rollins' batting line when his left arm bumped into something. A cardboard dump displaying semi-sweet morsels jumped out of nowhere, now teetering. Shawn tucked his phone into the pocket of his khaki cargo shorts, steadied the display with his left hand, and caught a pack of chocolate chips

46

about a foot off the ground with his right hand. No more hiding in the box scores.

He reached the back end of Aisle 6 without plowing over any cardboard displays or setting off any chain-reaction product spills. He turned left toward the milk refrigerator, but a movement from his right side caught his attention. Scott's co-worker, Missy (Michelle?) was leaning into the meat container, stocking for the next day. She had to be about Shawn's age, maybe a year or two younger. She turned toward Shawn, saw him standing there, smiled, and went back to work, reaching for another package of Italian sausage. She removed the blonde hair from her left cheek, revealing skin smooth like a bath of milk. She stretched her long, thin, left leg back as she leaned into the cooler. Shawn stood still, staring at the girls' face. They didn't know each other, had never met. She was tall, maybe just a few inches shorter than he was. Blonde hair. Too blonde. Skin too pale. Arms and legs too thin. By the time Missy or Michelle had reached for another package of sausage, Shawn was gliding toward the dairy refrigerator.

Shawn picked up the chilled pen and signed the receipt, balancing them both atop a gallon of milk. He pushed his grocery cart out toward the store with his left hand, closing the milk refrigerator with his right. Back toward Aisle 6. Missy or Michelle was still working in the meat department, but Shawn looked down the aisles, toward the front of the store. Make it to the parking lot, out into the darkness.

Aisle 6, empty. He rolled the cart over the shadowed floor, a foot to the left of the semi-sweets, charged toward the front of the store, the automatic door, the trunk of his car. There was nobody at the registers, nobody shopping for tiny American flags or patriotic cakes, nobody sizing up tomatoes, checking their ripeness.

Ginger snaps; now four boxes for five dollars. What a deal. They were always his favorite, eating Greta's off the aluminum foil-covered baking tray before they cooled. He used his hands like bookends, flanking four consecutive boxes, squeezing them in mid-air. He glanced toward the registers. Nobody. How would he pay? Who would he pay? The self-check aisle was closed from nine pm until eight am. He didn't want to go find Scott, didn't want to spend any more time here than he had to. He put the boxes back where they came from, then was up righted by a voice from behind him.

"Mine are better."

The four syllables wrapped him in a warm blanket and spun him around. "Mom," was all Shawn could get out before emotion caught up in his throat and tears wet his beard. The two hugged, and for a moment, Shawn forgot about everything, about the past four years, about the terrible thing he had done the last time he played baseball, about living alone; and instead, closed his eyes. He was in the living room, above McMaster's Restaurant, McMaster Field out the window and down below.

Then, he opened his eyes and he was hugging his mother, who he hadn't seen in four years, with whom his only communication had been through letters he sent her, telling her he was fine. No return address. "I'm sorry," he said, looking toward Greta through tear-filled eyes.

"Sorry? Sorry for what?"

"For what I did. For running away. For not coming back, or telling you where I was."

Greta took Shawn's shoulders in her hands. "What happened, happened. It's over now."

"It's over now? Something like *that* is never over." How could it be over? Shawn replayed the incident in his mind every day. And every day, each and every day, he reinvented the hatred of himself.

"Shawny, come home. Just come home. We can go right now."

"Home? I can't go back there."

48

"Of course you can!"

Shawn looked at Greta. Down at Greta. Farther down than he remembered. Had she shrunk? One thing was for sure, she looked older. There was more gray in her hair than he remembered. And her eyes. Wrinkled in the corners. Tired. "Mom, I can't go back there. Nobody wants me back there."

"Of course they do!"

"No, they don't. How could they? And, dad. Dad certainly doesn't."

Greta stepped toward Shawn again, grabbing his hairy chin with her hand. "Listen to me, of all people, daddy wants you home."

"Whatever."

"You know he could never say it, or show it. But I know. I know he misses you, he misses watching you play baseball. So do I. We all do."

Ha! Play baseball. "Mom, I can't play---" said Shawn, looking at his shoes.

"Don't worry about baseball right now. Just come home," said Greta, grabbing his beard just below his chin. "Look at me, right here in the eye. Nobody is mad at you."

"Mom, how---"

"Nobody is mad at you. Would I lie? Would I have you come home like a ram to slaughter?"

A small laugh escaped through Shawn's nose. She may have been a little older, but Greta hadn't changed.

Shawn shifted his weight to his right foot, then back to the left. "Um?"

Greta flashed a quick smile. "Yes. CeCe is still around. She just wants you to come home."

"Is she… does she have?"

"Look, that's a discussion for you and her to have. But she would really like you to come home. Let me leave it at that."

One of the Shawn's shopping bags shifted. An apple fell out, and bumped its way to the bottom of the cart. Mother and son both looked at it. The lights of a car from the parking lot flashed through the front window, then turned off. Shawn pulled his mother close, resting his chin on her shoulder. "I really am sorry," he whispered in her ear.

"I know you are, honey. Just come home."

"I'll think about it, ok?"

"OK, that's fair enough. Would it be too much to give me your phone number?"

Shawn deleted his old cell phone number from Greta's phone and added his new one. The two embraced one last time.

As he walked away, Shawn turned and said, "So, I guess that *was* Larry the other night?"

"Indeed it was, and I will never be able to thank him enough."

14

September 30, 2009 - 8:48 PM

The confidence, maybe cockiness, that Shawn felt during his first at-bat was all but gone. Paul Jackson took care of that with a blazing fastball on the inside corner, followed by a back door slider that Shawn could only wave at, lucky to get the bat in the way of it, and hit a weak grounder back to the mound. It was his first ever at-bat in the Final Exam, a game he had watched so many times from the crowd, from the dugout, and even from the scoreboard operator's room atop the restaurant. But now he was eighteen and eligible to play.

He stood in the batter's box and looked out at the Al's Everything defense. What happened to all the holes he saw in the infield? All the green gaps in the outfield? All the spaces had closed up, the infielders huge, Jackson enormous atop the mound. And he had to be closer than last time. Had to be.

Shawn inhaled through his nose, filling his lungs. Blew it out through his mouth. That was all ridiculous. Nothing had changed. *Just see the ball out of his hand. Just see the ball. That's it. Relax.*

"You suck, McMaster!" shouted a fan from behind the Al's Everything dugout. Laughter. Clapping.

From the lefty batter's box, Shawn could look up and see who yelled, see who was laughing, clapping. But he resisted. Instead, he peered out at Jackson. His shoulders now tensed, hands squeezing the handle of the bat. Tighter and tighter. Just see the ball. See the ball. See the ball.

Jackson rocked and fired the first pitch of the at-bat. A fastball exploded out of his right hand and screamed toward the inside corner. Shawn barely even saw it. Was that a golf ball, he just threw? He never strode, not one fiber of brain matter thought about swinging. Strike one.

51

"Yeah, Shawny, that's a baseball. Ever seen one before? Oh wait, you didn't even see that one, did you?" Laughter, clapping.

The catcher tossed the ball back to Jackson. Shawn didn't move his feet, and inched his hands back onto his shoulder. Breathing shallow. Moist palms slipping on the grip. Such a hot evening for the end of September. So hot.

From the dugout behind him, Billy said, "step out, take a breath, ok?"

15

Greta watched her son walk away. No question in her mind that he had grown. Maybe a couple of inches since the last time she had seen him, hugged him. And that hair. Oh, and that beard. She wanted to tell him to shave that thing off his face and go get a haircut. It was as though he had gone from age eighteen to forty. She longed to see the face of the handsome young man he had become. The twenty-two-year-old who should be sitting with her in the restaurant planning the next moves of his adult life. Talking baseball with Billy. Joking with Dusty and Chuck. Holding hands with CeCe.

She reached a hand out in his direction, and started to call his name, but, taking her own advice, stopped after two letters. And anyway, the squeal of the wobbly wheel on his cart drowned out her voice. Shawn kept walking, pushing his cart, until he exited the front of the store, walking out of her sight.

She wanted to follow him, but didn't. She wanted to run out into the parking lot and jot down his license plate number, or follow him to find out where he lived. So tempting to call in a few big, strong guys and kidnap him back home. Can somebody be kidnapped back home? Better, can somebody be transformed from their adult life back to their eighteen-year-old life, turning back time by four years. No, Greta had wished, hoped and prayed to turn back time, not four years or even four minutes. Four seconds would have more than done it.

Push it down.

She would have to wait. She would have to hope that Shawn would come home. Can't force these things. Can't make anybody do anything. That much she had learned. If he were meant to come back home, he would come back home.

Greta walked out of the air conditioned supermarket and out into the humid night. The rain had stopped and the sky was clearing. She watched Shawn drive away, his hair and beard flowing and flopping around his face. His car halted, if only for a second, at the stop sign at the exit of the supermarket parking lot. He turned left and drove into the night.

As the tears she'd been holding back flooded her cheeks, movement to her rear caught her attention. It was a car she recognized. It snapped and splashed across the parking lot, faster than a car could ever drive through a parking lot in the middle of the day. It didn't stop at the stop sign at the exit of the supermarket. It made a screeching left onto the main road and only the growl of its engine escaped the darkness.

16

December 13, 2007 - 10:13 PM

"Give me your hand, at least I can keep that warm," said Shawn, taking CeCe's much smaller hand into his, then pocketing them both into his varsity baseball jacket.

It was a little uncomfortable for CeCe, a funny angle for her arm to rest, but it was worth it. "We have to pick out a *really* good one, my mom is very picky about her tree."

"Then, we better walk down every row and look at everyone,"

CeCe knew there was a basketball game Shawn wanted to watch, and it was going to start in a few minutes. But here he was, walking around, reaching past the branches of this tree and that, grabbing the trunk, giving them a shake. "What are you doing, Charlie Brown?"

"Well," said Shawn, turning toward her, squinting his eyes as if he were trying to hold back years and years of Christmas tree knowledge, "I have no idea."

CeCe grinned. This guy who she had just met over the summer, so quiet in his everyday life. So focused on the baseball field. But so silly. No, open, *honest* with her. CeCe thought there was something wrong with him after they met, after her first few days working at his family's restaurant. He would look at her, for seconds that felt like minutes, not saying a word. Was he freaked out by her thousands of freckles? Her flaming head of hair? Shoulder muscles?

But when they were alone, just the two of them, he opened up like an umbrella in a windstorm. He had so much to say, and she was honored that he saved it all for her.

"It needs to be full. Lots of branches and stuff. But not too.... Tall. KnowwhatImean?" CeCe explained.

Shawn shook his head slowly, as if he were calculating the perfect height to width ratio right there in the dark of mid-December. "Short and fat, like your friend's mom."

"Shawn! She has some sort of problem."

"Eats too much?"

"No! Some sort of chemical --- wait, now look at this one."

"Oh, good eye, girl. And look, it's in the reduced price section. $49 instead of $79. Winner-winner-chicken-dinner."

"What the heck does that mean?" CeCe asked through a foggy laugh that floated through the late fall chill. There was so much to love about Shawn. But he was already focused on getting that tree from where it was to the back of Dusty's father's truck. He dragged it right past her, and the smell of pine filled her nose. She picked up the thick stump at the base of the tree to help Shawn, and her hands got sticky with sap. They tossed the tree into the back of the truck and walked over to pay.

"$79," said the guy behind the table. He had to be in his fifties. Or at *least* a few years older than CeCe's mom. He was wearing a red and black flannel jacket, and his breath smelled of alcohol. The scent turned her stomach.

"I think that one is $49," said Shawn, pointing to the sign.

"I said $79."

"See the empty space, that's where we got it from. Clearly, in the $49 section," said Shawn, the volume of his voice increasing.

"Look, this is my lot, and I say that tree is $79," said the man, pointing to a sign that said Earl's Xmas Trees.

Shawn didn't say a word, slapped two twenties and a ten on the table. Earl shook his head and waved his fingers at Shawn, asking for more money. Shawn reached down, gripped the edge of the table and flipped it over. The transformation of Shawn from discussion to action was like a rayon shirt exposed to a flame. The table landed on Earl's feet, bruising his shins on the way past. "Keep the change," Shawn said as he took CeCe by the hand and led her back to the truck.

CeCe could feel Shawn's quick pulse through his hand. He looked down at her with a nervous grin.

There was so much to love about Shawn....

17

A crescent moon slipped past thinning clouds as Shawn drove home from the supermarket, from the meeting with his mother. Was he met, or was he waylaid? Either way, it was the push he needed to consider a return to Quail.

Rain water sprayed off his tires, sprinkling the fingers on his left hand, which tapped the door panel as he drove. The scent of rain and worms and grass and mud, of summer, poured in through the windows. Usually he would keep his windows closed, the air conditioning on, the radio down low or even off. Stay hidden. Get home. Lock the door.

But he had been found. Could he believe Mom? Could he believe that he had been forgiven, that Quail had moved on? Or was a mother telling her son anything to get him back home. Four years in solitude had dulled his sensitivities. He wasn't sure.

Shawn made a right hand turn and the moon, clouds gone, hung like a badge on a navy blue uniformed chest. He knew that Greta wanted to grab him by the ears and drag him home, but held herself back. He was glad she didn't, but maybe that would be the easiest way to get the job done.

All the talk of the restaurant and his family and CeCe... made him want to go back. Certainly he couldn't play ball again, but that was just one part of his life on the McMaster property. A big one, no doubt. But only one.

Go back. Why not? What's the worst that could happen? If the children of Quail banded together and beat him with long, ice cream sundae spoons, or if all the mothers of the borough encircle and whipped him with dampened dish towels, or if CeCe, feigning affection, caresses his bearded cheeks, then yanks his chin into her rising knee, or at a hint of any such thing, he could leave.

Drive back to his apartment. Lock the door. Answer some emails. Do some push-ups. Press play again on his simple adult life.

But the thought of staying in hiding sucked, especially after talking to his mother, after hearing stories of what and who he had left behind. That settled it. In the next few days, he would travel back to Quail, look over McMaster Field, walk into McMaster's Restaurant and face whatever music the people of Quail would play for him.

Headlights appeared in his rear view mirror, bleaching out more and more of it each second. A low rumble increased in volume, the roar of the car's engine, an engine he had heard before. Countless times. With the car just feet behind Shawn's, the howl of the engine drowned out Shawn's radio, and vibrated his windshield.

Instead of turning right to go to his apartment, Shawn turned left. Maybe it wasn't who he thought it was. Who would have sent Bubby after him anyway? Certainly not Greta, she hated him for all the punishment he had inflicted on Shawn as they grew up in school together. Neither would Larry. Nobody would. Bubby Tate was good for two things: driving the fastest car in Quail and driving the loudest car in Quail.

Bubby turned left behind Shawn, and followed closely. So as Shawn approached the next intersection, he put on his right turn signal, but turned left. Bubby did the same. There was no question in Shawn's mind, Bubby was tailing him.

It made sense. Word had spread around the restaurant. Somebody overheard Larry, who, at some point, must have told Greta about running into Shawn, and about where Shawn was. This was the welcoming party. Or the unwelcoming party.

A car passed in the other direction, and as its lights shined into Bubby's car, Shawn could see that there were two people inside. One to watch Shawn, the other to drive. One to hold Shawn, the other to punch.

Shawn had to laugh. Return to Quail. What was he thinking?

Shawn closed his windows, turned off his radio, and popped on the air conditioning. There a few quick turns he could make up ahead. A left, followed by a sharp right. Then a dirt road that paralleled a creek. Shawn had found it within his first year of hiding out, late at night, out for a drive, not yet used to holing up in an apartment for days at a time. It would be his best chance to lose Bubby and his accomplice. There was no way he could outrun him; he would have to outsmart him.

No turn signal. Shawn ripped the left turn, then spun the wheel back right. Lights off, crawling along the creek, waiting for the sound of Bubby's car to fade away. Hoping it didn't pull up behind him.

Shawn cracked his window, held his breath, dipped his chin to his chest, and listened.

His rear-view mirror stopped vibrating. The cry of Bubby's engine faded away. Shawn had escaped again.

Return to Quail. "What the hell is wrong with you?"

18

Shawn sat at a square table in the back corner of a twenty-four-hour coffee house. He was wearing shorts and a t-shirt that he found in the trunk of his car. After sleeping in his car for two nights and a sink-shower in the men's room of a Turkey Hill convenience store, he had had enough of his own stink. Luckily, he had enough change in the ashtray of his car to run a washer and dryer at the Suds-O-Matic Laundromat and enough guts to ask a woman for a capful of detergent to wash his current outfit. He sipped at a small paper cup of some coffee and mostly milk that was slipped into a cardboard hot beverage sleeve advertising the Fall Fling Wine Tasting Event at the local Catholic Church. And somehow, he was much happier and more relaxed than the guy at the next table.

The man looked to be about forty, or at least a few years younger than his own father. He wore a shirt and tie, the top button of the shirt unbuttoned and the tie loosened and leaning to the left. Sleeves rolled up. Two empty mugs behind his laptop. Two elbows on the table, two hands running through his thinning brown hair. He looked as if he were ready to type the first paragraph of a horror novel, murderer's manifesto, or suicide note. He noticed Shawn noticing him. "Don't open your own business. Ever," he said to Shawn.

"I'll keep that in mind," said Shawn, shrinking into his shirt, hiding under his hat. He had managed to be invisible for more than forty-eight hours. He forgot that other people could see him. Apparently, the man wanted to vent.

"I have this software business. I supply a few companies, big companies, with this program I created for inventory and crap. It's great. Brilliant really, but I am

61

constantly updating and upgrading it, so I send out electronic upgrades. And each one is specific to the department of the company." The man stopped for a sip of coffee and came up empty.

Shawn nodded and sipped and listened.

"I'm a programmer, not an emailer. Not a secretary. I don't have the time or patience for this. There is a good chance my program goes big time. But I don't have the money to pay a staff yet. These emails need to go out. Every day, all day. I promise to get the upgrades and updates to the different departments within twenty-four hours of the request. I'm up all night, I barely sleep anymore." Again he lifted an empty mug.

Shawn thought for a moment. He could send emails. He just needed enough money to get by. Oh, and a place to live. Shawn from four days ago would never have been so bold, but sleeping-in-his-car Shawn suddenly had some stones. "So, basically, you need somebody to deal with all the emails and electronic updates or whatever?"

"Yeah."

"But you can't afford to pay anybody?"

"I can afford a little. But not enough for somebody to come work full time."

"This might be a lucky day for both of us."

The man lowered his laptop screen and looked at Shawn. "I'm listening."

"I can send an email. Lots of them. Train me to do the crap you don't have time to do."

"I can't pay you that much---"

"Pay me what you can," said Shawn, "but there's one thing."

The man raised his eyebrows, sign language for, "I'm listening."

"I need a place to live."

The man stood up, picked up his laptop, walked over to Shawn's table, and sat down. "You're right, this is our lucky day," he reached out his hand toward Shawn, "My name is Steve."

19

"We need to do something about this now," said Chuck.

Dusty reached for his fork. "Now?"

"Now."

"Now… I'm going to eat this fuggin' waffle."

Larry watched the two bicker from his seat at the counter. It was like they were married. Argue, argue, argue, then go out onto the field and turn double plays like they invented ground balls, baseball gloves, and underhand tosses.

"Do you understand, my little moron, that if we don't pay this bill soon, they will turn off our electricity?" asked Chuck.

Dusty dragged a wedge of waffle through the syrup on his plate. "They gonna turn it off today?"

"No."

"Is their office open today?"

"No," said Chuck, leaning back in his chair.

"Then, you eat your fluffy little omelet, I'll finish my waffle, and on Monday morning you can use those lovely green eyes and your stupid English degree to look up their number and give them a call."

"I generally hate you, and I hate you even more when you're right," said Chuck, reaching for his fork and knife.

"Calm down, your chocolate shell is going to melt."

"In your mouth, not in your hands."

"Dream on," said Dusty, and the two smiled at each other, then continued eating.

Larry spun his chair to look outside. The two Teener league teams that would play this morning were crowded around the flagpole, caps off, heads bowed, listening to the National Anthem. Larry waited for the song to end, for the teams to put their hats back on and march down to the field. He pushed through the front door and walked out toward the flagpole and monuments. The sun was evaporating last night's rain off the walkway, and the grass wet his shoes as he crossed toward the plaques. It was the top of the first below as he looked down at all the Wilbur Ryan McMasters. Rain water dripped off the electrical box, off the old lock, and onto DJ's plaque. Larry stood still and watched the water drip. He listened to the sounds of teenage boys cheering, parents and friends clapping, the ting of the ball off an aluminum bat, and the cry of the home plate umpire. Warm sun on the side of his face.

'To understand everything is to forgive everything.'
Forgive yourself, love yourself, and enjoy each and every moment of the rest of your life.

Breathe in, then out. In. Out.

Larry resisted the temptation to swipe his hand over the top of the electrical box. The rainwater was fine right where it was. It would drip off, or evaporate, in its own time. Instead, he walked toward the field, toward the top of the bleachers on the first base side. Down below, the batter laced a line drive into center field for a base hit. The clap of a man sitting off by himself toward right field caught Larry's attention. "Atta boy," called the man. Larry walked toward him.

"If it isn't Larry Schneider," said District Judge Buddy Cahill, extending an enormous paw toward Larry. "Or what is it they are calling you now-a-days? Larry Last?" asked Cahill, pulling his glasses low on his nose, smiling at Larry. The glasses looked like a child's toy in his hand.

"You know people, they make mountains out of molehills," said Larry, easing onto the bleacher next to Cahill. Cahill was at least forty years past his high school state championship season as a heavyweight wrestler, but he still had the size and presence. Larry was ready to confess to several crimes he didn't commit.

"I'd say it's been a year since we've spoken, Larry. Asking about the McMaster property."

"That's right," Larry looked over his shoulder, then leaned in. "You haven't mentioned October first to anyone, have you?" He jerked back in his seat, as if he had realized his head was in a lion's mouth.

"I said I wouldn't, and I haven't. And it hasn't been easy. Muldoon is in and out of the office all the time." Cahill pivoted toward Larry.

"What does he know?"

"Only that he would pay a king's ransom for the McMaster property," said Cahill, removing his glasses. "My question, Larry Last, is what do you know?"

"I know what DJ told me, as he lay there dying," Larry forced his mouth into a frown.

"OK, cut the crazy crap there, Faulkner. I know the good people of Quail figure you went nutso when you watched your buddy die, but I know better. What did he really tell you."

Cahill grew as he turned his attention away from the game and focused on Larry's face. Larry felt like a lightweight stepping into the circle with the former state champion. He exhaled, then looked Cahill right in the eye. "He told me he tried to save the property, and that Muldoon knew, that's all." Larry uncrossed his legs, then re-crossed them in the other direction. He rubbed his mouth with his right hand.

"Knew what?"

"I'm not sure."

Cahill stared at Larry, rubbing his temples. The vibration of his cell phone distracted him. He picked it up off the bleacher, looked at it, then put it right back down.

"All I can tell you is that you have until October first to produce the deed, a will, a letter from DJ. Hell, I'll take a bequeathment written in chocolate sauce on a used place mat from the restaurant if it says he willed the property to Billy and Greta," Cahill looked down at the field, then back at Larry, "and DJ signed it."

"There's no paperwork, no nothing," Larry said, counting the fingers on his right hand.

"Well, find something. Anything. The McMaster property is the last bit of good, old Quail we have left. I don't want to have to put it up for public auction, but if I don't have something concrete by the beginning of October, I have no choice."

Larry nodded his head as he shook Cahill's hand again. He stood up and walked away, to take a seat right behind home plate. He could take in the game from there with perfect perspective. He rubbed the laminated, triangular sheet of paper in his left breast pocket. He would wait for the bottom of the third.

20

The breeze shook the bottom of the curtain in Shawn's bedroom, rippling it from bottom to top. He had opened the window before lying down to sleep, but his eyes hadn't closed for more than a minute at a time. He sat up on the edge of his bed facing the window, wearing mesh shorts and a t-shirt. Moonlight filled the backyard, lit up the trees like dusk, floated on the surface of the creek like a raft.

Shawn looked passed his window, around and through the curtain rustling in the breeze. He looked over the creek and passed the trees onto the baseball field. For minutes he stared, the curtain moving in and out of sight. He stood up and stepped toward the window. Four in the morning. Emails populating his in-box. Two dishes in the sink from dinner. He threw the curtain over his shoulder and leaned his hands on the sill. He listened to the creek rush by, water hitting rock. The white blotch on the surface stayed in one place. Breathing, pulsing. But not progressing with the water. Shawn shut the window and flopped back into bed.

Three minutes on his back. His mother's face appeared on the ceiling. Shawn pressed his closed eyes with his fingertips. Opened his eyes, then closed them again. Paul Jackson, standing on the mound. Growing, grinning. Shawn opened his eyes and smoothed his beard from his mustache to his Adam's apple. He rolled onto his side, back to the window, back to the trees and the creek and ball field. A deep breath in through his nose and out through his mouth. He closed his eyes. His dad standing behind the counter at the restaurant, white t-shirt, white apron, eyes locked on Shawn, the right corner of his mouth curled.

"What the hell is wrong with you?" Shawn yelled, flipping his legs onto the floor. He grabbed two socks out of the bottom drawer and pulled them onto his feet. Then, he pulled a pair of sneakers out from under his bed, without looking, and slipped them on. He walked through his dark room and into the living room, which was dimly lit through the sliding glass window. Out the door, down the steps and into the backyard. Shawn stopped by the one hundred yard track he had cleared, with Steve's permission, to run sprints. He looked down the path he had sprinted so many times, his footsteps exploding on the dirt in the quiet overnight.

But tonight, he continued passed the track and hopped across the creek on three protruding rocks, wetting only the right toe of his sneaker. He stood on the other side of the water, now able to see more of the baseball field than he ever had. He crept toward it, as if he was stepping onto a lake that he wasn't sure was frozen. With each step, the field grew. The entire outfield appeared, then the infield, then the backstop and the dugouts. Shawn walked onto the field in foul territory, down the right field line. His shoes moistened with each step in the dewy grass. He stopped with his toes inches away from the right field foul line.

It had been four years since Shawn stood on a baseball field. Four years since he did the unthinkable, four years since he stormed off, out of Quail, out of the lives of his family and friends, and CeCe. Shawn removed his hands from his pockets and looked up. The moon had shrunk since he left his room, and it had moved higher in the sky. He took a deep breath, closed his eyes. So many things had happened in the last week. Twice, twice! He was discovered at the supermarket. Perhaps his patterned life was starting to fail him. Maybe it was time for something different.

He blew out the breath and stepped over the foul line, into fair territory, onto the field.

"Come talk to me," said a voice.

Shawn leapt into an athletic position, as if a line drive was hit right toward him. He looked around, but saw no one.

"Come in here and talk to me," said the voice again. The voice sounded very familiar to Shawn, but he couldn't place it.

"Where?" asked Shawn, loud enough to be heard, but no louder.

"In the dugout. On the first base side."

Shawn closed in on the dugout, looking up and down an empty bench. "I don't see you," he said.

"Well, I'm in here, genius. Come look."

Shawn grinned, but only for a second. Then, he stepped through the opening between the backstop and dugout fence and turned the corner. Nobody. The dugout was empty. Except for countless sunflower seed shells littering the floor, an empty sports drink bottle with no lid, and a wooden baseball bat, cracked just above the handle, leaning in the corner.

"I'm no genius, I can tell you that. But I am sure that there is nobody in this dugout," said Shawn.

"You just looked at me, dummy."

"What?"

"Yeah, over here, in the corner."

"Ha, ha, funny," Shawn said, walking to the back of the dugout to find the ventriloquist.

"Laugh all you want, dope. It's me. Wood. Tape grip. Red stripe so you know where to put your fingers when you bunt. Oh, and this little crack above the handle. No big deal, it was an accident. I'm over twenty years old, if I do say so myself."

"Yeah, you look about twenty years old," Shawn replied. "Wait! Why am I talking to a bat? What the hell is wrong with me?" Shawn tore out of the dugout and into the woods, looking high and low, squinting in the moonlight.

70

Then, he stepped onto an overturned five-gallon bucket and looked on the roof of the dugout. Nobody.

Shawn walked back onto the field, near home plate, facing the pitching mound. "This is a great trick, whoever you are, but it's time to come out. I can't find you, you can come out now."

Maybe Bubby had done a better job of trailing than Shawn realized. A speaker, or a phone in the dugout, positioned near the bat? That had to be it. Shawn marched into the dugout and hunted above and below and behind the bat. Nothing. Maybe it was attached to the back of the bat, or inside. That's why it was cracked. Shawn reached his right hand out, then stopped. "Um, no thanks." He leaned close to the bat, his nose, no more than an inch away. Shawn saw no evidence of anything, no speakers or wires, nothing but an old wooden bat, cracked above the handle.

"Are you satisfied yet?"

"Ah, no," said Shawn. "Not until I figure out who is playing this trick on me. And how?"

"Hmm, ok, but you're wasting your time."

"I'm going to walk around the field a little bit, then come back in here. Between now and then, I hope to wake up or come to my senses, or whatever. I know I see things lately, but I've never spoken to any of my visions." Shawn stopped at the gap in the fence and looked back. "I'll be back in a few minutes."

"Good. We need to talk."

Shawn raked his right hand over his forehead and his right eye, tugging at the bottom lid in the process. His hand continued down his face as he walked toward left field, folding his bottom lip as he passed on the way to his chin. Shawn started to turn his head back toward the dugout, then stopped. Instead, he jogged out into left field, turned toward home plate and stood.

Well over a thousand days since he last stood in left field, but the view was the same. The size of the mound, the angle of the dugout fences, the distance from home plate, the position of the bases around the diamond. Then, Shawn saw the metal bleachers behind home plate, bathed in moonlight, and a sour pit formed in his stomach. He stood up straight, and rocked forward and back with his hands on his head. Then, he slid his hands into his pockets and walked toward the dugout.

He sat on the bench, a couple of feet from the bat. Silence. Shawn giggled, and waved his hands close to the bat. Nothing. Then, he leaned in and looked closely at the bat. A long sliver of oak, tanned and treated, grains positioned around the trademark in textbook fashion. But Shawn looked at the crack more than anything else. His eyes only inches away from the damage, straining to see in the moonlight.

"I know, I'm a beauty," said the bat, and Shawn jumped to his feet. He braced himself and dragged both hands down the sides of his face.

"OK, seriously, what is going on here," He turned to the field, "I must have completely lost it."

"What's going on here is that I am trying to talk to you, and you keep questioning your sanity and peeing in your diaper."

"What the hell do you expect me to do?"

"Listen."

"Fine, I'm listening," Shawn crossed his right arm in front of his body, using it to prop his left arm, which was holding his face. "I have no idea who I am listening to, but I'm listening," Shawn looked around the dugout and back out at the field.

"Why has it taken you so long to come out here? I mean, four years. C'mon, man."

"How the heck do you know I've been here four years?"

"Can you stop with the 'why is the sky blue, daddy?' questions and start answering mine?"

72

"Fine," Shawn said, opening his hands toward the bat, widening his eyes. "I haven't stepped on any ball field since I moved here."

"Why not?"

"I don't want to talk about it," Shawn said, his voice lowering with each word.

"Okay."

"Okay?"

"Yeah, are ya deaf? You said you don't want to talk about it, so we won't talk about it. When you want to talk about it, we'll talk about it."

"Thanks," He slid his foot back and forth on the floor of the dugout, clearing a path through the sunflower seeds.

"So why did you come out here tonight, flapjack?" asked the bat.

"Not sure," said Shawn, moving his eyes from the bat to the wall above it.

"I think you are."

"Well...." said Shawn, moving more shells.

"Just tell me. Does it look like I am going to run off and tell anybody?"

"No, I guess not."

"Good thinking, toolbox," replied the bat.

Shawn told the bat that he saw his mother tonight for the first time since he left Quail, after having been found by Larry Last. And that he couldn't sleep. "Something pulled me out here."

"And then you met me. How lovely," said the bat. "What's with the beard?"

"I guess you could say I'm hiding."

"From?"

"From.... Anybody from Quail."

"I see that worked well, dirt-nose."

"Worked for almost four years," Shawn said, "but I guess it didn't work when I needed it to."

"Perhaps... So, you saw your mom...." continued the bat, stretching out the word mom so Shawn could continue.

"And she wants me to come home."

"So go."

"I can't go back there. Those people must hate me."

"For whatever happened, or whatever you did, that you aren't ready to talk about yet?"

"Exactly." Shawn sat down on the bench next to the bat. He looked east and noticed the navy blue sky had lightened a shade on the horizon.

"Did your mom say that everybody hated you?"

"No, she said they all forgave me a long time ago. Any of them that needed to forgive me in the first place."

"So...."

"She's lying. She just wants me to feel better. She's my mother for crying out loud." Shawn kicked a pile of sunflower seeds into the fence. He didn't have a college degree, but he could see right through his mother's psychological trick.

"So, you've been holed up in an apartment in the middle of nowhere for the past four years, looking like a guy who makes clothing out of used paper towels while planning his next Dungeons and Dragons adventure, and you think you know what's going on in Quail. You need to look at yourself in the mirror. Soon. Now."

"Perhaps."

A minute passed with no words. Then, "Maybe it's time you went back."

"I told my mom I might stop by this week."

"There you go," said the bat.

"I was lying, I can't go back there," said Shawn, standing up and leaning in toward the bat, pounding his chest each time he referred to himself. "If I don't go back there, I won't see anybody. If I don't see anybody, I won't hurt anybody. I don't want to hurt anybody anymore."

"So, you hurt somebody?"

74

"Many people, I'm certain. Oh, and CeCe," Shawn leaned his head back, shaking it left and right, closing his eyes.

"Yes… CeCe," said the bat, again dragging out the last syllable.

"Never mind."

"Next time," said the bat.

Silence again, this time broken by Shawn. "Mom said my dad is sad."

"Does your dad get sad a lot?" asked the bat, speaking the word sad for an extra beat.

"Not for no reason."

"Maybe your mom is sad. I'm sure she misses you.... Dipstick."

"I know. I miss her too. And.... I miss them all. Quail."

"Then go back."

"I can't," said Shawn, quieter than last time.

"Yes, you can."

"What if they hate me?"

"Then they hate you. What's the worst that can happen? They banish you to an apartment in the middle of the woods so you can train to be a body double for Ted Kaczynski?"

Shawn laughed and looked at the sky. More light blue than last time, and a thin, long purple cloud cruising above the tree tops. "I guess I'll think about it. I mean, maybe my mom was telling the truth. Maybe they have forgiven me."

"That's the ticket, old boy," sang the bat. "Only one way to find out."

"Don't get too excited, I just said I would think about it."

"Oh, I'm dewy with anticipation over here.... It's your decision. I'll be here in the corner no matter what you do."

Shawn laughed. "I guess so." He looked at the sky again. "I have to go."

"OK, Edward. See you soon," said the bat. "Oh, by the way, did you ever think you would step on a baseball field again."

"No way!" said Shawn, then softer, "No, I didn't."

"And did you?"

"Yes."

"Are ya dead?"

"No, no, I'm not."

Shawn yawned as he walked back toward his apartment, stopping to look back to the dugout every few seconds. His head bobbed as he walked, and he missed the second stone in the creek, stepping ankle deep into the cool, rushing water. Inside his apartment, he used his big toes to force his soaked sneakers off his feet, flinging them toward the front door. One came to rest sole side up in the opening to the kitchen, the other leaned toes up against the wall. He sat between two cushions of the couch, teetering left and right, and left again as he yanked off his wet socks. He fell left, closing his eyes, asleep before his head hit the cushion.

21

"Are you going to take her to see Shrek 2?   .
comes out next week," said Chuck.

Dusty shook his head, and buried his spoon in his ice cream. Shawn was about to offer up the Spring Dance, but wasn't sure that would be funny. Was it just jumping on to Chuck's joke? Would it turn the attention on his love life? He ate a scoop out of his bowl, some rocky road ice cream, mostly whipped cream.

"She did look lovely today and---"

"Oh my God, Chuck, shut up. We worked on a lab together in school."

Shawn was about to jump in. He had noticed that they were sitting close to each other at the lab table. Practically shoulder to shoulder. There had to be a joke---

"Well, your right shoulder and her left shoulder went on a date today already," said Chuck. Dusty looked up from his bowl, forehead wrinkled. Shawn looked too, with mouth hanging wide open. How did Chuck do that? And more importantly, what was the punch line? "They touched all through science class today," finished Chuck.

They all laughed, then returned to their celebratory ice cream. "I don't see Amanda here, do you guys?" asked Dusty. "But we did win a game this evening. You're a jerk, but that was a nice hit."

Chuck had smoked a line drive to center field to drive in the winning run. It was his only hit of the game. In fact, he had struck out in his two at bats before that. How did he do it? Shawn would never have recovered from two consecutive strikeouts to get a hit. Especially the game winning hit. Shawn had dunked a fly ball double down the left field line. He was over-matched by the pitcher, but managed to get enough of the bat on the ball to hit it far enough to be out of the short stop's reach, and shallow enough for the left fielder to have no chance at it. Shawn's legs did the rest. But that first at bat had psyched him out. His final three at bats: ground out, strike out, ground out.

"I know, I know. I am *the man*," said Chuck as he flicked imaginary dust off each of his shoulders with the backs of his hands. "But, my brothers, what about the glove on this ma'an," Chuck continued, pointing his strawberry ice cream coated spoon at Shawn. "Can I get an amen?" Occasionally, Chuck would try to imitate a black, Southern preacher. Try.

"Yeah, but what about my hitting?" asked Shawn, looking over at the swinging door between the restaurant proper and the kitchen.

"Buddy, what about running, about a hundred miles from left field to catch that fly ball after Tummy fell down in center? That was ridiculous," said Dusty

"You mean Timmy?" asked Chuck.

"No, Tummy. Timmy and dummy put together."

Shawn smiled, "I guess that was pretty good." He was jogging over in the direction simply because that's where the ball was hit. But when the center fielder got tangled up in his long, evening shadow and tripped, Shawn knew there was no way Timmy could recover. There were two outs, the tying and go-ahead runs on and circling the bases fast. If the ball had hit the ground, they would have both scored easily. But Shawn took off in a dead sprint at the perfect angle and backhanded the ball when it was about a foot off the ground, then tumbled over. Before breaking into riotous cheering, the crowd hushed, wondering if a human being could have covered that distance to make that catch. And not an adult, not a high school kid, but a seventh grader. Shawn had shown the ball in the pocket of his glove and ended the mystery.

The kitchen door flew open and Shawn jerked his head in that direction. Just a waitress delivering a late evening burger and fries. "I just wish I could hit the ball a little better."

"You had a double, my brothaaa," sang Chuck. The last syllable had lasted seconds and increased in volume.

"Oh my God, Chuck," said Dusty.

"My God! My God! My loooving God!"

"Seriously, shut up. If you bought a couple of flannel shirts, you'd be as white as me."

Shawn ate ice cream and giggled at the exchange of his friends and kept watch on the kitchen door. Billy would slide through it any time now.

"Are we still friends, my redneck pal?" asked Chuck.

"Sure are, my light-skinned, African-American brother."

Chuck looked at Shawn. "What do you think?"

"You guys make a lovely couple---"

The kitchen door blew open and Billy stormed through.

"Hey, Brother McMas-ter," Chuck started to sing, but he trailed off when he made eye contact with Billy.

"Fellas," said Billy, sliding in next to Chuck, across from Dusty. "Nice win. That'a way to hit the ball," he said, backhanding Chuck on the shoulder. Then he looked at Shawn. "See how relaxed Chuck stays. Just see the ball and hit it."

"He did have a double," said Dusty.

"Yeah, but it wasn't a well hit ball. Luck runs out on those types of things," said Billy.

Chuck slid away from Billy, turning his body on the bench seat to face him. "How about that catch, Mr. McMaster? Your boy went forever to get that thing."

"It was a great catch," Billy said, reaching across the table, softly bumping knuckles with Shawn. All three boys breathed out. Smiled. "But you have to hit to get to the next level."

Shawn looked into his bowl and knocked the cherry into the melted ice cream pooling in the bottom. It landed and sat half submerged, sinking slowly.

22

May 28, 2001 - 10:15 AM

The fourth grade girls' hundred-yard dash was next. CeCe lined up with the other girls in her class and Mrs. Stokley's class. Mrs. Stokley was the other fourth grade teacher. CeCe was glad she wasn't in her class. She smelled like the water that pooled up in the tire swing in the backyard. And she gave too much homework.

CeCe looked at the two girls to her left and the three to her right. She was the tallest, but only by an inch or two. The other girls' legs looked like straws falling out of the bottom of pink, yellow, and purple athletic shorts. CeCe's were muscular, toned and strong.... Her arms too. She had never lost a race. She turned her head toward the finish line, toward Mr. Smith, the gym teacher, who had both his hands above his head. The race would start when he dropped them down. She wasn't going to lose this race either.

CeCe stared straight ahead, but she could see the other girls out of the corners or her eyes. Mr. Smith let his hands fall to his sides, and CeCe blasted off. The other girls disappeared. She would win again. By a mile. A small grin leaked onto her face as she approached the finish line. Winning never got old. CeCe finished three and a half seconds ahead of the girl who came in second.

She walked toward the moms, dads, grandparents, and other adults who were there to watch. CeCe scanned the crowd for mom, then remembered that she couldn't get out of work. Mom's boyfriend Mitch was there somewhere. She couldn't see him yet, but she could almost feel him looking at her. He always gazed at CeCe. Too long, like he was watching something he liked on TV.

She heard his voice before she saw him.

"Nice race there, stud," Mitch said.

81

"Thanks." CeCe looked around for her friends.

"You're really fast. Must be those legs," Mitch said, tilting his head to the right, as if to take a better look.

"I guess so." CeCe was looking for her best friend Molly, or her teacher, Mrs. Williams. She would even settle for Mrs. Stokley at this point. Anybody to pull her away from Mitch.

"Your arms are really strong too." Mitch gave CeCe's left biceps a squeeze. "Amazing."

CeCe forced a smile and pulled away. Why couldn't he act like other adults, or at least the way he acted when mom was around. When mom was in the room, he would ask about her homework, or about soccer. Mitch would look her in the eyes. "I have to go find my class now. Thanks for coming." She spun and jogged away from Mitch. Toward anybody. CeCe heard him giggle, then say "My pleasure." She couldn't see it, but she was sure she didn't like the way he was watching her.

23

Shawn eyeballed each rock in the creek as he skipped across, more carefully than the last time he passed in the opposite direction. The moon was half of what it was last time, and last time it was full, bright, gleaming, spreading light across the backyard, the creek, the trees and the baseball field.

Tonight was darker. More clouds. Less moonlight. Wispy, cool fog hanging and drifting, hiding some leaves on the trees, some leaves hiding the fog. It covered the entire outfield as Shawn walked toward the dugout.

The floor was still covered with the empty, broken shells of sunflower seeds. Was that sports drink bottle in exactly the same place? The bat was, cracked and leaning, like the most obtuse of angles waiting for a bus. It said nothing.

Of course it said nothing. It was an old, wooden, cracked baseball bat. Shawn sat on the bench next to it, extended his legs out in front of him, ankle over ankle. He wove his hands together and rested them behind his head. He closed his eyes and inhaled and exhaled the moist, summer night.

"Boo!" yelled the bat.

Shawn twisted away with the top half of his body and slid away with the bottom half. The combination of the two deposited him on the ground, shells digging into his palms. "Are you kidding?" asked Shawn.

"Quite a bit of the time, yes. But not always."

Shawn knew what he meant. Everybody complained that Shawn didn't talk enough, but on the rare occasion when he did join into a group conversation, people took his dry humor as honest observation, and vice versa. And he came up with his best lines when he was talking to himself, anyway. Silence was an easy choice, most of the time. "I almost ended the life of these Jockeys."

"Almost is a double in the gap," said the bat.

"That's what my dad says."

"Imagine that."

Shawn pushed himself off the ground and clapped his hands together like cymbals. He leaned against the fence, facing the bat.

"So," said the bat, "you decided to come back."

"I wanted to see if you were real. Or if I was crazy."

"Is 'all of the above' a choice?"

"I'm not ruling anything out," said Shawn, turning toward the field, away from the bat.

"That's the spirit!"

"What? Admitting that I'm crazy? And that you are real?" asked Shawn, stepping toward the bat.

"No, no, no, dummy. Not ruling anything out. Realizing that anything is possible."

"I see. Your daddy was a tree and your momma was an elementary school inspirational poster," said Shawn through a crooked smile.

"Now we're getting somewhere," said the bat.

"Really?"

"Yes, *really*," said the bat, as if somebody were squeezing his cheeks together. Not that it had any. "You finally showed some backbone."

"I usually have no reason for higher confidence."

"*And we're back*," said the bat in the tone of a radio announcer, "*on the Shawn Thinks He's Not Good Enough Program.*"

"What are you talking about?"

"Figure it out."

Shawn walked out of the dugout and took a few steps toward home plate. Then stopped. No way he could step back into the batter's box. He couldn't even figure out what the bat was talking about.

The bat called out to Shawn, "OK, sweetie, why are you here?"

"I guess I needed to talk."

"I don't have any hands to tape your mouth shut."

Shawn walked back into the dugout and sat next to the bat, leaning his head on the wall, looking out toward home plate, toward the pitcher's mound, at the rest of the field. "I really want to go back. Go home."

"Did you forget the way? I think I can get you directions."

Shawn turned his head toward the bat without removing his head from the wall. "I know how to get there."

"No shit."

"I'm not sure that kind of language will help my situation," said Shawn, hoping that the bat would appreciate the sarcasm.

"Attaboy, give it right back to me," said the bat.

Shawn walked to the other end of the bench, toward first base and hooked two fingers from each hand into the fence. "I want to see CeCe so bad."

"But?"

"But what if she has a new boyfriend?"

"Did your mom say she had a new boyfriend? Or husband? Or a girlfriend?"

"So you think I pushed her to the other team?" Shawn asked, hanging air quotes around other team.

"Wow, brother, I was just making a joke. The earth spins around the sun, not Shawn McMaster."

"Oh, I know that. I can barely get a hula hoop to spin around me," said Shawn.

"*Welcome back*," said the bat, back in the announcer voice.

"I know, I know," said Shawn, walking back toward the bat. "But if she looks at me with disgust or hatred, it will kill me."

"And if I had a testicle, I'd be more of a man than you."

Shawn forced a laugh through his nose. "Really? What if I flung you against the fence?"

"You won't."

The bat was right, he wouldn't. Instead, he leaned in toward the bat, "Seriously, what if everybody still thinks I'm a jerk? Or worse, forgot about me all together."

"That's a good point," said the bat. "Much better to stay out here in the middle of nowhere, sprinting through the woods like Jacob, talking to a bat in the middle of the night, fantasizing about your high school English teacher in the morning. Letting life pass you by."

"How did you---? Never mind. I get your point. This has gone on long enough."

"That's right."

"I need to go take my life back."

"Can I get an amen?" yelled the bat.

"Get my woman back."

"Amen, amen, I say!"

Shawn looked at his shoes. "Or at least check in on her."

"Well…"

"Make sure she is ok."

"Mmm, not exactly…"

Shawn walked out of the dugout and stopped on the other side of the fence. "I guess I'm not going to be able to do any of this sitting here talking to you."

"Not exactly the testosterone-laced bravado, I was hoping for, but it will do for now."

24

Larry looked at his watch as he walked out of the garage port and toward the front door. Plenty early for dinner. Should have stayed for a few more hands of poker. Or maybe popped in on DJ over at the restaurant, just to see what was going on.

Cynthia was waiting in the living room when he walked in. She looked like she was waiting for a pot of water to boil, arms crossed, sitting on the edge of the couch.

"Told ya, home in plenty of time for dinner. We going to the smorgasbord?" asked Larry. This had become the routine in Larry's first year of retirement. Breakfast out with the fellas, maybe some cards or golf in the afternoon. Dinner with the wife, sometimes out, most of the time Cynthia would throw something together. Occasionally, Larry would grill some burgers.

"Yes, Larry. I guess so," said Cynthia. The tone of her voice brought Larry back into the room.

"Cyn, you ok?"

"Fine."

"You don't sound fine."

"I'm fine."

Larry took Cynthia's left hand in his right. "Did I do something wrong?" Larry asked, moving his head to stay in Cynthia's line of sight. "What did I do?"

Cynthia reclaimed her hand and walked to the front window. Peered out, as if she wished she could fly through the window, out into the late summer sun. "I've been waiting," she said. It sounded like she was going to say more, but she stopped there.

Larry looked at his watch. "I'm home early, hon. We're not going to leave for another two hours. I coulda fit in nine holes."

87

Cythnia turned back to Larry, arms crossed again, eyes closed.

Larry sat on the couch. "C'mon, Cyn, talk to me. What's wrong?"

"You were in the typical summer mode for the last few months. Breakfast or golf in the morning. Or both. Ball games in the evening."

"That's my time off as a teacher. That's one of the perks."

"I know. But you are retired now. This is what we've been waiting for."

"I've developed a fall routine. Breakfast in the morning, cards or golf through lunchtime, then dinner with you. Maybe a ballgame on tv in the evening. Or we can watch one of your reality shows or something."

Cynthia was looking out the window again. Larry couldn't read her. What was the problem. "So that's the plan now?"

"Yeah."

"So that's what you're going to do every day?"

"Pretty much."

Cynthia stormed out of the room, into the kitchen. Larry followed. "What do you expect me to do to pass the time?"

"Pass the time?" asked Cynthia, eyes wide open, shoulders leaning forward toward Larry.

"Yeah, pass the time. What else am I going to do? I've been working all these years. This is my time now."

"Your time?"

"Yes. Retirement. My time to not work. My time to relax. You stopped working a few years ago."

"I retired."

"Yes, you retired. What have you been doing? While I worked? Stuff you wanted to do, right?"

Cynthia turned her back and started washing a glass in the sink. "Yes, Larry, I guess I have."

Her voice wasn't angry. It wasn't happy either. It was just a voice. Perhaps she was focusing on washing the glass. "I think it's clean, hon." Larry removed it from her hand and placed it upside down on the drying rack. "I'm gonna go take a shower. I'll be ready in plenty of time for dinner."

Cynthia looked at Larry with a smile, the type of smile you see on driver's licenses, or school pictures. "OK," she put her hands on the edge of the sink, soapy water dripping off her fingers. She turned and looked out the window into the backyard as Larry left the room. "I'll be waiting, I guess."

25

The blade of the straight razor was longer than he thought it would be. Sharp. It balded an area on the back of Shawn's hand without much trouble. He looked at the blade, and the hair on it, then caught his reflection in the mirror above the sink. The bat was right; Shawn looked like something the garbage man had accidentally left behind. Or maybe not by accident.

Shawn bought the razor at Wright Pharmacy, an old-fashioned drug store in the middle of a small town Shawn passed through on occasion. It had a soda fountain like the one Shawn had seen in a movie set in the 1950's, and it still appeared to be operational. *Central Apothecary* was painted on the wall above the bar and stool seats. It reminded Shawn of McMaster's Restaurant.

The middle-aged woman behind the register, Marge, according to her name tag, said, "You have a lot of work to do there," motioning to his face.

"You have no idea," said Shawn, as he walked out.

"Wait, don't you need some shaving cream?"

"Nope, I'm good. Thank you," said Shawn from the doorway, holding the door open with his foot, stuffing a few dollar bills back into his pocket.

Shawn refocused his vision on the face in the mirror. He recognized the eyes, but who the hell was the rest of him? The shaggy beard. The shaggier hair. Pale skin. Typically, Shawn's face, neck, and arms would be a golden brown, much darker than his hair, from playing double-headers, catching a bunch of fly balls after lunch, before an evening game, or just wasting away summer afternoons with CeCe. Those summer afternoons and evenings would rush by (how was it midnight already?), but there would be another one lined up behind it. Another

90

day of late breakfast down in the restaurant, a ballgame in the evening, then a movie or a ride around the countryside with CeCe. Sun down, sun up. Restart from beginning. Press play.

That was a summer day for seventeen-year-old Shawn. Twenty-two-year-old Shawn's life had ritual to it as well. Stay hidden during daylight. Open email, reply, attach, send. Pushups in the bedroom. Sprints in the woods after sundown. Conversations with a bat in the dugout overnight.

Shawn stared at himself in the mirror. "Conversations with a bat, what the hell is wrong with you?" He squeezed the handle of the razor, and held it close to his eyes for inspection. It was sharp enough to do the job.

For four years, Shawn had sleep-walked through life. He thought that's what being an adult was. He had watched his parents do it for years. Mom up way before dawn (or had she not been to bed yet) making way too many pies. Dad cleaning the grill, raking the infield dirt, mowing the outfield grass. Sacrifice.

Shawn had given up on ever again, smelling a golden brown pie crust just out of the oven, or ever again collecting freshly-mown grass clippings on his cleats jogging in the outfield. He had been certain that he couldn't face his family again, CeCe again, the people of Quail again. Not after what happened, after what he did. But seeing his mother again, the warmth of her words, her gaze, the forgiveness in her touch, made him realize he couldn't do this anymore. Hide. Stay secluded. Alone.

Hence the razor.

Changing a habit, ending a lifestyle, required a drastic move. "The ultimate commitment," his father had always said. It was usually in reference to becoming a better hitter. Shawn had his moments, a four-hit game here, a home run there, but the pressure, the move-by-move scrutiny of every single thing he did from the time he stepped out of the dugout to the time he walked back in never allowed for much improvement.

But that was over now. Baseball was over. No more worrying about making it to the "next level." He wasn't eighteen anymore. Twenty-two was passed his prime. He hadn't swung a bat, hit a ball, thrown a ball, or caught one in four years. And the "mental side" of the game, as his father called it. Forget that.

Shawn took a deep breath. This was it, the drastic move. The events of the last ten days made him realize that he couldn't go on like this. He put the razor up to his neck, forced it through his beard, to the skin below his jaw line. He started to pull down. Then stopped. This wasn't right, something was wrong. It shouldn't feel like that.

He bent over and opened the cabinet below. He pulled out a can of shaving cream he had been saving for this occasion. He had pulled it out a handful of times before, only to leave the cap on, to put it back in the cabinet, and close the door. But this time, he popped off the lid, depressed the button on top, and poured a white dollop onto the palm of his hand, like whipped cream on top of an ice cream sundae.

26

Shawn didn't recognize the girl scooping ice cream. All he could see was the Phillies cap on the top of her head, two strong, toned arms (muscular, but not masculine, not to Shawn) reaching from the sleeves of a brand new, white McMaster's Restaurant polo shirt, and glittery red and golden hair spilling over her shoulders. The noises of the late lunch crowd: voices, forks, plates, and laughter, filled the room.

He stood five paces in front of her. Watching. How? How is it possible? How can such beautiful hair come out from under a baseball cap? And a Phillies cap! Shawn had seen hot girls with baseball caps on, even Phillies caps. But they were in bikinis, on posters, holding a bat behind their neck. Prizes for games on the boardwalk at the beach. This was a real, live person.

And those arms. His brain was telling him that he shouldn't like them. That if his buddies were around, he would be elbowing them so they could see, and start the verbal assault. But his heart was telling him otherwise. The opposite, in fact. He couldn't stop looking at them. He wanted to… touch them, if only to see what they felt like. Can you fall in love with forearms at first sight?

The brim of the cap jerked up a bit, revealing the girl's mouth. She was still digging into a tub of chocolate chip cookie dough ice cream, dripping and dropping partial scoops into a medium cup. More evidence that this was her first day. Each time she forced the metal scoop into the nearly frozen solid ice cream, her mouth changed shape. It would go from neutral to something that resembled sadness, from happy to deep thoughtfulness, from concern to complete disappointment.

There was no way it could be any cuter, right?

Wrong.

The brim lifted to further reveal cheeks with thousands (millions?) of orangey freckles. Some lumped so close together that they looked like one big freckle. Some spaced just so, as if to model the stars of a constellation. Others lonely, spread out, white skin in between. Room for Shawn to run the tip of his finger through.

Wait, what? Shawn obsessed over footwork in the outfield, balls and strikes in the batter's box, even which flavors of ice cream to toss into his ice cream pie. But firm yet feminine forearms? Fondling forbidden fields of freckles on a female's face? Inadvertent alliteration? What was going on? What was that feeling in his stomach? Like when the Phillies lost the final game of their season, a hunk of melting ice cream aching in his gut.

But it felt... good. No. Great. What in the world was going on?

Then it happened. Greta walked through the swinging door and saw Shawn. "Oh good. Shawn, this is Celine."

The girl shifted the ice cream scoop from her right hand to her left, then extended her right hand to Shawn, "I go by CeCe," she said with a small smile.

Shawn double-clutched, then took her hand in his and squeezed. "Shawn." He looked into her eyes.

The restaurant went silent, like the woods beyond the right field fence at McMaster Field in the middle of the night. Or maybe it exploded, and disappeared. Maybe the roof was ripped off by a tornado. Shawn could have no idea. He was falling, swimming, drowning in the bluest eyes, he had ever seen. Whatever he thought was blue before, a cloudless sky on opening day, the ocean on the first day of vacation, the cursive letters on the front of the Dodgers' home uniform, had immediately become less blue. CeCe's eyes welcomed him, not judged him like he was used to with other teenaged eyes. He would have to look up what shade of blue they were, if there was even a name for it.

Shawn let go of her hand because he knew he had to. But he didn't stop gazing into her eyes. Couldn't. CeCe smiled, and dropped the brim of her cap again, reminding Shawn that this amazing creature with the golden red hair and attractively toned arms and billions and billions of adorable freckles, was wearing a Phillies cap!

CeCe finished scooping the ice cream into the cup and handed it to Greta, who peered inside and said with a wink, "not bad. Not bad at all for your first day. And you'll get better at it."

Shawn had walked around behind the counter and was standing below a picture of himself in a baseball uniform holding a trophy. CeCe was facing the other direction, acquainting herself with the soda machine. If her arms were attractive, her legs were a perfect ten. Precisely proportioned quads and calves, thin ankles, precious little feet.

She turned and stopped in her tracks, noticing Shawn standing there, mouth ajar. She smiled again, then tugged at her skirt, apparently trying to make it as long as possible without ripping it off her hips. She slouched a little, and crossed her arms in front of her midsection, then dropped them to her side, then crossed them again.

Shawn opened his mouth to say something, anything, but nothing came out. He closed his mouth, smiled, then shook his head, agreeing with who-knows-what. Then he scurried through the swinging door, through the kitchen, up the stairs to the residence, and back into his bedroom.

27

"Your boys ready for next week?" Muldoon asked DJ, who was looking at the selection of orange extension cords in the only Kmart in Quail county.

"Just another game, Al. Just another game," said DJ, turning around to face Muldoon.

"We've lost, what, five games between us this year? I think this game is a winner takes all," said Al, knowing full well that his team, Al's Everything Shop, had lost three and McMaster's Restaurant two. He also knew that McMaster's had won their annual meeting eight of the last nine years, and seventeen of the last twenty. This year, the schedule maker, DJ McMaster himself, placed the Al's versus McMaster's match-up on September 30. It would be the last game played on McMaster Field until next spring. Given recent history, he was sure DJ wanted to make sure that Al's entered the long off season---chilly fall, from Halloween trick-or-treating, through Thanksgiving dinners around a family table, and frozen winter from opening presents in the tree light-pierced darkness of Christmas morning, through the first time backyards were dry enough for a father and son to have a catch sometime in March— with a loss.

DJ removed his hands from his shopping cart and crossed them in front of his chest. The cart containing a box of kitchen rags, two spatulas, and an orange extension cord drifted, coming to a stop against a display of surge protectors. "Feels like there should be something else at stake, doesn't there, Muldoon?"

"Sure does," Al replied, empty-handed and without a cart. He didn't look at DJ as he spoke, but instead looked at the corners of the store, at the shelving units, at the ceiling and floor. The Al's Everything Shop team needed a change. They needed to start winning for a change, but maybe if there were some stakes involved... But it was DJ's world. His field, and his dominant team winning on it. Muldoon would have to follow his lead and hope that DJ's hubris would kick in. Despite the on-field rivalry, Muldoon always envied DJ. DJ was a great family man, and he treated everybody who walked onto his field or into his restaurant as part of that family. One time Al was in the McMaster's Restaurant before a game to grab a soda on a steamy July evening. A little league team was having an end of the year ice cream party. The coach had recently lost his job, so instead of charging him what had to be upwards of seventy-five dollars for the ice cream, he only charged $7.50. Muldoon would never forget the look of relief on the coach's face and how he was able to enjoy the rest of the party with his team. The extended McMaster family. DJ was beloved in Quail for moments like that, but the recognition had gone to his head. Muldoon knew that DJ, if given the opportunity, was willing to open himself up to risk. And the shrewd businessman that he was, Muldoon was more than willing to let him do it.

"How's this, Al?" DJ said, having thought in silence for a few minutes. "I'll make sure that each year our game is the last one of the entire season. We'll shut down summer."

The tone in DJ's voice told Al there was more. "I'm listening." Al removed his glance from the construction of the back wall of Kmart, and fixed it on his rival's face.

"And the winner of this game," continued DJ, sounding like he was trying to convince himself of his own idea, "will assume sole control of the home locker room for the entire off season and next season." He paused, thumb and index finger rubbing his chin, "The only way to gain control of the locker room is to win the game. We'll call it 'The Winner's Locker Room'."

97

"Let me get this straight. My team wins next week, and the home locker room is mine, my team's, until you beat us again."

"That's right."

"So that part of your building become mine?" Muldoon checked how far he could push DJ.

"Not technically, you can't live in there or anything. But the locker room is yours, I won't go in."

Swing and a miss. But Muldoon continued the negotiations. "Well, how can I be sure you won't go in there when I'm away?"

Another pause. "Each year, if we have a new winner, Jack will install a new deadbolt. The winner gets the only key. Jack'll keep one at his locksmith shop. Just in case."

The two shook on the deal as DJ got on the end of the express aisle queue. Muldoon walked out empty handed, but he left with much more than he walked in with. A new era in the Muldoon-McMaster rivalry had been born. He turned to DJ before he walked into the parking lot. "Let's call the game 'The Final Exam.'"

28

June 18, 2013 - 8:21 PM

The bleachers beyond the fence in right center field were never used. The small thicket of trees had grown up to it, allowing Shawn a place to stand. Out of sight. The darkening evening, the shade from the trees, the worn, green wooden bleachers, the plain navy ball cap pulled low, the charcoal t-shirt and jeans all provided camouflage for Shawn, allowing him to see Quail before Quail saw him.

The second game of the evening, the eight-thirty match up, was about to begin. Shawn smiled as he heard the National Anthem, same recording as 4 years ago, as 14 years ago. After hearing the first note, his head remained still, but his eyes moved to the flag. Another grin as he looked at both teams positioned around the flagpole, heads bowed toward the padlocked electrical box.

The windows on the front of McMaster's Restaurant shone yellow in the twilight, shadowy figures moving here and there. Occasionally the doors would open, and words and laughter would escape, would roll down the hill toward Shawn. He studied the silhouettes, turning his body toward the restaurant, leaning and squinting. Grinning.

Then he pulled back, turned toward the game, covering the bottom half of his face with his right hand. He looked at the batter, he looked at left field. His stomach turned sour, and sweat formed on his brow, even in the gentle warmth of nine at night. He didn't watch baseball until the Spring following his late September departure from Quail, and only then on TV. This was his first live game. The batter struck out looking. Shawn watched him walk back to the dugout, remove his helmet, replace his bat, then sit on the bench. Shawn shook his head and looked at his feet. Such a simple thing to do, walk back to the dugout, place your equipment on the ground, and sit down.

The sky darkened and color was added to the shapes in the window, white shirts hustling back and forth. From this distance, it looked like a team huddled around three or four tables pushed together, eating ice cream. Another booth or two occupied with late diners or dessert eaters. Shawn pressed his fingers into his eyes, then pulled his hands down his face. A deep breath, held. Then released. Ball cap pulled low. Moist palms slid into his jean pockets.

Shawn walked outside the fence in right field, never getting close enough to touch it. Head dipped, hands tucked, shoulders rolled forward. Six-foot-two sneaking forward at five-foot-ten. Nobody knew he was there. Much different than the last time he was at McMaster Field. The stunned crowd hushed, Billy screaming, then the sounds of confused questions circling the McMaster Field bowl. Shawn had put his head down and marched to the parking lot. He could do the same right now. Nobody would know he was there. Was back. Jump into his car, drive back to the apartment, sit on the couch.

Wait. He hadn't nearly sliced off his chin with a straight razor for nothing. Hadn't moped into a barber shop, looking like a sheep dog, taking a little ribbing from the locals-- walking out with a "grown-up" haircut for nothing either. At some point, you have to press play and see what comes next. He had come this far.

Into the bleachers behind the first base dugout, past the pockets of fans, head ducked, and up the steps toward the restaurant. His childhood home and stomping grounds grew out of the hill with each step. In the front window was his mother, sliding a six-scoop sundae in between a male and a female. Teenagers, cell phones on the table, traded in for long, silver spoons.

Shawn reached the top step, and then stopped. Took three steps toward the front door of the restaurant, and stopped again. He could see his car in the far corner of the parking lot, practically out on the main road. Nobody would know if he hopped right back in, jumped back on the highway, pulled off for a drive-thru cheeseburger, then sat on the balcony of his apartment late into the night. But what would the bat say?

What would the bat say? The bat. Ha. "What the hell is wrong with you?" whispered Shawn. Instead, he turned right and walked onto the grass, looked up at the flag, down at the plaques places for his ancestors. He hovered over the mulched and maintained bed, which contained the plaques for the three passed McMaster men, some empty space for one or two more. He crouched down, traced the M on his grandfather's plaque, and sighed. The door opened behind him, and a loud laugh and the sounds of dishes and silverware slamming filled his ears. He stood up and turned. "What would the bat say? Enough is enough already."

Shawn walked through the grass, onto the macadam path, and up to the glass front doors. A course he had traveled thousands of times before, but not once in the last four years. Behind him, the eight-thirty game was going on, as it had for decades upon decades. In front of him, the people of Quail ate, drank, talked, and laughed. Above him was the home in which he grew up. All he had left behind, everything he thought he could never see again, have again, was all around him.

Four years of anonymity were about to end; he would be recognized. By his mother or father. Or Larry. By somebody who knew him from way back when, who wondered where he went, who wondered why he did it, who probably hadn't forgiven him yet. He grabbed the handle of the door and pulled. The smell of waffle and cake cones, of coffee and French fries attacked his nose. The clanging of plates, forks, and knives in plastic tubs, the voices of young baseball players recounting their victory, sounds slipping out as the kitchen door swung open and shut again, pelted his ears. The supermarket at two in the morning was quiet, his apartment always silent. The trees and creek only whispered, and not during the day, only at night. Not like this.

A discussion in the back corner, which was a few syllables from a full on argument, garnered much of the room's attention. As did turkey club sandwiches and banana splits. Shawn stepped into the restaurant undetected.

29

"I am telling you, they *are not* the same person," said Chuck.

"Whatever. That's the whole point of the commercial," replied Dusty, turning his attention to his peach pie.

Seconds of silence, pie eating, coffee sipping, then Dusty and Chuck, in unison, "We treat you like you'd treat you."

"Treat *you* like *you'd* treat *you.* YOU, YOU, YOU!! Clearly, they are the same actors, that's the only way it makes sense. Search, Discover Card commercial on your stupid phone," said Dusty.

"Dumbass… who will treat you like you'd treat you?" asked Chuck.

Larry rotated on his counter stool to watch the two argue. As ridiculous as they were, many of their discussions were entertaining. It reminded him of his old teaching days. Larry gently shook his head, refocusing himself on Dusty and Chuck.

"We."

"Who is we?"

"Discover Card, I guess," said Dusty.

"Right. It's not 'you, treat you like you'd treat you.' It's we. WE!" said Chuck, leaning back in his seat, sipping coffee as if there was nothing more to say.

"You can play your big 'college degree' word games with me. Just go watch the damn commercials again. It's… It's…"

"Now we're doing scenes from The King's Speech?" asked Chuck.

"It's… Shawn," Dusty was finally able to spit out.

Chuck spun his head around. Larry swung back on his chair as well. Greta must have gone to see her boy, and he must have once again been where Larry said he saw him. For the second time in two weeks, Larry needed to convince himself that he was seeing whom he thought he was seeing. Two weeks ago, he had to look past the long hair and beard, and identify Shawn using his memory of DJ's eyes. The young man in front of him was clean-shaven with no hair jutting from the bottom of his plain blue ball cap. Larry took a deep breath, reminding himself that he wasn't looking at a young DJ, or even a young Billy. It had to be Shawn.

Greta burst through the swinging door, tossed a rolling pin onto the counter near Larry, and dashed across the dining area toward Shawn. She hugged him close, quick and firm, then pushed him away, holding him by the outsides of his shoulders. "I hope you didn't shave on my account?"

"Maybe, but it was time," said Shawn. He stood still, eyes darting to all parts of the room, leaning a little backwards, like Greta was an aunt who was looking for her annual kiss.

"Well, I'm glad you did, and I'm glad you're here."

Larry sat on his stool, holding a rolling pin in his left hand. What he just saw, that moment, was perfect. Larry remembered the night Shawn left, remembered watching Greta let him go, remembered Greta, then Billy, dialing, then redialing and redialing his cell phone number. What must it be like to reunite with a loved one after years of separation? Larry didn't know, but he wished he did. "Welcome back," he said, extending his hand toward Shawn.

"Thanks," said Shawn, who then pointed to Larry's left hand, "Um, rolling pin, huh?"

"Yeah," said Chuck, approaching from the side. "Larry is thawing out all of the dead former students in his basement and cooking them in pies."

104

"Some sort of freaky, old man, three-fourteen worship crap," said Dusty, wiggling his fingers around his head. Then quietly, "I might try some though."

"Why wouldn't we?" asked Chuck, who reached to shake Shawn's hand, then pulled him into a hug bear hug. "I have missed you so much, my little boychik," he said, trying to sound like Dusty's Russian grandmother.

Dusty was next. "The pedagogical son returns!"

"Prodigal," said Larry.

"The prodigal son returns!" said Dusty, and he and Shawn launched into a short but crisp handshake, high five routine, ending with a quick chest thumping, back slapping hug.

Greta sent Dusty and Chuck back to their booth, and pulled Shawn to the side. "Look around," she said, and then raised her eyebrows. Then she turned to Larry, "My son here thought that everybody hated him, and that nobody would want him back."

Larry looked as though he was trying to remember why he walked into a particular room in his house, then said to Shawn, "What happened could have--- well, it was an accident"

Greta jumped in, "We don't need to worry about any of that right now. Go be with your friends."

The most difficult person to forgive is yourself; you are with that person all the time.

"Yes, yes, right," said Larry as he watched Shawn join Dusty and Chuck in their booth. He had watched the three of them grow up in that booth, around this restaurant, and down on the ball field. All three of them good ball players, but Shawn, gosh, could Shawn track down a fly ball. Larry shook his head as he turned and reached for his cup of coffee. The poor kid was gone for four years, and Larry tried to talk about the reason he left. He didn't mean any harm. In fact, he wanted to let Shawn know that all was okay. But the past was the past. This moment was about

Shawn reuniting with his family and friends. Yes, this moment. Larry decided to finish his coffee and eavesdrop on the fellas' conversation.

"I'm glad you're back," said Dusty. "We haven't won The Final Exam since you... since you were---"

"Since you were gone," Chuck interrupted, singing, "I can breathe for the first time."

Dusty shot, Chuck a look, "We need you back in left field because---"

"I'm so moving on, yeah, yeah."

Dusty, who had been facing Shawn, turned toward Chuck. "If you don't let me finish, I'm going to have two lovely green eyes hanging from my rear view mirror, and you're gonna be walking around Quail like you're filming Night of the Living Dead, Light-Skinned Black Man."

Chuck looked at Shawn, and using his stuffy, professor's voice, "You see, students, it's always the African-American who goes first."

"I see things haven't changed," said Shawn.

"Nope, not really," said Chuck, who then pointed to Dusty. "You shut up," then pointed to himself, "and me, shut up," then pointed to Shawn, "and you talk."

"Where the hell have you been?" asked Dusty.

"And what the hell have you been doing?" said Chuck, imitating Dusty's voice as best he could.

Then Dusty and Chuck, pointing at each other, and in unison, "Shut up."

Shawn told his friends about his job, his apartment and how he came to have both. He told them about picking up his groceries in the middle of the night, and sleeping through a lot of the days. Larry had to strain to hear his voice, and he was no more than ten feet away. All the while he was talking, Shawn kept eying the kitchen door, and looking over his shoulder, scanning the room.

"So all you have to do was make sure to reply to each email within twenty-four hours?" asked Chuck.

"And other than that, you just hang out in your place, sleep and eat stuff?" asked Dusty.

"And clearly work out," said Chuck.

"Yeah, look at the size of this guy."

"Spectac---" stated Chuck, interrupted by Billy blasting through the swinging door.

Shawn stood up, took a step toward the counter, then stopped. Billy also stopped on the other side of the counter and looked at Shawn. Larry could almost read his mind, mostly because Larry was thinking the same thing: Damn, the kid looked like a ballplayer. A professional ballplayer. He had grown a few inches, both in height and in width.

Billy continued out around the counter and hugged his son. Neither man said a word and both left the embrace with tears in their eyes. Billy grabbed Shawn by both biceps and nodded with approval. Shawn smiled.

"How are you, dad?"

"Never mind about me, how the heck are you?"

Shawn smiled, and at Greta's urging, both men sat down at the counter next to Larry. She uncovered a cherry pie, and then cut three slices. As she slid them down on the counter, she paused and looking upward, squinted her eyes, as if she were trying to hear if somebody was going to ring the doorbell again. "Shoot, my pies," she said, and ran into the kitchen.

The conversation continued, Larry and Billy filling Shawn in on what he had missed; games down at McMaster Field, things around the restaurant. Folks from Quail who had died, people who had gotten married, had kids, or moved away. Shawn listened, looked around, ate pie and drank coffee.

Some other people from the town of Quail popped over to say hi to Shawn, clapping him on the back, leaning in to hug him across his shoulders. Greta had returned from the kitchen.

"Do you have your glove?" asked Billy.

"Wilbur Shawn!" yelled Greta, giving her husband the look. The look only a wife can give her husband.

"Maybe the kid wants to catch some fly balls," said Billy.

"Can our son at least get his shoes wet?" asked Greta, interrupted by the front door flinging open.

CeCe blasted into the restaurant, and stopped a step inside. She was wearing pink flip-flops, tiny white shorts, and her chest was heaving in a purple V-neck t-shirt. She looked at Shawn, and Shawn back at her. Her phone slipped out of her back pocket and landed face down on the ground.

"Number one versus number two," said Chuck into his spoon.

"It doesn't get any better than this," said Dusty.

30

CeCe bent over at the waist, legs straight, and reached for her phone. But she didn't take her eyes off Shawn, so she grabbed and missed twice. And when she decided to look down, she lost her balance, and it took all the strength in her hamstrings, ankles and toes to keep her from toppling forward.

Oh CeCe, you're such a good athlete, and so beautiful at the same time, most guys would say to her at times like this. Shawn would say something like *nimble,* but CeCe would know he really meant *nimble, but not unbelievably agile like me.* Other guys would kiss her ass in hopes of one day seeing it. Shawn took pleasure in kicking it. And CeCe delighted in the challenge.

But Shawn, this Shawn standing in front of her, said nothing. Just stood there. He looked older. Well, of course, he was older. But his boyish face had turned into that of a man. He looked tired. But at the same time wired. That's how Shawn's body would react to a situation like this.

CeCe took a step forward, then stopped. As soon as she stopped, Shawn took a step forward. Then stopped. They looked at each other and the little smiles leaked out, like a smile on the face of a shy child on the first day of Kindergarten, after they realized everything was going to be alright. Then they rushed toward each other and hugged.

It was strange, at first. She knew it was Shawn, she could feel it in his touch. Smell it in his scent. But everything on him was… higher. His chin and shoulders. His arms and ribs. His belt buckle jabbed her much higher above her navel than she remembered. Her lanky, handsome, competitive, sexy baseball star boyfriend (was he still her boyfriend?) had returned, but super-sized.

They used to hug like this all the time. Sometimes a goodbye hug would last for five minutes. CeCe would fall asleep, her cheek resting on his chest, his heartbeat a lullaby. But now, their arms were rigid, backs straight. They were in the middle of a restaurant, after all. But muscle by muscle, fiber by fiber, CeCe felt Shawn relax, which allowed her to relax in turn. Shawn had come home, and in that moment, with her eyes closed, with her arms wrapped around Shawn and his arms wrapped around her, she was home too.

She expected to open her eyes as an eighteen-year-old. All the evidence was there. Shawn and his arms and his smell and his chin resting on her forehead. The clang and thud of plates, mugs, and silverware bouncing in plastic tubs. The smell of coffee, apple pie, French fries, and gravy. Her head felt light, and her feet had vanished.

"I believe this hug is heading for overtime," said Dusty.

"No question, this one is deadlocked," Chuck said into the shovel end of a spoon dripping with vanilla ice cream.

During the play-by-play Shawn stiffened, then pulled away. CeCe opened her eyes, and she wasn't eighteen and Shawn was still a man and still looked tired. And what happened between them had still happened. And what happened to cause him to leave her had still happened. And what she had done while he was gone had still happened, as well.

Shawn's hands were buried in his pockets and his eyes bounced around the room like a class ring hanging from the necklace of a jogger. He looked like the guy in that movie who lost his memory and felt like a stranger to his wife and family in his own house. "Let's sit down," said CeCe, pulling them off center stage. Greta had already walked around the room, politely urging people back to their cherry pies, back to their conversations and coffee, "This isn't dinner theater, folks."

110

They sat across from each other in CeCe's--- in ShawnandCeCe's--- favorite booth. Many an evening had ended there, and some had started there. The two spent a lot of time on the McMaster property, not much at CeCe's house. CeCe always told Shawn that she loved the restaurant and being around the baseball field. That was true, but not the whole truth.

Nothing was said for a minute. Awkward, to say the least. They used to tell each other the tiniest toenail of a detail about their day, and the other would soak it all up. Now they looked like two high school sophomores on their first date, with their parents two booths away.

Shawn used to gaze into her eyes for ten minutes, fifteen minutes at a time, describing a fly ball, or something somebody said in class, or something somebody did at the restaurant. He once told her that her eyes were the only place he truly felt comfortable to be himself. CeCe had said, "That's the freakin' most romantic and poetic thing anybody has ever said to me," and he replied, "It's just the truth."

Now he wouldn't look at her for more than a second or two. Had he fully retreated, even from her? Or did he hear about how CeCe had been getting by over the last four years? Either way, if somebody was going to start this conversation, it was going to be her.

"So, here we are."

"Yeah," said Shawn, looking at CeCe. Then he looked out the window, then at CeCe for a second, then he scanned the restaurant, then back at CeCe, but only for a moment, then he looked over his left shoulder, over the counter, toward his pictures and articles hanging on the wall.

"Hey!" said CeCe, a touch louder than she wanted. Shawn's head snapped back and his eyes locked with CeCe's.

Chuck spoke into the end of a dripping straw, "One time, my father went out for eggs and milk."

"In o-six?" asked Dusty.

"'o-five."

"Right."

"He didn't come back until two days later," said Chuck, speaking as though he were announcing a ground ball to third base.

"Bet your mom had something to say about that," said Dusty, adding on a cheesy, morning show laugh.

"It was a lot more than, 'hey!' I can promise you that."

CeCe turned and looked over her left shoulder. "Would you two shut up?" Then, as she turned back toward Shawn, "Why don't you two go on a date for once?"

Dusty and Chuck both dropped their microphones. "Wait, does she mean with each other?" asked Chuck.

"I do love you, man."

"Likewise." Chuck lowered his voice a click. "I don't think we're ready to date yet."

"Maybe in the fall?"

"Oh, the leaves---"

"Enough!" said CeCe, and the guys stopped. There was no joking in her tone. "Shawn--"

"I'm sorry," Shawn said, interrupting CeCe, as if, at that particular moment, and only that moment, he had the courage and the strength to speak.

"There's nothing to be sorry about," said CeCe, looking down at the table. She did want an apology from Shawn, although that anger had morphed to concern as the weeks that Shawn was gone turned into months; and desperation as the months turned into years. "I'm just glad you're back."

Again, Shawn broke eye contact.

"You are *back*, right?" CeCe said, sliding a little lower in her seat.

112

Shawn leaned in, and spoke loud enough for only CeCe to hear, "The only thing I am sure of is that I am sorry. I'm sorry about what happened."

"What happened was an accident."

"Maybe, but I caused it. And I'm sorry I--- disappeared. I just. I didn't. It was just... easier, became easier."

"Easier?" asked CeCe. Easier for Shawn to be away from her than with her for the last four years? That didn't sound like much of an apology anymore. CeCe's eyes narrowed and her smile went neutral.

"No, not easier. Not easy to be away, just easier not to... Not to."

"Not to?" CeCe asked. Her tone was not forgiving. "No to, what, Shawn? What? You've been gone four years. I've waited..." Her voice trailed off. Tears welled up in her eyes.

"Not to face everybody. Easier to just stay in hiding. Easier to miss everybody and everything and miss you, especially because I couldn't deal with what I did."

"Everybody knows it was an accident, Shawn. You didn't mean for that to happen."

"Of course I didn't, but it did."

"Shit happens. Shit happened. Now it's over. It's been over for four years. Four years!"

"I thought that the townspeople would swoop down on me the moment I showed my face back in Quail."

CeCe cranked her head as far as she could to the right, eyes wide open. Then leaned far to the left and looked out the window. Then she looked at Shawn and raised her eyebrows ever so slightly.

Finally, a face that CeCe could recognize. It was the Shawn ok-you-got-me face. The only thing Shawn and CeCe liked more than each other was competing against one another. Running, throwing, hitting, passing, eating, holding their breath, kissing... Whatever. But there were times when Shawn would just talk until he proved himself wrong, and all CeCe had to do was watch and listen. Then make a sarcastic face of some kind, and Shawn would have no choice but to admit defeat. Not verbally, but with a face of his own. It was somewhere between, I just found my car keys and I just stepped in dog crap. But it was adorable as hell. And it was great to see it again.

"Then there's what I did to us," Shawn said. He didn't avert his gaze.

But CeCe did. What was this "us" now? She knew what it was then. It was high school sweethearts. It was ShawnandCeCe. One name was rarely said without the other. They were rarely without one another. After school. All weekend. Even before school. Before and after baseball practice. Before and after track practice. Off to college together.

Then nothing. Not a call, not a text. No, "hey, I'm ok." No, "Just need some time to cool off." Nothing. Gone.

Now back.

Shawn continued, "Is there... Is there still an 'us'?"

"That's a really complicated question, don't you think?"

"So there's somebody else?"

"I didn't say that," said CeCe. This was exactly where she didn't want this conversation to go. Not yet. Christ, she wasn't even used to how damn big he had gotten.

"So there's nobody else?"

"I don't have a boyfriend. Can we leave it at that for right now?"

Shawn nodded his head, and ate a few bites of pie. Every noise grabbed his attention. A clanging plate raised his eyebrows, made him jump. Somebody coming through the front door, or through the swinging door, swung his head. He was like a baby, experiencing new sensations after new sensation. CeCe could tell by the relieved look on

114

his face that Shawn hadn't fully processed what she had said.

"So you graduated college?" he asked.

"Yeah, barely. I hit some low spots, but I made it through," CeCe said. Shawn deflated as she said that, and CeCe knew her little message hit home. She knew it was no picnic for Shawn living alone all that time. No, living with himself, and with the way he felt about himself all that time. He was so hard on himself. But she wanted him to know that it had an effect on her too. Mission accomplished. "What did you always tell me when I would pout after I messed up playing field hockey?"

Shawn grinned, which veiled an ok-you-got-me look. "Move on, there's nothing you can do about it."

"Exactly. Let's move on," CeCe said, looking at something on her arm. "I'm ready," she said, unable to look Shawn in the eye as she lied.

They talked a while longer, Shawn about his job and his apartment, CeCe about college and Quail. Shawn was filled in on all the gaps while CeCe knew she was leaving out some important details. But that was always the case, even back in high school. She knew it was better that way.

Silence again at the table, and CeCe noticed it was quiet in the restaurant as well. All the patrons had left. The only other people in the dining area were two waitresses wiping down tables and filling up ketchup bottles.

"I've got a two-hour drive. I better go," said Shawn.

"You're not staying here?"

"The clock is ticking on those emails," Shawn said as he stood up.

The two hugged again, and Shawn gave CeCe his new number. She walked him to the front door of the restaurant as if he was the guest at her house. The sour, sick feeling in her stomach grew as she again watched Shawn walk away from her, get in his car, and drive off.

115

31

Shawn cruised through the warm evening, windows down, music loud, fingers drumming on the steering wheel. He felt alive. Because he was alive. Nobody set up a claymore land mine to blow off his legs as he crept around the outfield fence. There was no sniper waiting to pluck him off when he reached the top of the bleacher steps. And nobody threw the deadbolt on the front door to keep him from entering. In fact, he was welcomed with open arms. By his mother, and to the extent he could, his father. Larry, and the rest of Quail too. At least the folks who were in the restaurant didn't seem to mind he was there.

Then, there was CeCe. Shawn could tell she was about sixteen percent pissed off, and eighty-four percent relieved to see him. That was a split he could live with. At least for now.

The road descended and Shawn felt a cool breeze rush through his car as he passed a large pond. He repeated the words aloud, "I don't have a boyfriend." That's all he needed to hear. All this time he had been afraid that CeCe would meet somebody, get married, move to the Philly suburbs and have two kids. But not even a boyfriend. Shawn cranked the music up even louder and pressed a little harder on the accelerator. What a night.

Another thing: that body. It was great to see it in person again. He had been looking at the picture of CeCe's beautiful face for four years. But her athletic, sexy body. Back in high school, most guys were intimidated by it, some made fun of it, and a few worshipped it. Shawn knew CeCe hated that, and tended to dress rather modestly, in public anyway. On a rare occasion when they were hanging out at her house, during their junior year, she came out of the bedroom in a bikini. It left Shawn speechless, and before she initiated the make out session, she said, "I love the way you look at me. Only you."

Shawn couldn't help but notice that he got more of a public eyeful of CeCe than he was used to. She would never wear a V-neck t-shirt, or at least not one cut that low. And never shorts that short. Usually mesh athletic shorts. Sometimes old jeans cut off an inch or two above the knee. The shorts she was wearing tonight showed an inch or two of pocket. Maybe that was part of growing up, becoming an adult. Confidence or something. Four years was a long time.

Shawn pulled into the driveway next to his apartment and crawled around back to his parking space. He sprinted up the stairs, taking two at a time. He walked through his apartment, the dry, cool conditioned air pointing out where he was sweating. He pushed the curtain on the back window to the side and peered out through the trees, across the creek, to the baseball field. That evening went better than he ever could have hoped for. He felt lucky, his family and friends welcomed him back, and CeCe was waiting for him. Or at least, didn't move on.

Shawn squinted to see some of the infield dirt or the outfield grass. Half of a moon was starting to rise, illuminating the night, if only just a little bit. Shawn left the curtain open, sat down in front of his laptop, and flipped open the screen.

32

September 5, 2006 - 12:11 PM

CeCe scanned the cafeteria for a path to the corner table. Why couldn't all the freshman have lunch together? Did there really have to be sophomores and juniors and seniors all over the place? Scurrying through this room with all the tables and all the people, all the eyes, was like running in the woods. Roots, mud, and holes all over, ready to trip, ready to twist an ankle.

CeCe decided on a route. It would keep her far away from the tables teeming with upper class-men. They had facial hair, and deep voices. They feared nothing and they had things to say to CeCe. Comments to make. She was holding her tray with both hands. She would have to trust that the zipper on her hoodie was up all the way, that the waistband was covering her butt.

"Kinda hot for that sweatshirt, don't you think?" asked a voice from the middle of a crowd at some table. "It's over ninety degrees!"

CeCe felt every single degree of those ninety. Sweat formed on her back between her shoulder blades, in the crease on the back of her knees. Lunch and three more periods. Then she could go out to field hockey practice where her ripped arms and her calves that looked like bell peppers when flexed were assets, even sought after, instead of sections of a dartboard for the nasty comments, or the sexual comments.

Then she heard it. A boy, or young man maybe, junior or senior, with a goatee was following her along, serpentine, between tables and around the chairs. He was holding a carton of milk out in front of him. Laughter erupted at each table CeCe passed. She didn't know he was doing behind her.

118

"Lemme rest my carton upon your buttocks," he announced. "Plenty of room for it to rest right on top there." Roars of laughter.

It was the same type of comment that her mother's ex-boyfriend used to make all the time. When mom wasn't around, that was. "Come 'ere, CeCe, and turn around, I need a place to rest my beer." Then he would laugh. And CeCe, who was ten at the time, had no idea what to do. No idea what to think.

Then, he would apologize. Call her over for a hug. That hug lasted forever. Maybe that was the tradeoff for having a body like this. Maybe to be the best athlete on the field, she would have to endure all the comments, all the laughing behind her back. And everything else.

Finally, she reached the corner. She dropped her tray onto the table and pulled her sweatshirt down as far as she could, careful to keep it down as she took her seat looking out the window, facing away from the rest of the room so nobody could see the tears. In a few hours, she could go out on the field, hit the ball around, and run. Run faster than anybody else out there.

33

June 20, 2013 - 11:12 AM

"Key Lime today, right?" asked Larry.

"You know darn well that Thursday is Key Lime," said Billy.

"Just making sure," said Larry, but Billy was right. He did know Thursday, every Thursday, was Key Lime Pie day at McMaster's. Greta was up well before dawn making sure she had enough. And she always did. Too much, most of the time.

"Believe it or not, she's running behind a bit. She said she'll be out with the first batch by noon."

"I'll be back," said Larry, then he walked out the door.

He shielded his eyes from the glare of the light blue sky. Sky covered with a gauzy layer of clouds, thicker in some spots, others clear. Within ten steps, sweat formed on his brow and on his back. Spring had ended; it was summer in Pennsylvania.

Larry stepped halfway down the bleachers and took a seat above the first base dugout. He spaced his feet, about shoulder width, then placed his hands on his knees. He closed his eyes, and breathed. In and out.

Accept and respect yourself; don't deny your screw ups, accept them, and move on.

He listened. Birds in front of him, car doors behind. The restaurant door opening, voices and clanging escaped, then dissipated. In and out, in and out.

But before long, his mind drifted. He was back on the night DJ died, died right there in front of him. The shortness of breath, the pain he must have been feeling, slurred his words. DJ told Larry that he tried to save the property. That made sense, the restaurant and ball field. He also told Larry that Muldoon knew. Knew what? That the property needed to be saved, or that DJ tried to save it.

Then he made Larry swear that he wouldn't tell a soul what he was trying to do, what he was looking for. That was easy enough, because Larry had no idea what he was looking for.

Before he collapsed, DJ had reached up to Larry and had handed him a slip of paper, which looked like the corner ripped from a larger sheet. Out of breath, in obvious pain, about to die, he said, "rrrr McMaster's… Will rrrrrefuse the key… rrrregret…a win. Look, it's rrrright there."

Larry tried to make sense of it all for the first few years after DJ's death. But he couldn't ask anybody for help, so he was on his own. Bouncing ideas off the guy in the mirror. The guy in the mirror knew exactly what Larry knew. Not much. Frustrated that he had let his friend down, and that he was going to let Billy and Greta down, and with nothing really to live for, Larry sunk into a cycle of ballgames, ice cream, and pizza; and ball games, pizza, and ice cream.

Larry's digital watch beeped, signifying high noon. Key Lime pie time. Larry hopped up, and again shielded his eyes, which were now sensitive to the light after being closed. Three steps up he stopped and said, "Refuse the key. Key Lime pie!"

Maybe there was something to the meditating. His mind had cleared and made this connection. After ten years, finally a lead. To be sure, it was a ridiculous one. Vague to say the least. But a riddle that took ten years to solve would have a crazy answer, wouldn't it? He skipped up the stairs, and into the restaurant.

Nobody refused the Key Lime pie. Folks came to McMaster's on Thursday because of the Key Lime pie. So somebody who refused the pie would be easy to spot. This was fantastic. It was late in the game, but Larry was figuring this thing out. Find the person who refuses the pie, then…

121

Then what? Who knows? Who cares, one thing at a time. The person who refuses the pie has to hold the next clue, one way or another. Larry pulled open the door, marched into the cool air, and up to the counter where Greta was waiting with Larry's slice. He sat down, and forked off a large hunk.

"Pretty much everybody gets a slice?" Larry asked Greta, nodding at the counter.

"Just about," said Greta, who had been drying her hands on the dishtowel since the moment she handed Larry his pie.

"Just about?"

"Yes, Larry, just about. But don't worry, I've got plenty more in the back. I can even send you home with a few."

Larry leaned in, looked left, then right. Then left again. "Who doesn't?"

"What do you mean, who doesn't?" chirped Greta.

"SShhh, just keep it down," whispered Larry.

"What the heck are you talking about?" asked Greta, now leaning in too.

Larry had another bite. "This is really good, you nailed it today--- Wait." Larry held up his hands. Focus. "Is there anybody who eats here regularly but doesn't get Key Lime pie?"

"Andrew Wilcox has been eating lunch here on Thursdays for twenty years---"

"Grampy Wilcox?"

"Yes, Grampy if you must. One Thursday, had to be over ten years ago. Maybe fifteen. Billy wanted to give him a free slice, for being such a great customer. But he refused."

Larry dropped his fork. "He what?"

"Refused. You know, didn't want any. But that was because---"

122

But Larry hadn't heard anything after 'refused.' He spun off his chair and scanned the room for Wilcox, whom he found sitting alone in a booth on the other side of the restaurant. He dropped on the seat across from him.

"Would you care to join me?" asked Wilcox, looking up only for a second to see who had already invaded his lunch.

"Thanks, Gram--- Thanks. I will." Larry watched Wilcox eat a salad with croutons and grilled chicken. Oil and vinegar bottles in the middle of the table. Part one of the plan: completed. Part two: there was no part two.

"I'm assuming," Wilcox said, pausing to stuff a crouton and spinach leaf into his mouth, chew and swallow, "that there is a reason you are sitting here with me, Larry? It can't be fascinating to watch an old man eat like a rabbit."

"Going to have dessert?"

"Doctor makes me eat salad for lunch every day. You think he told me to wash it down with an ice cream sundae?"

"But the pie. Thursday is Key Lime pie day. It helped put McMaster's on the map."

Wilcox put his fork down on the table and leaned back in his seat. "It smells and looks fantastic. But it's not for me."

"You've never had any?"

"Nope."

"Have you ever been offered?"

"I'm assuming anybody can order a slice, Larry, nobody needs an invitation."

Larry dipped his chin and leaned forward with his right eye, then winking it, said, "Are you saying you refused the Key Lime pie?"

"I'm saying, I never ordered any. I've never had any. If you call that refusing, then yes, I refused it," said Wilcox, the volume of his voice increasing with each word.

Larry nodded, and leaned back in his seat. Wilcox had picked up his fork and was shuffling a cherry tomato around an otherwise empty plate. Finally, Wilcox stabbed it, stuffed it in his mouth, then locked eyes with Larry, who had been sizing him up.

"What is this all about?" asked Wilcox.

Larry sensed that he had touched a nerve. He leaned forward, his forearms on the table, "Anything you want to tell me?"

Wilcox squirmed in his seat, and covered his mouth with his hands.

"DJ wanted you to tell me," said Larry.

"DJ?"

"Yes."

"DJ McMaster?"

"Yes, DJ McMaster."

"He's been dead ten years, what's he care what I eat?"

"He cares. Well, he cared. Trust me. You can tell me. Tell me what I need to know."

"Why do you need to know?" said Wilcox, lowering his voice, squinting his eyes as if Larry had sprouted a second nose during this inquisition.

"I can't tell you that. But trust me, I need to know. It's going to make a lot of people around here really happy?"

"Happy?"

"Yes," The smile on Larry's face grew.

Wilcox picked up his fork, looked at his empty plate, and put it back down. Rubbed his hand over his mouth. "And you say DJ, who has been dead ten years, wants, wanted me to tell you why I don't eat Key---"

"Refuse," interrupted Larry, speaking as if he had played a ninety-point word in Scrabble.

"Fine, why I refuse Key Lime pie?" asked Wilcox.

Larry looked at Wilcox like a girlfriend who was about to become a fiancée. After ten years, the mystery was about to be solved. To think that he had all but given up on life that night at the ballgame, the night he found Shawn.

Wilcox leaned in toward Larry, and a click above a whisper said, "I have a citrus allergy."

"A citrus allergy?" asked Larry. Louder than Wilcox would have liked.

"Keep it down," Wilcox said, looked around, then continued, "After I eat any citrus, I have about twenty minutes, thirty tops, to get to a bathroom. Preferably at home."

Larry slumped in his seat. "So you don't eat Key Lime pie because you have a citrus allergy?"

"That's what I said, didn't I?"

"How disappointing," said Larry.

"You're telling me. You should see the color of what comes out of me. Oh, and the smell."

Larry left the table and walked outside. He didn't say goodbye to Wilcox, or to Billy, or Greta either. Instead, he walked through the grass to the plaques and peered down at DJ's. Leaning on the flagpole, then the electrical box with his hand, he lowered himself to one knee. Under his breath, for only DJ to hear, he said, "I finally followed your clue, and it led me to a bowel movement. A terribly colored, foul smelling crap. You said, look, it's right there. How am I missing it?"

Again, he used the flagpole and electrical box to hoist himself up. As he walked toward the parking lot, he dug through his pocket for his car keys.

34

From the dugout behind him, Billy said, "step out, take a breath, ok?"

Shawn took his father's advice, but not because he heard him. He needed to get out of the batter's box for a second. All he could hear were the barbs and laughter from in front of him, from the Al's Everything crowd.

Shawn took a deep breath. In through the nose, out through the mouth. Or was it in through the mouth, out through the nose. No, that felt stupid. Oh, shut up and get back in the batter's box. Brave, be brave. Get pissed off at Jackson. He's a jerk.

Shawn dug in, deep breaths, having escaped to somewhere in the universe, replaced by shallow, sick pants. He looked out at Jackson, who looked like he was seven feet tall. Eight feet tall. His right arm a rifle. The baseball a bullet.

The crowd buzzed as Jackson stepped back on the rubber, ten seconds after Shawn stepped back in. "C'mon, Shawny, you got this. Pick one out," from the McMaster's dugout.

"Pick one out? He has to see it first!" Laughter.

The muscles in Shawn's arms and legs tensed. Swing at this pitch. Just swing at this pitch and get out of here. Shawn was a contact hitter. Make contact. It had to be another fastball coming. He had frozen on the first one. Barely saw it. Jackson would try to embarrass him again. He's going to throw a fastball right down the pipe. He had to know Shawn was scared to death.

Jackson rocked back, kicked his left leg into the air, then dropped it toward the front of the mound. See the ball, see the ball, see the ball. The baseball blasted out of Jackson's hand like a spitball out of a straw. But Shawn

126

had a good look at the location. He stepped, planted, and pulled his hands around his body, whipping the bat toward the path of the ball. But Shawn felt no contact. Not even a foul tip. He looked around like a child who had just fallen for the shell game on a city street corner.

"It's in the catcher's glove, Shawny," said the voice from in front of him.

Another voice. "Shawn, let me introduce you to Curve Ball. Clearly you've never met." Laughter, clapping. Knee slapping.

Shawn turned and took three steps toward the McMaster's Restaurant dugout. He looked at Billy, who extended his hands out in front of him, palms down, then pumped them up and down. Shawn knew his father was trying to calm him, but it looked like he was slamming on a piano.

Shawn stepped back into the batter's box. "Oh, and two," yelled the home plate umpire.

35

Shawn slid the door closed while looking out toward the trees. He sat on the singular chair on the deck and sweat formed on his brow before he had tasted his first swallow of beer. The sweat on his forehead, the sweat on his bottle of beer, and the babbling creek were the only things moving this night. After midnight. Sultry. Only the brightest of stars visible through the haze. The moon a buttery stain on the sky. Shawn's mouth turned up slightly at each end as he took in the scene.

Three days and nights had passed since he went back to Quail, to his family, to CeCe. Speaking to his mom felt natural, like throwing with the correct hand. Just the way it was. And seeing his dad, talking to him, listening to him, felt like it always did. Like brushing your teeth. And CeCe. To see her again. That she would see him again, talk to him.

Talking. Talking to people. Not something Shawn had done a lot of in the past four years. He was a talker growing up. Whispering during class.... "Mr. McMaster, something you would like to share with the class?" All hours of the night on the phone with girls from school, then, of course, with CeCe.... "Shawn, time to hang up." He would… Then, start texting.

It was frustrating to Shawn how he shut down in groups, could not think of anything to say, felt like everybody was judging his movements, his comments, and his hair. Especially when, one-on-one, he couldn't stop talking. To his mother, about life. To his father, about baseball. With Dusty and Chuck, they were almost like one person, he could talk about sports, girls, and overeating. But sometimes, even then, it seemed like Dusty and Chuck were out to get him, ganging up on him.

128

"We're just a comedy team, don't take it personally, brother," Chuck said to Shawn one day back in high school when Dusty was on vacation. "Ever notice that we do that to *everybody*?"

That made sense to Shawn, but he still had a difficult time remembering it when he was in their play-by-play cross-hairs.

But with CeCe... With CeCe he talked about everything. School, his parents, taking over the restaurant and field someday, and not wanting to take over the restaurant and field someday. About being scared to death a lot of the time in the batter's box; but then how the ball looked like it was the size of a basketball when he was hitting with confidence. Cockiness. About how easy it was for him to track down a fly ball. Always.

There was also the Shawn McMaster persona that took over on the baseball field. Losing himself in the moment, batter-dipped in cockiness and competitiveness. During the summer after his sophomore year, playing Legion ball, after smoking a single right passed the pitcher's head into center field, he spoke to the first baseman. "Tell your buddy over there the next time he throws that pitch I'm going to hit him right between the eyes with it." His next time up the pitcher threw one right at his head. Shawn didn't duck, didn't jump out of the way. Instead, he caught the ball with his right hand. Reached out and grabbed it. As he ran to first base, he rolled the ball to the pitcher. "Hit or be hit. I guess you made the right choice."

But the same guy could sulk in the corner after going oh for four, or after striking out. Inconsolable, even if he had saved the same game with his always-perfect fielding. It would even take CeCe a few hours to perk him up.

Shawn tilted in his chair and reached into his pocket, pulling out his phone. Pressed the home button.

129

Twelve-twenty-three in the morning. Too late to call anybody. Who would he call? He rested the phone on his thigh, looked out over the creek, through the trees. The ball field. Shawn had returned to Quail, had walked into the restaurant, spoken to his mom and dad, and CeCe. Saw many others from his past. But didn't step on McMaster Field. Couldn't.

He finished the rest of his beer in one big swig, and went inside to fetch his shoes. His apartment felt like a walk-in freezer. He tied his sneakers, then walked outside, heading for the only place he could possibly talk to somebody. Someone. Some... thing. Shawn laughed as he hopped over the creek.

The summer night was moist, but the grass on the field was bone dry. Summer had set in. The infield dusty, cracking as Shawn stepped in toward the dugout. A summer night, the sounds of baseball. He turned the corner, and there was the bat. Still leaning in the corner. Still cracked just above the handle. Shawn stood still, the leaves on the trees silent. Only the bugs and tree frogs providing their white noise.

Shawn moved toward the bat. Leaned in. Nothing. His stomach clenched with a laugh as he sat down on the bench.

"Boo!"

Shawn jumped to his feet and pressed his chest to keep his heart in place. "What the!!"

The bat laughed. "Gotcha!"

"You did.... you did." Shawn sat back down, right leg bent, left leg extended out in front of him.

"So you went back to Quail..." said the bat.

"How the heck did you know that?" asked Shawn, sitting straight up.

"I'm a freakin' talking bat, and you're asking me how I know what you've been up to?"

130

Shawn nodded, raising his eyebrows. "Yeah, so happy I went."

"That's terrific. How's your mom and dad?"

"They're great! I talked to my mom for at least an hour. It was like I never left."

"Oh, so you talked to your mom and dad for an hour?" asked the bat.

"Just mom. Dad had to, you know, work. He kept working. He came by when I talked about my job though." Shawn stood up, walked to the other end of the dugout, stuffing his hands into his pockets. He gripped his cell phone.

"And...."

"I talked to CeCe." Shawn said. He walked back toward the bat.

"How is she?"

"Amazing. She hasn't changed a bit," said Shawn, yanking his hands out of his pockets, his hands signaling safe like an umpire.

"She's just like she was when you disappeared?"

"She looks a little older, dressing a little more... grown up, I guess, but not --- I didn't exactly disappear," Shawn said, dropping his hands to his sides.

"I'm sorry, when you left. I was just using your word."

Shawn thought for a moment. He didn't remember using the word 'disappear' last time. Finally, "She's still beautiful."

"I'm sure she is."

Shawn walked to the end of the dugout and back again. No words. There and back again. Quiet. Shawn looked at the bat. "It was great to see her."

"I'm sure it was, bingo chip," replied the bat.

"That's all you have for me? I'm sure she is, I'm sure it was?"

"I'm waiting for you to be honest with yourself."

131

"I am! It was great to see her."

"I believe that," said the bat. "Are you sure she is 'amazing'?"

"We had a great conversation, I felt terrific when I left." Shawn looked at the bat, then down. "I said I was sorry. She said she knew I was."

"Boy, pop tart, that was a great conversation you had with CeCe about you."

Shawn extended his arms toward the bat, head tilted. "I asked if she finished college, and what was happening around Quail."

"I'm sure that made her fall in love with you. All. Over. Again."

"What the heck do you want from me?" asked Shawn, kicking at the ground, clearing a path through the dirt and sunflower seed shells.

"The truth."

"I told you the truth!"

"No you didn't," said the bat, voice slightly raised.

"How do you know? Wait, what's the truth then, you're so darn smart?"

"The truth is; you have no idea how she is. You know she's still beautiful, you know she still has a perfect, athletic body that looks terrific in shorts. Shorts that were shorter than you were used to seeing her wearing in public. But you have no idea how she *is*."

"I know she doesn't have a boyfriend," said Shawn.

"Did you do the math on that one, Captain Ridiculousness?"

Shawn took two steps toward the bat and raised his left hand to take a swipe at it. He froze like that, hand shaking, then dropped it to his side. "Darn it!" He stormed out of the dugout and marched into left field. He turned back toward the dugout, and stood there with his hands on his knees. The bat was saying something, but he couldn't hear it.

Shawn twisted his legs a bit, but didn't move his feet. Didn't take his hands off his knees. His shirt was sticking to his back, and the night sky, grabbed his arms, legs, and neck. A cloud of gnats surrounded him. Shawn stood up and swatted in front of his face with his right hand. He took three quick steps toward the dugout, then made a sharp left turn toward right field, toward his apartment.

Shawn stepped slowly over the creek, lips pursed, eyes squinted. Tired. The moon overhead, almost full, a sliver missing and still tucked behind some clouds. He took one step at a time up to his apartment door, missed the dead bolt with his key three times. "What the hell is wrong with you?" he said. He closed the door behind him, locked it, and leaned up against it. The dark of his apartment, the cool air, surrounded him. He closed his eyes and let out a deep breath.

36

Larry mashed the accelerator to the floor of his super-duty pickup truck. He was at least fifteen miles over the speed limit, but he was an hour and fifteen minutes late getting home. Cyn would be waiting on the couch, face twisted into half a frown, half a scowl.

He had driven this road that led up to his house at high rates of speed before. He felt invincible in his American-made vehicle, invincible as America herself. The local police recognized his truck. They wouldn't pull him over. And he needed to get home. 'One more hand' of cards led to three, four, five more. Fifteen more. Ah, the life of a retiree.

Cyn would be pissed, but she would get over it. She has the stuff she liked to do: keep the house in order, laundry, doing the dishes after each and every meal, and she would get to spend the rest of the evening with him. It was no big deal. He would take her to the lake after dinner, instead of watching the Phillies' game. Gestures like that had cheered up Cyn in the past.

Larry pulled into the driveway, hopped out of the truck, and jogged up to the front door. He twisted the handle, which he expected to turn, and then he expected to walk through the door and see Cyn sitting there.

He dug his keys out of his pocket and searched for the house key. He rarely used it, because Cyn had been almost always home, so the front door was unlocked most of the time. He found the correct key on the second try, then pushed through the door.

"I'm sor---," Larry started to say, but stopped. Cyn wasn't sitting there. Maybe she was a little angrier than usual. "Cyn!" he called out. His voice echoed in the hallway. There was no response. Dinner, then the lake, and

134

he would have to think of something else. She was clearly pissed off.

Larry walked through the kitchen to see if she was in the backyard, sitting or gardening, straightening up. As he walked to the back door, a single plate with crumbs, a single coffee cup and one empty glass in the sink caught his eye. The sink was usually empty.

Cyn wasn't in the backyard. Or the basement. Not in the bathroom nor taking a nap. She wasn't anywhere in the house. Larry sat down on the edge of their bed and looked around. The closet door was opened a few inches. One of Cyn's drawers was off its track, so it was sitting crooked in the dresser.

Larry walked around the house. It was quiet. Quiet enough to hear the conditioned air blowing through the vents. Cyn was not at home, and she had not left a note. He had no idea where she could have gone and no clue how to find her.

37

Shawn sat and watched. CeCe hadn't noticed that he was there. She was scooping some *Calculus Makes Absolutely No Sense* Chocolate into a cup. Lips curling, right eye squinting, left forearm flexing. Her hair was in a ponytail, shooting out from underneath her Phillies cap. Her McMaster's white polo shirt was worn thin on her right shoulder, and stained on her left hip.

Then, Shawn noticed something odd. Delicious, but odd. None of the buttons on CeCe's shirt were fastened. And every time she dug in for some *What Did Miley Do Now?* Wanilla (DJ's joking way of saying Vanilla, which stuck), she revealed at least an inch of cleavage. Back in high school, CeCe always made sure two buttons were fastened before scooping anything. Again, Shawn chalked it up to adulthood, and missing the last four years.

As CeCe rinsed her ice cream scoop before heading for another flavor, she noticed Shawn sitting there, watching her. A small smile moved some freckles around her mouth, and then she stood up and looked at the ceiling. Shawn knew this look… She forgot the final flavor for the sundae. He rested his chin in his palm and watched the show. Try as she might to hide it, to hide anything, CeCe's eyes were a screen to practically every thought she had. Shawn couldn't imagine how she could ever keep anything from him. That made him feel worse and worse, for every day of the twelve hundred plus he was gone.

CeCe finished up the sundae, passed it over the counter, and looked around. Having grown up in a restaurant, Shawn knew she was checking to see if she had a second to talk. CeCe hustled out to the table where Shawn was sitting.

"So, one visit and a bunch of texts each week? You have to do better than that," said CeCe.

136

"I, too, have a job," said Shawn, right hand on his chest, posing in a way that he thought made him look grown up. "A job which gives me an apartment."

CeCe waved her hand at the ceiling. "I bet you could still live here,"

Shawn leaned forward. "Can you keep a secret?"

"I promise," said CeCe, leaning in. Shawn couldn't help but peek.

"I'm working on leaving that job. But Steve invented the position for me, or me for him. Either way, I can't leave him high and dry. I have to make sure he's set before I move on. He really helped me out these past few years." Shawn leaned back again, "I'm in the process."

A smile grew on CeCe's face. "That's great," she whispered. Then, she looked over her shoulder. A man and his daughter were standing at the counter. But Greta, drying her hands on a dish towel, waved to CeCe, telling her to stay.

Shawn soaked in CeCe's smile, and downloaded her 'That's great.' But here is what would really be great. If Shawn could return, back to Quail, back to his family and friends. Back to CeCe, pick up right where they left off. Return to everything. Everything except baseball.

CeCe continued, still in a whisper, "So, you're in the process…"

Shawn explained how he needed to find somebody who could live off from a rather small salary, it had grown since Shawn started and Steve's business grew, but it was not very much, even considering the apartment was included, free of charge. "If I could only find another… me. Somebody that is hiding from something."

CeCe wriggled in her seat as Shawn finished talking, as if she had a mouthful of medicine that she was trying to choke down. He had to stop with the running and hiding talk. The last thing he ever wanted to do was run and hide from CeCe, but the desire to run away from what

137

happened trumped everything. However, CeCe clearly didn't see it that way. Shawn ran away from her. Hid from her. For four years. He had to try to see it the way she saw it, and talk about it in a way that didn't make her look so darn uncomfortable. He was trying to make fun of himself, to look weak, to take the blame, but it was backfiring.

The two were silent, staring into each other's eyes. Not unlike one evening during their junior year of high school, when the two of them had a quiet moment, locked in each other's gaze, and it was comfortable. Enjoyable. Anything but awkward. Perfect really. Like it was meant to be. And like the muscle memory of a baseball swing, the two fell into the same type of trance at that moment.

But after four years apart. Awkward. And anything but enjoyable.

Shawn looked away first, and hunted for anything to talk about. He picked up the napkin dispenser and held it in front of CeCe's face.

"Ice cream on my mouth?" she asked.

Shawn said nothing, just shook the red plastic back and forth in front of her.

CeCe raised an eyebrow. "No thanks, I'm good."

Shawn pulled the dispenser back toward his face, then thrust it toward hers, stopping it no more than six inches from her nose.

"Oh! Male, definitely male."

"Darn it, I thought female."

"Nope, male."

"Why?" Shawn asked, putting it back on the table, leaning in for a closer look.

"You know this, Shawn. When I look at it, I see a male."

"What the heck is male about it?"

"I don't know, straight up and down, strong shoulders," CeCe said, turning her palms to the ceiling.

138

This back and forth felt like old times, which is what Shawn wanted to get back to. But CeCe had only ever known, liked, loved, Shawn the baseball player. Could she love Shawn, the former baseball player? He was dying to ask, but afraid of the answer.

"I want to try 'us' again, CeCe."

"We're off to a good start, don't you think?"

"Yes, but do we have to start all over?"

"I don't think that's possible," said CeCe, who averted her eyes, and shifted in her seat, as if her butt was falling asleep.

Shawn took a moment to process that comment. Not possible to start all over? That was good. He didn't want to go all the way back to 'just friends' or 'dating' or 'going steady' or whatever the heck was short of ShawnandCeCe. But why did she look so uncomfortable as she said it? It sounded like a good thing. Why did it look so bad?

Of course, like he could never forget what he did, neither could she. There would always be the baggage of the pain and horror he caused that night at McMaster Field. "No, I guess it's not."

"But again, that's all happened, and there's not a God damned thing we can do about it now," said CeCe. "Except move on. Try again. We're different now. Older. Things have changed, but it doesn't mean we can't give it another shot. But I need... to take it slow, ok?"

"Ok," Shawn said. "Then, you understand I need to ease back into this slowly too. I'm not the same anymore, and there are things that... I won't be able to... do anymore." He decided to start with that. No talk of baseball. If CeCe wanted slow, Shawn could do slow.

"OK, then. To slow," said CeCe.

"To slow," said Shawn. But hopefully not too slow.

139

38

June 24, 2013 8:15 PM

"OK, then, to slow," said CeCe, but her mind moved elsewhere.

"To slow," said Shawn.

CeCe hopped up out of her seat and hugged Shawn around the head. She could only do that when she was standing and he was sitting. "Gotta get back to work."

"I have to head out also," Shawn said, looking at his phone.

"Keep going with that *process*," CeCe said, hanging air quotes around it. Shawn smiled as he walked toward the door. At some point, she was going to have to tell Shawn that her "what he did" was different than his "what he did." All Shawn could focus on was what happened after his last at bat, right after. But it was the four years after that CeCe was dealing with.

CeCe grabbed a damp rag and walked from table to table, wiping each one down. Most of them were empty. It was the lull between the dinner rush and the late evening or after-the-game snack crowd. Soon, these very tables would be smeared with ketchup or gravy or hot fudge, but Greta wanted them spotless for every new set of customers who came in.

She swiped her knuckles against a napkin dispenser and thought of Shawn. Thought of the male/female game. Discussing it was like the old days, before they went away to college, before Shawn's last at-bat, when they were still falling in love. Flirty, competitive, sweet. Before all the other shit happened. CeCe squeezed her eyelids together tight, then opened them. She looked around. Nothing had changed.

CeCe cleaned off the last table, then walked behind the counter, stopping to look at the pictures of Shawn. He had come back, but it felt to CeCe like holding a butterfly. Or a bird. Or whatever the hell they say. She had to tell him how hard it was on her when he left. But that could crush him, and send him running again. Perhaps for good.

But, she had to start with that. Because if they were going to get back together, there was a ton more CeCe had to tell him.

39

Albert Muldoon visited the city hall at least once a week. Building ordinances, requests for property boundary lines, interpretations of local zoning laws. The occasional speeding ticket. Today, he marched straight to District Justice Cahill's office, dressed in a suit, handkerchief in hand.

Cahill's secretary showed him in, closed the door as she left. Cahill did not get up.

"Muldoon," said Cahill, greeting the old man, pointing to the chair in front of his desk. Muldoon sat down, extending his hand across Cahill's desk. Cahill accepted the hand, shaking it once.

"So what's the good word in the Borough of Quail, your honor?"

"Cut the crap, Al, and get to the point. We both know why you are here. Do we really need to waste any more time on this?"

"I'm afraid we do," said Muldoon, leaning back in the chair, touching his hands together at the fingertips.

"I'm afraid I have nothing to tell you. The McMaster's aren't behind in taxes, aren't breaking any laws. The only thing to feel guilty about in there is how damn good Greta's apple pie is."

Muldoon leaned in. "Rumor has it you spoke to Larry the other day."

"I did."

"About?"

"Just a little chatter during a baseball game. And my dealings with other citizens of Quail are none of your business." Cahill rocked forward, and Muldoon's eyes got big so he could take him all in. "You may own most of Quail, but you don't own this office."

142

"Don't be so sure," replied Muldoon. Cahill's body froze and he squinted his eyes. He was up for re-election in the fall. "I have money to spend, however, I see fit. And lots of it."

"Al, look," said Cahill, shrinking back into his chair.

"Cut the crap, Buddy," said Muldoon. "I know Larry spoke to you about the McMaster property. I want to know what he knows. And I know you want to sit in this chair for a few more terms before you ride off into the sunset. My influence can make or break that."

"Are you threatening me?" asked Cahill, but with a ninety-pound voice.

"Promising," Al said, sitting up in his seat, steady and firm, looking Cahill square in the eye.

Cahill slumped forward in his chair, leaning his right elbow on his desk. He exhaled slowly, rubbing his right hand from his forehead to the nape of his neck. He opened his eyes and looked at Muldoon, "Fine, I will tell you what Larry knows, which is all that I know." Cahill closed his eyes for a few seconds, then opened them. "The night DJ died.... Larry saw him."

Muldoon pressed his palms together. So had he.

Cahill continued, "DJ told Larry to protect his family by saving the property."

"Why would the property need to be saved?" asked Muldoon, a grin growing toward his ears.

Cahill leaned back in his chair and folded his arms. The muscles in his forearms quivered as he squeezed his rib cage. "Because as of October first, the McMaster's will no longer own the property." Cahill's eyes closed and his chin hit his chest, as if somebody had yanked out his spine.

"What?" asked Muldoon, leaning forward, placing his hands on Cahill's desk.

"The McMaster's have occupied that property since before God invented dirt. Nobody ever questioned it, and in fact, except for you, everybody celebrates it. But the state audited this office a little over ten years ago and told me that DJ needed to produce some sort of documentation for the land. They didn't question his ownership; they just needed something on file, willing the property forward to Billy and Greta."

"DJ didn't produce anything before he died, did he?" asked Muldoon, but he knew the answer. He finally knew what DJ was up to the night he died.

Cahill shook his head. "The state gave the McMaster's a grace period, a rather generous one, during which to produce documentation. Billy and Greta don't have anything. Larry said, it doesn't exist. The grace period runs out ---"

"October first," interrupted Muldoon, bulldozer wheels turning in his head. The room was quiet for a minute, Cahill was moving a pen around on his desk, and Muldoon was staring out the window. Then, "So if no paperwork turns up, no documentation is produced...." Muldoon said, leading Cahill.

"Then, the property goes up for public auction."

Muldoon smiled, showing all of his teeth. He leaned back in his chair, "and I ---"

"I know," interrupted Cahill, "you have money to spend, however you see fit. And lots of it."

Muldoon left the office, left the building, and floated toward his car. He had known that DJ was up to something the night he died, something he wouldn't show Muldoon. And now, Muldoon knew what it was. But, Muldoon didn't know where it was. However, there was good news: Larry Last, the only person who could possibly know that something existed to give Billy and Greta ownership of the McMaster property, had no idea that anything existed. Muldoon tapped his fingers on the steering wheel as he drove toward that delicious little sliver

144

of land tucked between his two housing developments. He would drive by it, just for a look.

40

Larry lugged the foldout beach chair through the trees, over some brush, and into the clearing that not more than a handful of people knew about. It was beyond the left field fence at McMaster Field, past the batting cage and down a foot or two into a depression. He opened the chair, and positioned himself so he could sit, could meditate, and follow the progress of the game on the scoreboard.

Larry lowered himself into the seat, wiggled into a comfortable position, placed his feet flat on the ground, his hands on the armrests of the chair. Closed his eyes. Breathed. In front of him, the hum of the crowd was interrupted every so often by the sound of baseball against an aluminum bat. From behind, the sounds of crickets and tree frogs from the woods, and the occasional car door or backyard conversation from Muldoon's housing developments on either side of the McMaster property. Larry heard all the sounds, but tried not to listen. Tried to let them come through his consciousness, then out. Sound with no meaning, no purpose. Just sounds bouncing around in the warm, muggy summer evening.

The most difficult person to forgive is yourself; you are with that person all the time.
Time passed. Innings. Hit, runs, and outs. Larry sat amongst it, his mind clearing, emptying. *To forgive is to set a prisoner free and discover that prisoner was you.* He felt like a tree in these woods. No, a leaf. Moving and swaying, not by choice, but by the whim of the universe. Calm. Quiet. Free. *Remember what the Buddha said, 'To understand everything is to forgive everything.'*

Then, through it all, over the hum of the crowd, in front of the sounds of the woods, he heard DJ's voice: "Rrregret a win."

Regret a win. Who would regret a win? It didn't even make sense. Everybody loved to win. Some people may not like or be able to eat Key Lime pie, but nobody would prefer losing over winning. So, if there was somebody, it should be easy to spot them.

Larry opened his eyes and checked the scoreboard. The bottom of the third had begun. He hopped up, folded the chair, leaned it against a tree, and headed up toward the field. As he walked, he reached into the chest pocket of his shirt and pulled out a laminated corner of a piece of paper. The words Last of the Third were written vertically, so that 'Last' had its own line, 'of' had its own line, and 'the Third' had its own line. Larry read it, as he had thousands of times over the last ten years. Rubbed his fingers across it. Then slipped it back into his pocket.

When he was three steps onto the landing of the bleachers in left field, Larry belted out, "Last of the Third!" A few fans turned their heads, but most continued to watch the game, all but ignoring Larry. This form of investigation, of inquiry, had netted no information for Larry. He used to get shocked or dirty looks. Then, he was labeled as the crazy town crier. Now, he had become background noise that fans had to endure during the bottom of the third inning.

What else could "Last of the Third" mean? It was an old fashioned way of saying the bottom of the third, and DJ, who had written it, had handed it to Larry on the night he died, as he died, was an old fashioned baseball guy. Larry had hoped that at some point over all these years something, anything, would happen in the bottom of the third inning of some game at McMaster Field. "It's right there," DJ had said. Larry wished he knew where.

But, he had a new idea tonight, a new mission, a new lead. Look for somebody who wasn't happy about his team winning. Maybe somebody on the field. Maybe in the crowd. At the very least, it should be easy to find

147

somebody who wasn't enjoying the fact that their team was winning.

The game was close; the home team of the affair winning by one or two runs the entire game. By the top of the seventh, the last inning, with the score seven to five, Larry made his way into the home bleachers. He scanned the crowd. All the parents, family members, and friends of these middle school aged kids on the field were cheering and smiling; worried that their team might give up the lead. The winner of this game would move on in the Quail county playoffs. The loser could hang their cleats up in the garage or the basement and start thinking about football season.

With two outs and two runners on, his team still down, seven to five, the batter hit a long, high fly ball to center field. The center fielder drifted back, deep, toward the fence. The home crowd held its breath, the visiting crowd stood up. But the center field slowed down three or four steps in front of the fence, turned, reached both hands into the air and caught the ball in his glove, ending the game. The visiting crowd groaned, and clapped for its team's effort. The home crowd cheered. Their team was moving on, still alive.

The coach of the home team was pulling his players out into right field to talk to them, to celebrate, to talk about what would come next. The parents and families hugged and high-fived. Then, Larry saw him.

One of the fathers was standing near the fence behind first base, calling to his son. The son kept walking toward his coach, every step or two peering back over his shoulder to look at his father. Finally, the father pointed at the ground in front of him, as if he were calling for a dog to come sit beside him. The son looked at the coach, then turned, head hung low, and walked toward his father.

Larry casually walked over toward the two, and followed them up the hill toward the parking lot. He listened to the conversation as best he could.

"This is absolutely ridiculous," said the father.

"It's no big deal. We won," said the son.

"That's not the point."

The son looked at the ground as he walked. Larry didn't know what regretting a win was if he wasn't watching it here. It seemed that the son wanted to enjoy the win with his team, but the father had some sort of axe to grind. Larry closed in on the two as they approached the car. He had been retired from teaching for quite some time, but he could still think on his feet. "Great win, huh?" he said to the father, the son already slumping in the passenger seat. It was such a simple question, but the father would have no choice but to show his hand.

"Oh, terrific, whoop-de-doo," the father said, reaching to open the driver side door.

Larry probed. "I guess you're ready for the season to be over? It's been a long time coming since March."

The man walked around the car toward Larry, and his speed and the angle of his head put Larry back on his heels. But maybe he was finally getting to the bottom of something. Or the beginning of something. He would take the butt end of anything right now. October first was bearing down on him like a high and tight fastball.

"That's not it at all," said the father through gritted teeth. Then, his face relaxed, and he took a step back and sat on his car. He crossed his arms.

"Then, I don't understand. Your son's team just moved onto the next round of the playoffs, why do you look like, like, you regret it."

As soon as Larry said 'regret,' the father perked up again, like turning on the fan below one of those wind tube puppets they use to advertise stores and car dealerships. His hands flailed in front of him. He stepped toward Larry, who

149

thought the process of finding information was about to get painful.

The father wagged his index finger above Larry's nose. "The only thing I regret was paying for my son to play on this team. He's their *best* pitcher, and he didn't get an inning today. How is he supposed to get noticed? How is he supposed to get a scholarship, or get drafted?"

Larry thought, "really, that's it? That's what this is about?" But, unfortunately, he thought it out loud.

"Yes, old man, that's what this is about! Do you know how difficult it is to get a young player noticed now-a-days? Everybody has YouTube clips and highlight videos. Back in your day, if you had talent, they found you. Now it's a beauty contest."

"But, they won. Aren't you happy about that?" Larry asked, his voice trailing a bit, hoping against hope that he could still get helpful information.

"My God, have you been listening? A county championship doesn't mean anything anymore. Who cares? Your team won. Big deal. It's about getting to the next level, Pops," said the man as he dunked into his car seat. Then, his head popped up again, "You're stuck in the old days. Why don't you go sit at the counter in there and have a malted?"

Larry watched them drive away, screeching the tires as they hit the main road. Then, he headed toward the restaurant. He might as well have a malted, or some pie, while he still had the chance.

41

The game had ended with a ground ball to
Chuck at short, who flipped it to Dusty covering
second for the force out. Chuck didn't even look
at second base, or if Dusty was there covering. He
knew he would be.

"That's some chemistry for a couple of thirteen year
olds," Shawn heard somebody say as he slipped through the
crowd. He had noticed something recently; his mother
wasn't around immediately after some games. And he had
looked into the bleachers after the last out was recorded
tonight, and saw Greta scurrying up the steps toward the
flagpole and plaques, toward the restaurant. What the heck
was she up to?

Shawn followed from a safe distance. He hid among
the fans at the top of the bleachers, putting himself where
he could see her, but she could not see him. He felt his
heartbeat and the sweat drying on his face as he watched
his mother move passed the lit front of the restaurant, into
the darkening, blue evening around the side. Shawn darted
through the twilight, and positioned himself around the
corner from Greta. He peeked, relieved to see that her back
was to him.

Greta leaned on the door to the Winner's Locker
Room with her left palm and forearm, and knocked with
the knuckle of the middle finger on her right hand, like
somebody trying to crack an eggshell without demolishing
the entire egg.

Then, she said, "Shawny won again, Al. Watch out,
he's coming for you." Now standing a step away from the
door, "I'm sure I'll be back again real soon," and she
pounded on the door once with the butt of her right hand.

Shawn barely pulled his head back before Greta
turned and started walking toward him. He would have to

hide, or at least have a reason for being where he was. Usually, he would be down with his teammates.

Greta pulled the door of the restaurant open and saw Shawn sitting at the counter, facing her.

"What are... Why aren't you down with the team?" she asked.

"I got a little overheated, needed to cool off," Shawn lied.

"Ah, you're just like your father. This heat gets to him too. Let me get you a drink."

Shawn spun around and watched his mother get him a bottle of water from the small refrigerator under the counter. From behind, he could hear the rest of his teammates pouring through the door.

42

"Just come, you didn't talk to daddy that much, I think he wants to talk to you," Greta said, wall phone in one hand, body wrapped in the cord, bacon cheeseburger and fries on a round, white plate in her other. "OK, sweetie," she said, hanging up. She delivered the lunch plate to Larry, who was sitting at a table for two in the middle of the restaurant.

"Here he comes," said Chuck into the end of a straw.

"The champ?" asked Dusty, speaking into the business end of a fork.

"You better believe it."

"He's ready to go, Chuck. Look at him, he's been working hard in the locker room already. Covered in a glaze of sweat, determination and apple pie."

Billy walked over to Greta and Larry, sweat soaked through his white t-shirt and apron, shooting Dusty and Chuck a dirty look. He looked at Greta and raised his eyebrows, tipping his head toward her.

"I don't know." Greta looked at Billy. "He seemed a little distant, kind of like the first time I spoke to him at the grocery store, I suppose."

Billy squeezed his hands together in front of his chest, staring at something on the floor. Then, he turned and walked back toward the kitchen.

"He said maybe later," Greta called out, to Billy's back.

"It'll take time." Larry picked up his burger. "Boy's been gone a while."

"I know. It's just that we're flying through the summer, and," Greta's voice trailed off, more words caught in her mouth, which is where they stayed. Greta and Larry both stared off. Quiet. A mid-July afternoon was inching toward evening, the sun dropping through the sky, customers leaving and entering as the two daydreamed for a moment.

The jumping of the chair across from Larry awoke them both. Muldoon plopped his tied and suited body down into the seat, toothy grin on his face. He eye-balled Larry as if he were trying to read his mind, then turned to Greta. His smile stayed. He said no words. Then, Billy arrived, and Muldoon smiled at Billy. The three then traded looks with each other.

Dusty pointed at Muldoon. "Oh look, it's the challenger."

"Not a drop of sweat on this guy," said Chuck.

"But he is covered in ugly," said Dusty.

The guys were ignored this time, the four staring at each other across the lime green table. Larry decided to break the silence. "What?" he asked Muldoon.

Muldoon leaned in and looked them all in the eye one last time, like a poker player about to drop a full house on the table. Then he said it. "October first, huh?"

Billy and Greta looked at each other, faces turning pale like Billy's t-shirt. Larry just stared at Muldoon, elbows on the table, two hands on his burger, grease and ketchup dripping on the plate. Billy moved in on Muldoon. "What about October first?" he asked.

"You know, Billy. Larry does too. And now, I know as well." Muldoon stopped talking and instead looked in all the corners of the restaurant, and out the window, down to the field. Billy and Greta looked at Larry, who nodded, and searched for the perfect French fry.

"They're in there close, I can't tell what's going on," said Chuck.

"Lots of body blows, I imagine, but I can't see. Or hear," said Dusty.

Billy leaned on the table with both hands, breathed in and out deeply, then looked at Muldoon, "Seating is for customers only."

Muldoon stood up and smoothed his tie, top to bottom, slowly. Smiled at Billy, and started toward the door. Greta looked at Muldoon, eyes glassy and said, "Al, don't tell anybody." Muldoon turned to her, pinched his index finger and thumb together and dragged them from one end of his mouth to the other. Then, he turned and walked out. He patted his stomach as he walked across the parking lot, a hop in his step.

Billy sat in the chair Muldoon vacated. Greta pulled in beside him, leaned her hip on his shoulder, and combed his hair with her fingers. "So you know there's nothing willing this place to us," Billy said to Larry, waving his hand over the restaurant and the field. It wasn't a question, more of a statement of fact.

Larry nodded; there was no denying it. But DJ had told him not to tell anybody. Anybody is anybody, including Billy and Greta. *Beauty is truth. Truth beauty... Live in this moment.... Plead the fifth.*

Crap.

Billy leaned on the table with his forearm, which left a sweaty smudge, "You were there the night my father died. What did he tell you?"

Chuck said, "They're checking on the champ."

Larry looked at Billy, then back at Greta. He took a deep breath, stalling. "Well, nothing really."

"Nothing?" Billy asked, leaning closer to Larry.

"Well, nothing more than you already know," Larry leaned back in his chair. He tried to look like he was telling the truth, but he looked like the guy who farted in church.

"Just tell me what he told you," said Billy.

His tone brought Greta into the conversation. "Wilbur Shawn, that's enough." Billy retreated into his chair. "I'm sure that was a difficult night for Larry. And why wouldn't he tell us everything he knew?"

Dusty said, "Definitely a debate of some kind, but I can't hear. Perhaps training table discussion? Apple pie or cherry."

The interruption gave Larry a chance to think. How could he keep his word with DJ and show Billy that he had been trying to help all these years? "Listen, there's one thing that I know that you don't. Well, you know, I know it, but you don't know that it has anything to do with this."

"Larry," growled Billy, causing Greta to place a hand on his forearm.

Another deep breath. Before he exhaled, Larry pulled the laminated corner of paper from his chest pocket, looked around the restaurant, then handed it to Billy.

"Last of the third," Billy read.

"After he told me about October first, and to help you guys out, he handed me this. Then, then he---"

"So you're not crazy," said Greta, as if she had found a missing shoe where she had looked a hundred times.

Larry leaned into his burger and fries. "I'm not sure I'd go that far…"

Billy held the paper in his hand, and looked out the window down toward the field. "So, last of the third, bottom of the third. I get it. That's always when you start hooting and hollering. But what does it have to do with this place?"

"I have no idea," said Larry, happy, for once, to be telling the truth.

"So, we have exactly what we had before. Nothing." Billy held the laminated paper between his thumb and first two fingers.

Greta grabbed it out of his hand. "Wrong. For once, we have hope," she said, waving it in his face.

"What is that she has there?" asked Chuck.

"Mouthpiece?" asked Dusty.

"Hair piece?"

156

"World peace?"

"Carrots and peas?"

"Carrots and sticks?"

"Fleas and ticks?"

"Speeding ticket?"

Then, in unison, "Lottery ticket?"

Billy popped up and stormed back toward the kitchen, blasting Dusty and Chuck on the way by, "For once, would you two SHUT UP?" Billy stopped by the counter, leaning on it with both hands for a moment. Took a deep breath, then continued to the back, more slowly than he was moving before.

Greta passed Dusty and Chuck on the way to the kitchen herself, "Muldoon has that effect on him, I suppose. Don't take it personally."

"Yuck, Muldoon," said Chuck.

Dusty squinted and wrinkled his nose. "The worst."

Larry finished his burger and headed for the door. He would go watch some batting practice, soak in some afternoon sun. Maybe just sit. Be. He didn't like lying to Billy and Greta, but that was over now. All he could do, in this moment, was hold the door open for the young couple approaching.

Accept and respect yourself; don't deny your screw ups, accept them, and move on.

43

"Why don't we go for a walk instead?" asked Shawn.

"Where?" asked CeCe.

"Anywhere," said Shawn, waving his hand away from the restaurant.

CeCe took Shawn's hands in hers and looked him in the eye, which now caused her to crank her head back and him to drop his forehead forward. It was worth the strain for Shawn. Those eyes were medicine. Drugs. Like street drugs. Addictive. "You can do this," she said.

The two moved through the front door of the restaurant, which was held open for them.

"Thanks, La-Ray," said CeCe.

"Thank you," said Shawn, ducking his head toward his chest.

"Well, look, there they are," said Greta through a tired smile. "Dinner?"

"Sounds great, Mrs. M.," said CeCe.

Shawn said nothing, just nodded. Made eye contact with Greta. He had sensed that CeCe was keeping something from him the last time they were together, and now it looked like Greta was doing the same.

Greta slid through the swinging door, and before it stopped swinging, Billy blasted through. "Let's go," he called to one of the waitresses, who was taking an order. "This has been sitting here forever," he said, pointing to two platters of food on the counter.

CeCe turned and looked at Billy, then snapped her head back to Shawn.

"Is he always like this now?" asked Shawn.

"No. No, he isn't." CeCe peeked over her shoulder again. "You know he's always short with people, but he's joking, his sense of humor. This is different."

158

Billy slammed a plastic tray of glasses, still dripping from the washer, onto the counter. The crash turned most heads in the restaurant. Shawn thought about leaving. Just getting up and walking out. It was strange to be around people again, and he was sensing that it was strange for them to have him around. CeCe and Greta were hiding something from him, and Billy was angry about something as well. The only thing new around here was... him.

CeCe stood up, walked around the counter, and started putting away glasses with Billy. She said something that Shawn couldn't hear, but caused Billy to look over at him. Billy walked over and sat where CeCe had been sitting.

The two looked at each other. Shawn started to let a smile slip, more out of discomfort than anything, and Billy followed suit. His father looked older. Grayer. The skin around his eyes more creased than Shawn remembered. Baggy underneath.

"So," Billy started, "you sell software?"

"It's more like I distribute it."

"Don't they have to buy it first?"

"They're already part of Steve's company. The software needs to constantly be updated and upgraded for the company to keep doing what it does."

"I see," said Billy, the sweaty white t-shirt clinging to his chest and shoulders. He wore the face of somebody who knew the punch line of the joke somebody was telling.

"They email me, I email them back what they need," said Shawn. That made it sound so simple. Like anybody could do it. He could see the wheels grinding out that fact in his father's head.

"So you send emails?"

"Yeah, I guess that's what I do." Steve had credited Shawn with helping take his company to the next level over the past four years. Billy made it sound like he made money for sending letters to old friends…

Don't leave. Don't run. Talk. It's ok. "So this place looks like it is jumping, as usual," said Shawn, changing the subject to something Billy could be more positive about.

"We're doing ok," said Billy, looking over Shawn's shoulder.

"OK? Looks like you are doing great! The place is packed."

"Business is good."

"Good? Every table is filled right now!"

Billy reestablished eye contact with Shawn. "If you were so damned worried about how this place was doing, maybe you shouldn't have run off for four years," Billy said, then stormed off to the kitchen.

Perhaps Billy hadn't forgiven Shawn for what he did to him.

Shawn felt like somebody had ripped every bone out of his body. And that every eye in the restaurant was on him. CeCe scurried over at sat down across from him, and Greta arrived just in time to keep Shawn from sliding out of the booth.

"Shawny, stay. He's just… having a bad day," said Greta.

"He's right, I let everybody down."

"That's not true," said CeCe. Shawn looked at her, but she had nothing else to say.

"You've never let anybody down," said Greta, looking at Shawn, then at CeCe, then back at Shawn. "Daddy's missed you."

"Yeah, right," said Shawn.

"We all have. He just doesn't know how to show that he's happy you're back," said Greta.

Shawn looked at CeCe. She smiled at Shawn, but the look in her eyes wasn't what he was used to. Then he

160

said to Greta, "So he's going to yell at the waitresses and slam glasses every time I show up?"

"No, honey---" Greta grabbed his wrist.

"I shouldn't have come back," said Shawn, staring at the table.

"That's not true."

"Everybody is edgy and angry, and it's because I am here. Everybody is better off with me back in my apartment, hiding."

CeCe gasped, then sprang out of the booth and hustled through the front door.

"Now what?" asked Shawn, watching CeCe go.

Greta turned her body toward her son. "It's going to take time, Shawn. You were gone for a while. People... made due."

"Made due?"

"Did what they had to... To get by," said Greta, seeming to pick each word like steps across an icy walk.

"Get by," Shawn said, almost under his breath. He wanted to ask what was going on. What was everybody keeping from him? What was everybody trying to "get by?" Things seemed normal around the restaurant, around the baseball field, when he had first returned. Now, as time had gone by, things had gotten worse. Billy was angry, and something said made CeCe run off.

"Just promise me you'll give this time. Give everybody some time," said Greta, standing up.

Shawn said nothing, looked around the restaurant. Looked at his pictures hanging on the wall. Looked at the fake smile on his mother's face, wondering what she was hiding behind it. She *had* to want him back, she was his mother. Billy was honest with his feelings. And CeCe, well, she escaped from his presence. "OK, I will."

"Promise?" Greta asked.

Shawn nodded his head in response, and watched Greta walk away. He had lied to his mother, but at least he

161

hadn't done it with words. He thought about his apartment, the soft whir of the air conditioning unit. The balcony off the back, overlooking the brook. The soothing babble of the water rushing over the rocks. The comforting rustle of an evening breeze through the trees, through the leaves. He stuffed his hand into his pocket, searching for his keys.

44

"I just wish," said Shawn, while pulling CeCe close with a hug around the neck, "that you could know how it feels to run that fast."

"Oh, shut up. It was a great catch, OK? Let's leave it at that," said CeCe.

Billy turned to the two eighteen year olds, "A great catch that in the last inning of the game. A four-for-five game."

Greta walked behind all of them as they moved toward the front of McMaster's Restaurant. She knocked lightly on the door of the Winner's Locker Room as she passed it, muttering "Won't be long now, Al." Her son was playing the best baseball of his life, just months before he would be eligible to play in his first Final Exam.

Billy was not a step past the front door when he announced, "Everybody's bill, thirty percent off!" The late dinner crowd, filling a little more than half of the tables, cheered. "Sit down, everybody," he said to the other three, "I'll get our drinks."

"How about that, Mrs. M? Mr. M'll get the drinks," said CeCe, sliding across the booth seat so Shawn could sit next to her.

"He must be in the best of moods, I suppose," said Greta. She enjoyed all four of them spending time together. Quality time. She wondered why it couldn't always be like this.

Billy returned to the table squeezing four glasses, filled with soda, in his hands. Cokes for the kids, Sprite for Greta, Diet for himself. "So, your first at-bat. You smoked the first pitch up the middle. Were you expecting that pitch?" asked Billy. Most of the time his gruff voice pervaded the dining area like a splash of hot oil, but every

163

one of these syllables bounced around the room like a little leaguer giving high fives after his first-ever home run.

"I wasn't expecting anything. I just… saw it, and hit it. I felt really good after BP, and I guess I kept it going," said Shawn.

"See, it's all about your mindset," said Billy. "Back when I played---"

"You never hit like that," Greta interrupted. Then, imitating Billy, "back when you played."

Greta looked around the table after delivering that jab. Shawn smirked while investigating the knuckle on his right ring finger. CeCe stared at Greta, then turned her attention to Billy, her enormous, beautiful blue eyes as big as Greta had ever seen them.

Billy shook his head ever so slightly, and took a sip of his soda. "Mom's right. I never came close to hitting like that." Billy pointed at Shawn as he said, "Son, guys who make it to the next level have games like that."

"I just felt so… good. So comfortable in there," Shawn said, looking up as though he was trying to see into his own brain to find the right words. "Today, when I was hitting, I felt the way I always feel when I'm fielding."

"In the zone," said CeCe.

"Oh," Shawn pivoted his body toward CeCe. "You've read about that?"

CeCe slapped Shawn's arm with the back of her hand. "CeCe," Greta said, sounding astonished. "That deserves at least *three* slaps."

CeCe obliged, then said, "I've been in the zone before, Shawn. Sometimes, in soccer or field hockey, I swear there were days when I could tell how the goalie was going to move before she moved."

"Alright," said Billy, as if he hadn't heard or seen anything that just happened, "your second at-bat, you hit a double on an oh-two pitch."

164

Shawn drilled a finger into CeCe's neck, and said, "I knew he was going to try to drop a curve ball on the outside corner in that at-bat. I barely fouled that pitch off the first time around, so I knew he was coming back to it. I waited for it. The third pitch he gave it to me, and I went with it down the left field line."

Billy turned to Greta, and as he dug into the huge plate of nachos a waitress dropped off, "That's how a hitter thinks."

"Let's not stop there," said CeCe, sliding a chip covered in cheese, tomatoes and sour cream around the plate. "Tell us about the rest of the at-bats," she said, burying her chin in her hands, batting her eyes at Shawn.

Greta loved the way CeCe teased Shawn. But, she also knew that Shawn's athletic ability was one of the things that CeCe found irresistible. CeCe looked like a girl who could play any sport better than every other girl out there. But, the way CeCe would describe some of Shawn's more amazing accomplishments, like many of the catches he made in left field, showed that she was a little in awe of, a little jealous of, but mostly in love with, Shawn McMaster, baseball player.

Shawn finished talking about his last at-bat, "… was probably the ball I hit the hardest, the second baseman just happened to get in the way."

"Get in the way?" said Billy. "He had to save his own life. That ball might have killed him if he didn't catch it!"

Greta watched everybody laugh at Billy's commentary. The conversation hit a lull, and all four of them worked toward the bottom of the plate of nachos. Then, a guy who lived in Quail stopped by the table to tell Shawn that he had been at the game, and that it was the best he had seen anybody play all season.

"Gosh, Shawn," said Billy. "It's moments like these when I am so darn proud of you."

165

Even though Greta watched a huge smile erupt on Shawn's face, like the sun rising over the Atlantic Ocean, she added, "But we're always proud of you, honey, no matter how you do."

"Oh, no, yeah," Billy said, trying to iron out the wrinkles in his unfiltered praise. "Of course. Of course we are." But then, he leaned toward Shawn, and whispered as if Greta couldn't hear, "but after games like that, it's pride that could explode out of my chest."

"You sure that's not the nachos trying to escape?" said Chuck, having snuck up on the table unnoticed.

Dusty, who must have dropped out of the ceiling, joined in, "Another Pathmark---"

"Hallmark," said CeCe.

"Another Hallmark moment, ruined by Chuck," said Dusty.

Greta piled the empty glasses onto the empty plate, and carried it back to the kitchen. Billy slid out as well, making room for Dusty and Chuck to join ShawnandCeCe. The two stood hip to hip in the kitchen.

"You have to watch how you say that kind of stuff," said Greta.

"I know, I know," said Billy. "It's just that when I see him play like that, to his full potential, it's so exciting. He could be the first McMaster to make it to the big leagues."

"Easy there, papa. What if he doesn't even want to play baseball that long?"

Billy's mouth dropped open like a college kid setting foot on the beach on his first trip to Spring Break. "Honey, he's a McMaster. What else could he possibly want to do?"

"I suppose," said Greta, pushing through the swinging door. She stood behind the counter, watching Shawn with his three closest friends. Dusty and Chuck talked and talked, and laughed, and talked some more.

166

CeCe talked a little, laughed a lot, and put her head on Shawn's shoulder. Shawn's eyes moved around the table, his mouth turned up into the smallest of grins. He didn't say much, he laughed a little, but there was no question that the universe of this conversation revolved around him.

45

Shawn drove right by the parking lot of the McMaster Restaurant and Field as several cars filled with high school kids pulled out. An afternoon practice must have finished recently. Shawn knew CeCe was working that afternoon, and he saw her car in the lot as he passed. She was inside, white skirt revealing tanned, toned legs. Strong yet feminine arms delivering meals, snug white t-shirt hugging her slender midsection. White sneakers. This he knew.

That's all he knew. They used to talk for hours, about anything, about everything, up in the Scorer's Loft, as Billy and Greta cleaned up and closed up the restaurant. CeCe knew that his favorite hitting count was two-two, even though the pitcher had the advantage. Shawn knew that the moment she felt most alive was when she was toward the end of a run, and she had to dig deep to keep going. They hadn't seen each other for four years. Hadn't seen each other, hadn't talked.

Shawn turned into one of Muldoon's housing developments that bordered the McMaster property. At the first three houses, adult men wearing shorts, wearing ear buds, wearing sneakers with greened soles, the fathers of the homes, mowing lawns. The mother at the fourth house, a house with trimmed bushes equally spaced in beds that had mulch and didn't have weeds, opened the mailbox and looked inside. A father and son shot baskets in the driveway at the fifth house, the black driveway marked with a slate blue foul line, key, and three-point line. At the next house, teenage brother and sister wore running sneakers and ankle socks, athletic shorts and shirts, leaning on each other as they stretched their quads.

Shawn used to traipse through the developments surrounding the McMaster property dressed in Halloween costumes, or dressed in dark clothes playing Man Hunt with the neighborhood kids, or in shorts and a t-shirt while going for a jog with CeCe.

But that felt like a lifetime ago. Or, at least, a long time. A long time that should have been filled with four years of college, four years of college with CeCe. Four years of dates, spats, and making up. Where could they be now? Engaged? Maybe even married. Would they have been in the car together shopping for a house. Would he still be playing baseball?

Like a ball hit a country mile, but foul--- it didn't matter. Those years were gone, his career was gone. Shawn always thought there was a slight chance he would return to Quail, and he did. He had great people in his life who forgave him, who waited for him. But like Billy always says, "father time is undefeated." Four years is a long time to go without playing baseball. If he couldn't get back out there to play four years ago, there was no way he was ready now. And he knew it would take some unimaginable convergence of events, like a Phillies player hitting... four hundred, during the same year the Eagles won their first Super Bowl, during the same year that the 76ers went the whole season without losing a game. The chances were slim and none, and slim hadn't quite left the building, but he was digging through his pockets for his car keys.

Shawn had to admit, Muldoon's development was quaint. The sidewalked streets lined with wrought iron lampposts, winding through undisturbed clumps of trees, leading to one picture perfect home after another. It looked like something out of a movie or television show. Shawn reached the back of the development, passed by Al's Everything Shop, then circled back. That was a funny place for a store; out on a main road would have to be better. Shawn always thought McMaster's Restaurant was in the perfect location for just that very reason.

After two quick lefts, Shawn was in the McMaster's Restaurant and Field parking lot. He could see Billy standing by home plate holding a fungo bat, his apron draped over a five-gallon bucket, which held several baseballs. John Bair, McMaster Restaurant's DH, stood in left field inspecting his glove. Billy pulled a ball out of the bucket and lofted it through the air toward Bair. Bair took two steps in, then three back, then one to the left, then two quick ones back. He lunged toward the sky. The ball nipped the middle finger of his glove, and then rolled off. Bair jogged after the ball, picked it up, and slammed it into the pocket of his glove.

Billy crossed his legs while leaning on the bat like it was a cane. He turned and looked at the restaurant while Bair hunted the baseball. He didn't see Shawn leaning on his car. Watching. Such a strange feeling, wanting to put on a glove, run into the outfield and catch fly balls. But knowing that stepping on that field, walking passed that dugout, would make him vomit right then and there.

Bair was back in position, so Billy skied another fly ball in his direction. Shawn knew that swing. It was the one Billy used when Shawn was still getting loose, still stretching out his legs. Billy could still do it, drop fly balls or line drives wherever he wanted in the outfield. Shawn marveled as he walked toward the flagpole. Shawn could practice for a million years and he could never hit fungos like that. Or make an omelet like Billy either, for that matter. The man was amazing, Shawn stood and watched as Billy hit the kindest, softest, gentlest fly balls toward Bair, who looked like he was trying to avoid them, not pull up underneath them. Even from the top of the hill, Shawn could tell almost instantly, on every fly ball, that Bair was heading three steps, four steps, or even just one step out of position. Bair stabbed at the fly balls as if they were balloons he was trying to pop.

Again, Billy turned as Bair hunted down a ball he had missed. He saw Shawn standing in the grass near the restaurant, watching. Billy reached into the bucket for another ball and turned to Shawn. He arched his back and took a steep swing at the ball, sending it high into the air. Shawn sensed it was going to land somewhere in the grass as soon as it was twenty feet up. A pit formed in his stomach as he moved toward where the ball would land. Shawn wiped his sweaty hands on his khaki shorts as the ball closed in on him. His heart moved his shirt. He was right where he needed to be to catch the ball. But he stepped to the side and let it land in the grass with a thud. As Shawn retrieved the ball, Billy took a deep breath, then turned back toward Bair.

Shawn walked down the steps toward the field holding the ball in his hand like a waiter carrying a full mug of hot coffee. Billy hit a fly ball to Bair, and before it hit the ground three steps in front of the lunging, lumbering power hitter, walked over to the fence. Shawn tossed the ball to his father, lobbing it high into the air. It landed in Billy's left hand, right in front of his stomach,

Billy tipped his head toward Bair, "Couldn't catch a train at the 30th Street Station."

"I think he got that one on a bounce," Shawn said, smiling. He sat on a bleacher seat in the first row with his hands pressed under his thighs.

"I need his stick in the lineup. Bobby is a much better fielder, but he hits like his son."

"Isn't his son, like, six?"

"Yup." Billy walked over and hit the ball Shawn had tossed to him. It only made it out to shortstop, landing in the dirt, stopping before it reached the outfield grass. Billy clutched his lower back and struggled to catch his breath.

Shawn stood up, walked toward the fence, then stopped, "You alright?"

"Yeah," Billy said, then breathed a few shallow breaths. "Musta tweaked my back when I… hit that ball up to you."

171

"Well, come sit down," said Shawn, motioning to the bleachers behind him.

Billy grabbed his apron and dried his face as he walked toward Shawn. "The Final Exam is right around the corner," Billy said as he looked out at Bair, who was collecting balls in the outfield like a four-year-old at an Easter Egg hunt.

Shawn looked at his sneakers. "I know."

Billy turned and looked at his son. "It's good you came back.... Your mom really missed you."

"I missed everybody too."

"I think CeCe missed you a ton, also," Billy looped the apron over his head. Bair walked to home plate and dumped a shirt-full of baseballs into the bucket. Billy and Shawn watched him put the bucket back in the dugout.

Shawn decided to avoid any conversation about the restaurant. He remembered how that went last time. "Dusty and Chuck playing good ball?"

"I'd never say it to their face, but they really are the best middle infield combination we've ever had."

"I'll tell them for you."

"Don't, those boys are one thought between them away from leaking out of their ears, they're so full of themselves. We don't need a jukebox, because those two sing their own praises non-stop."

Shawn scanned the outfield from foul pole to foul pole, still green, deep into the summer, mowed as if it was the set of a fertilizer commercial. The sun was dipping toward the trees, bathing the Pennsylvania countryside in gold. For just a moment, Shawn felt like a ballplayer again. He forgot his troubles, and imagined taking left field.

The buzz of a text message rattled in his pocket, waking him from his trance. He looked at the time, then looked at Billy, "No games tonight?"

"Just a late one. We've lost a game or two here and there to some newer fields in the area."

172

Shawn waited for Billy to say more, it looked like he wanted to, but he said nothing. Shawn jumped in, "You're losing your touch with those fly balls. You can't make any of them land in Bair's glove."

Shawn expected some sort of snide comment back from Billy, but he got something much worse. "Not everybody was born to catch fly balls like you, Shawn. In fact, hardly anybody could catch a ball like you."

Shawn was taken aback by the tenderness of his father's comments. He was used to a quick pat on the head for the fielding, then a swift kick in the rear for his hitting. But for some reason, the compliment felt worse. It was time to talk about what happened.

"I'm sorry about---"

Billy cut him off with the palm of his right hand.

"I didn't mean for that to happen."

Billy shook his head as he listened. "I know.... Of course I know."

Shawn looked at his father as they sat below the sounds of the restaurant and among the buzz of the bugs and birds. "I can't play."

Billy turned toward Shawn, and his shoulders slumped forward, his chest, stuffed into a sweaty, white t-shirt, came to rest on the top of his belly, a belly that was bigger than Shawn could ever remember it being. Then he looked back at Bair and yelled, "more tomorrow!"

"I'm not ready."

Billy looked like his mouth was filled with swamp water. He peered up at the restaurant, then out toward the field, as if he were trying to find the best place to spit it out. Shawn filled the silence with the lectures he would have gotten in the past. "You have to stop swinging at bad pitches," or "you look like you are afraid up there," or "one for four isn't going to cut it if you want to make it to the next level."

"I know, Shawn," Billy said instead, standing up. He walked to the steps, and without looking back at Shawn, said, "I know."

Two steps up, Billy looked at the restaurant. Then, he stopped and looked down at his feet. He turned and walked back toward Shawn. "Listen, son, don't waste your time running or hiding from life. It's too short. Listen to your heart." He tapped Shawn on the chest a few times, and Shawn stepped toward him beginning to lift his arms. But Billy was already turning back toward the steps.

"Thanks, Dad," Shawn said, not sure if Billy heard him. He watched his father plod up toward the restaurant, each step slower than the last. Near the top, Billy only stepped first with his right foot, the left foot always following, always the second to reach. He gripped above his right knee with his right hand, causing his upper body to lean forward. The sun was reflecting off the front window of the restaurant, casting a glare at the top of the bleachers. Upright again, Billy walked into it, disappearing from Shawn's sight.

46

May 15, 1955 - 7:23 pm

"I know, baby, but daddy has the car, and I have your little brother," said Mom.

"But it's the last game," said Albert Muldoon, sitting on the couch in the living room wearing his little league uniform.

Mom sat down next to him on the couch, pulled off his baseball cap, and kissed him on the head. Maxwell Muldoon, chubby with baby fat, sat straddling Mom's left leg. The three of them sat in the quiet house, Muldoon and Mom looking around the room, toward the front door, as if they expected somebody to jump out and yell "surprise!"

Muldoon lugged himself off the couch and dragged his feet back toward his bedroom. He pulled off his jersey, and threw it on the floor in the hallway. He wouldn't need that anymore. Dad was supposed to take him to the game. But it had started almost an hour ago.

Muldoon walked back out toward his mother, his ribs sticking out of his exposed chest. "It was my only chance to play on McMaster---" He stopped when he saw Dad sitting on the couch next to Mom, exactly where he had been sitting a minute ago. Dad was whispering things in her ear. It didn't look like she wanted to hear it.

Dad turned to Muldoon, "Oh, McMaster Field, McMaster Restaurant." He lunged over to Muldoon and took him by the shoulders. "What happened to your shirt, there, Richie Ashburn?"

"I don't need it anymore," said Muldoon, shaking away from Dad's grip.

"You guys playing topless now?" said Dad, laughing, turning to Mom. "Honey, you should join that team."

Mom jumped off the couch and carried Max into the kitchen. Muldoon could hear her fasten Max into his high chair, then slam cabinets closed, toss plates on the table.

Dad followed Muldoon into his bedroom. "I don't know what her problem is."

Muldoon sat on his bed, facing the wall, away from Dad.

"Look at me when I'm talking to you!"

Muldoon turned toward his Dad, tears welling up in his eyes.

"What the hell is wrong with everybody around here? Now you're crying," Dad said, knocking a baseball off the desk as he flung his arms.

"You were supposed to take me to my baseball game."

"What game?"

"My last game!"

Dad walked over and sat on the bed next to Muldoon, placing a hand on his shoulder. "Sorry, boy, but you have no idea what it's like to run a business. I can't be worried about taking you here and there. We're about to be rich, boy. We are about to have tons of money, to spend however we see fit."

"It was my only chance to play on McMaster Field."

Dad stood up and kicked at the ball on the ground. "Why don't you go move in with the Goddamn McMasters and live their little "Father Knows Best" life? You don't like the way shit runs around here? You can hit the road!"

Mom appeared in the doorway. "That's enough, Gordon!"

Dad turned around to face Mom, looking like a penguin waddling on ice. "Don't you dare yell at me, woman. I'll do whatever I want in my Goddamn house." He hobbled after her, chasing her into the living room.

Muldoon closed his bedroom door and locked it. He hid under his blanket, under his pillow, squeezing them tight over his ears. He knew the yelling, screaming, and fighting would end soon enough. Dad would be passed out on the couch, or on the living room floor. Mom would be sleeping on the bed with Max at her side. Makeup would be smudged on her face. A lamp might be overturned, a chair on its side. Maybe a broken glass on the floor.

Muldoon wondered if there really were families like he saw on TV. Maybe the McMasters were like that. They always seemed happy. Maybe that was the trade-off for Dad having a successful company and lots of money. He would have to put up with nights like this. It wasn't always like this, sometimes Dad would come home and they would have a catch. Maybe the TV shows only showed the good parts like that, and they leave out these types of nights.

Muldoon dozed into sleep as the noise in the other room settled down. He thought about family dinners, baseball games, those picture perfect houses he saw on TV, and a scoop of chocolate ice cream.

47

"She's pretty," said Chuck.

"No doubt," said Dusty.

"Who?" asked Shawn.

"Miley Cyrus," said Dusty, dripping soda onto his bunched up straw paper, watching it wiggle and grow.

"But she's lost her mind," said Dusty.

"Indeed," said Chuck.

"Yup," said Shawn, then caught a glimpse of CeCe behind the counter. Now that is a pretty girl. Gorgeous. She smiled at a customer, and Dusty and Chuck's voices evaporated. He watched CeCe scoop some *What was that actor's name again?* Strawberry into a cone for a little girl.

Chuck's voice brought him back to the table. "What the hell are you talking about?"

"She's had a tough go of it," said Dusty.

"A tough go? She's a billionaire's superstar daughter of another superstar," said Chuck, leaning back, crossing his arms, shaking his head.

"She grew up without her mother," said Dusty.

"What?" asked Chuck, who then looked at Shawn as if he couldn't identify what he had put into his mouth. Then, after a few seconds, the look turned to that of a boy about to pull a girl's ponytail.

"Her mother died, when she was little," said Dusty.

Shawn started to speak, but Chuck cut him off. "Who was her mother, Dusty?"

"Oh, damn it. Shoot, what was her name?"

Shawn and Chuck shared a glance across the table. No words needed to be said. Chuck nodded toward Shawn, who felt great being on the inside of the inside joke for once, instead of inside his own head.

Shawn looked at Dusty. "Brooke Shields?"

"Yes! Exactly."

Shawn and Chuck burst out laughing, and the rattling of plates, glasses and silverware as Chuck slammed on the table turned heads all around the restaurant.

"What?" asked Dusty. "It's got to be hard growing up without your mom and being in the spotlight all the time."

"It's got to be hard being you, dumbass!" said Chuck.

Shawn leaned toward Dusty, "That's Hannah Montana's mom who died. Brooke Shields played her mother on the show."

"Nuh uh," replied Dusty.

"I'm afraid so," said Chuck. "Miley's mom is alive and well."

"Who is her mom?" asked Dusty.

"Who the hell knows? Mrs. Fuggin' Cyrus!" shouted Chuck through his laughter.

The laughter died down, then the three of them looked at each other again, inciting another round of hysterics.

Then, after a minute or so of silence, "But she is pretty," said Chuck.

"And in great shape," said Dusty.

"Is she your type?" asked Shawn, looking back and forth between the two of them.

"Nope," said Dusty, finishing a French fry.

"Not at all," said Chuck, stirring ice with a straw.

Dusty smacked Shawn on the shoulder, "She's your type," he said, pointing at CeCe.

"Yeah," said Shawn.

"Yeah?" asked Chuck, moving to Shawn's side of the table. "Yeah?" he asked again, sliding in against him, pinning him between Dusty and himself. "Yeah?" he asked again as he rubbed Shawn's neck.

Now Dusty, while feathering back Shawn's hair with his box-moving, cardboard-ripping, bat-choking

179

hands, "Yeah? Then why are you sitting with us? Are we your type?"

"No," said Shawn, who pushed his way past Chuck and out into the middle of the room. "Not even close. Although, Chuck's eyes..."

"Oohhh! Another zinger for Shawny. What a day for the comeback kid," said Dusty.

Shawn walked toward the counter, toward CeCe. But he was looking back over his shoulder, enjoying the sudden praise of his wit. A chair got in his way, catching him in the upper right thigh, causing him to stumble to his left.

"Hard to believe that used to be the best defensive left fielder in the state of Pennsylvania," said Dusty.

"Shut up, Lily," said Shawn.

"OH!!!!" yelled Chuck. "Three for three for Shawn! The hits just keep on coming."

"I don't get it," said Dusty.

Shawn walked toward the counter, toward CeCe, trying to hide a smile, as if he were circling the bases after hitting a home run. It was an accomplishment any time he could get a smart comment across in a discussion with Dusty and Chuck.

"You ok there, Tony Dovolani?" asked CeCe.

"Wow, tough crowd today." Shawn smiled. "I would never, ever attempt to be on Dancing with the Stars."

"I think they're happy about that." CeCe pulled the apron over her head. "Walk?"

Shawn nodded and the two headed out the door. The eight-thirty game was about to begin, and both teams were huddled in the grass around the plaques in the mulch, near the flagpole. Shawn and CeCe stopped behind them and listened to the National Anthem. After the teams walked back down toward the field, Shawn and CeCe walked over to the plaques.

"What did your grandfather call this again?" asked CeCe, pointing to the electrical box.

"The fuse box. He just couldn't get it through his head that there wasn't a single fuse in there." Shawn stepped into the mulch, in the large empty space to the right of the three plaques and squatted down like a catcher. He leaned forward and traced the letters on DJ's plaque. "I miss him."

"I'm sorry I never met him," said CeCe.

"Me too," Shawn stood up and pointed to the flagpole.

CeCe caught on quicker this time. "Oh, male. Definitely male," she said with a grin.

"I figured," said Shawn. "Let's walk."

The two walked down through the bleachers, then out into the grass down along the fence near right field. They passed the light stanchion, and hugged the fence in right field. Each step beyond the light took them further into the evening dusk. Beads of sweat formed on Shawn's brow as the muggy July air surrounded them. Short of going back in the restaurant, they couldn't escape it.

"I told my dad," said Shawn.

"Told him what?" asked CeCe.

"That I can't," Shawn said, nodding his head toward the field, "do that anymore."

The two sat on the old wooden bleachers at the edge of the tree line. CeCe turned her body, her entire face, both of her eyes toward Shawn. "How did he take it?"

Shawn took a deep breath and peered into her eyes, those eyes that for years had accepted Shawn, and everything he did, and everything he said. No judgement, honest advice, love. "OK, I guess. He said he knew. Then, he told me some stuff about listening to my heart and not hiding from life. I'm used to, don't step in the bucket, or, you're rolling your wrists too early, not life advice. Then, he just… walked away."

CeCe didn't respond, didn't break eye contact either. She never did. Usually, she would just stare back, then a small smile would grow on her lips, jiggling her freckles, and leak some commentary that would make Shawn feel better. Today, she just stared back. Her face remained steady, but her eyes might be looking past him, or through him. Shawn couldn't tell. Maybe he was out of practice in reading CeCe. Maybe she didn't have anything to say to twenty-two-year-old Shawn. Or maybe she felt she couldn't say it.

"Anyway," Shawn said, fighting through a stammer, "It's, g-, nice to spend time with you again."

A smile returned to CeCe's face, her freckles unfrozen. "Same here."

Shawn was able to breathe a little deeper, and the two sat in silence for a while, turning and watching the game. At the end of an inning, they simultaneously turned and said each other's name. CeCe motioned to Shawn for him to go first.

"I told Steve that I need to move on."

"Move on?"

"Move back to Quail. Back home. I can tell it's been killing my mom that I haven't been here. And my dad seems to be slowing down. I think they can use a hand, maybe I can pitch in a little bit. And…" Shawn stopped, and just nodded his head, blinked to hold back tears.

"And…" CeCe rested her small hand on his muscular forearm.

"And I need you. I didn't," Shawn stopped again, looked up into the darkening sky, "become me, until I met you. Nobody, nobody gets me like you do."

"I know… You know," CeCe stopped, and wiped a tear from her left eye, then looked away. She took a deep breath, and then continued, "Nobody knows more about me than you do." She put her hands on his and looked into his eyes. Not through him, or over him, right at him now, "How soon can you move back?"

"It's going to be a process. Steve is looking for my replacement." Shawn changed his tone to overconfident, sarcastic, "You know I'm hard to replace." Then he stopped as he saw the look on CeCe's face.

"Impossible to replace," she said, her words trailing off, tears picking up. She looked at the game for a second, then off into the woods. The sky was dark, the woods darker.

Usually, a comment like that would be followed by a freckle-rattling grin, then a hug, or a kiss. But today CeCe broke contact. The words were sweet, but the aftertaste must have been bitter. Maybe they were out of practice.

Before he realized what he was doing, Shawn reached out and turned CeCe's head toward him by her chin. Then he used the back of his fingers to wipe away some tears. CeCe closed her eyes and leaned into his hand. The touch of her skin. No, the touch of her soul, her desire to lean in, felt better than a grand slam home run to win the World Series ---three seasons in a row--- would.

CeCe opened her eyes and looked at Shawn. There it was. That was the look, he was allowed back in. She didn't break contact, she didn't look away, and she didn't blink. Their heads crept toward each other. For the moment, the humid July night was gone, the field and the game too. The noise of the crowd dissipated. All of it faded away. So did Shawn and CeCe. So did the last four years. Back came ShawnandCeCe. Their heads, their lips moved closer and closer. Shawn put the palm of his hand on her jaw line to steady his aim. Closer.

Then CeCe hopped up off the bleachers, and started to cry. "I can't," she said. "I can't yet." She backed away and said, "I still… There's still something I have to tell…" She sobbed and stopped speaking. Then she turned and ran into the darkness, up the side of the hill beside the bleachers, and out of Shawn's sight.

The sound of the bat hitting the ball caught Shawn's attention. Fly ball to left field. He looked into the sky and looked at the arc of the ball. Then he looked down to where it would land. Two seconds later, the left fielder jogged right to where Shawn was looking, and recorded the third out.

48

Shawn sat on second base of the ball field by his apartment. Clouds moved overhead on the midsummer midnight breeze. Warm and wet. The moon overhead, when not hidden, was almost full, just a small sliver missing from its left side. Shawn's heels were pressed against the base, his knees pulled toward his chest.

Shawn squinted in the direction of his apartment and picked out the window to his bathroom. Fatigue buzzed around his head. Life was more complicated than ever. Not only did he have to run his household and do his job, now he was running to Quail practically every day. Rekindling relationships with his family, friends.

And CeCe. She didn't seem to understand how difficult this was for him. Living all but alone for years, then, all of a sudden, trying to fit back into a life that had moved along without him. And she was right in the middle of it. She didn't miss college, she graduated. She hadn't been away from the restaurant, from Greta and Billy, from Dusty and Chuck. But, somehow, she was the one who wasn't ready.

He stood up and faced the creek, the path through the trees. His apartment. But he was drawn to the dugout. He walked toward the bat. Shawn needed to talk.

"No scary business this time," Shawn said, flopping onto the bench.

"As you wish, cupcake," said the bat.

"I'm tired, dude," Shawn said, rubbing his eyes with the heels of his hands.   "Being social can be exhausting, especially for a hermit."

"I wouldn't say I've been a hermit."

"What would you say, then?"

Shawn stood and looked down the right field line. Some leaves that had started to dry, rustled in the breeze.

He turned to toward the bat, "I'd say I sacrificed myself for everybody around Quail."

"Oh yeah?"

"Sure. When I was there, my dad got hurt. Since I left, nobody else got hurt. Simple."

"That makes sense," said the bat.

"See," said Shawn, sitting back down. He smiled through a yawn, then said, "sometimes I make the right call."

"So your mom took your newspaper clippings and pictures off the wall of the restaurant?"

Shawn crossed his arms, tucked his hands in his armpits. "What do you mean?"

"Since you caused so much pain around your family's property, I'm sure they removed any reminder of you. You know, for everybody's sake."

"Well, no," He walked away from the bat to the other end of the dugout. He kicked his right foot up onto the bench and leaned on his right knee.

"Ok, well, certainly nobody talked about you. That would have been too much for everybody to handle."

Shawn breathed out through his nose, his lips pursed. Then he said, "No, Larry told me my mom and dad looked for me, asked about me and talked about me all the time. And CeCe too." Shawn looked at the bat, standing with his hands in his pockets.

"Imagine the panic had you stayed, beef jerky," the bat said with a chuckle.

"I had to leave," said Shawn, his voice raised a level, his arms flailing with each word.

"Did you?"

"Yes! Nobody wanted me there."

"You said they were looking for you."

"My mom and dad. Nobody else!"

"Did they come after you when you returned? Did someone beat you up, yell at you, throw anything at you? Look at you funny?"

Shawn stepped back and dropped his hands to his sides. "No," mumbled Shawn. He sat on the bench, leaned his forearms on his thighs and lowered his head. "No, they didn't." A duck took flight off the creek. Shawn peered into the night toward the sound of it flapping through the sky. "But what about CeCe?" asked Shawn, some volume returning to his voice. "She'll talk to me, but she pulled away, wouldn't let me kiss her."

"Oh, poor Shawny," wailed the bat.

"Great comeback," Shawn stood up. "She's obviously hurt by having me around." Shawn's shoulder dropped as he spoke the words, his voice trailing off.

"I'm sure your *return* is what hurt her," said the bat.

"What's that supposed to mean?"

"You seem to be the expert on comebacks, you tell me."

Shawn turned and took three steps away from the bat, then spun back, "Look, the best thing for her at that time was to be away from me, from this monster," said Shawn, shaking his hands above his head. "We were just starting college together, she didn't need me, the guy who did *that* hanging around. Imagine the ridicule, the embarrassment for her."

"In addition to comebacks, you also seem to be an expert on predicting the future."

"Huh?" asked Shawn, focusing in on the crack in the bat. It was more pronounced tonight. Perhaps the bat had shifted since they were last together. Or maybe Shawn was more observant.

"*Imagine the ridicule, the embarrassment,*" the bat said, doing a very good imitation of Shawn's voice. "You have absolutely no idea what it would have been like if you stayed. For CeCe, or for you. Or anybody else, for that

187

matter. And maybe more importantly, you have no idea what it actually *was* like for everybody in your absence."

"I'm pretty sure it was business as usual. The restaurant is still running; there are still ballgames down on the field. CeCe and Chuck finished college, Dusty and Chuck still work at the flooring place, CeCe at the restaurant."

"Your crystal ball tells you that?" asked the bat. "Look, you know where a fly ball is going to land pretty much right after it is hit. I'll give you that. But every other prediction is a story you've created in your head."

"Well, here's something that's definitely true. I was the one who was in solitude for the last four years. Isolated. Ostracized," said Shawn, walking around the dugout, like a teacher lecturing to his class.

"Solitude? Yes. Isolated? Definitely. Ostracized? I don't think so. You did that to yourself. You could have come back at any time."

Shawn walked toward the bat, some of the confidence removed from his voice. "Oh really?"

"Yeah, really, trash can. You came back, didn't you? When you chose to?"

"Yeah, but because Larry saw me, and then because Mom asked me to."

"You were gone for four years, by your own choice, and you came back by your own choice as well."

Shawn opened his mouth and started to say something, then stopped. Instead, he sat down on the bench next to the bat and looked out into the night. The moon fought to be seen, pushing through the clouds, desperate to show its face.

Shawn turned to the bat and said, "Look, I was the one hurting. I was the one who was gone." It was a statement, but sounded more like a question.

"Oh, I see," said the bat. "So Mom, it was easy on her… having you missing."

"She knew I wasn't missing. I kept in touch."

"I'm sure a letter every few months is very fulfilling for a mother, from her only son. Her only remaining son."

Shawn's butt slid toward the front of the bench and his head and shoulders sunk toward the ground. He hadn't thought of that. He thought he was doing everybody a favor by leaving. "She seems ok though. Still working, still baking all those pies."

"Yeah, all those pies..." The bat, let the words float in the overnight air. "Did you ever think that she's ok because you are back?"

"No, I guess I didn't," Shawn said, standing up, turning toward the bat. "But what about Dad. I saved him a lot of trouble."

"How so?" asked the bat, sounding like he already knew the answer.

"All he ever did was nag at me about my game. My swing, my stance, my batting average. Making it to the next level," Shawn waved his hands in the air.

"Sounds awful," said the bat.

"He was obsessed with me and my game."

"Say that again."

"Huh?"

"Say what you just said again," said the bat.

"He was obsessed---" Shawn cut himself off. He put his hands on his hips and looked at the sunflower seed shell covered ground.

"Yes, sweetheart, you were saying?"

"I suppose that left a little bit of a hole in his life," said Shawn. "But I almost killed him."

"What did he say about that when you guys talked?"

"Nothing, he brushed it off."

"So the reason you hid for four years, which was an accident anyway.... Your dad just brushed it off."

"I guess I may have overreacted," Shawn said through a soft chuckle.

"I think your crystal ball may not be completely cracked after all."

Shawn's grin evaporated. "Oh boy, CeCe," Shawn waited for the bad news.

"Yes, CeCe. And how about Dusty and Chuck. Her boyfriend disappears, their buddy disappears. You said they are still at their jobs, still doing what they were doing. Four years ago. Still."

"They could have done something different, moved on," Shawn's voice trailed off. Moving on to different jobs, growing up a little. That sounded fine. "They were waiting, weren't they? Waiting for me?"

"Honestly, Dusty and Chuck are probably doing exactly what they want to be doing," said the bat, "but CeCe..."

Shawn walked toward the end of the dugout, then back, dragging his feet, leaving dirt trails through the empty shells. The bat was right, Dusty and Chuck loved playing ball, loved hanging around the restaurant, loved working at the flooring place, and seemed to love rooming together. For a moment, Shawn wondered how the bat could possibly know all that, but his thoughts quickly returned to CeCe. "But it was just going to be one kiss."

"Oh, Shawn, really? Just a kiss?"

"Yeah, just a kiss."

"You are dumb. And you're an ass. But you're not a complete dumbass. Think about it..." said the bat, going silent.

Shawn thought for a moment, but didn't know what the bat wanted him to think about.

"Oh for God's sake," said the bat, his words rattling around in the trees. "I want you to think about the events right before you left."

"I don't want to think about the game."

"Not the game, fart breath. Before that. At school. With CeCe."

Shawn sat down again and thought. He remembered the first month of college with CeCe. Going to classes, then eating together, or hanging out together in her room or his. They were in love when they arrived on campus, but had fallen deeper and deeper in the month they were there together.

Then, it hit Shawn, like a weighted bat on a helmeted head. What they had become, what they had done, what they had shared. Then he had run away, disappeared. He thought about what that must have been like for CeCe. For everybody really.

Shawn hopped up, tucked his chin to his chest and stretched his back like a cat. Then he stood straight up, his spiky hair at least two inches above six feet high. He reached his hands toward above his head, and was surprised how easy it was for him to touch the ceiling of the dugout.

49

July 23, 2013 - 9:43 am

Muldoon paraded through the parking lot of the McMaster property toward the front door of the restaurant. Seventy days? Seventy-one days? Soon. Not soon enough, but soon, this small sliver of Quail Township would be his, and the pie would be complete. The restaurant would be gone, and the field too, replaced by houses down below, and Al's Everything Shop up where he currently stood, hands on hips, legs spread wide, like Superman or Tarzan, or even Mr. Clean. Somebody who was in charge of things.

There was one potential problem: Larry Last. Muldoon knew Larry was the last person to see and speak to DJ before he died. Muldoon also knew that Last of the Third business had to have something to do with what DJ told him, and be the key to whatever paperwork, if any, DJ left. Muldoon strode in through the front door, and much to his pleasure, but not to his surprise, Larry was sitting at the counter eating breakfast.

Muldoon sat in the corner, almost hiding behind the menu. He had already eaten breakfast over at his store, so he would nurse a cup of coffee and hope that neither Larry nor Billy nor Greta would see him. He was not a peacock today; he was a spy. Anything to win. He had done that on McMaster Field, controlling the Winner's Locker Room for the last nine years. The rest of the property was the final battlefield, his chance to once and for all drive a stake through the heart of the McMaster family. He would provide the families of Quail Township with a happy life, but on his terms. Modern, convenient, cost-effective and profitable.

Greta hipped her way through the swinging door carrying four pies at one time to the display case. She put them in, removing the old ones. A waitress nearby wondered aloud if Greta had just put them in there an hour ago. "Yeah," said Greta, "but I have plenty more to put out there. Got to keep them fresh." The high school aged waitress rolled her eyes, and Muldoon agreed with the sentiment. Quite a waste to throw away perfectly good pies and keep making new ones.

Muldoon, needing to hide from Greta, who was passing by, held his coffee cup up to his face for what must have been a forty-eight second sip. He watched her flit by, drying her hands on a dishtowel. She retreated behind the counter. Muldoon's cover had not been blown. Then he turned his attention to Larry, his breakfast platter empty, his coffee cup refilled by Greta, or whoever else passed by at the opportune time. Damn, what did he know? And what did Greta and Billy know? It had been ten years, if they knew something, they would have acted on it by now. But if there was something Larry knew, some late-inning, game-saving diving catch of a clue that could spoil Muldoon's victory over the McMaster's? Muldoon needed to know about it. Decipher it. And destroy whatever evidence it pointed to.

Another long draw of coffee out of an empty cup for Muldoon as Billy stuck his head out from the kitchen. He said something to Greta, who spun, then sought out a waitress. The waitress shook her head as if she understood. Then Greta walked through the swinging door into the kitchen.

Eyes back to the counter. A waitress offered Larry a refill from what looked to be a fresh steaming pot, but he covered his cup with his hand. Odd. Then Larry looked over his left shoulder, then his right. After the waitress walked out into the main restaurant area, forearm quivering as it balanced the steaming pot, Larry hustled behind the counter, then through the swinging door and into the kitchen.

This was it, Larry was making his move, and Muldoon was there to make it with him. He knew he was taking a huge chance moving in behind enemy lines without an invite, without a plan, without even a map or clue where he was going. But, he knew ultimate victory required the ultimate sacrifice, or at least a ballsy jaunt into the belly of the beast.

Muldoon waited for the counter area to clear, walked over doing his best imitation of a coat rack, fence post, or highly competent home plate umpire. That was a change for him; usually, he was brash, obnoxious, like a new kid in the neighborhood trying to stake his claim.

He slipped behind the counter and through the swinging door without stuttering a step, without looking back. Anything to win.

50

Larry tiptoed up the steps to the McMaster residence. Billy and Greta were on their way to the Green Dragon, the local farmer's market to pick up the fresh ingredients they used in many of the restaurant's dishes. He knew he had a couple of hours, which was good because he had no idea what he was looking for.

Larry had been up there plenty of times. At the top of the narrow, steep steps from the kitchen of the restaurant was a door that the McMaster's could lock to seal off anybody who might gain these stairs and enter. But they never, ever locked it. Who would ever enter the swinging door, pass the kitchen, and climb the steps?

Well, Larry would. Larry did. And he was in the largest room in the residence (can you call it a house if it sits atop a restaurant?), which was really three rooms in one. To his left, and in front of him for that matter, was the living room. Couch, chairs, television. The wall above the front of the restaurant, facing the field, was all windows. The wall above the parking lot had one large window, big enough to spy on the entire parking lot. Most of the time, however, blinds were drawn, covering it. To his right was the dining room, which was really an extension of the living room that contained a dining room table. And beyond that, toward the back right of the room, was a small kitchen area, mostly sink and counter space, but there was a small range and microwave.

Larry decided to sit on the edge of the couch to gather his thoughts. He planted his feet under his knees, and rested his hands on top of his thighs. He closed his eyes and took a breath in through his nose and out through his mouth. He forgave himself the intrusion, the invasion, the breaking and entering, or entering anyway.

To forgive is to set a prisoner free and discover that prisoner was you. Remember what the Buddha said, 'To understand everything is to forgive everything.' Forgive yourself, love yourself, and enjoy each and every moment of the rest of your life.

He forgave himself because he was working for the good of the McMaster's. This search was necessary in this moment, and in a few moments would be over. Relieved, peaceful, Larry decided to repeat the words, if only under his breath, that DJ had said to him, hoping for any clue, any inspiration. "McMaster's... will refuse the key, McMaster's... will refuse the key, McMaster's will refuse the key." Over and over. His mind cleared until all he saw was those words bouncing in darkness. Over and over he muttered them. Over and over.

His eyes flew open when he thought of it. Of course. Of course, and what a great place to hide something. A place nobody ever went. Not "McMaster's... will." No, "Will McMaster."

Larry stood up and walked toward the back of the residence, down the hallway toward the bedrooms. Billy and Greta's was straight back at the end of the hall. Shawn's room, or what used to be Shawn's room, was on the left. And across the hall from Shawn's room was Will McMaster's room, which was frozen in time as a shrine. Will was Shawn's older brother. Will died when he was two years old. Shawn had never met Will.

Larry had never been in the room, but he had looked in, once or twice when baby Will was sleeping. Larry knew what to expect, a crib and other baby furniture, and whatever else was in there twenty-five years ago when he passed. Larry took the doorknob into his hand as if he were handling a baby chick, looked back out into the living room, then twisted and pushed.

The door opened and Larry stepped in. He was met by a fog of dust and the faint scent of baby powder. The circus was the theme of the room, pictures of elephants and tigers, trapeze artists and clowns. One step into the room, Larry scanned past all of that, ignoring the crib, ignoring the dresser with the diaper changing pad on top, looking for files, or folders, or papers.

Larry crept toward the middle of the room and noticed a brown cardboard box, colored to look like wood. He removed the lid and inside was a mess of papers and cards, a tiny winter cap that would only fit a baby's head, a long, thin rectangular box that contained a candle, and various other items. Larry reached in and stretched his hand around all the papers and cards, grabbing and lifting them, as if he were handling the Declaration of Independence. On his knees, he laid everything on the floor, and he picked up what appeared to be a birth announcement. He looked at the front, then as he turned it to inspect the back, he heard a sound from the living room. It sounded like the door of the residence closing. Billy and Greta shouldn't be back already, but maybe they were. Maybe it was Shawn.

What would he say? How could he explain this? Looking for some baby powder… Taking a stroll down memory lane… Falsely admit that he had lost his marbles. No, he would have to tell the truth, finally tell Billy and Greta that he knew more than he ever admitted. Not much more, and nothing that he understood even in the least. But more.

Larry shallowed his breathing and rested his rear back onto his heels. Listened. Waited. Listened for footsteps down the hall. Waited for the door to fling open. Hoped that he would go undetected. He wasn't ready to talk about this, to share everything DJ had told him. Not even with Billy and Greta. DJ hadn't wanted him to, he at least wanted to keep that word.

He heard no footsteps, and the door never opened. Larry closed his eyes, inhaled and exhaled, then thumbed through each and every document in the pile. Opened every card. Inspected the corner of every single item, looking for a rough edge that matched what DJ had given him. All he found was a birth certificate, several cards of congratulations, and many, many more notes of condolences.

But nothing that said anything about the McMaster property. Another swing and a miss. Larry piled everything back into the box, replaced the lid, and put it back exactly where he found it.

51

Shawn stepped back into the batter's box. "Oh, and two," yelled the home plate umpire.

"Here comes another curve ball, McMaster," yelled a voice from the Al's Everything Crowd.

"Here comes the fastball, Shaw- Nee."

Shawn didn't look up at them. They didn't matter. Focus on Jackson; focus on this at-bat. Focus. He kicked his left foot back into the groove he had made for it in the back end of the batter's box. Then right foot in, right arm extending with the bat to touch the opposite front corner of the plate. Deep breath. He turned his head toward the mound looking like a shivering child peeping into a dark room in the middle of the night.

Jackson stood with both feet on the rubber, his right hand gripping the ball in the pocket of his glove. He jerked his elbows in and out and the sleeves on his sweaty biceps and triceps popped up toward his shoulders. He had to be ten feet tall now, had to be only twenty feet away. He glared over the top of his glove like a bull ready to charge.

The voices in front of Shawn, mocking him, came from a speaker attached to the brim of his helmet. So close, so loud.

From behind, Billy said, "C'mon, Shawn, this is what we've worked for."

Shawn rocked the bat toward Jackson, then back toward the catcher. Toward Jackson, then the catcher. Hips moving left and right, up and down. Stay loose. Relax. He dropped his hands into place, an inch above his left shoulder.

"OK, Shawn," called CeCe, barely loud enough to be heard. She never cheered for him before a play. Always after. The sound of her voice straightened Shawn up. He extended his left palm back toward the umpire and said, "time, please."

"Time!" the home plate umpire yelled, raising his arms, taking two quick steps out from behind the catcher toward the Al's Everything dugout.

"Good idea, McMaster, no way you were ready," said the voice from in front of him.

"No way."

Shawn tapped the barrel end of his bat on the side of his cleats, knocking loose some dirt. Inhaled and held it, then blew it out. In each and every other moment of his life, CeCe's hugging gaze, musical voice and field of freckles were his safe house from the rest of humanity. But for some reason, the sight of her, the sound of her, even sometimes the thought of her was distracting, especially in the tensest moments of a game. She knew this. If she called out to him, she must have thought he needed a little safe house at that moment, more than he needed his focus. Scary thought.

Shawn stepped back in, left foot, right foot, bat tap, and looked out at Johnson, who was already set on the mound. He looked like a fifteen-foot domino that was tipping forward, ready to crush Shawn.

From the bleachers in front of him, in rapid succession, back and forth, "fastball," "curveball," "fastball," "curveball," over and over and over.

Shawn rocked the bat and swayed his hips. Hadn't seen the fastball. Looked like an idiot on the curve. What was coming next? Maybe neither change up did Jackson even throw a change up? no, had to be a fastball because Jackson knew he couldn't catch up to it no had to be the curve because it would humiliate Shawn in front of everybody literally in his backyard no had to be a changeup wait does he even have a change up?

Jackson stepped back with his left leg, kicked it forward into the air, then dropped it toward Shawn, lugging his entire body behind it. Shawn's eyes tried to find his

200

right hand, tried to focus on the ball, but the arms, legs, torso, and head of the lunging monster confused him. He finally found the ball as it cleared Jackson's fingertips.

Fastball did it shoot off his fingers or curveball did it flip over the top of his index finger and roll out of his hand or something else or change up did it escape from Jackson's palm? This is what we worked for OK Shawn this is what we worked for OK Shawn fastball curveball fastball curveball fastball curveball.

Before even one single muscle in Shawn's body considered twitching, the ball slammed into the catcher's glove.

"Strike three!"

From in front of Shawn, clapping. Laughter.

52

The evening was warm, but the air was dry.
Shawn knew it would cool off quickly after the
sun disappeared. Great baseball weather.
Playoff baseball weather. The Fall Classic. The
Final Exam.

CeCe opened the front door of her house and
stepped out onto the front stoop. White keds, denim cutoffs
that stopped an inch above her knees, plain purple t-shirt,
unbuttoned white sweater. Her hair rich red in the twilight,
golden highlights hidden till another time. Her mother,
Fran, grabbed the door before it closed and stepped out.

"Don't I get to meet Shawn?" she asked.

"Yeah mom, of course you do."

"I could have come inside," Shawn said to CeCe.

CeCe stepped off the front stoop and onto the
walkway. "It's beautiful out here, I just couldn't wait.
Don't you love this time of year?"

Fran danced on the front lawn with an imaginary
partner. "Oh, yes, I do."

"Not you, mom." A smile leaked through onto
CeCe's fake angry face, freckles hopping on her right
cheek. Mother and daughter hugged, exchanged "love
yous."

"Be good, be careful," said Fran.

CeCe shouted a "we will" over her shoulder as they
got into Shawn's car.

Shawn started talking as he pulled out of the
driveway. "Here's what I was thinking. First, we head back
to the restaurant for a bite to eat because, well, it's free.
Then some mini-golf out at Davis'. Then, after I whoop
you, we can see what time it is and decide what to do from
there. Maybe dessert. I was--- what?" Shawn asked,

stopping mid-thought, noticing that CeCe was staring at him, mouth ajar.

"You never, ever talk that much. Not with your friends, not with your family. You're not, like, on drugs right now, are you?"

Shawn laughed. "No," he said, then paused, peering out to his left to see if it was safe to turn. "You're just... easy to talk to."

"Easier than talking to Dusty and Chuck, whom you've known since you were little?" CeCe tugged her shorts down to her knees. "Easier than talking to your family, who you've known your whole damn life? You've only known me for, like, a month."

Shawn looked at the road in front of him, didn't say anything. Those were two excellent questions. He turned his face completely in her direction and said, "Yes. Honestly, you are the easiest person to talk to that I have ever met." The two gazed into each other's eyes for a moment, then Shawn turned back to the road.

CeCe smiled. "Yeah, my mom said to be careful."

Shawn looked at CeCe out of the corner of his eye. A wisp of hair fell onto her cheek, covering about a thousand freckles. Then he turned his attention back to the road, but he could feel CeCe's eyes, bluer than the Microsoft Word background, looking at the side of his face. That sort of thing would typically make Shawn squirm a little, then look at the person, then say something stupid. Or look at the person, saying nothing, and look stupid. But her gaze was fine. No, it felt good. Great.

Shawn pulled through the McMaster Restaurant and Field parking lot, and into the residence parking spaces. He sprung out of the car and hustled around the front. Jumping across the hood would have been quicker, but it didn't seem like good first date etiquette. Despite his efforts, CeCe was standing outside of the car when he arrived.

"Shall we?" he said, then started toward the front door, keeping himself one step ahead of her the entire way. Her legs were strong, but her strides short. She almost broke into a jog as the two sped toward the front door of the restaurant. Shawn arrived a step ahead, the length of his stride proving too much for CeCe to overcome.

He pulled the door open with his right hand, and invited her in with his left. CeCe rolled her eyes as she passed him.

"Well, there they are." Greta floated out from behind the counter, wiping her hands on the dishtowel every step of the way.

"Mom," said Shawn, pushing the word through a half-opened mouth.

CeCe smacked Shawn's shoulder with the back of her tiny hand. "Hi Mrs. McMaster, don't mind him," she said, then wiggling her fingers at everybody in the room, voice fluttering, "People."

"You know my boy, don't you?"

"Easiest book I ever read," CeCe winked.

Shawn watched CeCe in action. She spoke to his mom like she spoke to her own. As far as Shawn could tell, from what he had learned in the month he had known her, CeCe could talk to anybody.

No, it was more than that. She could talk to anybody in the fashion that they needed to be talked to. There was friend CeCe, who could be caring or caustic; employee CeCe, who could be obedient or apologetic; waitress CeCe, who could punish the advances of a flirty teenager with an incorrect drink order, or reward the flirty repartee of a World War II veteran with a wink, dimple shaking grin, and flip of the hair. Shawn wondered what girlfriend CeCe could (would?) be like.

Shawn had one gear, one pitch, one strategy. Get in and get out, don't get hurt. And, for goodness sake, don't hurt anybody else. Low risk, small reward. A ground out to

204

short was fine as long as he didn't strike out. Shawn McMaster, the living, breathing cliché.

Greta vanished, the kitchen door swinging in her wake. Before it could stop, Billy came through and leaned on the counter with both forearms. "Ah, CeCe, good, I could use some help tonight," he said, no laughter in his voice, no smile of punctuation.

CeCe turned her body towards Billy, tugged her short bottoms toward her knees and adjusted her shirt. "Um, no, we" pointing to Shawn, "oh, yes, I can work." She started to slide out of the booth, but Shawn lunged across the table and grabbed her right arm above the elbow, vibrating some soda out of a glass.

Shawn looked toward Billy, "Dad, tell her you're kidding." Then to CeCe, "He's kidding. You have to live with him for a hundred years before you can sense his sarcasm."

CeCe turned back toward Shawn. Her swimming pool irises were frozen, surrounded by rings of snow. The chill locked her body. Her biceps was flexed in Shawn's hand, pulsing.

Shawn slid his hand down her arm and took her hand as if he were capturing a butterfly. "He's kidding," he whispered, and squeezed her hand, melting her eyes, allowing Shawn to dive back in. Her freckles quivered and her grin grew. CeCe was back, but where had she gone?

Greta slid two platters onto the table, along with a serving bowl. "Cheeseburgers and fries, and some gravy for dipping."

"For dipping what?" asked CeCe.

Greta and Shawn looked at each other as if they had just found out Aunt Cindy was a man. As she walked away, Greta said to Shawn, "I'll let you handle this."

"Handle what?"

"So let me get this straight," Shawn leaned back on the bench seat, stroking his chin. "You're in a diner-style restaurant, and French fries and gravy have been placed in front of you, and you have no idea what to dip in what?"

"No, Mr. Outfielder," said CeCe, back in her own creamy, freckly skin, "I don't. Why don't you explain it to me?" She leaned over the table, resting her chin in the cradle formed by her palms and fingers.

"Oh, girl, are you in for a treat. French fries dipped in gravy, are you kidding? You've never had French fries and gravy? My goodness," said Shawn, his voice one click louder, which was about a three on the radio scale, "I should announce to everybody in this place that we have a gravy fry virgin over here." He waved his right hand across the rest of the room like an opera singer.

CeCe's left eye squinted as a smile scattered hundreds of adorable freckles. "Go ahead," she said, leaning back, mocking Shawn's hand wave.

"Um, right, I'm not going to do that," he said, leaning further in, backing the volume down to two. Maybe one. "But fer realz, dip a few fries in there… and then prepare to thank me."

CeCe obeyed, dragging two steak fries through the gravy, then placed them into her mouth like a zookeeper feeding a lion. She chewed like a county fair judge. Swallowed. Her lips halted, followed by her freckles. Two more fries, same experiment. Same expression.

Shawn waited. Seriously? No reaction. He couldn't take it. "Well?"

"It pains me to tell you this," she said, leaning across the table toward Shawn, lowering to a whisper, "but that is fuckin' amazing."

Shawn had already closed the passenger side door behind CeCe, despite her efforts to do it herself, when two familiar voices froze him at his left front headlight.

"Mr. McMaster, Mr. McMaster wait, just a quick question or two," said Chuck.

"Mr. McMaster, look over here, a picture," said Dusty.

Shawn shook his head, laughed, said nothing, and tried to get into the driver's seat before they made it over to the car. But, Dusty's rear end beat Shawn's hand to the door, and he was stuck outside.

"Rumor has it you are treating Celine Easter to a round of mini-golf at Davis', is this true?" asked Chuck.

"Why don't you just look in---" Shawn started to ask.

"I'm jotting that down, I'm gonna put that in my story. Shawn McMaster avoided the question, told me to shove it up my ass."

"I never said that," said Shawn. He peeked inside at CeCe, but couldn't see her face. Could she hear any of this? Was she laughing? Was she going to hop out of the car and escape this date by taking Billy up on his offer?

Chuck looked at Dusty. "Did you hear him say it?"

"Better," said Dusty, "I have it on video."

"No, you don't," said Shawn, and he took a lazy swing at Dusty's empty hand that had the phantom video camera. That was his comeback? 'No, you don't.' Seriously? Good work, Shawn. And you wonder why even your best friends bust your chops all the time.

"Enough of the evasive tactics, Mr. McMaster," said Chuck.

"Look out, university words."

"You and young Ms. Easter will be playing eighteen holes tonight," continued Chuck. "Is that correct?"

"Oh, you know that's correct," said Dusty.

"Care to comment?"

"Um, yes, uh, that's the plan," said Shawn, wondering why he was talking into Chuck's thumb.

"Do you believe you will leave victorious?"

"Well, sure. Um, but, I don't know," said Shawn, talking into his chest, not Chuck's thumb.

"C'mon Chuck, get to the hard hitting stuff," said Dusty.

Chuck smirked at Dusty. "I see what you did there."

"McMaster, do you think you will get a Hole in One?"

Shawn knew his buddies were messing around. This is how they showed affection. He knew that. Maybe he could fire back, 'Maybe, maybe not, but you two won't even be on the course tonight.' That wasn't bad. Shawn opened his mouth to start to speak, then stopped. What if CeCe hears that, 'maybe, maybe not.' How will she take that? She would know he was joking, right? But maybe not. Shawn looked at Dusty and said nothing.

"Well?" demanded Dusty. Shawn shuffled his feet, and began to open his mouth again. Captain Cliché, Shawn McMaster, was about to say, 'shut up' or 'you'll never know' or 'are you going to get a hole in one?' But instead, CeCe popped out of the car.

"OK, Tirico and Gruden, you have this all figured out. Shawn and I will be spending the evening together. And what are your plans?"

"Oh, well, we are going to…" stated Chuck.

"Yeah, we have to… Oh," finished Dusty.

Chuck pointed toward the restaurant. "Ice cream."

Dusty started toward the front door. "Cherry pie."

And the two disappeared, like dogs called back by their owner. CeCe fired the discussion right back at them like a line drive hit right back at the pitcher. Shawn was standing in the batter's box, taking their abuse, dumbstruck. CeCe ended it with one simple question. A fastball down the middle that nobody was expecting. Shawn would have to take notes. Sometimes the answer is right under your nose, you just have to look in the mirror to see it.

The first six holes of mini-golf were played with laughter and talking, compliments on good shots, and nice tries. But on the seventh, when CeCe sent her ball through the tunnel, off two walls, and right into the middle of the cup, she had built up a four shot lead. A fact that the scorekeeper, Shawn, was keenly aware of.

CeCe hit her first shot on the eighth hole to within two feet of the cup. "Oh, would you look at that, Shawny."

But Shawn did not reply, didn't even acknowledge the playful banter. He bent over and placed the ball in the exact spot he wanted it, instead of dropping it and playing it from wherever it stopped. Two practice swings, the first two of his round, then a look at the hole, then back to his ball, hole, ball. Then a swing… and the ball careened off the back wall, and came to rest about a foot closer to the hole than CeCe's ball. "Yes!" Shawn said as he looked at CeCe, and then walked passed.

"Oh, I see," was all CeCe said.

Both of them knocked their second shots into the hole. As CeCe walked passed Shawn toward the tenth hole, she said, "Your first shot was great."

"Why, thank you," said Shawn.

"Even better than mine."

Shawn smiled and nodded.

"But we tied on the hole, sucks for you. I still have a four stroke lead," she said, bending over to place her ball for her next shot, peering back at Shawn upside down, the golden highlights in her red hair catching the sun as it spilled toward the ground, her shorts riding up her thighs, and her shirt creeping up her torso. The smile disappeared as she popped up and tugged her shirt and her shorts lower. Shawn didn't know much about girls, but he was pretty sure that if he was a girl, and had a body like that, he would let it hang out every once in a while. But what did he know? He had enough trouble being a boy.

Shawn inched closer as the back nine wore on. He picked up a stroke on twelve when CeCe's second shot rimmed out. "Oh, tough break, that," Shawn said, in a terrible English accent.

CeCe grinned, but didn't back down. In fact, all the banter seemed to motivate her. She hit a long putt on fourteen to save a two, tying Shawn.

On fifteen, CeCe hit her first shot to within six inches of the cup. She stepped away, the freckles on her left cheek vibrating as she held back a smile. "All yours." Shawn proceeded to knock his shot right into the cup, a hole-in-one. "You're right, it is," was all he said.

Disaster for CeCe on sixteen: her first shot took an awkward right-hand turn after hitting the back wall, almost like a football bouncing on the ground, and spun right into the water hazard. One stroke penalty. Shawn started to say, "We don't have to---" but CeCe cut him off with a look. Her face blank, her eyes wide. Somewhere between Are you kidding me? And Better protect your privates. The penalty would be assessed. No special treatment for this girl. She managed a four, Shawn a two. Tie score.

Seventeen was a wash, both players carding twos. Tie score moving on to the last hole. CeCe and Shawn each hit first shots that left them with putts that were about ten feet or so. CeCe would hit first. She hunched over her ball and took practice swings. Looked at the hole and then back down at her ball. Shawn forgot about the tie score, the eighteenth hole, and that they were golfing at all. Instead, he focused on the way her cut-off jeans hugged her athletic bottom, the way her legs swelled out at the calves, then darted back in at her thin, but strong, ankles. Her cute little feet. His head told him no, but his heart couldn't resist. Before she hit, Shawn snuck up behind her and grabbed her by the shoulders and said, "don't miss," in her ear.

CeCe jumped and shrieked, shaking loose from Shawn's grip. Shawn was startled, and fell backwards. CeCe ran off to the bathroom. Shawn was sure he heard her crying. He didn't follow. He stood there near the eighteenth hole, looking at the women's bathroom door, burning heat emanating from the center of his body, a cool sweat leaking from all his pores. Why couldn't he just leave it be? Let her putt. Then putt himself. See, this is why he spoke very little in public, if at all. It was better for everybody if he kept his mouth shut. Nobody gets hurt. Enjoy your day.

Shawn picked up CeCe's club and pocketed both of their golf balls. He didn't know what to do, but he did know he wanted to get the heck off that golf course. He returned the clubs, and the balls too. He decided to stand out in the parking lot, waiting for CeCe, as if he was the boyfriend waiting for his girlfriend to go to the bathroom. His car was ten miles away, with each step, his feet filled up with more and more sand. He stopped in the middle of the parking lot and looked up into the sky. Why was he such an idiot? Why was---

"Boo!" said CeCe as she sped by him to the car. She opened the passenger door and hopped in.

Shawn sat down, put the key in the ignition, stopped, and turned to CeCe. "Are you... I'm sorry, um."

"It's ok, seriously. You just surprised me. That just freaked me out, knowwhatImean?"

"Yeah, I didn't mean to---"

"I know. Seriously. That was all me. It's just," CeCe faced front and looked out the window. "It's ok." She reached over and turned the key, starting Shawn's car. "How about some ice cream?"

Shawn put the car in drive and glanced over at CeCe, "I know a place."

211

53

It had been about four years since Shawn had seen Fran, but by the looks of her it could have been ten, or even fifteen. She answered the door, not CeCe. "Oh, hi, Shawn," she said. "It's really good to see you," were the words that came out of her mouth, but the look on her face was that of somebody who was drinking water, but wasn't thirsty.

Shawn stepped past Fran who was holding the screen door open. "Hi," was all Shawn could squeeze out. Then, one click softer, "how are you?" He stood up against the wall in the hallway, marveling at the wonder that was the shoelace. It wouldn't have bothered him one bit if the wall engendered a mouth and swallowed him. CeCe must have gotten her eyes from her father.

CeCe smiled as she passed Shawn and walked toward the front door. She yelled "bye" to Fran, who was already in the kitchen. Fran yelled "bye" back. Shawn didn't move until CeCe pointed out the front door with her chin. He dug in his shorts pocket for his car keys as he walked out into the deep summer evening.

CeCe was already down the front steps, the last rays from the setting sun wiggling through the trees, searching for the golden highlights in her hair. Shawn watched CeCe walk, her micro short denim cutoffs working overtime. She was still athletic, but slenderer. The muscles in her quads and calves had softened and shrunk. Her rear end was smaller, but still shapely, still tight, still fantastic to look at, especially in those shorts.

After one last peek, Shawn slipped past CeCe and beat her to the car by five steps. He opened the door for her, and waved her in.

"Why, thank you," she said as she dropped into the passenger seat.

As Shawn backed out of the driveway, he reminded CeCe of the plans. "If we're going to do this right, it's cheeseburgers and gravy fries at McMaster's to start."

"Damn straight."

"OK, then. Dinner at McMaster's, mini-golf at Davis', then back to McMaster's for ice cream."

CeCe looked at Shawn and laughed.

"What?" he asked.

"You looked like a statue of a goddamn miserable little boy in my house. Now you are, like, animated and talking a mile a minute. Smiling."

"You know why that is," said Shawn.

CeCe looked at Shawn, who looked back at her. She smiled, then looked out the window. Shawn opened his mouth to speak, released a noise that could have been the combination of any two letters of the alphabet, then stopped. When CeCe had turned, Shawn's eyes were drawn to CeCe's top. Tight, sleeveless, with a plunging neckline. Cleavage again.

CeCe turned back and caught Shawn in mid-creep. "Um," was all she said as she pointed at the red light they were approaching like a sprinter toward a finish line. He slammed on the brakes, they anti-locked to a stop, and they sat in silence for a moment. Shawn's face flushed and sweat beaded on his forehead. CeCe looked forward. Smiling.

Shawn eased his car into a spot in the middle of the parking lot. He hopped out of the car and scurried to the passenger side. CeCe had the visor pulled down. She was staring in the mirror, putting the finishing touches on her face. Shawn opened the door and waited for CeCe to get out. And waited.

She tossed her lipstick in her bag as if she were trying to hide a cigarette from a parent, and sprung out of the car. "Thanks," she said.

"Kitchen's open until ten," said Shawn, falling back as if CeCe had knocked him over.

"I know I was keeping you waiting. Sometimes I take too long."

"It's fine. I mean, I understand, you have to keep up with this," said Shawn, motioning to himself with his chin as they walked.

CeCe smiled, then sucked her top lip into her mouth, making most of it disappear. She watched her feet for the rest of their walk to the front of the restaurant. Again, Shawn opened the door for her. CeCe dipped through, peeking at Shawn for only a second. Shawn followed her in.

"Well, look who it is." Greta walked across the room toward them, drying her dry hands on a towel.

"Hi, Mrs. M.," said CeCe, stepping into a hug.

Shawn also hugged Greta, but didn't say anything. Walking in here again was still strange. He felt like the last piece of a puzzle that you just can't turn in the right direction to make it fit, but it has to be the one to finish things off.

"You two have a seat. Cheeseburgers and gravy fries coming right up."

"How did you know?" Shawn asked, each word of the question softer than the previous.

"Women have a way of knowing things, I suppose." Greta winked at CeCe. "Hold on." She dug into her pocket for her cell phone. "Text from your father. He said, 'Is Shawn ready for some batting practice?'"

Shawn shifted his butt forward, then backwards on his seat. "Oh, um, no, I, um, told him---"

"Christ, Shawn, relax. He's just kidding," CeCe shook him by the wrist across the table. "Where is Mr. M.?" Greta pointed up, to indicate the Billy was in the residence.

214

Shawn chuckled, then looked up at CeCe. She left her hand on his wrist for a few more seconds, then pulled it away. Shawn gazed across the table at CeCe's hair, and the way it fell across her face, hiding some freckles, framing others. Then into her eyes, and passed them. Into her soul. Or whatever the heck it was that made him feel so good when he looked at her. The room and everything, and everybody in it faded away. The four years between them evaporated. Shawn breathed in and out, and he couldn't tell if he was twenty-two or eighteen, or somewhere in between. Or even sixteen again. The center of his chest felt light, but not hollow. Full, but not a burden. Like pushing away from the dinner table after the perfect amount of food, then taking a nap that was not a second longer or shorter than it needed to be. It had been so long since he had experienced that feeling.

"Would you look at what we have here," said Dusty.

"Yes, my brother," sang Chuck. They must have sprouted through a crack in the floor.

"ShawnandCeCe, back again."

"Can I get an Amen?" Chuck asked, at a volume that might have elicited a response from all corners of the restaurant.

Shawn looked at Dusty, then Chuck, then CeCe, then at the placemat in front of him. He wanted to say, *Yup, we're back*. He wanted to say, *Relax, punk, it's just a date*. Or, *Amen, now move along so we can pick up where we were interrupted*. The first option was presumptuous; the second, blasé; and the third, so loaded with potential misunderstanding that it almost made Shawn's brain bleed. So instead, he looked toward the kitchen, praying that the door would swing open.

"And look at you two," said CeCe, "still together after all these years."

215

Shawn laughed. Because it was funny, because CeCe spit it out so quickly, because it took the pressure and the focus on him, and turned it on the fellas.

"We don't waste a moment." Dusty shot a melodramatic glance in Chuck's direction, placing a hand on Chuck's shoulder.

Chuck fired his arms up into the air, which threw Dusty back a step. Chuck hovered his palms over Shawn and CeCe's heads, tilted his own head back, and squeezed his eyes shut. "My children," he chanted, again, loud enough to imply that he had fathered the entire populous of the room, "you never know what will happen. Bad hops---"

"Hmmm, beer," said Dusty.

"Broken bats---"

"Broken hearts."

"None of these days are promised to us," preached Chuck, now resting his hands on Shawn and CeCe's heads. "Ashes to ashes, dust to dust---"

"Pocket full of posy."

"Would you get your hands the hell off of us." CeCe smacked Dusty's hand away from her head.

"We are going to enjoy the rest of this day. With dinner, and mini-golf." Shawn's shoulders dropped. Really? Lay out the itinerary as a comeback?

Dusty looked at Chuck. "Something about a hole-in-one. Too soon?"

"Definitely too soon," said Dusty.

"Perfect. Going for a hole-in-one, Shawny?"

No, no, he wasn't. Not tonight. Not that he wouldn't want to. Because he would certainly want to. But this was just the first date. Well, their second first date. Shawn sat there with his mouth sealed shut, making sure he didn't insult anybody inside his head.

"Oh, wait. Maybe you are going for the hole-in-one, Celine," continued Dusty.

216

"What the shit does that even mean?" asked CeCe, right on the tail of Dusty's accusation.

"Anything is possible on God's green Earth," sang Chuck.

"Clearly," said CeCe, "look at you two."

"Amen," said Shawn.

CeCe looked across at Shawn, freckles bouncing on her cheeks, and let out a resounding, "Ha!"

Shawn leaned back in his seat and looked at the guys. Two syllables. He had gotten in two syllables, but they were perfect. He could tell by CeCe's reaction. The strange thing was, it just flew out of his mouth. He didn't think. Didn't plan it. Just came out.

"Excuse me, boys." Greta placed a tray on the edge of the table. "Cheeseburgers, fries, and a bowl of gravy."

Dusty reached for a fry on Shawn's plate. CeCe slapped away his hand.

"Aw, fries and gravy," said Chuck.

"Why does this always happen to us?" Dusty looked at Chuck.

"Look over there." Greta pointed at a booth on the other side of the room. Two piles of fries and two bowls of gravy sat on the table.

"That's a long walk," said Dusty.

"Exactly," Greta winked at CeCe, then smiled at Shawn.

The two walked away, Chuck with his arms raised, hands extended out as if to bathe the patrons of McMaster's Restaurant in his aura. He was saying something about the blessings of potatoes and the wonder of gravy thickener.

Shawn chose a fry and dragged it through the gravy, and popped it into his mouth. He looked over at CeCe through half-opened eyes. She was smiling.

It was the best thing he had tasted in a long time.

217

CeCe would play first. She strode to the tee area and, keeping her legs straight, bent over to place her ball. Taken out of context, and in spandex instead of tiny denim shorts, it would have looked like she was stretching her hamstrings. She addressed the ball, swung the club back, then stopped and turned to Shawn, "I think I ate too many fries, not sure I can do this."

"Nice try, Easter. Just hit," he said, fiddling with the handle of his putter. "Let's go."

CeCe turned around, addressed the ball, wiggled the club, wiggled her butt, took a deep breath, brought the club back, then swung forward as if she were fending off an attacking mountain lion, missing the ball by three feet. "Ooops!" was all she said, then lunged forward as if the putter were attracted to a huge magnet.

Shawn smiled, but said nothing. CeCe used to be a vicious competitor, and a proud athlete. The eyes, the smile, the hair and the freckles were still there, but where was the rest of her?

"OK, OK, I'm just screwing around," said CeCe as she stepped next to the ball. Without looking up, she smacked the ball toward the hole. She didn't watch it roll, didn't see where it stopped. She just walked toward Shawn and said, "Your turn, sport."

Shawn stood over his ball, looked at the hole, and took two practice swings. Glanced at the hole again, then tapped the ball, rolling it right toward the cup. It rolled right, two feet from the hole, then came to a rest. Shawn watched it the entire way, leaning left as it bent right.

Shawn stood by his ball and watched CeCe. She had her club resting against her inner thigh as she used both hands to put her hair in a loose ponytail. "Good ahead."

Shawn sunk the three footer, pumped his fist, and pulled out the scorecard. "Two. Let's see what you got."

"Oh really?" asked CeCe. She leaned forward over her ball, giving Shawn another great view down her shirt, and swung. The ball flew off her club, screamed past the hole and caromed off the back wall, coming to rest farther from the hole than where she just hit from. "I haven't played much golf over the past few years."

Shawn grinned like a ten-year-old who hadn't received the gift he wanted for his birthday. Then watched CeCe finish up the hole. He wrote a five next to his two. "You're down three already," he said.

"Uh oh," said CeCe, into the screen of her phone, which she was using as a mirror.

Shawn surveyed the next hole, placed the ball on the ground, looked at the cup, then moved his ball eight inches to the right. Two practice swings. Then he rolled the ball toward the cup with a swing as smoothly as the arc of a grandfather clock pendulum. The ball hit the edge of the cup, jumped into the air, and came to rest six inches from the hole. Shawn turned to CeCe sporting a tiny grin, but she was fixing her front, left pocket, the bottom of which was hanging below her shorts.

Finally, she looked up. "Oh, good one." She dropped her ball and whacked it in the general direction of the cup. Hole 2: Shawn 2, CeCe 4.

Shawn was readying for his next tee shot, was aiming to fire through the windmill, timing the movement of the blades. CeCe had said something, but he didn't hear it.

"Your dad spends a lot of time up in---," said CeCe.

But Shawn interrupted her with a raised hand, as if he were asking the home plate umpire for a time out. He swung and rolled the ball under the windmill as if the rotating blades weren't even there. "Yes!" he said as he pumped his fist. Then he looked at CeCe, "What were you saying?"

"Nothing. Don't worry about it," she said, looking around for her ball. "Nice shot."

The scorecard didn't leave Shawn's pocket after the sixth hole. He had an eleven stroke lead, and he could tell CeCe was more interested in how her tank top lay on her shorts, or how her ponytail was holding up. He decided to compete against the course. He would keep his score in his head, remembering where he stood relative to par.

"Miss playing baseball?" CeCe asked, as she was getting ready to hit her tee shot on the eleventh hole.

Shawn nodded his head.

"Your dad hasn't been able to find a left fielder that comes even close to replacing you."

Shawn tapped the head of his putter on an ornamental rock. "Bobby is a very good fielder."

"Very good is freakin' very far away from how amazing you were. KnowwhatImean?"

"Yeah, *were*." Shawn rested the putter on his shoulder like a baseball bat, then pulled it off as if he had a terrible case of sunburn. "And he's giving Bair a shot. He's a good hitter."

CeCe marched up to Shawn and planted her club on the ground. "Bobby is a very good fielder," she said through her scrunched up nose.

"I don't sound like that."

"Bair," she said, nose still scrunched, head bobbing, "he's a good hitter."

"He is."

"Yeah, no shit he is. CeCe's nose was no longer folded freckle over freckle. Her eyes were wide, coming at Shawn, like the deep end of a pool rushing at a diver. "What the hell happened to, 'I could carry Bobby on my back and Bair in my lap and still catch every fly ball, CeCe?' Where is *that* Shawn?"

"He's gone," Shawn said into his chest.

"Bullshit. He's in there," CeCe poked Shawn in the chest with the handle of her putter.

"I can't anymore."

220

"Have you tried?"

"No." Shawn crossed his arms. "I can't."

Her nose was scrunched up again. "I can't, I can't."

Shawn lurched forward and clawed CeCe's shoulder with his right hand. CeCe shook loose and scurried away. "Don't run away from me!" yelled Shawn.

CeCe stopped immediately. "Don't run away from me? Don't run away from me? Are you fucking kidding me?"

"You don't know what it's like."

"What what's like?"

"Having something burning, melting inside you. Day and night. Something you can't undo. Ever!"

"Maybe I do, Shawn. Maybe I do. But you wouldn't know, because you ran away."

"I did that for the good of everybody."

"Bullshit, you did that for yourself. You ran away from what happened. The rest of us, all of us were left behind." CeCe pushed past Shawn, dropped her ball on the ground, and whacked it toward the hole. CeCe turned away, but Shawn watched the ball ricochet off the back wall and roll into a fake sand trap lined with tan carpet.

The remainder of the round was played in silence. But CeCe's eyes warmed and her freckles smiled more and more each hole. And the eye contact between the two of them increased each hole as well.

CeCe tapped her ball into the eighteenth hole as said, "I think it's time for a drink."

"Um, ice cream?"

"Yeah, I mean, ice cream." CeCe grabbed her ball out of the hole and walked toward the parking lot. She dropped her ball in the barrel, rested her putter on the counter, and slid her phone into her pocket. She took Shawn's arm and said, "I know a place."

54

July 25, 2013 - 2:23 am

Shawn woke up on the couch in his living room, the Los Angeles edition of Sports Center shouting on the television. Enough noise for today. At the restaurant. At the mini-golf course. Back at the restaurant. Shawn reached for the remote. Pressed mute.

The plastic crinkle of a vertical blind wiggling above an air conditioning vent kept the apartment from silence. Amber light from the desk lamp highlighted the carpet below it, brightened the wall above it, left hints in the corners of the room. Shawn slid his feet off the couch, and attempted to raise his upper body. The first attempt pulled his feet off the ground, and his shoulders back to the couch. Second attempt, too. The third time, he used his legs and his arms, and his head, to set himself upright. He chuckled in the overnight peace of almost silent and minimal illumination. "Just do it right the first time."

He remembered what caused him to fall asleep: The moment-by-moment replay of the date, and more analysis than was ever inflicted on any Super Bowl game. His head was calm when he woke. Clear. Even empty. But as he rubbed his eyes and recovered from his nap, the thoughts popped back into his brain, like programs starting up on a rebooting computer.

"Why did she just let me win?" he asked. "The CeCe I remember would have battled me to the end."

He stood, steadied himself, and began pacing around the room.

"And with the hair. And the makeup and the clothes all the time," he looked out the window at the creek. "Not that I mind, she looks amazing."

Shawn turned back toward the middle of the room, dim light from the lamp not strong enough to light up his face. "Wait. Who in the heck am I talking to?" He walked

222

over to his desk, flipped up the screen of his laptop. Then pressed it closed again.

"I'm talking to myself. And you know what? I like it. I like talking to me. I like listening to me. I *understand* me. I don't understand most anything else. I don't understand CeCe anymore. I don't understand how to get myself back on the baseball field. I don't know what I'm going to do once I leave this place. Quit my job. Move back home. No idea."

Shawn walked back into his bedroom and pulled off his shirt. He looked in the mirror and inspected the muscles in his chest and arms, his flat stomach. "I guess I'm a little different too. I wonder if CeCe noticed?" He smiled at himself. Flexed. Decided against pushups. He didn't need them. Not tonight anyway.

He changed into a pair of mesh shorts and threw on a faded blue t-shirt that had a picture of a baseball glove on the chest. Shawn rubbed his fingers across the decal. It was cracking and faded, but still recognizable.

CeCe had asked him if he missed playing baseball. "Why would she ask me that? I grew up with a baseball field in my darn backyard. I didn't even make it through my first full Final Exam." He reached up and grabbed the doorjamb with the fingertips on both hands. "Of course I miss it, CeCe. I haven't played in four years! Of course I miss it."

He marched into the living room. "Why can't anybody understand that I just can't get back out there? Nobody has any idea what I went through. What I'm going through."

Shawn sat down on the couch again and dug his fingers into his hair, dragging his fingernails through his scalp. CeCe's words scrolled across the screen in his mind. *Maybe I do, Shawn. Maybe I do.*

"What the heck does that mean?" He slid his palms toward his eyebrows and stretched the skin on his forehead.

"The only thing she knows about now is hairspray, mascara, and blush, or whatever. And tight tops and short shorts." Shawn leaned back on the couch, crossed his arms, and looked at the ceiling. In a whisper, "But man, it does all look good."

Shawn walked into the kitchen and pulled open the refrigerator door. Bright white, like the headlights of a car that turned a corner, filled half of the room. The rest remained shadowy. He pulled out a can of soda, then returned the room to darkness.

"So now what, Shawn?" he asked himself as he returned to the living room. "Now what, me?" He toasted the empty room with his can of soda. "I move back. I have to move back. CeCe liked that idea. Mom obviously does too. Dad, well... I think deep down he likes it." Shawn sat on the couch, placed his can of soda on the coffee table.

"Dusty and Chuck? Who knows what they are thinking? But they seemed genuinely happy to see me. And even happier to bust my chops. They didn't even break stride." Shawn leaned forward, took a long draw from his soda, rested his elbows on his thighs, and caught his chin in his hands.

"OK. OK, here it is. Move back. Live with Mom and Dad. Live at home. Nice and easy, low responsibility. I got thrown into the real world, right? Doing a job, taking care of this place. Just ease back in. Work around the property a bit; get used to Quail again. Let Quail get used to me again. Take it day by day with CeCe. Hopefully, she, and everybody, can understand what I've been through. They know what I caused, but they also have to understand what I've been through. Maybe I can figure out what she thinks she's been through." He stood up and walked into his bedroom, slid open the door to his closet. He reached in deep with his right hand and pulled out a cardboard box. He dropped it on the bed. His baseball glove, along with batting gloves, wrist bands, and a worn out, salt-sweat stained McMaster's Restaurant baseball cap, hopped, then came to rest again.

He looked into the box. "And this." Not touching anything. "Maybe." He looked into the mirror. "Maybe next year, Shawn. Maybe next year, me, we think about getting back on the baseball field." He looked at himself in the mirror. "I know, I know. Maybe that's too soon. Maybe the year after that. Whatever. Whatever feels right. My pace."

Shawn's phone vibrated on the coffee table in the next room. "Ah, CeCe calling to apologize for yelling at me. I knew she would come to her senses." He looked at the clock on his nightstand as he left the bedroom. Two-forty-eight in the morning. "Pretty late for a call, even from CeCe."

It was Greta. "Hello," he said after tapping 'accept.'

"Shawn, sweetie," Greta said through sobs.

"It's really late. Why---Is everything ok?"

"I have terrible news."

"What?" Shawn asked, without thinking. His legs had already gone numb. Warm prickles exploded all over his body. Terrible news. What? What terrible news?

"Daddy had a heart attack."

"Heart attack? Is he ok?"

Of course he was ok. Billy could make fly balls land on a blade of grass. He could flip pancakes and scramble eggs at the same time. He could convert an umpire with a glance.

Of course he was ok.

"He didn't make it. He's gone," said Greta, who then burst into tears.

"No. No, Mom. That can't... No. I don't... No."

"I know. But it's true."

Shawn dropped onto the couch. Then stood back up. "You were there? You saw… him. Did somebody try…"

"They did, sweetie. The paramedics."

Shawn reached to place the phone on the coffee table, but missed. It fell to the floor, bounced to the right and landed, face down. Shawn walked into his bedroom and stood in front of the mirror.

So many times growing up, playing ball, after a bad at bat, after another speech on commitment, or the next level, he had wished death on Billy. But not seriously. Not really. He always took it back. Always regretted it. Always felt guilty. Even hated himself when Billy would sit on his bed with him, later on. Put his arm around him. Pump him back up. Greta sent him, most of the time. But, whatever.

Shawn leaned forward and looked at himself, but all he could see was his dad. His eyes filled with tears. He stepped backwards and fell back onto the bed. He wiped tears out of his eyes, sobbing. What the heck was he going to do now?

He sat on the edge of the bed, an occasional spasm launching from his chest, escaping through his mouth. He looked over the edge of the box, like a child, glancing into the pool, his first time on a diving board.   He reached in and pulled out his baseball glove. Inspected it. Slid it onto his hand for the first time in almost four years. Inspected it again. Looked at the palm and the webbing. Looked at his right index finger sticking out of the hole in the back.

Shawn was away from his father for four years, didn't see him again until recently. He had survived, did just fine. But this was different. Billy wasn't two hours away, making an omelet, or softening the dirt around second base with a rake.

He was gone.

Not watching over Shawn from the kitchen, from the other side of the batting cage, or from the dugout.

226

Not upstairs in the residence, while Shawn, Dusty, and Chuck raided the ice cream supply.

Not down in the restaurant, while Shawn and CeCe looked at the summer sky from the Scorer's Loft.

Gone. And instantly, Shawn was the only McMaster man left.

He stood up and looked at himself in the mirror, wearing his glove. He lowered into his ready stance, his elbows up and his hands out in front of his chest, knees bent. He reached over with his bare left hand, pulled the glove off his right hand, and whipped it at the kid in the mirror.

55

"And how are we going to fit stairs into this corner?" asked Billy, looking at DJ, then looking back up at the right, front corner of the restaurant.

"Can you trust me? I have this all figured out," said DJ.

"Of course you do. There's nothing wrong with the scoreboard system we have right now."

"Except that some unlucky soul has to sit outside in the cold, or in the rain, or in the summer heat."

"Just like the fans," said Billy. "Just like the darn players."

"Calm down, son. It's time to upgrade this. Times are changing." DJ pointed to the poster on the wall behind him. Pictured was an American flag hanging vertically, fading into the New York City skyline. Two of the stripes that should have been white, instead showed clouds in a blue sky. The twin towers should have been there. Below it said: IN MEMORY, 9/11, white letters on a black background.

"An indoor scoreboard operator's loft is not going to prevent terrorist attacks," said Billy.

"Oh, Wilbur, sometimes you have to make things better, even when you think they are good enough; or even perfect already. And this is the perfect plan, the perfect idea. Trust me."

"Fine. Tell me where the stairs are going to go."

"This corner booth comes out, and we install a spiral staircase. Cut a hole in the ceiling, frame out a room up top. All windows. Sliding, with screens for when the weather is nice. You can see the whole field from up there. I checked," said DJ, leaning his hips up against the table in the corner, looking up.

"And I guess this means a fancy new scoreboard as well?"

"No, no, no. I want to make what we have better, not erase what we have. Same scoreboard. Same operating system. Just instead of storing it in that stupid fuse box, we'll keep it inside."

Billy walked to the front door and looked out toward the pole. He and DJ had attached the metal box to the pole when Billy was just a kid.

"Look, we'll leave that box out there. Padlock it. It will be part of that whole monument area. Flagpole, plaques, and the fuse box."

Billy turned to DJ. "There are no fuses in there, Dad."

"I know. E-lec-tric-al box is way too much for me to say."

56

Greta pressed the pie crust into the metal pan while looking toward the swinging door. Every time a waitress pushed through with an armful of dishes, or ketchup bottles, she could see Shawn and Billy sitting at the counter talking over ice cream sundaes. The expressions on their faces were important. Both looked happy. Giddy, even.

The restaurant was all but empty, but she couldn't hear their conversation over the sound of the dishwasher behind her, or the clang of glass on metal to her left as a waitress refilled ketchup bottles. Greta was happy because her boys looked happy, but she was dying to hear what they were saying. One more pie and she would have a full load in the oven. She spun the crust like a machine, pressing a fork into the edges to define what would become the crust. She poured and spread her famous peach filling into the crust, slid it into the oven next to the other nine, set the timer, and walked out front.

"OK, that batch is in the oven."

"Another set of ten pies? Don't we have enough?" Shawn waved his hand at the display case, which was still half-full.

"Leave the restaurant business to us." Billy made brief eye contact with Greta. "Why don't you tell your mother the good news."

Greta already knew there was good news, but what was it? Did Shawn get a hit every time he was up in today's JV game? Or did he hit his first home run? Or did he make another great catch to save the day for his team? She stood in front of Shawn, drying her dry hands on her apron.

"Coach called me up to varsity, starting with practice tomorrow. I'm the starting left fielder now."

"Oh honey, that's fantastic. There can't be too many freshmen out there who are the starting left fielder for the varsity team."

"Exactly." Billy grew in his seat. "Coach said they can't ignore his speed and defensive ability any longer. They need him patrolling that enormous left field."

"The pitching is going to be really good up there." Shawn looked at Billy as if he had just asked him for the keys to his car for the very first time.

"Look, play great defense, zip around the bases with your speed, and use the rest of this season to get used to the pitching at this level. Then, next year… Look out."

Shawn nodded and smiled into his sundae, scooping out a helping that he couldn't fit into his mouth. Some whipped cream escaped onto his cheek and some sliced almonds fell to the counter top. He looked up at Greta and smiled.

She decided to enjoy this moment with the fellas, knowing that Billy's tone was sure to change once Shawn played through his first varsity game. No matter what Billy said, she knew he would analyze each and every one of Shawn's at-bats, then the pressure would mount as he recorded every single one of Shawn's muscle twitches in the batter's box.

But tonight, Greta smiled. She tossed a soapy rag on the counter in front of Shawn and Billy and cleaned the counter top as best she could.

57

CeCe hung up her apron and walked past the office in the back of the kitchen. No sound came out of there. No pulling of drawers. No scratching of pens. No smart comments that CeCe knew were hugs from Billy. Nothing. Nobody was in there.

Greta was rolling out a pie crust, moving the rolling pin as if it were a hundred-pound dumbbell. Two hundred pounds. CeCe took a step in her direction, opened her mouth to speak, but said nothing. Stopped and turned around. Greta didn't react to her presence. It was better that way. CeCe had no idea what to say.

She pushed through the swinging door and walked into the dining area. Their booth, Shawn and her booth, was empty. He must not have arrived yet. She turned and grabbed a glass out of the plastic crate. It was still warm from running through the washer. She added ice, then soda.

"I'm back here." Shawn was sitting in a booth back in the corner.

CeCe would have never thought of looking for him back there. "New booth, huh?"

"Trying to stay out of sight. I don't feel like talking about it anymore."

CeCe sat down and pushed the soda in front of Shawn. He picked up the straw and tapped it on its end as if to unwrap it. He wasn't hitting it hard enough, but he kept tapping. "So what have you been up to?" She felt like she had asked about Billy, even though she was trying to 'not talk about it anymore.'

"I've been doing a lot of work for Steve."

"Hasn't he found a replacement yet?"

"No, and honestly, the work, and being out at the apartment helps keep my mind off things."

232

CeCe shifted in her seat, leaning one direction than the other. She ended up in the same position in which she started. "They say it's good to keep busy, keep a routine when, well, you know."

Shawn nodded. Closed his eyes, then opened them. He put the straw back on the table, and turned his head to look out the window.

"Maybe we could get out? Tonight---"

Shawn leaned back in his chair, away from the table. If his face could have swallowed itself, it would have.

"Or whenever you want. You know, it's up to you. Whenever."

Shawn took a deep breath, and looked up at CeCe. "Thanks, I think I have to take this day by day. We'll see. I really don't know what I am going to do now."

"OK, I understand," said CeCe. But she didn't understand. Wasn't it freakin' obvious what he needed to do right now? Move home. Become the man of the house. Help his poor mother. But this wound was fresh. Like getting up off the ground with a brand new sprained ankle. It's hard to know how to step, how much to lean on it, whose advice to take. "I understand."

Dusty pushed into the booth next to CeCe. "Suck over," he said as he burrowed in.

Chuck waited for Shawn to make room, and eased into it. "How you doing, buddy?"

"I'm ok."

Dusty looked at CeCe, then over at Shawn. "Yeah, um. We were thinking about some mini-golf. Or, um, just cruising around."

"Look," said Shawn, loud enough for most of the restaurant to hear. "I'm not dead. My dad is dead. Not me."

"Yeah," said Chuck. "We know, buddy."

"Quit calling me buddy! You never call me buddy."

233

"OK, alright."

"How… What can we do?" asked Dusty.

"Can you make things go back to the way they were?"

Dusty crossed his hands together and squeezed.

"Can you, Dusty?" asked Shawn. "No, you can't. Can you, Chuck?" he asked, turning his body to the right, his knee digging into Chuck's thigh. "Can you bring my dad back? Can you erase all the stupid things I've done?" He pushed out of the booth seat and stood over them, leaning on the end of the table with both hands. He looked at all three of them, one after the other. With a softer voice, "Can any of you do that?" A tear ran down his cheek. "Can you bring back my dad? And for that matter, how about my brother? And can you keep me from swinging that bat?" He stood up again, and at full throat, "Can you?" He turned and stormed out of the front door.

Dusty turned to CeCe, "we didn't mean…"

Chuck continued, "We thought we would tone down our act. We thought that was the right thing to do. Honest."

"I know, guys. He's in a bad place right now. I think we're going to have to," CeCe stopped, and forced out the words as if they were a rotten egg she had stored in her mouth for four years, "be patient."

"Should we go after him?" asked Chuck.

"I'll go," said CeCe. She could be patient, but it didn't mean she had to wait around.

She found Shawn out beyond the right field fence, beyond the reach of the field lights. A game was going on, teeners, or maybe adults. The sky above was dark, like burnt toast, and seemed close enough to touch. The stars were hidden. No moon.

"The guys were just trying to help."

"I know." Shawn looked toward CeCe, but not into her eyes. "I just need... I need time."

"OK. But remember, Shawn. There are other people around here. Your mom. She needs help."

"I know. I know she does. I just have to figure this all out."

CeCe cocked her head toward Shawn, and leaned toward him. "What the hell is there to figure out, Shawn?"

Shawn took a step back and put his hands up, as if CeCe were a wild animal, approaching him in the woods. "You don't know what I'm going through," he said to the ground, as if she would have to pick the words up to hear them.

"I don't, huh?"

"No, CeCe. You don't. Did you ever lose your dad?"

"I never had a dad, Shawn! Did you ever think of that?"

Shawn stepped toward CeCe, then stopped. He opened his mouth to say something, then didn't. He pushed past her and took a few steps toward the parking lot. He turned and said, "I need some time." He walked up toward the parking lot, fading into the night until all CeCe could see were his movements.

She didn't realize she was crying until she touched her face. This happened to her sometimes. The ache emanating from her soul numbing the rest of her body. How could this be happening again? How could she be losing Shawn again?

She didn't want to do it, but she knew who she needed to call. She hadn't in such a long time. She was doing so well.

58

Shawn jogged across the bleachers, not on the floor, but on the bench one level above where CeCe was sitting. The clang of his feet on metal camouflaged the tinny clap of a baseball colliding with an aluminum bat down below on McMaster Field.

Shawn tossed the sweatshirt that he retrieved from his bedroom at CeCe. She yanked it over her head and straightened her arms, her hands not reaching the ends of the sleeves. How could she need a sweatshirt already?

"I'm not going to be warm again until next summer am I?" asked CeCe.

"It won't be that long. I'm thinking late spring," said Shawn, crashing hip to hip, putting his arm around CeCe and leaning in close. "Like, first week of June, late spring."

"Shit." CeCe tucked her chin, mouth, and nose into the collar of the sweatshirt.

Even with half of CeCe's face hidden, Shawn could still see more freckles than he could ever count. He tried, one by one, touching as many as he could with the tip of his left index finger. Other than a line drive base hit up the middle, what was better than doing that?

"Oh, come on, Shawn. Still?"

"I'm going to count them all."

"Better hurry, because I am going to have them removed." Shawn squeezed her tighter with his right arm as he laughed. "Seriously, I'm getting tired of them."

"You can't get rid of them."

"Like hell I can't. I think they can bleach them. Or like, laser them out, youknowwhatImean?"

"I don't care if you can get them off with dish soap, there is no way you are getting rid of them" Shawn leaned

236

in, and pecked her on the cheek like a chick eating seeds off the ground. "I love every last one of them."

CeCe turned and caught one of his pecks with her lips, and turned it into a long kiss. From down below in shallow right field, one of the players taking batting practice yelled, "Hey, don't swallow her, McMaster. She has to scoop us all ice cream in a little while."

Shawn pulled his head away. CeCe tried to follow with her lips. "Are you ashamed of me?"

"No."

"Or afraid of them?"

"No, no, it's just---"

"I know, Shawn. You're just shy. It's one of the things that makes you so irresistible. That, and how your ass looks in your baseball pants."

"YouknowwhatImean?" said Shawn, mimicking CeCe's voice, head tilt, and eye squint. He also leaned away from CeCe and onto one cheek.

"Why don't you come down here and hit some baseballs instead of trying to hit that girlfriend of yours?" called the voice from right field again. Shawn waved him off, as if he were shooting a basketball at him, with perfect follow through.

There was no question that The Final Exam ended games on McMaster Field for the season, but teams still reserved two-hour blocks to hit and field on the weekends throughout October and into November until the cold kept the players from wanting to hit because it stung their hands.

But this afternoon was made for batting practice, for fall baseball. Even getting a root canal out on the pitcher's mound would be a treat in this kind of weather. The sky was blue like a raspberry snow cone with half the juice sucked out. Mid-afternoon in fall, the sun was closer to set than that time of day in summer. Shawn was wearing a t-shirt and shorts, and sneakers, of course. But CeCe's need for a sweatshirt reminded everybody that winter was on

Pennsylvania's breath. Two hands worth of fingers were plenty to count the clouds in the sky, white and grey bordered in lavender and purple. Every once in a while, one of them would blot out the sun, spreading a chill over the McMaster property. But like the players down on the field, the sun wasn't ready to give up on baseball season yet. It escaped from behind the clouds, and Shawn and CeCe exhaled.

"What's wrong?" asked CeCe, looking over at Shawn.

Shawn was looking in the opposite direction, through the backstop and beyond. He had never kept anything from CeCe, until recently. It was time to talk. "You're going off to Susquehanna State next year."

"So are you, dummy," CeCe said, punching Shawn in the shoulder.

"Just listen," Shawn didn't turn and look CeCe in the eyes like he normally would. 'The safest place in his world,' he called those eyes. Instead, CeCe turned her body toward him. He could feel her stare on the side of his face. "You're going to be taking different classes than me---"

"There's tons of free time---"

"Please, just listen." Shawn turned toward CeCe. Their faces were a foot apart. The sun was setting behind Shawn, but it was still powerful enough to match CeCe's eyes to the sky, illuminate her freckles, electrify her hair. The soft, cool breeze pushed her bangs into and away from her right eye. "You're going to meet all kinds of different people."

CeCe opened her mouth, then closed it again. She put her hand over her mouth.

"You know everything about me. You're the only one. You're my safe place. I'm afraid that…"

CeCe tried to maintain eye contact with Shawn, but he looked down at the ground. She raised his face by his chin, reconnecting with his eyes.

"I'm afraid you are going to find something better. Somebody smarter. I think college is going to... expose me." CeCe took Shawn's hands in hers. He continued, "They want me there to track down fly balls. I can do that." A smile snuck onto his face, "Better than anybody."

"You got that right."

"That's all fantastic here on my family's baseball field, where there are pictures of me on the wall of the restaurant. Here in tiny Quail. What happens when you start meeting other Chemistry majors from all over the place? I'm just going to blend in. Fade away. I'll be like my hitting. Average. Sometimes good, but a lot of the time forgettable."

The door of the restaurant opened and the sounds of the early dinner crowd escaped. Voices and laughing. Silverware on plates. Shawn turned to watch the batter. He hit a pop up toward left field, then another to third base. Shawn and CeCe both squinted as they watched. "I don't want to lose you. I can't... lose you. How could I live without you?"

CeCe looked at Shawn for a long time. After about a minute of silence between them, "First of all, slugger," CeCe said, using the name he called her, "let's take it one pitch at a time. It's only October. We have our whole senior year ahead of us, and the summer." The batter squared one up, hitting the ball right on the sweet spot. The sound was unmistakable. Shawn and CeCe both turned, and all the players on the field cat called as the ball flew over the left field fence. "And I know I'm going to meet all kinds of different people, some of them that have the same love for the fucking periodic table that I do." She leaned in and reached her arms around Shawn's waist, at least as much as she could and still look him in the eyes.

Down on the field, somebody yelled, "Hey, get a room." But neither of them heard.

"And even if he looks exactly like Zac Efron, I won't be interested." She pushed her left cheek into Shawn's chest and said, barely loud enough for him to hear, "You have no idea what you've done for me. What you mean to me. I'm not going anywhere."

Shawn reached his arms around CeCe and hugged her tight. She fit in his arms like his hand fit in his baseball glove. He looked down at her adorable little foot, her flip-flop dangling. "Flip-flop," he said to her.

"Oh, definitely female."

"The feminine curves?"

"Absolutely. Even the one's that Dusty wears on his freakin' disgusting feet all summer after games. Female."

The two turned back toward the field. Batting practice was over. The players jogged around picking up the remaining balls. Shawn kept his right arm around CeCe, hugging it around her side and hip, pushing the tips of his fingers into her right, front pocket.

The team had gotten all the balls, but one. They forgot the one that was hit over the left field fence. They couldn't see it from field level, but Shawn and CeCe could see it from where they sat. They didn't say anything.

Shawn rested his cheek on the top of CeCe's head and closed his eyes. Breathed in slow and long. The smell of coconut from CeCe's hair, burgers from the restaurant, mown grass from the field, and burning wood from somebody's backyard filled his nose.

CeCe was right. He had no idea what he meant to her. He wondered what she meant as he opened his eyes and strained to see the darkening sky beyond the field, beyond the restaurant and through the dying leaving on the trees.

59

"So, somebody hits one down the line, stupid blues have no idea what happened. Fair or foul," said Dusty.

"Yup, so they go to the instant replay," said Chuck.

"And then what happens?"

"Well, Dustin," said Chuck, sounding as much like what he thought a sarcastic, white guy sounded like, "they get the call right."

"Then what?"

"What do you mean, then what?"

Larry pushed his plate toward the edge of his table so he could face the fellas and listen. It was about to get good. He would celebrate in the moment. Tuna on toast, and two knuckleheads banging into each other.

"So they figure out what the call should have been. Then what, Charles?" asked Dusty, imitating Chuck's version of what a sarcastic, white guy would sound like.

"Can you move your high school diploma away from your face? I can't understand what you are saying."

"Get your hands out from underneath your college graduation dress and listen." Larry chuckled, almost spitting toasted crust onto the floor. "Let's say there is a guy on first base. Line drive down the right field line. They think they need to check the call…" said Dusty, leaving the rest of the sentence blank for Chuck to fill in.

"They go to the ump up in the booth, or to somebody in the league office in New York. Or they consult with the baby Jesus. Can I get an amen?"

"Amen. Keep going."

Larry had to keep himself from tossing in an 'amen' himself. Instead, he kept listening. He knew where Dusty was going with this. And he knew Chuck did not.

"So Uncle Replay up in the booth looks, and says, you screwed up again, idiots, that was foul. Runner goes back to first, another strike on the batter." Chuck looked at Dusty as if he had to explain to him how to zipper his pants.

"And?"

"And?"

Larry watched Dusty flip and flop his right hand, almost as if it were jumping back and forth over a fence. Larry put the rest of his sandwich down, crossed his arms, grinned, and watched.

"What if it was fair?"

"Simple, dope."

"Dope?"

"Oh, sweetie, you know I love you, right?" asked Chuck.

"Yes. Yes, I do. And lover, I would like you to keep going."

"Well, if it was fair, they would just keep the results of the play. If the runner scored, and the batter ended up on second, then so be it."

"And?"

"And?"

Larry couldn't help himself. "What if the call on the field was foul, but the replay shows that it was fair?"

Dusty bowed his head to Larry, then looked at Chuck, "Yeah, what Nicky Rooney said."

"Mickey."

"Yeah, what Mickey Rooney said."

The grin on Chuck's face retreated into his mouth, leaving a wide-open space.

Dusty plowed into a slice of cherry pie. "When you figure it out, let me know. You know where I live."

Larry tossed the last bit of tuna sandwich into his mouth, and reached for his coffee cup to wash it down.

"You're not DJ McMaster, are you?" asked an unfamiliar voice from behind.

242

Larry turned away from the Dusty and Chuck show and faced the man standing in front of him. "No, I'm sorry. I'm not." The man had to be in his forty's, and most likely toward the end of them. He squeezed a white, legal sized envelope in his right hand. It was already creased and bent from the pressure.

"OK," said the man, who turned to walk away.

Larry couldn't let him walk off. Somebody who knew DJ, or at least, of him. Holding an envelope. Larry patted the laminated paper corner in his pocket. It was mid-August. He needed a break. Maybe this was it. "Did you know DJ?" Larry asked. The man stopped and turned. He manipulated the envelope with both hands now. The dinner crowd started to roll in, the front door opened and closed, ushering in waves of deep summer heat. Larry didn't notice, nor did he notice the smell of burgers and fries, the sound of plates and glasses and laughing and dinner orders. The man had his full attention.

"I would have to say that I knew of him. I played ball against his teams back in the day." The man stopped and tilted his head toward Larry. "Wait, you said, 'did you know,' not 'do you know.'"

Larry emptied his lungs through pursed lips. Interesting. This guy didn't know that DJ was dead. And he showed up looking for him, wringing the juice out of an envelope. "DJ died about ten years ago, I'm sorry to tell you." In through the nose, out through the mouth. Larry shifted in his chair, and inspected the man with squinted eyes. "I don't really look anything like DJ," Larry said, then stopped, allowing the man to speak.

"It's been a long time since I saw DJ. More than thirty years, I guess. But I was in and out of this place, and played on that field all the time. Honestly, you looked familiar. Were you around back then?"

Larry relaxed his shoulders and motioned to the chair across from him. The man sat down. Larry studied the

243

man, and the envelope he was holding, like a math problem Larry knew was wrong, but the mistake was invisible.

Accept and respect yourself; don't deny your screw ups, accept them, and move on.

Less than two months, he had to take a chance. "I've been around this place forever, and sometimes I sat on the bench with DJ. We were friends for a long, long time."

The man placed the envelope on the table, face down. "I'm Patrick Poole." He extended his hand across the table.

"Larry Schneider." Larry shook Patrick's hand, looking the man square in his envelope.

Patrick held it up for Larry to see. "I guess this is why I'm here."

Incredible. For ten years Larry had been hunting, then not looking, then poking around, and now searching again for whatever the heck DJ left behind that night. A couple of months ago, he was ready to ice cream sundae himself to death, having failed his best friend. Then he woke from a dream in a supermarket parking lot with a new outlook on life. He'd lost ten pounds. Was it all leading toward this? Toward this meeting with Patrick Poole? Cleansing exhale. Back to now. "What do you have there?"

Patrick placed the envelope on the table and slid it to Larry. "Look for yourself."

Larry folded back the torn flap of the envelope and pulled out a folded, white sheet of paper. Opened it. None of its corners were missing. It wasn't even the same color as the laminated paper corner in his pocket. At the top was a company letterhead: Abbott Paper Company.

"I'll save you the reading. They let me go after twenty-nine years of working there. I started there out of high school, sweeping floors. It was a little, family run place. Almost went out of business five times back in the eighties, but I stuck with them because they gave me my start. Old man Abbott moved along, and the new generation is replacing the old guys like me with younger guys with laptops thinner than a spiral notebook and tablets with credit card slots."

Larry's eyes shot around the room like the synapses firing in his brain. What did this have to do with DJ, with McMaster's, and with him finally solving this mystery? "So what brings you here?" Larry had a million probing, meaningful, burning questions he wanted to ask Patrick, but that's all that came out.

"Everything's gone modern. Like the paper company. Like signing for something with your finger on a damn computer screen. I haven't written a check in six months." Patrick pointed to both sides of the restaurant. "How about these damn Muldoon cookie cutter developments surrounding this place?"

The last question made Larry shift in his seat.

Patrick leaned in toward Larry. "This is the last little bit of old central Pennsylvania around here. I had to come back. Ask for a job. Or at least just have a sandwich and take in a game. Like old times, you know? I at least want to help keep this place in business."

Again, Larry shifted on the chair, and spread ketchup on his plate with his fork. He broke eye contact with Patrick. He said nothing.

"I'm sorry, did I say something wrong?" asked Patrick.

"No, no. Not at all. You in a rush or got some place to be?"

Patrick shook the letter at Larry. "I've got all the time in the world."

Larry inhaled and exhaled. Twice. Then pulled his hand across his mouth. He thought of the poster in the bathroom of the faculty room at school. 'Beauty is truth, truth beauty.' Underneath it, somebody had stuck a printout from an old dot matrix printer. It said, 'Sometimes you just gotta do what you gotta do.'

Maybe it was time Larry added a soldier to his one-man army. DJ told him not to trust anybody, but Patrick had the same goal. Maybe a fresh perspective was just what Larry needed? "Look at the menu, because I've got one heck of a story for you."

+++++++

Patrick dropped into the front seat of his car, leaned toward the passenger seat, and opened the glove box. He reached in and pulled out a large screened smart phone. He burped as he leaned back. He was stuffed. Muldoon was right, they did make a good burger. He unlocked the phone, pressed a single button, then put the phone up to his ear.

"It's me." He listened. Then said, "Oh, I've got a lot of information for you. How late is that bank of yours open, Muldoon?"

60

Greta could see the strength in her son's back and arms. Shawn was carrying his father's plaque in the warm pre-dawn. He rested the metal plate against his chest, holding it with two hands on either side. It was two weeks after Billy's death. Mother and son walked through the grass toward the flagpole and the electrical box and the other plaques in the mulch. The sky was one shade lighter than midnight. The only light provided by the restaurant, leaking through the front window and door.

Greta noticed Shawn's arms shaking as he neared the empty space in the mulch. She thought he might heave the plaque into place, eager to get it out of his hands. She knew the relationship between her husband and son was always touch and go, on and off. That stress could exist between parent and child when one coached the other. Both of her men were competitive, stubborn, and had tempers that lit quicker than Fourth of July sparklers.

Shawn didn't toss it into the mulch, not even close. Greta watched him sink into a squatting position like a catcher, the bronze colored plaque pressing into his thigh. She watched from a step behind Shawn as he looked at the three plaques that were already in place, then at the empty space, then back again. When Shawn was a young outfielder, Billy would move him into position from the bench. If Billy said two steps to the right, Shawn would go exactly two steps to the right. Move three in? Three in, it was. As Shawn got older, he would still listen to his coach, but he would also use his own intuition, his gut, as he called it, to position himself before the pitch. Greta wondered if Billy was telling Shawn exactly where to place his plaque, and if Shawn would obey, or put his own spin on things. Finally, Shawn lowered the plaque into place. No thud or explosion of mulch like Greta expected.

247

The plaque fit right in, another Wilbur McMaster, but this one did not have Ryan as its middle name like the other three. Wilbur Shawn McMaster, 1962 - 2013. Greta moved next to her son, putting her hand on his shoulder as he remained crouched. She and Shawn looked at the four plaques, and she caught her son looking into the empty space on the right side of the mulch. Her hand raised and fell as Shawn took a deep breath.

"Let's go inside, I need to tell you something," said Greta. They walked toward the restaurant, the first rays of sunlight peeking over the trees, reflecting in the spotless window. Greta pointed to a seat at the counter, and Shawn slid into it. Greta poured a cup of coffee for each of them.

"Are you.... Doing ok, mom?"

When she turned and looked him in the eye, he focused his attention on his cup of coffee, on the spoon that was leaning against the left side of the cup. Every night her heart ached for Billy, she missed him desperately, woke up from dreams where he was still alive, hoping that her dream was real life, and not the opposite. "I miss daddy.... But I'm ok. There's plenty to do around here to keep me busy, I suppose," Her voice trailed off at the end. She and Billy had never wanted to tell Shawn about October first, but she didn't see how she had a choice now. He had come out of hiding, and suddenly become the man of the house, restaurant and field, in a matter of weeks. She needed somebody to lean on. Larry hadn't found anything to keep them in the ownership of the McMaster property, and September was only days away.

Shawn kept stirring his coffee, but looked up at Greta. "You wanted to tell me something?"

Greta looked at the clock. The restaurant would be opening in a few minutes. The cooks and waitresses were arriving, so Greta led Shawn to the office in the back of the kitchen. She closed the door behind them. Shawn leaned on the desk and folded his arms, looking at his mother. Greta

248

wiped her already clean and dry hands on her apron, took a deep breath, and exhaled. "Your grandpa died suddenly, going on ten years ago now, just like.... Daddy." Tears welled up in her eyes. Shawn rubbed his mother's shoulder and upper arm. It was the first time she made that connection between the deaths, and the emotion took her by surprise. She gathered herself, and continued. "He didn't have a will at the time. And he died without leaving the property to daddy and me. Or to you. Or to anybody."

Shawn looked at Greta as if he was waiting for the rest of the story. She could tell the significance of this hadn't sunk in with him. The two stood in silence for a minute, the bustle in the kitchen the only noise. "OK," said Shawn, slow and drawn out, as if to ask, "so what?"

"Buddy Cahill gave us ten years to produce some sort of evidence that the property should legally be passed on to daddy and, well, on to me. Or to you."

"Why does it matter? Anybody can come look at those plaques out there. We've owned this property for as long as anybody can remember," Shawn's voice started to rise in intensity. Just like Billy's.

"There needs to be some sort of documentation, or Cahill has to put up the property for public auction on October first."

"Can't we convince everybody to not, like, bid or whatever?" asked Shawn, now standing in the middle of the room.

"You know there is one person who will bid no matter what, and has more money than everybody else put together."

"Albert Muldoon." Shawn leaned back on the desk again, crossing his arms in front of his ribcage. "There's nothing we can do? There's definitely no documentation or whatever?"

"Larry's been looking for the last ten years for something, anything."

"Larry?" Shawn interrupted. "Larry Last? Wonderful. Our only hope is a crazy old man."

Greta looked at the muscles in her son's arms flexing and firing, and decided to stay calm. "I think you need to give Larry a break, honey. Remember, he watched your grandpa, his lifelong best friend, die in his arms."

"True."

Greta watched as Shawn stared off into the corner of the room. The death of his father was fresh in his mind, she wondered if he was imagining what it would be like to watch somebody you love die. She hoped he would never have to see that. Shawn refocused on Greta. "He hasn't found anything?"

"No, but he got a good lead recently." Greta went on to explain how Larry yelling in the crowd all these years has been his way of looking for information. He never meant to sound crazy, but it became a good cover for what he was doing, how he blended into the restaurant and ballfield like a cup of coffee, a slice of pie, or second base. "But Shawny, you can't tell anybody. There's only five of us who know at this point, and it's best if we keep it that way, I suppose."

Greta watched Shawn do the math in the corner of the room again. "Me, you, Larry.... Cahill. And?"

"Muldoon."

"He knows already? Great. That's just great," Shawn paced around the small office. He pulled open the filing cabinet. "You looked through all of this?" Shawn pointed to file after file in the drawer.

"Sweetie, we've looked everywhere."

"Cahill can't do anything?"

"Not really. He's been great through all of this. He held off Muldoon as long as he could. Lied to him for years. And he said if we find anything, he doesn't care what it looks like, as long as it says that grandpa left this property to us and he signed it."

250

Shawn rubbed his eyes with his fingertips. Greta wondered if he wished he had stayed in hiding, living alone in his apartment, selling software by email, or whatever it was that he did.

"Is there anything I can do?" asked Shawn. "I'll do anything."

"Well, there is one thing," Greta walked forward and took Shawn's hands in hers. She looked up into Shawn's eye's "You could play in The Final Exam." She felt Shawn's hands stiffen. "Daddy would have loved to watch you play one last time."

"Mom, I can't. I can't play. I can't do it," Shawn pulled away from Greta, walking to the other side of the room. "And dad didn't want to see me play ever again. Not after what I did."

"That's not true!"

"Of course it is!"

Greta cornered her son so he couldn't pace anymore. "Shawn, daddy knew that was an accident."

"Yeah, right," Shawn said, crossing his arms, looking down to the ground.

"He did. He was upset after it happened, of course. But by the time he calmed down, you were long gone. He never had a chance to talk to you about it."

"He did these last couple of weeks." Shawn said, his eyes filling with tears.

Greta stepped toward Shawn and spoke in a hushed tone. "He didn't want to bring it up after you had been gone all these years. He didn't want you to.... Go again." She grabbed her son's hand and didn't let go.

"Mom, I can't play again. Out there," Shawn pointed toward the front of the restaurant, toward the field. "I haven't touched a bat, or a, well, a bat in four years."

"That's doesn't matter Shawn. Just being out there." Greta looked up toward the ceiling. "He'll watch you play. I would love to see you in uniform again. I don't care how well you play. I never did."

"I'll think about it."

"I think it would mean something to Quail if you played," Greta pointed at his pictures on the wall.

Greta went to work, pouring juice and serving breakfast. Taking orders and refilling coffee. She kept her eye on Shawn, who was sitting in a booth in the front of the restaurant, overlooking the field. He had eaten a few bites of pancake, and had finished off one piece of bacon. A sip or two of coffee. Mostly he looked out the window, down toward the field. The sun was low in the sky still, an orange circle pinned on a background of solid grey. Slowly it rose, bringing more and more light to the field, to the restaurant, to the entire McMaster property.

61

As far as Shawn could tell, the bat hadn't moved a hair since they starting "talking." The knob at the end of the handle leaned on the bench, and the top half of the bat rested against the wall of the dugout, angled because of the crack. Shawn hadn't touched it, didn't want to. Talking to it was strange enough, he was afraid what might happen if he actually took hold of the darn thing.

"Mom wants me to play. In The Final Exam. Oh, The Final Exam is---"

"I know what The Final Exam is, dummy. What do you want to do?"

"I can't play. I haven't been able to pick up a bat, not to mention swing one. I haven't thrown either."

"I didn't ask what you can or can't do, dope. I asked what you wanted to do."

Shawn turned and looked out toward the field, "Mom said Dad wanted me to play." He chuckled, "Said he would be watching me from up there." Shawn extended his thumb and pointed it toward the ceiling twice.

"Wow," said the bat, "I know you're not this dumb."

Shawn turned back toward the bat.   "What?"

"I've asked you twice now what you wanted to do. Not your mommy or your daddy." Then the bat quickly added, "God rest his soul."

Shawn paced back and forth in the dugout. Away from the bat, then back again. He missed playing ball, thought about it night and day. Watched it on tv, read about it. He dreamt about catching fly balls, ripping line drives back up the middle. He also had nightmares about striking out and storming into the dugout, eyes closed. Enraged. He would wake up in a cold sweat, the ache in his stomach

253

keeping him awake. "I want to," Shawn said, practically to himself. "But I just can't."

"Well, technically, you can."

"Yeah, I can," said Shawn, mocking the bat. "I can put on a glove and---"

"I know you can put on a glove," interrupted the bat.

"How did you know? Oh, never mind." Shawn knew not to ask how the bat knew what it knew at this point. Somehow the bat knew that Shawn had rummaged through his closet to find the glove he hadn't slid his hand into in four years. In the comfort of his apartment, on the bedroom floor, with the pain of Billy's death coursing through his body, the glove had calmed him. Calmed him from his right hand, up his right arm, through his chest, then all over his body. The previous time he had worn the glove, felt the leather encase his hand, he was still a ballplayer, still part of the McMaster family, still together with CeCe. It was before he struck out, before he rushed into the dugout, the anger melting his face and scalp. Before he closed his eyes and swung.

"It's your decision, Shawn. It always has been, it always will be."

"Look." Shawn sat on the bench, almost close enough to the bat to bite it. "The last time I played baseball, I almost killed my father. Now that I think about it, maybe I did. I'd love to play again, to feel the rush of hitting a fastball, the joy of tracking a long fly ball and pissing off the batter by catching it. But I can't take the chance, I can't risk doing that again. I can't let CeCe see me do that.... See me like that again. We're starting over."

"You know what you need to do?"

"Play baseball?"

"No, write freakin' children's novels, you dungle."

Shawn walked toward the opening in the dugout by home plate, then stopped. "What the heck is a dungle?"

"You tell me."

Shawn walked out toward home plate. The night was clear, stars pulsing in the sky, some bright, visible with peripheral vision. Others could only be seen when inspected directly. A steady cool breeze blew from the north, delivering the coldest night since late May. Shawn thought of October, of the restaurant closing and his mother moving out. He looked up and thought about his dad watching him play, not able to say a word, not able to coach or comment, not able to recommend or correct. Just looking down.

Shawn stepped into the lefty batter's box and wiggled his feet in the dirt. He reached for an imaginary bat toward the opposite corner of home plate. He made fists of his hands, putting the left on top of the right, and hung them just above his left shoulder. He took a deep breath and looked out toward the mound. In the moonlight, he could see the hump of dirt sixty feet away, the white pitching plate peeking out. Above it, darkness. Nothing. Nobody. "Can I do this again?" Shawn asked, under his breath, up to the sky.

"It's your decision, Shawn. Always has been, always will be," said the bat from the dugout.

Shawn took a deep breath and raked his hands, still in fists, still one on top of the other, in front of his body. Toward the mound, then back toward the catcher, and back again. He exhaled through puckered lips, and looked into the darkness toward center field. He rested his hands by his left shoulder, then swung as if he was holding a bat. Slowly, as if he were trying to guide the bat through a narrow opening between two shelves of crystal and china. Then he threw open his hands and turned toward first base and started to jog. Halfway to first he bubbled out to make a proper turn and hit first base so he could run directly toward second. He touched the left inside corner of first base with his left foot. The dirt exploded under his feet with

255

each step, the sound of a double, or a triple, or a stolen base echoing in his ears. He picked up speed as he rounded second base and headed for third. He was at full speed by the time he reached third base, stepping on the front half of the bag, turning his attention toward home. The last ninety feet were at top speed, leaving divots in the dirt behind him, the sounds of a thousand horses hitting the backstretch. He stepped on home plate, and his momentum carried him all the way to the fence of the dugout, right in front of the bat.

Shawn jumped onto the fence, hung on like a monkey, then lowered himself to the ground. He breathed a few deep breaths, and looked at the bat. "Should I do this?" He turned toward the field and took two steps forward. He tipped his head back and stared at the endless dark blue sky, freckled with more stars than he could ever count, framing a full moon. "Can I do this?"

62

August 21, 2013 - 10:19 am

Larry could hear them shuffling up from behind, but he ignored them. Kept walking toward the plaques. They would attack soon enough. It was part of the McMaster's experience for Larry. He used to fight it, or try to avoid it. He had come to realize that, like a sunset, or the last finger of coffee, he should enjoy it while he could.

"New shoes, Lawrence?" asked Chuck.

"No, no, no, he shaved those pork chop sideburns off," Dusty placed a hand on Larry's shoulder. "Good move. We're closer to the twenty-seventies than the nineteen-seventies."

"Not really," said Larry. He knew what they were up to. He would let them bob and weave, and jab a little more.

"I know; you finally chopped off those frosted tips. Those killed in the nineties, but they went out when Tony Fernandez hung 'em up. I'm glad you moved on, brah," said Chuck.

The guys circumnavigated Larry, one to his left, the other to his right. They cut him off, blocking his path toward the flagpole. He had something to do, but it could wait. This moment would be followed by another moment, and that one by another.

Chuck slid his arm around Dusty's waist as they ogled Larry. "Shit, Larry. Subtle, but very effective. Do you see it, Dusty?"

"Indeed, I do."

"New belt. Larry, you dirty dog."   Chuck gave Dusty a high five. "It's transformed you. Seriously. You don't look seventy-five years old."

"I'm only sixty-eight," said Larry.

"See?" asked Dusty.

257

"Okay, okay, I've lost about fifteen pounds this summer. But it was fun to listen to your observations. Gosh, I love you guys."

"Did he?" asked Dusty.

"He did," said Chuck.

"That's it. You are moving in with me and Chuck." Chuck waved his palm across the sky. "Baseball on the flat screen all night long."

"Baseball video games all morning long," said Dusty.

"Knight Rider reruns."

"Night swimming."

"Swimming trunks."

"Bikini waxing."

"Waxing nostalgic."

"Waning Gibbous."

"John Gibbons," said Chuck, unable to hold back laughter.

"Enough boys, enough," said Larry, sweat dripping off the side of his diet soda. "I'll give it some thought," he said with a wink.

"He said he'd think about it," said Chuck.

"Richey Wall said he'd think about it too. We're still waiting for him to decide. That was six years ago," said Dusty, hands on hips, looking down at the ground.

"Let it go, sometimes the pitcher stabs those line drives we hit back up the middle."

"The circle of life?" asked Dusty.

"Nahhh, lasagna, bag of ziti, baba," sang Chuck.

"Close enough." Dusty pulled Chuck by the elbow. "We'll leave you to it," he said to Larry.

Chuck looked over his shoulder as they walked away. "Let us know your decision by sunset. I'm not making any beds after the third inning of the Phils."

Larry found himself alone in the grass between the restaurant and the mulch that housed the plaques. Deep summer. The chirps of birds blended with the moist heat, which blended with the creamy blue sky. Background. Almost ignored by this point of the summer. Larry strolled across the grass, watching the first base disappear behind the dugout as he went.

He placed his bottle of soda on the electrical box, then knelt down and scanned all four plaques. Wilbur Ryan McMaster, Wilbur Ryan McMaster, Wilbur Ryan McMaster, Wilbur Shawn McMaster. Billy's plaque fell right in line with the others. The watchmen of this property, of the restaurant and ball field for four generations. Larry closed his eyes and breathed in, then out. In through the nose until no more could fit in his lungs. Then out until there was nothing left.

To forgive is to set a prisoner free and discover that prisoner was you. Remember what the Buddha said, 'To understand everything is to forgive everything.' Forgive yourself, love yourself, and enjoy each and every moment of the rest of your life.

"Refuse the key. Refuse the key," he said to himself, to the mulch and grass. "Refuse." He changed the emphasis to the other syllable, changing the word from verb to noun. "Refuse! Garbage. Refuse the key."

Larry fought gravity enough so that he could stand, then strode toward the back of the restaurant. He passed the Winner's Lock Room and pounded once on the door. Around the back of the building was a small, metal garage door. He lifted it, revealing a series of garbage cans. None of the Wilbur's ever wanted to pay for a dumpster. Instead, they used an army of plastic, ninety-six-gallon hard rubber cans. They kept them in the small garage to keep the animals away. They left the garage door unlocked so the trash collectors could access the space. There was a door that led to a hallway, that led to the stairs, that entered the kitchen of the restaurant, and that led to another set of stairs that led to the McMaster's residence. That door remained locked at all times so nobody could enter from that side of the building.

Unless they had the key. Or, more accurately, knew where the key was kept. In the back corner of the garage was an old fashioned, metal milk box. Rusted and dented. In retirement for forty years. Maybe more. Well, not a full retirement. Hooked on the inside wall of the box was the key to that door. Refuse the key. Key. Refuse. It was a strange way to say it, but it was one place Larry had not checked in all these years.

He kneeled down in front of the box and gripped the lid. Larry felt like he was holding the last forkful from a slice of cherry pie. The last taste. The last chance, then it was all gone.

He opened the lid and inched his head forward, allowing him to inspect more and more of the cube. The rattle of the key clanging against the side of the box echoed in the otherwise empty milk container, and ricocheted to all corners of the garage, silencing itself somewhere in the trash cans.

63

November 8, 2003 - 8:17 PM

CeCe was thrashing around in her room looking for her Super Mario Bros. 3 cartridge for her Game Boy when Mom called her out into the living room.

"They called me in to work, hun. You're going to stay with Mitch, ok?"

CeCe frowned. "It's Saturday night. Can't you say no?"

"You know I can't," said Mom. She looked at CeCe's feet. "You'll be fine." Then she turned to Mitch, her boyfriend for a few years now. "I should be home around midnight. Nine-thirty bedtime for her."

Mitch pointed his beer bottle at Mom like a magic wand. "I'm all over it. I'll just be sittin' here watching the game."

Mom kissed CeCe on the forehead, long and hard. "Be good, ok?"

"OK." CeCe said, then retreated to her room. Closed the door. Continued the search for her game. Maybe she would go to bed early. And when she woke up, Mom would be back. She kneeled down on the ground and looked into the darkness under her bed. Thrust her arm in and felt around. No game.

"Hey, CeCe, come on out here!" called Mitch from the living room.

CeCe thought about pretending she didn't hear. But that would only last so long. And maybe Mitch would come to her room. That would be too weird. She decided to go see what he wanted. Get it over with.

"Come on, watch the game with me."

CeCe sat on the couch across the room from Mitch... "Is it the Phillies?"

"No, dummy, baseball season is over. This is college football. I coulda played if I didn't get hurt my leg junior year of high school."

CeCe looked back toward the door to her room. "Oh." Her desk lamp spilled golden light into the hallway as if her room were filled with jewelry and other treasures.

"You can't see the game from over there. Come over here."

"I'm fine here. I can see."

"No, no, you can't. Come on. Come sit with me."

CeCe looked over at the reclining chair. "There's no room. I'll just stay here."

"You'll sit on the arm of the chair. Get over here. Now."

Mitch's voice sounded funny, like it usually did when he drank beer. His mouth had a little smile on it the entire time, whether he was watching the game, or talking to CeCe. When he looked at CeCe, up and down her body, it felt like snow falling down her back under her shirt. She walked over, faced her body away from Mitch, her bottom barely making contact with the armrest.

"See. Isn't that better?" asked Mitch. He finished his beer, and reached over the other side of the chair to grab another one. He took a big gulp, almost spitting it out to complain about a penalty the referee called in the game.

They watched for a while, long enough for Mitch to finish another beer. Then he rubbed the empty bottle on CeCe's arm. She shivered, and pulled away.

"Now relax. Your mom said we should get to know each other better. You guys might be moving in with me. Wouldn't that be nice?"

CeCe didn't say anything. She tried to move so Mitch couldn't touch her with the bottle anymore.

"Now quit wiggling around there. Come on, come sit with me. Just right here on my leg."

"No. Um, I don't…"

262

"I said!" Mitch shouted, then lowered his voice. "I said come sit with me. Your mom left me in charge. We're going to get to know each other a little better." He grabbed her arm above the elbow and pulled CeCe onto his lap. "That's some arm you got there."

CeCe remained silent. A tear built in her left eye. She was too afraid to cry.

"You're so pretty. Just like your mom. Mitch dragged his fingers through her hair. "And you're so athletic, so far ahead of the other girls your age. You know what I mean?"

CeCe allowed a tiny 'mhmm' to pop into the top of her throat. Mitch's breath stuck to the back of her neck and smelled like wet tree branches and rotting leaves.

He put his hands on her hips and pulled her closer to him. Her strong arms and legs were useless. She couldn't breathe. Couldn't scream. He had hundreds of fingers and she felt each and every one of them on her bare skin. All over her body.

Damn this body. She would give back every trophy; lose every race, every game for the rest of her life to not have this body.

CeCe smelled damp leaves and trees and the sound of cheering. The warm sun on her back. She was at the park. She was on the playground. Slides. Swings. There was a game nearby. Lots of cheering. The sun was so warm. Why were the leaves, trees, and the grass wet? She climbed the monkey bars and sniffed the metal on her hands.

Cheering.

Sun.

Wet.

Then a jingle. Like bells. And her mom's voice. Was Mom at the park? At the game.

"Got all the way to work and realized I forgot--- What the hell?" Mom screamed. CeCe fell forward in front of Mitch, on the ground at his feet. She lay there covering her head. Crying, reaching for her shorts. She heard Mom screaming, but couldn't understand what she was saying. There was the sound of glass breaking.

"Come on... OK, OK, OK." Mitch said, his voice shrinking. The front door slammed into the wall.

"Get the fuck out of my house!"

"Sweetie, listen. It's not what."

"Shut the fuck up. Just get the fuck out of here. Get out of here before I call the goddam cops."

The door slammed. CeCe sobbed on the ground. She smelled the carpet. And the scent of Mom's perfume.

64

August 28, 2013 - 7:59 am

Shawn sat four rows down in the bleachers on the first base side of McMaster Field. He could only see the field from this spot. Trees blocked Muldoon's developments on both sides, and all he could see behind him was the sky above the restaurant. He looked toward the east, toward the sun rising above left field. The sky was striped with low clouds, stained various shades of red, like a Band-Aid ripped from a scabbed knee.

CeCe would arrive soon. Greta told him that her shift started at eight. They hadn't spoken face to face in weeks. A couple of times on the phone, handful of texts. A few weeks ago, he told her he needed some time, that he was having trouble adjusting. He expected her to--- as she usually would--- hug him with her eyes, wrap him in a golden red and speckled blanket.

But she had taken a different tact. One Shawn wasn't used to, and didn't expect. For four years, Shawn had focused on his own pain, assuming that going into hiding was best for everybody. He didn't have to face what happened, or face any of the people who still had to be angry with him. CeCe pointed out that his running away, not having his presence around, hurt a lot of other people. And even though he lost his dad, she never had one. It was time to apologize, to grow up, to move on. Twenty-two-year-old Shawn wished eighteen-year-old Shawn could have had this vision.

A car pulled into the lot, Shawn stood up to see if was CeCe. It wasn't her mom's car. He began to sit back down, but froze when he saw CeCe hop out of the passenger seat. The driver was a man, appeared to be their age, maybe a little older. She bent over and leaned in to give the man a hug around the neck. He returned the hug, patting CeCe on the upper back.

Shawn was at the top of the steps when the man pulled away, and CeCe turned to jog into the restaurant. She took two quick steps, then stopped, stood upright when she saw Shawn standing there, like a kid who was caught sneaking in after curfew. Perhaps all the growing up Shawn did over the past month was for nothing. He stood on the top step of the bleachers, hands in his pockets, shoulders slumped, head tipped forward and to the right.

CeCe started moving again, but not at a jog, and not toward the restaurant. She stepped toward Shawn as if each time one of her feet hit the ground, she downloaded another sentence of explanation. Or excuse. Lie. Shawn wanted to lash out with something sarcastic, some clever words or comment that he could only conjure up when speaking to CeCe, one on one. Instead, he stood in silence, straightening his neck and head so he could look at CeCe approaching.

"Shawn---" CeCe stopped, waiting for the rest to download. "It's not what you think."

Shawn took a deep breath and kept his mouth closed. Exhaled. Then, "I don't know what to think."

"This is a long story, and I have to go work." CeCe turned and pointed at the restaurant. But Greta was standing between the two doors, the top half of her body leaning out. She waved her hand at CeCe like a coach telling an outfielder to move back a few steps. She was telling CeCe to stay and talk. "Seriously, this is a long story."

"I don't have anything to do." Shawn walked back down the steps, sitting in the exact spot he was before, his body angled toward the left field line a little more than before.

CeCe sat a step below, turned and looked up at Shawn. The red of her hair mixing with the sky flooded by the rising sun, which struggled to burn through the morning clouds. She started to speak, then pursed her lips and looked away.

"Home plate."

CeCe turned her head a click farther and said, "Yup, there it is."

"Home plate," Shawn said again, as if it was CeCe's cue to walk on stage.

"Oh, male. Definitely male."

"I don't understand," said Shawn.

"Pointy, angular. Definitely male," said CeCe, like a teacher explaining a homework problem.

"No, I don't understand. I thought we were giving it another shot. Is he," Shawn pointed toward the parking lot, "your boyfriend?" Then, as CeCe shook her head, he continued, "Have you had a boyfriend all along? Or just in the past few weeks?" Twenty-two-year-old Shawn was losing grip; eighteen-year-old Shawn was taking over.

"Neither." She rubbed her tiny hands all over her face as if she was putting on sunscreen. "That's kind of the end of the story. I think it's better if we start at the beginning, knowwhatImean?"

"No, I don't know what you mean, CeCe. I think I'd kind of like to know what that is all about," Shawn said, pointing at the parking lot again. It was moments like these where CeCe would protect Shawn, shield Shawn, say what Shawn needed to hear, do what Shawn needed her to do.

But the look in her eyes was different. "OK, you're going to know what *that is all about*," mocked CeCe, motioning to the parking lot, "but you are going to hear the whole story first. I should have told you this a long time ago, but I didn't. So here goes."

CeCe's tone startled Shawn. He felt like a little kid getting yelled at, and he didn't like it, but he knew enough in the moment to shut up and listen.

"From the time I was about nine until the time I was twelve, my mom had a boyfriend who lived with us on and off. He was creepy, but Mom never saw it. Or didn't want to see it," CeCe stopped and looked at her legs, down to her feet. "He came to all my sports, Mom thought it was sweet. You know I kicked ass as an athlete when I was little. I was stronger, faster. Everything. My body developed faster than all the other girls. In every way. He noticed. He commented on it."

Shawn rocked back and forth on the bleacher. What the heck did this have to do with the guy in the parking lot. This all happened over ten years ago. That guy was long gone, as far as he knew. CeCe had stopped, Shawn interjected, "I don't see what---"

CeCe showed him the palm of her hand. "Listen, you're just going to have to settle in and listen to all of this. Haven't I earned that?"

Earned it? What the heck was she talking about? Shawn decided to nod. It seemed like the best move at this point.

CeCe looked at the field, at the sky, and at the ground as she spoke the next part. "One night, I was twelve at the time, Mom got called into work on a Saturday night. She had never left me with him---"

"Did this him have a name?"

CeCe reestablished eye contact, the pace of her speech quickened, and her volume increased. "Yeah, Shawn, he did. I haven't said it since that night. Neither has my mom. And I won't." The sun broke through the clouds and ignited CeCe's hair. "Just shut the hell up and listen."

Shawn leaned away. He thought about his car, his apartment, even the living quarters above the restaurant. Terrific places to hide. But he decided to stay put.

CeCe focused on the floor. "He was drinking. He got a hold of me. I think he started to…" CeCe stopped, moved the words around in her mouth like the first taste of a new food. "The next thing I remember was running into my room and my mom screaming at him. I never saw him again."

Shawn stared out at the baseball field, but his eyes unfocused. The reality of the situation, of everything over the years attacked his brain. Without thinking he said, "all the clothes?"

"Yup. I was so ashamed. I blamed myself, my boobs, my freakin' ass for so long. It took my mom a while to figure it out, and then she finally got me into counseling. It really helped. And I met this guy."

Shawn looked up at the parking lot, where CeCe had been dropped off today, then back at her.

"No dumbass, *you*."

Again, without thinking, Shawn said, "Oh." Then laughed.

"You have no idea how refreshing it was. I could tell you liked me," she said, pointing to her head. "All of me, not just…" and she pointed at herself from her neck down. "And I saw how quiet you were around everybody else, but how you opened up to me. Completely. You needed me. I was tired of needing help, of hating myself. I loved focusing on you."

That felt better, but CeCe's tone hadn't changed. And her face didn't soften. And he still didn't know who that guy was.

"Gosh, Shawn, we were perfect for each other. I was so in love with you."

"I was in love with you too."

"I know." CeCe raised her hand to Shawn. "We had all those plans, we went off to college together. Then we…"

"Made love."

"Yes, and that's exactly what it was. I finally felt safe enough to completely open up to somebody. To you. Then…"

It hit Shawn like an elbow drop in the stomach at a sleepover in the middle of the night. "Then I disappeared."

"And I understood why, I really did. But I just couldn't convince myself, deep down, that you hadn't rejected me."

"I didn't reject you! It had nothing to do with you, everything to do with what an idiot I am."

"That's where you're wrong. That's where you've always been wrong, Shawn. I know, we all know," CeCe said, waving her hand across the McMaster property, "that you were ashamed and scared, and that's why you ran away." CeCe grabbed Shawn's shoulder. "But don't think for a second that it didn't have a tremendous effect on me. On your mom and dad. Even Dusty and Chuck."

An ache grew in Shawn's stomach, like an organism that had been growing for years. It took some tough love from CeCe, but he could finally see it. He wasn't protecting everybody in Quail by running away. He was protecting himself. Hiding. Hiding from what he had done. And he hadn't kept the ones he loved safe. He hurt them.

"I understand," said Shawn. "I understand what I've done. It seems too late to apologize."

"It's never too late to apologize."

Shawn pulled CeCe close and whispered in her ear, "I'm so sorry."

"I know you are." CeCe hugged back.

"But…"

CeCe pulled away and took a deep breath. "Like I said, no matter how hard I tried, I couldn't convince myself that you hadn't rejected me. I sort of went the opposite direction than I did when I was little. I found myself seeking out partners. It made me feel better at the time, but then I hated myself later on."

Shawn crossed his arms and looked at the ground. So he was supposed to believe that to make herself feel better she slept around. He looked at CeCe.

She stood up, paced away, then back. "I can tell that you don't believe me. That's fair, you're not the only one who thought it was a great excuse to slut around whenever I wanted."

"I wasn't thinking that."

"Yes, you were. It's ok. I was addicted to it. I know I was."

"I never even thought…" said Shawn, defending himself. He stopped mid-sentence because it was the end of his thought. He didn't know how to continue.

"Look, I know you didn't, Shawn. You didn't… do that to me when I was twelve. I know you didn't sleep with me and then disappear on purpose." CeCe sat down next to Shawn again. "But it happened. It all happened. I should have told you all of this, about what happened to me when I was little. All those years, it was easier for me to deal with you and your stuff than to come clean and deal with my own junk, youknowwhatImean?"

"So this," Shawn said as he waved again up toward the parking lot, "has been going on all this time?"

She stood up again and looked toward the field. "No. More counseling. I had it under control. God bless Dr. Withers, she helped me understand all of this. It was so hard to crave something, get it, and then hate myself for it."

It was Shawn's turn to talk, but he said nothing. He wanted to ask if she was 'cured,' and if so, what the heck was up with that guy? She must have read his mind.

"So you were back, and it was great, but it brought back a lot of difficult emotions. Robbie understands it all." CeCe pointed up toward the parking lot. "I needed… him. Shawn, I'm always going to be recovering from this. Always."

Shawn's mouth made a decision for him. "Well, tell Robbie, thanks for, whatever. I'm back, and I'm not going anywhere. Mom needs help around here. And I'm going to help you, for all the help you've always given me."

"OK," CeCe said, and that's all she said. Again, she looked away from Shawn, out toward the field.

Shawn looked up above the restaurant to the McMaster living quarters. He'd be moving back in. He was going to tell CeCe that, but she was still looking away. Shawn swore she was looking exactly where he used to position himself in left field, the only place to which he still could not return.

65

Al's Everything Shop sat behind one of Muldoon's developments, less than five minutes by car from the McMaster property. It did a brisk business, mostly with the suburbanites who lived in the general vicinity. The store's location was its major flaw, off the main road, requiring patrons to drive through a neighborhood to get to it. Folks on the main drag that passed in front of the McMaster Restaurant and Field that didn't know Al's Everything was back there had no chance of seeing it. The other flaw was its size. It was too small for what Muldoon wanted it to do, which was to sell just about everything.

Muldoon unlocked the front door of the store, and dragged a sign out to the front walkway. The sign featured a picture of him, beaming, positioned behind a family of four, mother and father, daughter and son, and even their dog. The family was looking at each other, smiling. The father was tossing a ball into the air, the son nearby with his hands extended... Mother and daughter were sharing pieces of an orange. The dog had a treat hanging out of its mouth. Muldoon looked directly at the camera with a satisfied grin. He caused all that joy. The type on the sign read "YOUR FAMILY WANTS TO BE HAPPY. LET ME HELP!"

Muldoon was halfway to his office in the back of the store when he heard a customer enter. Typically, he wouldn't open the store, or really be involved in day to day operations. He had a manager and an assistant manager and plenty of clerks to do that. But lately, he wanted more hands on knowledge of how the store ticked. How he could make it better? What he would do if he could move it to a better location and make it bigger. He needed to see things from the floor of the store to figure this all out. Sitting in

273

his office, or just popping in to shake the hands of some customers.

"Mr. Muldoon," said the customer. "Can I talk to you for a minute?" The young man, lanky and strong, had to stand over six feet, but his head, which was hidden under a beat up old baseball cap, leaned forward. The brim of the cap prevented Muldoon from seeing his face.

"Sure," said Muldoon, "what can I help you find?" The two walked toward each other, meeting next to a display of pencils, pens, notebooks and rulers, topped with a sign that read "Back to School!" The young man looked up and Muldoon recognized him immediately. Shawn McMaster. But not the young, skinny Shawn McMaster he had last seen playing baseball four years ago. The boy had grown into a man, shoulders broader, arms stronger. Taller. Muldoon was glad he didn't play for McMaster's Restaurant any more. Shawn had the body of a major league outfielder, but Muldoon felt like a few strong words would blow him over. His shoulders rolled forward, his neck bent, his voice only loud enough to be heard. "Oh, my, Shawn, how can I help?"

"Mr. Muldoon," Shawn looked down at his sneakers, then Muldoon's shoes, then the floor, as if he were eying a fleeing bug, or searching for a trap door. "I know you know about October first."

"Yes, I do." Muldoon had a good idea where this conversation was heading. He'd been preparing for it for weeks. But he had expected to joust with Billy.

Shawn shuffled around like a junior high kid fixing to ask a girl to dance. After thirty seconds, and a few squeaks on the polished linoleum floor, "Don't buy our property." Shawn looked Muldoon in the eyes for the first time, then, "Please."

Muldoon started. It couldn't have rolled off his tongue better if he had teleprompters attached the book bag display. "Shawn, first of all, I'm sorry about your father. I

274

know we were always rivals. In many ways. But he was a good man."

Shawn looked away when Muldoon mentioned Billy. He nodded at Muldoon in response, and then said, "I know you know the restaurant and the field were his life. Just like they were my grandfather's life, and my great-grandfather's life."

"I know that, Shawn. "Muldoon crossed his arms in front of his chest. In this moment, he felt bad for Shawn, and he looked out the window for a long time before speaking again. "But I think it is time for something different out there." Muldoon pointed toward the McMaster property. He knew exactly where it was from exactly where he was standing.

Shawn shifted his weight from one foot to the other. "My family has been there forever."

Two of those words hit Muldoon like a punch in the stomach: my family. LET ME HELP! It had been the motto of the store for as long as it had been open. Modern families were busy, running here and there. Al's Everything Shop was designed to help. Supplies for a school project, a pair of athletic socks, and a hot meal already prepared for them. All in one store. Everything the busy family needed in one quick stop on the way home from school, or on the way home from practice, or on the way to a lesson. Let me help. "I know they have, Shawn. But look around, this place is stuffed to the gills. I need more room."

"There's plenty of room out that way," said Shawn, waving in the opposite direction Muldoon had pointed a minute ago.

"Shawn, that's out in the middle of nowhere. This store needs to be in the middle of Quail. Do you know how many people I could help if we were out on the main road where the restaurant is?"

"Do you know how many people eat at our restaurant? Play ball on our field?"

"Quite a few, Shawn, quite a few. But nowhere near as many as would shop at the store. Times are changing, people need convenience. They need to get what they want quickly. In and out. Not a sit down, slow, home cooked meal. That's nice, but nobody has time for it." Muldoon turned and pointed to where Shawn had pointed, "We can build three or four or five baseball fields out there. No more waiting for the field. We can have several games going on at once. Don't you see the potential?"

"No, Mr. Muldoon, what I see is families coming for a meal, then ice cream, then a game. Talking to each other." Shawn paused and stared off for a moment. "Look around, you own most of this town. You've given people nice homes. Why don't you just leave our little slice of Quail alone?"

Muldoon rubbed his hand across his face, and paced a bit. Shawn painted a nice Rockwellian picture of what life used to be like in central Pennsylvania for a lot of people. But that doesn't work anymore. It never worked for the Muldoon family. His mother would cook dinner, expecting his father home at dinner time. But he wouldn't get there until eight o'clock, or nine o'clock, or after the young Albert Muldoon had gone to sleep. Sometimes the yelling would wake him and his brother. Sometimes Muldoon wouldn't make it to baseball practice because his mother had to cook, or shop, or watch the younger brother. Or babysit the neighborhood kids. That was how she brought in some extra money. Most of the time, the roadblocks of family life got in the way of Muldoon's dreams. Of playing ball. Of spending time with his family. His father. Of normal family life.

"I'm sorry, Shawn, I really am," said Muldoon, recognizing the frustration Shawn was feeling. "But this has been my goal for a long time. It's going to help families live better, easier, happier lives."

276

Shawn moved toward Muldoon, suddenly looking every inch of six-foot-two. His neck was upright, his head held high, tipped toward Muldoon. "My family has made families happy for a long time."

"I know, Shawn."

"And we're going to keep doing it."

"Well---" Muldoon leaned back a little as Shawn leaned in. Muldoon was now looking at a major leaguer through and through. Shawn's eyes were on fire, leading with his chin. Hands at his sides, not in his pockets. Shoulders back, the muscles in his arms twitching. Ready.

"I don't care what I have to do, I'm not losing this property to you. We're not losing." Shawn put his finger an inch from Muldoon's face as he said his last words. Then, he turned and stormed out, flipping the door open with a flick of his wrist.

Muldoon watched Shawn glide out into the parking lot and hop into his car. He appreciated the young man's spirit, even heard his message. Taking care of your family, it's a high calling. It's the key to a happy life. The McMaster Restaurant and Field had done that for a long time. But times have changed. That property was in the perfect location to aid the people of Quail, and beyond. It was time it joined the twenty-first century, to help families of the twenty-first century. Muldoon was the person to take it there. And there was nothing Shawn McMaster, or anybody else, could do to stop him.

66

Before even one single muscle in Shawn's body considered twitching to start his swing, the ball slammed into the catcher's glove.

"Strike three!" yelled the home plate umpire.

From in front of Shawn: clapping. Laughter. "You let us down, McMaster! We wanted to say swing and miss, but you didn't even do that!"

Shawn turned and stepped toward the dugout. Warmth grew from his core. Not from running in the field or swinging the bat in the on deck circle, but a burn, like alcohol on a cut. Growing, filling every pore. Strike three. Looking! His hands squeezed the handle of the bat tighter as he approached the dugout.

"Ha, ha, ha, Shaw- Nee. Fantastic at-bat."

"Good thinking, McMaster, don't swing. Save your energy for later."

Shawn entered the dugout, still choking the bat. Dusty was there waiting for him. "It's ok, bro. He's throwing darts out there. Get 'em next time."

Shawn eased his grip. Ok, alright. Next time. Get him next time. This happens. Guys go down looking.

Then Billy called across the dugout, "Geez, Shawn, haven't we talked about this forever. You've got to be ready with two strikes. Protect. Little leaguers know that. You gotta swing."

The heat sprinted from his core toward every cell on his skin like a wildfire spreading in a parched, windy forest. Swing. Swing? Here's a swing. Shawn cocked the bat back over his shoulder, squeezed his eyes shut and swung.

The crash and thunk of the bat hitting a support pole in the dugout opened his eyes. Opened them so he could

278

see the jagged edge of the broken aluminum bat puncture Billy's arm at the crease in front of his elbow.

Billy yanked the bat out of his arm and tossed it on the ground, looked at Shawn and said, "What the hell is wrong with you?" The question still dominated the dugout as blood began gushing from Billy's arm.

Every single set of eyes in the dugout found Shawn, who was holding the other end of the weapon in his right hand, dangling down by his waist. The heat attacked him from the outside now. The full weight of the crowd. He dropped the handle of the bat, grabbed his glove, escaped the dugout, hopped the fence down the right field line, and scurried up the hill toward the restaurant. CeCe left the crowd and sprinted after him.

As Shawn hopped in his car, he could hear CeCe yelling, "Why, Shawn, why?" He grabbed the keys from above the visor, fired up the engine, and tore out of the parking lot.

67

September 9, 2013 - 6:57 pm

Larry leaned back in his chair and soaked in the moment, and the last drops of a cup of coffee.

"This isn't even an argument," said Chuck.

"That's the first question you got right," said Dusty.

"No question was asked."

"Don't distract me with your college bullshit. Look, there is no way they would take you over me."

Chuck stood up. "Look at me, son. I don't care what the reality show is, they're taking this," he said, cascading his fingers from head to toe as if he were flicking water off his hands in slow motion, "over that," he finished, with a look on his face like somebody was holding a pile of dog dirt under his nose.

"America is looking for this," said Dusty, looking like he was pouring oil out of his thumb into his ear.

"Dusty... Sweetie," Chuck rubbed the back of the hand.

Dusty's eyes closed and he nodded. "Crap, you're right," he said, putting down his fork.

Then together, "Token black guy."

Larry inhaled the scent of pancakes, coffee, bacon, and pie, experienced the voices and clanking of silverware and plates, absorbed the colors, the light, and the faces in the room. He detected a body moving toward him. DJ.

No, stay in the present. Shawn. *Forgive yourself, love yourself, and enjoy each and every moment of the rest of your life.* Shawn. Darn, but with DJ's eyes. Larry took a deep breath and returned to the present moment.

"Ladies and gentlemen," said Dusty. "The quietest," said Chuck.   "Quickest left fielder to never play the---"

280

"Guys, can you leave me and Larry alone for a bit?" asked Shawn.

Dusty and Chuck looked at each other. Chuck rubbed the back of his hand. Dusty pointed at his work boots. They nodded, then stood up and walked away.

Larry turned his body toward Shawn. "How are you doing?"

"Fine," said Shawn, as if the word only had one letter. Then he looked into Larry's eyes. "I know," he said, motioning at the restaurant and beyond with the crown of his head.

Larry tried to taste coffee, smell bacon, and see the sun glinting off the windows of the cars in the parking lot. But DJ's eyes, Shawn's eyes, put him in a trance. DJ said not to trust anyone, but how could he not trust Shawn?

"I'm out of ideas," said Larry. "I've been looking, on and off, for ten years."

"Last of the third, thank goodness that had something to do with this."

Larry smiled at Shawn. "It was my best lead."

"Everybody thought you were crazy," said Shawn, looking as if Larry had just swallowed a whole peach.

"Bugged me at first, but it became a good place to hide. I figured people would mostly ignore me, but if the phrase meant anything to anybody, they would pipe up."

The two watched a waitress refill Larry's coffee cup. Then Shawn's eyes returned to the counter. "Thanks."

Larry wanted to ask *for what?* But instead said, "You're welcome."

"There are still a few weeks left," said Shawn.

"There are."

"There has to be something we can do."

Larry leaned forward and tapped the middle of Shawn's chest with his index finger. "Of course there is. Do what you do." Shawn leaned back in his seat. Larry could tell what Shawn was thinking: What is it that I do?

281

The thoughts of a twenty-two-year-old, what do I do? Bag groceries, teach school, drink beer, play ball, chase girls.

Larry would leave him to the meditation. He stood up, threw a ten-dollar bill on the table, and walked toward the door. Left foot, then right. Left. Right...

68

September 30, 2003 - 10:59 PM

Larry shook his head as he slid his hands all over his couch, down into the grooves between the cushions. A pen? Sure. Half a cookie? Why not. The TV remote? Of course not. How is it possible that something he used all day, every single day, could find such a tremendous hiding place?

Larry leaned back on the couch and crossed his arms. The real question was: How is it possible that Al's Everything beat McMaster's tonight? McMaster's has owned this match-up for ages, winning all but three of the matchups in the last twenty years.

Light spoiled the darkness on the living room wall, jolting Larry off the couch, which released the remote from below a cushion, dropping it onto the floor. But Larry was looking out the front window at the car that was idling about thirty degrees from straight in his driveway. The driver opened the door and leaned on the front fender, clutching his chest, his head bouncing up and down like a bobber in a rippling creek.

Larry hustled down the steps, into grey-skied night, and toward the man. DJ McMaster. Struggling to breathe.

"DJ, what the heck is---"

DJ clawed Larry's forearm, stopping him mid-thought. "I tried to save… rrrrrr… the property."

"Are you ok? What are you talking about?"

DJ continued as if he didn't hear Larry's questions. "Muldoon knows… never tell… rrrrr… anybody, don't trust anybody." DJ fought to take a full breath.

"Never tell who? Don't trust---"

"Just look, it's right there… rrrrr… McMaster's will… rrrr… fuse the key… rrrr gret…. a win."

"This doesn't make any sense. We have to get you to the hospital. No, call 9-1-1."

DJ slumped to one knee, but managed to reach into his pocket. He pulled out a ragged, torn piece of paper and reached it up for Larry to take. As soon as it was out of his hand, he fell face first onto the driveway.

Larry stood above his friend, who had died from a massive heart attack, right in front of his eyes. He read the ripped corner of a baseball score sheet that DJ had handed him. From top to bottom it reads: Last of the Third.

69

September 13, 2013 - 10:22 pm

Nobody knew that Shawn was sitting in the brush and small trees out beyond center field. Not Greta. Not CeCe. Not Larry, nor Dusty, nor Chuck. He had parked his car over in Muldoon's development and walked between two houses, and through the woods to gain this position.

Shawn had gotten used to this scenario: Sitting somewhere safely, stealthily. So safe, in fact, that not even his loved ones could find him.

There was no game tonight, so the field lights were off. Shawn could out himself right now, walk across the field, turn on the lights and march out into left field. Greta was finishing up in the restaurant; she would look out and see him. Her son, her only remaining McMaster man, back on the field where she wanted him.

Word of Shawn's return to the field would spread like a puddle around home plate in the middle of a downpour.

Greta had never given up on her son in all these years, and was left to work and wonder, bake and bustle, plead and pray.

Billy had worked himself to death; cooking, watering, and mowing. And looking for answers.

Dusty and Chuck continued to do what they loved, selling floors and turning two. But they had always put Shawn up on a pedestal with all of their play-by-play announcing theatrics and their defense of Shawn's game to Billy. They were satisfied with their lot in life, but they always wanted to see Shawn achieve super stardom.

CeCe just wanted Shawn to be happy. And to be with Shawn because that made her happy as well. They filled in each other's blanks without even trying, just by being themselves.

285

Shawn had molded this living darkness like a stage crew assembling a midnight backdrop. It was time for Shawn to flip on the lights.

It was time for Shawn McMaster to return to Quail, to McMaster Field and Restaurant, and to the beautiful patch of grass between shortstop and the left field fence.

70

Shawn leaned on the counter in front of the soda machine, sipping Coke through a straw. Larry had decided to eat his breakfast in a booth by the window. Shawn watched him eat. Something was different. Larry used to wolf down his meals like a kid late for a six o'clock little league game, and flood it with coffee. Cup in left hand, fork in right. Timing as good Rollins and Utley around second base.

Chuck called it 'Larry Last presents: The Platecracker Suite.' Dusty saw nothing wrong with it. Speaking of those two, the restaurant was rather quiet this morning. Or at least, lacking some of the usual sounds. Of course, there was the silverware on plates, cups on tables, friendly chatter, occasional laughter. But the two dork jesters weren't there yet. Shawn knew they would be soon, though. Down on the field.

The two dork jesters. That's pretty good. Shawn would remember that for next time. Why the heck couldn't he come up with this stuff when they are all eating cheeseburgers and gravy fries?

Shawn watched Larry, who clipped off a piece of omelet, slid it into his mouth, put his fork on the table, closed his eyes, and chewed. Opened his eyes. A sip of coffee. Cup down.

Strange--- Wait. Dork jesters. Is that even funny?

Larry's omelet was only a few bites big. It was time. Shawn walked over and slid onto the booth seat. "I know what I do."

Larry put down his fork, leaned back and crossed his arms. Said nothing for about three hours, just stared into Shawn's eyes, then, "And what is that, my boy?"

"I play baseball."

287

Larry said nothing, nodded his head like a heavy tree limb in an August breeze.

"Well, I mean, I haven't for a few years. But that's what I am, deep down inside. A baseball player."

Larry smiled, continued to nod. Continued to look at Shawn. Said nothing.

"I guess what I'm trying to say is, if the team will have me, I'd like to play in the Final Exam," said Shawn.

"I'm sure they will have you."

"And I bet they will have you, too."

"What do you mean?" asked Larry, leaning forward.

"If this is going to be it, the last Final Exam ever on McMaster Field, and my father and grandfather can't coach the team, then I want it to be you."

"I've watched a ton of baseball over the years, Shawn, but I've never coached."

"You know the game, and I know you know the game better than Muldoon. Wouldn't it be nice to beat him?" Shawn paused for a moment, looking around the restaurant. "Beat his butt on the field one last time?"

"Yes, it would, but---"

"Then, it's settled." Shawn reached his hand across the table, grabbing Larry's and shaking it with two large pumps.

"Yes, I suppose it is," said Larry, who put his hands on the edge of the table, then reached for his coffee cup, and took a long sip. "This coffee is fantastic."

"Um, I'm glad you're enjoying it."

Loud noises and disruption approached from the front of the restaurant. "There he is, Mr. Lefty Leftage Left Fielder," said Dusty.

"Easy champ, alliteration is dangerous for farmers," said Chuck.

Dusty pushed Chuck by the shoulder. "Watch I don't litter you all over the parking lot."

288

"Well, if it isn't the two dork jesters," said Shawn.

Dusty and Chuck stopped and looked at each other, as if they were both tasting a foreign food they had never tried before... and liking it. "Dork jesters," said Chuck, putting his hands together above his head and spreading them apart in slow motion.

"T-shirts," said Dusty.

"YouTube videos."

"Green ball caps with Dork Jesters stitched in yellow."

"A Twitter handle."

"A line of energy drinks."

Chuck paused, then, "Dork Loko!"

"Oh my goodness, enough," said Shawn. "Let's get started, shall we?"

"Indeed." Chuck bounced up and down where he stood. "Indeed, indeed, indeed."

"I'll meet you guys down there," said Shawn, walking toward the counter.

"OK, don't wuss out." Dusty tapped Chuck on the shoulder. The two left the restaurant, arguing about the sacrifice bunt.

Shawn walked behind the counter and toward the swinging door. He hesitated for a moment, looking at the picture of himself in his high school baseball uniform. He nodded, then continued through the kitchen, through the stairwell of the residence, and into the driveway. He opened the back door of the car, and pulled out a shoebox. He balanced the shoebox on his right forearm, and flipped it open with his left hand. He reached in and pulled out a pair of brand new metal cleats. He threw the box onto the back seat, grabbed his glove, slammed the door, and walked toward McMaster Field.

71

CeCe still had on a sweatshirt, still jeans, but she had to admit it was warm. Not warm like summer, but warm like, here comes baseball season. In a few months, everybody would consider this day freezing, but as the last of the snow melted, this day felt great. She sat on the bleachers above the first base dugout so she could look straight ahead and watch Shawn catch fly balls.

Billy stood just in front of home plate, picking a ball out of a large white bucket, and launching fly balls toward left field. Some high and back by the fence, some lower and to Shawn's left or right, some really high and far from Shawn, close to the infield, or over toward center field. Every once in a while, Billy would mess up. Hit one over the fence for a home run, or hit a sky high pop up that landed only a few feet in front of where he stood.

But Shawn. Perfect. He caught every ball that was hit in the air in left field. And most into center field. Even some that Billy screwed up and hit a mile high that landed on the infield dirt. But it was more than that. It was Shawn's speed. Or pace. Always consistent. In a group of people, or even a handful of people, Shawn could be completely clueless as to how to handle himself, but out in left field, he knew exactly where he needed to be, exactly how long he had to get there, and exactly how fast he needed to go. Exactly. No speedup at the last second. He arrived at the ball precisely when he needed to be there.

Billy held up two fingers and Shawn nodded. Billy rocketed a ball toward left center field, high and deep toward the fence. CeCe shielded her eyes from the sunlight, thankful for the warmth, but trying to see Shawn. He didn't take off immediately like he normally would. He nodded his head twice in rhythm, the sprung to his left like a jaguar chasing down its prey. Shawn was at full speed within two steps. His long, slender body, chewing up the territory between where he stood and where he knew the ball was going to land. Arms pumping, legs churning, but the torso, neck, and head still, as if Shawn were a bust out of a museum come to life, with mechanical legs that knew precisely how far to go and how long they had to get there, and arms and hands that knew right when to grab the ball out of the air.

CeCe grinned to herself. A bust out of the museum of eighteen-year-old hotties, by the way.

Shawn arrived on time, of course. His right hand, covered with his glove, springing out at the last possible moment to snatch the ball, like the tongue of a frog snagging a fly.

CeCe grinned to herself again. Like the tongue of a frog.

She looked down and shook her head. How does he do it? She kneaded her denim-coated thighs with her tiny hands. Thighs that were too short, but too big at the same time. And her boobs and butt, held her back and slowed her down. In so many ways. CeCe developed young, and dominated on the athletic fields. But she finished her high school field hockey career as an average player. Honorable Mention in the league. Not first team or even second. One of the better ones of everybody who was left.

She looked back at Shawn in left field. An aura of confidence, joy, fun, and excellence surrounded him out there. Out there, in front of the see-through cage that was the left field fence; to the right of the easily jumpable but definitive left field line; behind the rough, beige skin of the infield near shortstop; to the left of whoever would be in his way in center field. Out there. In left field. Ruler of the land. Undefeated. Gorgeous. Sexy. Unstoppable.

72

CeCe positioned her left hand to block the rising sun. She stood at the top of the bleachers on the first base side of McMaster Field, paycheck creased between her thumb and fingers, peering out at Shawn in left field. Chuck was standing in front of home plate next to a large, white bucket, leaning on a bat like that silent film star leaning on an umbrella. Dusty stood one step into the grass, behind shortstop tossing a ball with Shawn, who looked like an eleven-year-old girl descending the stairs in high heels for the first time. Each move deliberate, cautious, as if his left arm might drop to the ground, his legs evaporate, his baseball glove shatter.

CeCe had dreamed about this moment. Shawn, she thought, back in left field, would mean that things were back to the way they were. If he made it all the way down on to McMaster Field, he would have returned to Quail, to the McMaster Restaurant, to his family and friends. To her.

Then why this feeling like the Earth was pressing down on her shoulders at the same time that all the crap in her stomach wanted to come up? Perhaps it was the jumble of emotions that would have to arise when something she dreamt about, yearned for, even prayed for, materialized in front of her eyes.

Shawn turned his back to the infield and jogged out to left field. Without seeing his face, CeCe didn't recognize him. Or at least didn't remember him this way. This *size*. She was used to a slimmer, shorter Shawn zipping around the outfield, with the spunk and energy of a boy. This was a man. Tall, broad shoulders, body filled out. He reached his destination and turned, confirming for CeCe that it was, in fact, him.

Chuck reached into the bucket and held the ball up for Shawn to see. He twisted it and turned it, like he was displaying a ten carat diamond that he had just dug out of the right handed batter's box.

"For God's sake, he remembers what he's looking for, hit the damn thing," said Dusty.

"For God's sake, my children, I will hit this damn thing. Can I get an amen?"

"You want religion? You're gonna get a fist in the temple if you don't hit that ball."

Chuck pouted, and looked at the ground.

"I'm sorry, sweetie, I love you."

"I love you too." Chuck leaped back into hitting position. He tossed the ball into the air, swung and, ping, a high fly ball soared into left field.

Disobeying every baseball coach ever, CeCe took her eye off the ball and watched Shawn. He took a step back, then charged forward and to the right three steps, another step back, then two quick steps forward, lunging with his glove hand to swipe the ball out of the air in front of his thighs.

That also looked different. Not the same old Shawn, who knew exactly where to go in left field, and how fast to get there. He once told CeCe that Billy made him "Give the ball a head start." Before he hit a fly ball, Billy would hold up fingers to tell him how many counts he had to wait before he could track it down.

CeCe didn't think it would get that far today. In fact, Shawn's body was different, his game was different. Maybe this was a sign. Things are different. A fresh start. CeCe's body relaxed. She took a seat in the top row. Her stomach settled. A grin appeared on her face.

Chuck launched a similar fly ball to left. Shawn didn't move this time, peered into the sky as if he were studying the moon late on a gentle evening. Then he sprung forward, three steps, and then drifted back to the right, snagging the ball with an outstretched arm. He planted on his left foot, pushed off whirling his body around to toss the ball into Dusty.

CeCe had seen that move before.

Chuck hit another, this time to Shawn's left, and over his head. Shawn sprinted back, then slowed, then stopped and waited for the ball to drop into his glove, right above his shoulder.

Every ball that Chuck sent out to Shawn was another stroke of makeup on a movie star's face. With each ball, he tracked down, Shawn looked more and more like himself. His old, eighteen-year-old self. Chuck tossed another ball and angled his right shoulder toward center field. Before the bat hit the ball, Shawn had pivoted and started toward center... That's where Chuck hit it, a high arc dropping like a grenade. Shawn strode toward it, his speed constant like a car in cruise control, arriving in time to backhand the ball out in front of his left shoulder.

Dusty pounded his fist into his glove. "Oh, look at our boy!"

"Our boy is *back!*" Chuck waved his hands in the air.

The blender in CeCe's stomach started churning again. Shawn wasn't struggling to move forward; he was striding to get back. It made sense. CeCe, Dusty and Chuck had all lived as nineteen, twenty, and twenty-one year olds. Shawn entered a cocoon at eighteen, emerged with the body of a magnificent butterfly at twenty-two, but in his head, he still had to exist as a nineteen, twenty, and twenty-one-year-old.

CeCe swore to herself that she would wait for Shawn forever. But forever turned out to be four years. She was pretty sure she couldn't wait another four. Shawn pranced, bounced and strutted toward a dozen more fly balls. The computer analyst in hiding was gone, the First Team All-County left fielder was back.

Chuck waved the bat in the air, and motioned to Shawn, then to the batting cage. Shawn nodded as if he had agreed to go get a flu shot. Shawn was going to swing a bat for the first time since the Final Exam four years ago.

McMaster Field and Shawn parading in left field, and Dusty and Chuck laughing and cheering, the band back together again, was like a fifteen-foot wave crushing down on CeCe. Watching Shawn, the left fielder, reemerge was more than CeCe could handle. She definitely couldn't watch him hold a bat.

She stood up and took a step. Shawn waved to her. She could see the smile on his face. She waved goodbye, and walked away.

73

The bat felt heavy in Shawn's hands, even though he was at least two inches taller and much stronger than the last time he picked one up. Come to think of it, this bat was much heavier than the last bat, he held, considering that bat ended at a jagged crown an inch above the handle.

Shawn stood near the plastic home plate at the end of the batting cage. He decided to swing it. He hefted it up onto his left shoulder where it pressed into his skin, weighed down by the events and emotions of the last four years, from the disaster that started all this, to the gunk and plaque that was caked on all arteries that connected Shawn to all the people in his life. He squeezed the handle, then dropped his hands into the slot, left palm up, right palm down, and pulled them around his body, dragging along the barrel of the bat. It ended up behind him, draped over his right shoulder like an arrow in a quiver.

But all in one piece.

Nobody was screaming. Nobody was hurt. Aside from Dusty and Chuck, who were cranking up the pitching machine, nobody even knew he was there. He swung again, and it felt good. No. Great. He swung again and again. Like a dog shaking off water after a bath, or an engine running in a new part, each swing carried less fear, less guilt, and less sadness. After twelve swings, he was just a kid loosening up to take batting practice.

"You wanna, um, I don't know, try to get that bat in the way of a few balls there, lil' slugger?" asked Chuck.

"Yeah, yeah." Shawn settled into the left hand batter's box. Or at least the patch of dirt on that side of home plate, which was free of grass from the years of use. Not only by Shawn, but by lefty hitters from age six to sixty from all the teams that have used McMaster Field through the years.

Chuck held up a dimpled, yellow ball above his right shoulder, and then stuffed it into the sleeve of the pitching machine. It rolled down, and then shot through the spinning rubber wheels with a muted thump.

Shawn strode onto his right toe, dropped his right heel, fired his hips as he pulled his hands around his body, which set the barrel of the bat on a collision course with the ball. The bat smashed the middle of the ball with the center of the barrel, and the line drive dropped Chuck to the ground, protected by a screen. The ball hit the netting in the back of the cage, and fell to the ground like a bird that had been shot.

Dusty took a few pseudo-steps away from the cage. "I guess we're done here."

"No BP all this time?" Chuck asked.

Shawn didn't answer. He stood frozen in the batter's box, a statue of the finishing position of his swing. It felt so good he wanted to cry. First ball and he hits the perfect zero right over the pitcher's head.

Shawn made nice contact with the next pitch, but hit more of a fly ball. The ball hit the netting a few feet above and beyond Shawn's head, spun forward for a bit, then fell to the ground.

Next pitch, foul tipped into the back of the cage. Same with the next two. What the heck happened? He was right on it. The machine threw the same pitch every time. Why the heck couldn't he smack them anymore? Shawn stepped out of the batter's box, rested the handle of the bat against his thigh and the barrel on the ground. He removed his cap, ran his fingers through his sweaty hair, then wiped off his brow with the sleeve of his t-shirt.

Deep breath in through the nose.

Slow exhale out through the mouth.

He set his feet in the batter's box again, tapping the bat on the opposite front corner, as DJ taught him to do to make sure he could cover the entire plate with his swing.

Chuck showed Shawn the ball, then stuffed it into the machine. It looked smaller to Shawn. And faster. He swung and missed.

"On second thought," said Dusty, "I'll order us all some dinner. You know of any restaurants around here that deliver?"

Chuck looked at Dusty, closed his eyes and shook his head. Then raised an eyebrow toward Shawn. Dusty nodded, looking like a kid who got caught sneaking a cookie before dinner.

Shawn stepped out of the box again and looked toward the top of the bleachers on the first base side. Empty. He had just waved to CeCe a few minutes ago, and she waved back. Now she was gone. It was times like these when Shawn would find CeCe's face in the crowd at a game, and all she would have to do is lock eyes with him, and smile the tiniest little smile, and Shawn could hop back into the box with confidence.

Shawn hit about twenty more balls. Mostly weak grounders into the right side of the batting cage netting. A few that would have been decent fly balls. Nothing even close to the first two laser beams he hit. How in the world was he going to hit live pitching?

"That's enough for today, buddy boy." Chuck scurried around, tossing balls back into the bin. He stopped and looked at Shawn. "Excellent job for your first swings in four years."

Dusty walked through the cage with about ten balls balanced in his arms. "Yeah."

Chuck turned only his head toward Dusty. "Thanks for the commentary, Bob Costas."

"Whatever. How about some ice cream pies for these three hungry boys?"

"No thanks, guys, you go ahead, I have some more work to do out here." Shawn nodded his head toward the field.

Dusty turned to Chuck. "How about some *not free* ice cream pies for these two hungry boys?"

"I think we might get a freebie if we bat our eyelashes at Mrs. Greta," said Chuck. "What do you think, Shawn?"

But Shawn didn't hear them. He was already jogging across left field toward center. Alone.

74

September 21, 2013 - 11:09 am

Larry drained the last drops out of a white Styrofoam cup as the front door to McMaster's Restaurant closed behind him. God bless the Ethiopians for discovering this stuff. He stood flat-footed and observed the moment: Two teener fall ball teams gathered around the flagpole for the National Anthem before their eleven-fifteen game. The sun was well up into the sky to the south and east. It didn't climb as high as it did even a few weeks ago. Tomorrow would be the first day of Autumn. The sky was bluer, shadowed with clouds, like a wrinkled, azure pool tarp stretched out for the first time since May...

The field below was lined to perfection. Shawn had gotten good at it. It had always been Billy's job, at least after it stopped being DJ's job. Off to the left and right of the McMaster property, families in Muldoon's development mowed their lawns, kicked soccer balls, spread a Fall layer of mulch, sealed their driveways, and sipped iced tea and coffee on their back patios.

"Excuse us," said a voice from behind Larry, who was planted in the middle of the walkway down to the bleachers.

Larry turned and smiled, then stepped out of the way. This would be the last such Saturday. Ever. There would be no games on the field next weekend, the grounds will be in the midst of preparation for the Final Exam.

He walked over to the flagpole and rested his empty coffee cup on the electrical box. The teams were on the field playing the top of the first inning. White clouds, some with gray underbellies, sat on an invisible shelf in the sky, motionless. Cheers from the crowd, hoots and hollers from the field, the ball snapping in gloves, tinging off bats. Eggs, bacon, and pancakes wafting in from behind, and the first hints of rotting leaves all around.

Larry looked down at DJ's plaque, Wilbur Ryan McMaster's plaque to be accurate, and his breakfast became heavy in his stomach. Ten years. He'd had ten years to find what DJ had left for him. Nothing. He had not found a single thing. Larry reached down and crushed his coffee cup on the electrical box, slicing and tearing and crumpling it. He picked up the pieces in his hands and squeezed.

No. Today is not any of the previous days of the last ten years. Today is today. What could he do for DJ today, what could he do for the McMaster's today, what could he do for Quail today?

Not give up. Not to give up hope, nor give up looking. Larry said to his students countless times, "Keep trying, keep looking; if you quit, you'll never find out that what you were looking for was right under your nose the whole time."

Larry knew he had a big nose, but not ten years big. He decided to stroll the property, one last time. See if anything sent up a signal. 'McMasters will refuse the key, regret a win.' Larry walked the perimeter of the restaurant and residence building first. He dragged his fingers across the letters on the Winner's Locker Room door. He'd love to poke around in there, but Muldoon had the key.

Larry sauntered through the parking lot, ignoring the cars, but studying the lamp posts and the concrete parking space dividers, peeking down the water drains. He descended the hill and walked along the right field fence. He pushed on one of the scoreboard support columns, looked at the underside of the metal casing where the wires entered.

He continued around the outfield fence, picking up the loose netting at the bottom of the batting cage to go inside. Each time Larry thought he had found the bottom of it, there was a little more to pick up, like a magician pulling an endless multi-colored handkerchief out of his sleeve.

301

Finally, he stepped under and toed the plastic home plate so he could look underneath. He walked around the pitching machine twice, raked his hands through the yellow, dimpled, pitching machine balls.

Around the fence in the left field corner and back toward the bleachers. Nothing. He had tried again, and, nothing. He stopped and leaned on the fence with his forearms and watched the game for a bit. One-nothing after two and a half innings. He took a deep breath, in through his nose, then slowly out through pursed lips. There was only one thing left to do, one last time.

"Last of the third!" Larry called out as he walked in front of the visiting team's crowd.

75

September 26, 2013 - 9:12 pm

"We haven't spoken in a week. Maybe more. She won't return my texts. Nothing."

"Shawny, you have to understand…" Greta put down her rolling pin, drying her dry hands as she walked over to Shawn. "This is all very… emotional for CeCe." Greta leaned on the kitchen counter next to Shawn. "Has she… Did she---"

"Yeah," said Shawn. "I know."

"Everything?"

"Everything." Shawn pushed off the counter, walking over toward a bowl of peach filling. He didn't want to talk about what happened to CeCe or the 'everything' that came after it.

Greta walked toward Shawn. "You keep your fingers out of there." She grabbed his arms just above the elbows. She used to grab him by the shoulders. "CeCe waited for you, now it's your turn. You have something to keep you occupied for the next few days, don't you?"

"Yeah, I guess I do."

"Well, then worry about that. You know what they say; if you love someone, let them go… and God will open a door."

Shawn smirked at Greta, who smirked right back. "I have some stuff to finish up at the apartment, I'm going to sleep there tonight."

Greta nodded her head, but didn't look at Shawn. She was already sprinkling flour on the counter, reaching for her rolling pin.

Shawn lay in bed, exhausted, but his mind was whirling like a slot machine. Spinning and spinning, stopping for a moment, then spinning again. So many little things to worry about; positioning in left field, covering the

303

strike zone on outside pitches, watering the infield and outfield grass enough, but not too much. So many big things to worry about; moving out of the residence, closing down the McMaster property, finding a place for his mother to live.

And CeCe.

Shawn kicked his feet out from under the bed sheet, pulled them back in, rolled onto his stomach, then his left side. Right side. Asleep, but still somewhat aware. Hours and hours. How does he wait for CeCe when she's right there and they can just start in again? But Mom is right, he should be patient because she was patient, so patient for four years. For crying out loud, it's only been like four days since they talked. Just focus on the game, on the game, on the game. Baseball, baseball, CeCe, baseball, CeCe.

Shawn sprung up in bed. He knew exactly what to do. Time to go talk to an old friend. The clock read two-forty-nine in the morning as Shawn slipped on his sneakers. He straightened on the edge of the bed, and stretched his arms over his head. His back was sore. Swinging a bat used muscles that people just don't use in everyday life. Shawn liked the feeling, though. It reminded him of the beginning of every season he ever played.

He stepped over the creek, landing only for a moment on each rock. He reached the other side, sneakers dry. A few clouds zoomed across the sky, illuminated by the moon, which was itself only fifty percent lit, like it was sitting on a fence, unsure of which way to go. Shawn stepped out into right field, and jogged across through center, then left. His legs felt cold, stiff, but it still felt good to be out there. Even in the middle of the night.

Shawn walked toward the infield, toward the dugout, and toward the bat. "Hello in there," Shawn called. He couldn't hear the bat's response, so he walked into the dugout. "Are you giving me the silent treatment?"

The bat said nothing, just leaned its crooked lean against the wall in the corner.

"Oh, I get it, you want to scare me again," Shawn said with a laugh.

But the bat said nothing. Shawn looked at it closely, and it looked like.... A bat. Shawn saw a broken bat and nothing more. The dugout was quiet, and Shawn had to wonder if the bat had really ever said anything at all. But it had, of course it had. It urged him back to Quail, back to his family and CeCe. It called him a million different names along the way.

Now it said nothing, just tilted its head toward Shawn. He picked up the bat by its handle, and the broken barrel fell to the ground, lying in a pile of dirt and sunflower seeds. It didn't say a single word. It didn't launch into the air. It didn't pop up and smack Shawn on the head. It just lay there, powerless to do anything until somebody caused it too.

Shawn bent over and picked it up. He walked toward the opening in the fence on the way out to the field and dropped the barrel and the handle of the bat into the trash can. He walked down the right field line toward the creek and the trees, toward the apartment. He did not look back.

76

Over a thousand people crowded the McMaster property. Mostly in the bleachers, which hugged the dugouts and home plate area. A bunch filled the restaurant, not a table was vacant. About forty or so huddled around the flagpole, standing in the grass, hovering over the plaques. All of them were standing. Calves pushed up against the metal bleachers down around the field, families out of booths, shoulder to shoulder at the end of their table, mid-meal. The teams with their hats off, hats over their hearts, or tucked in their hands in front of their belt buckles, or behind their backs.

Soon the National Anthem, but now a moment of silence for Billy McMaster. The sun pierced the dry air, warm on Shawn's arms and neck and the right side of his face. But the early fall breeze cooled his entire body. It rushed the mesh top of his uniform, the first one he had buttoned up in a long time. It wiggled the ends of his pant legs, which rested on his black cleat tops. It shook the leaves in the trees; green turning brown, red, and orange; the only sound on the acreage. This rivalry was fierce, but everybody understood what the McMasters, and the restaurant, and the field, and this game meant to Quail.

The electric hiss of the recording of the National Anthem broke the silence, and the crowd remained still, some wiping tears from their eyes, off their cheeks. Shawn rubbed his eyes with his thumb and index finger, then looked at the four plaques, at the empty space to the right of his father's, then up at the flag. The enormous flag rolled slowly in the breeze, waving to show its stripes and its stars. So long since he had put on a uniform, stood with a team, played in a baseball game. Talked to his father. What would Billy say now? Take a deep breath? Stay within yourself? Don't swing the darn bat in the dugout?

Shawn felt like he was standing in line for a roller coaster that he swore he would never ride again. He wasn't sure if it was adrenaline, vomit, or a small wild animal that wanted to burst through his jersey.

The anthem ended and the teams headed for the stairs on their respective sides of the field, walking down through the fans. They would have to squish together to fit any more people onto the bleachers. The Final Exam always filled McMaster Field. Both teams brought a ton of fans, but the stands were also filled with folks who loved this rivalry, or who just loved baseball and wanted to watch the last local game before turning their attention to football season and preparing for the holidays.

But word had spread that this Final Exam was different. All week, a bulldozer had been sitting on the side of the road across from the McMaster property, and it didn't take much digging for the people of Quail to learn about DJ and his lack of a will, of Muldoon and his plans to take over the property and finish his takeover of the Quail countryside. Or that Shawn would be in left field, for the first time in ages, weeks after the death of his father. The crowd was no longer silent, conversation and anticipation coursing like a rumor through a middle school cafeteria.

The umpires and managers met at home plate, and Shawn decided to take one more lap around the outfield, to make sure his legs were ready, to make sure his feet remembered how to wear cleats, to make sure he didn't crumble into a pile of sand somewhere in the freshly mown grass. Just the opposite. His legs and feet felt light, cutting through the golden light of the fading day. The sun dropping toward the treetops. Shawn picked up speed as he approached left field, his cap pulled low. Don't look into the bleachers. Focus on the task. A hush fell over the crowd as Shawn sprinted, chewing up the grass on the way to the left field line. His footfall pounded drums in his ears.

Shawn angled his head so he could peek into the right field bleachers. He squinted as he scanned the crowd, frowned, and turned his head back to the left field grass.

77

September 30, 2013 - 7:01 pm

Strange feeling, wearing a baseball uniform again. Socks pulled high up to the knees, pants hugging the cleat tops, ankle-length for contemporary styling. He walked up and down the bench, past his teammates. The Final Exam about to start. Shawn smirked as he thought about his late night discussions with the bat. Dugout empty, field dark, vacant. Just Shawn and his thoughts and the bat. Somehow, for some reason, he was out here again.

Shawn hadn't looked out to the mound. He didn't want to see Paul Jackson yet, tall and lanky. Just like Shawn, he had become a man over the last four years as well. The difference was that he was playing all this time. Pitching. Adding miles per hour to his fastball. Adding bite to his curve ball. A slider. Magic to his changeup. His warmup pitches popped in the catcher's glove. Shawn had been away from the game for years, but he could hear eighty-five miles per hour behind him.

Bobby Leighton, the McMaster's Restaurant center fielder, led off. The pitcher burned a fastball right down the middle and Bobby sent it back past Jackson for a single. He swiped the ball out of the air with his glove when it was returned to him and stormed around the mound. McMaster's had decided not to fall behind against the flamethrower. They would look for pitches to hit early in the count. Especially fastballs. They didn't want to get late in the count and have to guess on the curve or a change, or decide if it was a backdoor slider or a two seam fastball that was going to stay outside.

Shawn could only see the Al's Everything crowd from his seat in the dugout. He was in the seventh slot in the batting order, he didn't expect to get up in the first inning. After the single, Bobby moved up on a wild pitch, slid over to third on a ground out to second, and scored on a

309

fly out to center field by Chuck. Dusty, the sixth batter, stepped in with two outs and a runner on first after a bleeder dropped in down the right field line. Maybe Shawn would hit in the first inning after all.

Shawn found a helmet that fit and swung a heavy bat in the caged area off the dugout. His heart pulsed against his tight, lycra undershirt and he patted his hands on some pine tar to counteract the sweat on his palms. He dropped the heavy bat, found the bat he was going to use, and stepped up to the backstop. Peering through the chain link, Shawn felt like he was at the zoo. Close to danger, but safe behind the screen. Soon he would have to step in, step back into the batter's box he last left after looking at strike three. Same game. Same pitcher. But so much life had passed. Both boys had grown into men. It was a moment Shawn both lusted after and feared, dreamed about and tried to not think about. Now, it was right in front of him. But it would have to wait a little longer, as Dusty grounded out to third base to end the top of the first inning.

Shawn grabbed his hat and glove and jogged out onto the field. He felt the weight of a thousand eyes as he trotted past the pitcher's mound, past shortstop and out into left field. As he stepped into the grass, he could see fewer and fewer people. It was just him, and left field. Just like when he was a boy and Billy would hit him endless fly balls. Buckets and buckets. Shawn wished this jog out to his position could last all night. Forever. He knew when he turned around, the rest of the team and his opponents, the backstop and bleachers, the restaurant and fans would be there. He was in the exact place he was exactly four years ago. Shawn put his glove up to his face, his eyes peeking over the web pocket. He breathed deep, the smell of the leather so familiar. Calming.

He looked above the McMaster's Restaurant dugout and picked out his mother, sitting amongst other mothers, wives, and girlfriends. Shawn looked left and right, up and down for golden red hair pouring out of the bottom of a Phillies cap. He couldn't find it. CeCe had to be there somewhere. Roger Ring threw his last warm up pitch, then retrieved the ball from Dusty after the infield had tossed it around the horn. The lead-off batter for Al's Everything dug into the right hand batter's box, and Shawn's stomach flipped and flopped like a base runner caught in a rundown. Over fourteen hundred days since his last live game action and now Shawn was patrolling left field again, in the Final Exam, no less.

Roger stood tall on the mound, both hands around his glove, his hands, the glove, and the ball in front of his face. Shawn looked at the leaves on the trees in right field, their edges crisp against the deep blue sky. Everything still looked like summer to Shawn, but the chilly breeze that rushed through McMaster Field reminded him that change was coming. September turning to October.

The ball was about to be put in play, and Shawn was one of the nine defenders on the field. Over the past four years, he had watched a lot of baseball on tv, thought about baseball, vomited thinking about baseball. But it had been from the sideline, not in the game, as a former baseball player. A ball could be hit to him, and he would have to field it. Think about where to throw it, and throw it there.

Roger rocked back and kicked his leg high. Shawn watched his arm drop toward the ground, then whip back around his head, past his ear, then toward home plate. Shawn stood flat-footed, as if he were standing in the middle of a department store watching a baseball game on a display tv. The ball zipped across home plate, right down the middle, strike one. The sound of the ball slapping in the pocket of Jimbo Jurges' catcher's glove woke Shawn from his trance, reminding him that he was playing baseball again, that he was in left field, that he was the left fielder, the one in charge of all that grass. No longer in charge of reading and sending emails, of picking up and paying for his groceries, of being invisible. Not talking to a bat anymore either.

Roger's third offering jammed Al's Everything's lead-off hitter causing him to hit a routine grounder to shortstop. Shawn forgot about everybody else and felt like the ball was coming right to him. His hair stood on end, and he felt his undershirt cool with sweat. He took two quick steps in, then slowed when Chuck surrounded the ball with his arms and legs and hands, fielding it cleanly, throwing to first in plenty of time for the out.

Roger walked the second batter, then struck out the third looking. Two outs, runner on first base, and Mac Green, Al's clean-up hitter lumbered to the plate. He dug a trench for his right foot in the right hand batter's box, shooting dirt behind him like a dog fixing to hide a bone, all the while extending his right arm and right palm back toward the umpire. As if anybody would dare start before he was ready. Finally, Green turned his attention to the mound as if Roger was a teacher delivering a homework assignment he had no intention of completing. Roger started him with a fastball inside. Too far inside, and as the ball approached the plate, Shawn leaned toward the left field foul line. There was no conscious thought. Just Shawn's center of gravity moving to the only place Green could hit that pitch. Ball one.

Green stepped out of the box and adjusted at least six items of clothing and uniform accessories. The umpire extended his palm toward Roger while Green, a local legend, refitted himself in the batter's box. Green had breathed smoke and infield dirt for eighteen years of intimidating baseball living, and eight others where he was reportedly an almost nice, if not over-sized, young boy. He had home run power to all fields, and there were rumors that at age sixteen he showed up to the first game of a Sunday doubleheader clean-shaven and hit the game

312

winning home run in the second game with a full beard. There is much more evidence to show that he was actually eighteen at the time.

Green was set and Roger dealt a curve ball that didn't dive as far outside as Jurges had called for it. Green took an extra-large cut at it, even taking into account Final Exam-level adrenaline, and lofted one down the left field line. He looked up at it for a moment and slammed the bat into the dirt just in front of home plate. He put his head down and trotted toward first.

Shawn picked up the ball right off the bat, planted his left foot, swiveled his hips, pointing his belly button toward the left field foul pole and pushed off. He found himself running, looking up at the ball and running, automatically. Like breathing. Right, left, right, left. The ball bounced in the sky with each step, a common problem for outfielders early in the season. Behind him, Bobby called "you got room, you got room!" Shawn took a quick peek at the fence, far away, then whipped his head around to find the ball again. He found it, just in time, catching it in the pocket of his glove, right elbow wedged in his hip. Out number three. Shawn looked at the ball in his glove and exhaled. It had been a while. The fear rushed out of his body as the blood ran back to his extremities. He was playing ball.

78

The helmet fit better and the bat handle was more comfortable than last inning. Shawn stood a step outside the dugout as Jackson finished his warm ups. He stepped into the lefty batter's box as if he were putting his cleats on a freshly waxed floor. He wiggled his left foot to make himself at home, and touched the bat head to the opposite corner of home plate. His breath was shallow, and his hands cooled, the blood rushing to his center of his body. He blinked slow and hard.

"Strike one!" called the home plate umpire. Shawn barely saw the pitch. He stepped out of the batter's box and adjusted his belt buckle. "Step out, take a breath, ok?" he could hear Billy saying. He moved back into the box, and looked out at Jackson. He couldn't have been more than thirty feet away. He could just reach in with his long arm and enormous hand and drop the ball in the catcher's glove. But that would be too easy. Wouldn't scare the crap out of Shawn, not enough for Jackson's liking. He kicked his left leg high in the air and spun the ball in, slower than the first pitch. A curve ball. Shawn recognized it too late, flailing at the ball, missing by a foot at least. Strike two.

Jackson turned his back on home plate, on Shawn, and rubbed the ball with two bare hands as he stared out at the scoreboard. Oh, and two. Shawn couldn't let Jackson strike him out again. Shawn twisted his left foot, as if a roach had crawled into the left-handed batter's box, tapped the corner of home plate a little harder, and stared into Jackson's eyes as he toed the rubber. Shawn gripped his bat tighter. A small grin snuck onto Jackson's face as he nodded at the catcher. It's a fastball. Definitely a fastball.

And it was. The hardest one Jackson had thrown thus far. Shawn swung and made contact, two inches above the handle, pushing a grounder just to the left of the mound toward second base. Shawn sprinted out of the box and covered the distance from home to first faster than he ever had in his life. First base flew toward his feet, a step or maybe two sooner than he was used to. The throw from shallow second base beat him by half a step, certainly out, but a hush came over the crowd. Both sets of bleachers. Shawn had almost legged out a hit on a routine grounder to second. The contact was nothing to call The Sporting News about, but the speed down the line was breathtaking. Even Shawn stopped and stared back toward home plate from shallow right field, trying to process what he had almost done. Then he jogged back to the dugout.

Dusty and Chuck sat next to each other on the bench, each holding a bat half way up, barrel just below their mouths.

"Did.... You.... See.... That?" Chuck asked Dusty as Shawn passed by.

"Barely, Chuck, barely. It was like a gazelle, but one that could start at full speed."

"No, Mr. Dusty, a cheetah. Going after a small wounded animal."

"Would a cheetah have to go fast if the animal was small and wounded?"

Chuck sat back and took note of the mental error he had made. Then, leaned back in, "Hey, fans, tweet me any animal you can think of that is faster than a cheetah. Then, I'll tweet back to let you know that the only thing faster than it is Shawn McMaster trying to beat out a grounder to second base."

"Lots of words," said Dusty. "Can you fit that into one-hundred and forty characters?"

"No, but Shawn McMaster is so fast that he could fit five-hundred and twenty-seven characters into one tweet."

"That, my good friend, is fast."

Shawn sat down on the bench in between the middle infielders. "That's a lot of talk about a ground out."

"Majestic," said Chuck.

"Gazelle," said Dusty.

"Cheetah," said Chuck.

"Shut up," said Shawn.

79

Greta cranked her head around to look at the restaurant from the top row of the bleachers. Old habit, worrying about the place when they--- she, wasn't in there. Not much sense in it anymore. She knew she would have time to say goodbye to the place where she spent the entirety of her adult life, either working in the restaurant or raising a family up in the residence. The McMaster family's only job at the moment was to beat Muldoon down on the ball field. Greta vowed to keep her back turned to what would soon be his, and instead, submerge herself in the game. The thought of Albert Muldoon marching around in her restaurant and, oh Lord, her home, made her want to spit.

The evening was crisp and clean, a fall day you dream about in the dead of the summer, or in the bottom of the winter… Leaves, branches, building, and people stitched seamlessly to the cobalt sky behind them.

Greta noticed some of the fans pointed out toward right center field. There was nothing there she could see, just the scoreboard, which read one-zip at the bottom of the third inning. But as more arms raised and hands pointed in that direction, the low rumble of a large engine vibrated through the air and the yellow of a bulldozer edged up against the trees that separated the McMaster property from the Muldoon development. Roger stepped off the rubber and all the players turned and looked into the trees as the murmur in the crowd grew. Greta could see the side of Muldoon's face as he stood in front of his dugout, a smile of contentment plastered on his face. He never could stand losing, even falling behind. With the score one-nothing, he had to do something to get back on top. He must have ordered the bulldozer to move into position. It was a direct

317

shot at the only people who could know the significance: Larry, Shawn and Greta.

Muldoon turned to walk back into the dugout as Roger climbed back onto the mound. Just before his head disappeared below the roof, Greta locked eyes with him. Muldoon stopped, glanced back over his shoulder at the bulldozer, then tipped his cap to her. She knew, had known for a long time, that nobody was going to pop up with information or anything that would will the McMaster property to Greta and Shawn. That game was lost a long time ago, but Greta had one more shot, she could fire over the mixed crowd. A majority of them were pulling for the McMaster's, the friends and families of the Al's Everything players were pulling for them, and the rest were there because they loved watching baseball at McMaster Field.

"Do you know what that bulldozer is doing there?" she called out. Heads turned toward Greta in the top row. Fans knew the voice, but weren't used to hearing it in the bleachers. For years and years, she had watched games and never uttered a syllable. It was time to be heard. It was time for her run-off home run, or whatever it's called. "I do. I know exactly what it is doing there."

"What?" and "Then, tell us!!" rang from the crowd. A fly out ended the third inning, but most people didn't see it. They were waiting for Greta to inform them about the bulldozer that had just taken aim on the trees, scoreboard and outfield fence.

"DJ McMaster, my father-in-law, Shawn's grandfather, died, ten years ago to the day, before he willed this property," she said, waving her arms left and right, "which of course includes the field and the restaurant." Now everybody had turned toward Greta, including the players down on the field, players from both teams, no longer playing, instead listening to her. "Tomorrow morning, the property will go up for public auction, and there is nobody around who can outbid that man." Greta

318

pointed at Muldoon, who was standing amongst his team, arms crossed, the smile gone from his face. "That bulldozer is his sick way of telling all of us what he plans to do with this field and that restaurant as soon as he can cut the check to do it."

The attention turned from Greta to Muldoon. "Is that true?" and "What the hell, Muldoon?" rained down upon him. He said nothing, just ducked his head and retreated to his dugout. Greta glided down the bleachers to hear what Muldoon's players were saying. She caught the tail end of the conversation.

"Never mind what I'm up to, just win this damn Game." His players just looked him, arms crossed. "Fine, I'll double the pay."

"Triple it, or we're done," said Mac Green, the muscles in his forearms rippling in front of his chest.

"OK, OK. Tell you what, if you win, I'll quadruple it!"

Muldoon's players all looked at each other and smiled. Some of them stopped in their tracks and looked at the ever deepening blue sky, closing left eyes and raising right eyebrows, mentally carrying ones, or at the very least estimating the potential pay day. They clapped their hands and flooded the dugout, ready to bat with a renewed vigor, but the crowd had come to life as well.

"Let's go, McMaster's!" chanted most of the crowd, in unison, then stomped their feet five times, also in unison, twice slowly, then three times fast. Over and over. Greta looked around at what she had done. The good people of Quail were rallying behind the McMaster family. Greta, Billy, and Larry hadn't accomplished what they had hoped, but the tribute gave Greta goosebumps.

Greta climbed the stairs back to her seat, her arms, shoulders, and back patted by fans on all sides of her, as if she were the crust of a peach pie, about to be slid into an oven.

80

Of course she was there to watch. But, she did it from the shadows of the scoreboard. She thought she was spotted last inning, everybody pointing in her direction. But, CeCe quickly realized it was the belching bulldozer they were astonished by, not a young woman watching the game from the woods, sometimes through binoculars. Sometimes through her fingers fanned over her face.

It was like watching Shawn back in high school, confidence billowing, an aura of confidence and, yes, sexuality about him. To see him in the outfield again was almost a sexual experience. Could that be healthy? Was it just love? Love she was feeling for him as he played catch with Bobby in center field before each inning? Catching the ball with ease, was he even looking at the ball, or did it just find his glove? And his arm, longer and stronger, spit the ball out much harder than it looked like it should go. CeCe always worked so hard to keep her body in shape, to sprint faster and faster, to smack the hockey ball. It never looked easy when she did it. Watching Shawn do it made her swoon a bit.

She had been keeping track, she was sure it was the bottom of the sixth inning. There was no doubt she cared deeply for the young man currently in left field, but those sexual feelings. How would she know if it was love, or just a coping mechanism? The first batter of the inning for Al's hit a single right in front of CeCe, dropping it softly into right center field. The small group of Al's Everything fans, friends and families mostly, cheered, but the rest of the crowd booed or remained silent. To CeCe, the crowd seemed split pretty much down the middle at the beginning of the game. But shortly after she thought she was spotted, after the crowd pointed in her direction, after the rumble of the bulldozer shook her off the tree she was leaning on,

320

most of the fans started to root for McMaster's. Chanted for them even.

The second batter of the inning hit a ground ball to the shortstop. Chuck flipped it to Dusty at second base for the force out; the first out of the inning. Dusty had no chance to turn the double play. The batter was too fast, and the runner did a nice job of sliding into his legs, causing him to hop toward the pitcher's mound to keep from falling down. Shawn had charged in to backup Dusty, then skipped backwards to his spot in left field. He once told CeCe that an outfielder should never turn his back on the infield when there is a runner on base, you never know what could happen when you're not watching.

The third batter of the inning saw nine pitches, fouling off three after the count was full. He finally hit one straight up into the air between home plate and first base, and first baseman Jackson Miller hauled it in. Out number two, runner still on first base. The scene was so familiar: an early fall evening pulled from a fairy tale, golden light playing in the trees, fading fast. The bleachers packed with fans in sweatshirts, toting blankets for the first time since early in the season. So similar to the night Shawn ran off. Disappeared. Left.

Mac Green stepped to the plate next, and everybody in the park knew he could give Al's a one run lead with one swing of the bat. CeCe watched Shawn and the other two outfielders take a step or two back, wave their throwing hands above their heads, palms down, to say don't let anything go over your head. Shawn had always told CeCe that with two outs and a runner on first, the only way the runner could score was on a double. The outfield would play deep enough to try to keep that from happening, clinging to the slim lead.

Mac didn't swing at either of the first two pitches, both balls. CeCe knew that Roger didn't want to walk him, even though he was their best hitter, because that would put the tying run at second base, and even a weak single could score a runner from second base with two outs. Shawn and CeCe would sit watching the Phillies all summer long through high school, feet up on the ottoman in front of the couch in CeCe's living room. It was impossible for her to not savor each and every one of his words. When he talked about baseball, when it was just the two of them, he was so confident, so relaxed, so funny. So handsome. Yes, so sexy.

The third pitch must have been somewhere Mac liked, because he took a mighty swing, and the sound the bat made colliding with the ball, and the sound the crowd made after they saw the ball launch on a line inches over Dusty's glove, a leaping Dusty deep at second base, one step into the grass. The ball skipped through right center field, no way for Bobby or right fielder Benny Lopez to reach it before it clanked off the fence. CeCe recoiled, both men looked like they were running right toward her. But she knew she could be standing there naked and they wouldn't have even noticed, not tonight. Benny whipped the ball into Dusty, who then turned and fired it to Jurges, but it was too late. The runner had scored; the game was tied. CeCe shook her head and let out a chuckle. Shawn always said the other team wants to win too when CeCe asked why the Phillies strategy didn't work.

The next batter lofted the second pitch into left field, and CeCe could follow the parabolic flight of the ball, rising, falling, as Shawn loped toward it. She watched him as if he were a moving mosaic behind the chain-link outfield fence (which is male, by the way. Another grin). Again, it looked like he was barely trying, but she could tell his glove was going to intersect with the ball at just the right time. It was such a plain thing, catching a fly ball, but it looked so delicious when Shawn did it. No, spiritual, maybe religious. As she watched him trot toward the dugout after recording the third out of the top of the sixth, that feeling arose in her once again. Deep in her gut, and lower too. Such a longing, but so confusing. To see Shawn play again was bitter sweet. Most of the time, Shawn was at his very best, his most confident, and most attractive, while on that field. But, she had also seen him at his worst, a lightning-quick tempered boy who ran from the trouble he had caused.

Without realizing it, CeCe had roamed a few too many steps forward. The light found her shoes and her denim-clad legs. She scurried back into the dark. She wasn't ready to be revealed, for Shawn to see her. She wasn't sure if she ever would be.

81

Larry watched Shawn slide his foot back into the groove he created the last time he was up. Everything looked different this time around. It was dark, the field lights were now necessary. Most, if not all, of the bare arms in the crowd had disappeared, hidden beneath sweatshirts, light jackets or blankets. The eye might miss the bulldozer if it didn't already know it was there.

Even Shawn looked different. In his first at-bat, Shawn looked like a student pretending to stretch while cheating off their neighbor: there, but trying not to be. This time around, he rocked and coiled, like a cobra ready to attack. Larry hadn't seen Shawn like this in years. So... ready.

Larry wished he were ready. The Final Exam was one-one heading toward the backstretch. He had done very little coaching in his life, and none in a game of this magnitude. What if he had to make a huge decision at the end of the game, what if it was the wrong decision, what if they lost---

Hold up. Larry had watched a million baseball games in his life. He knew the game, he second- and triple-guessed managers both on the field and on the TV. He could do this. Deep breath, in through the nose, out through the mouth. One pitch at a time, one play at a time, one inning at a time. Score one more run than Muldoon.

Jackson zipped a four-seamer on the outside corner, and Shawn reached out with the barrel, mostly arms, not much power at all, but made solid contact, and the ball zipped over the third baseman's head into left field, for a lead-off single. Shawn took a few quick steps toward first base, then bubbled out and rounded the bag. He stopped a few steps toward second base. His first hit in four years. He stood on first base and clapped his hands. His teammates called out to him: "Attaboy, Shawny!!" "Way to be a rabbit!" "Yeah, wheels!"

Jackson stared over at Shawn from the top of the mound, rubbing the ball in two bare hands, his glove tucked under his left arm. Shawn stared right back, locking eyes. A showdown in the top of the seventh. Jackson's fastball had lost a little; maybe he was getting tired. Maybe the pressure was getting to him. The crowd hadn't relented. Muldoon had become more of a villain, more of the bad guy, and all the players in his uniform were painted with the same brush. The fans of Al's Everything had been drowned out by the rest of the crowd. Any of their cheers swallowed up in boos. Or erased by another, "Let's Go McMaster's" chant. They erupted at any time, from any part of the crowd. Larry let it charge him up as though his last name was McMaster. Tonight, it was.

Shawn side-stepped off first base, right foot out, then left foot brought next to right foot. Then right foot out, like scissors opening and closing. Never crossing. Crossed feet were not athletic, and an invitation for even an average pitcher to throw over and pick a runner off. Shawn settled into his lead, about three and a half steps off first base. Jackson glowered at Shawn out of the corner of his left eye, over his left shoulder. He looked in at home plate, then back at Shawn. Larry knew Jackson was pausing so long to make it difficult for Shawn to steal. He fired home. Strike one. Shawn jumped off three or four more steps, a generous secondary lead, getting the attention of the catcher, who cocked his right arm back, anxious to fire to first. Shawn scurried back to the bag, ducking in, slamming his foot on the base. No throw.

The next two pitches were fouled off, and the third caught the inside corner for strike three. No swing. Shawn still on first base, one out. The nine hitter was up next, the light-hitting right fielder Benny Lopez. Lopez was a lefty, like Shawn, and he tried to slap everything to left field. Of course, Muldoon knew that, so he brought his left fielder in two steps, and two steps toward the left field line. The center fielder was way over in left center field. The right fielder was miles away from the right field line, charged with covering all of right and half of center in the extremely unlikely event that Lopez got around on one.

Shawn led, a good four and a half steps off now, drawing a throw from Jackson. Shawn dived back, his right hand reaching the base a split second before the first baseman slapped the tag on his shoulder. Safe. Shawn led back out again, maybe a half step further this time. Jackson went home, starting Lopez off with a curve ball. Lopez's eyes looked like scoops of vanilla ice cream. He had guessed correctly, and he smacked that first pitch on two hops past the diving third baseman and the lunging short stop. Shawn sprinted toward second base, and as he got close, turned out to round so he could head to third. With one out, he needed to get to third base on this hit so he could score on anything put in play by Bobby Leighton, who was coming up next. The left fielder had to charge to his left, toward center field to grab Lopez's single. Shawn was only one step past second base when the left fielder grabbed and planted, turned and fired. The crowd inhaled, all at once. The third base coach had two hands up, telling Shawn to stop, but he had never looked. Shawn was digging for third and was only a third of the way there when the ball flew out of the left fielder's hand. The view from the first base dugout was stunning. The throw was strong, and perfectly on line. It reached third base in the air, but Shawn had simply outrun it. His always-blinding speed matched with his new length had defied physics. He slid in under the tag, clearly safe. Muldoon stepped out to argue, then stopped, realizing that Shawn was actually safe. That he had outrun a thrown baseball.

Shawn kept his foot on the third base and raised his hand to call for time. Granted. He stood up and walked into foul territory. There was some clapping and cheering, but mostly the buzz of words, disbelief. How did he beat that out? The ball was already on its way, and Shawn, with just his long, lithe legs, his feet in metal cleats, chewed up the territory between second and third at an alarming rate. It was as if somebody lifted him up by his belt loop and tossed him to third base.

Shawn had just a second before play resumed. His eyes scanned the crowd, left, right, left, up, down. Then back to Jackson on the mound.

Bobby fouled off the first pitch, then sent a long fly ball to center field on the second. Shawn tagged and scored easily. McMaster's was back on top, two-one. Shawn jogged into the dugout and pulled off his helmet.

Larry tapped him on the shoulder several times. "Way to go, way to go. Back in the lead," he said, then, "Billy woulda been proud. DJ too."

Bobby wandered over after high-fiving everybody in the dugout. "What the heck does DJ stand for anyway? I thought all the McMaster men before you were Wilburs."

Shawn sat on the bench, grinned at Larry, then turned back to Bobby. "They were. DJ stands for 'Double Junior.' Somebody called him that when he was just a boy, and it stuck. Technically, his name was Wilbur Ryan McMaster, the third."

82

Greta knew that Shawn could do it, could lead McMaster's Restaurant past Al's Everything. All he had to do was show up. And he did. Now they were a few innings from winning the last game ever on McMaster Field, against the very man who was causing it to be the last game ever on McMaster Field.

Greta looked out at her son. What if things were different? What if what happened in the kitchen that night, the night Shawn's brother, Will, died, didn't happen? Would Will be out in center field next to Shawn? Would Shawn have run away after swinging that bat into the pole in the dugout? Would an older brother on the same team have kept Shawn from swinging the bat in the first place? Would Will have been a baseball player at all?

Sometime you lose a son, and you are powerless against it. Something happens, and he's gone. But sometimes your son slips right through your hands and he's gone. Greta had played the scene over and over in her mind, hoping it would end differently, but it never did. She was trying to do too much all at once. Get pies in the oven, wash the dishes, hold her infant son. To prove a point to Billy, that she was doing too much in the restaurant, that she needed help as a new mother.

Billy had even told her to slow down, to hand Will to him. But Greta said no, she could do it all. Her hands were slick with soap and peach filling. Will slipped right through her hands and hit his head on the edge of the counter on the way down.

People can find other restaurants, even other places to live, but they can't replace sons.

83

The sky was black, but vibrating with anticipation. Most of the stars were blotted out by the field lights, only the brightest shining through. Bottom of the eighth, still a two-one lead for McMaster's. More bundling in the crowd, hoods of sweatshirts covering many heads in the crowd. Shawn scanned the crowd after a foul ball, many familiar faces, but not CeCe. She had to be watching, she never missed his games. Shawn scoured the bleachers behind McMaster's dugout, looking for the golden red hair, the icy blue eyes, the face of endless freckles. Not there. Simply not there.

There exists a feeling when playing Al's, and it was made for the phrase: waiting for the other shoe to drop. No lead, no matter how late, felt safe, until the final out was recorded. The final strike out, or ground out, or fly ball like a sword slicing a monster's head from its body. Shawn stood in left field, squeezing his fingers in his glove, clinging to the slightest of leads. Two outs now, runners on first and second. Lefty Bobo Utkin skipped up to the plate. His full name was Boris Utkin, but sometime in his childhood a family member shortened it to Bobo... On the ball field, he was known as the Russian Rake. Not a ton of power, but he would spray line drives from foul line to foul line, always hitting for a high average.

Larry whistled out to Shawn, waving toward center field, then putting two fingers in the air. He wanted Shawn to shade over two steps away from the left field line. The Russian Rake had a single up the middle, a double to right center field, and long (uncharacteristic) fly out to right field. With Roger running out of steam, Larry must have thought that the furthest toward left that The Rake would hit the ball would be left center. Shawn hadn't seen the rake

329

hit in four years before tonight, but he knew with his bat control, and Roger was loosing miles per hour with each pitch, that the next ball in play could go anywhere. And with that enormous Al-scented boot hanging over McMaster Field, Shawn expected the ball to be sprayed where they would least expect it, so he dutifully obeyed by moving two steps toward Bobby, but turned his body just a touch so he could sprint toward the left field line if necessary. A reasonable compromise: Listen to the coach, but also to his gut.

With the count one and two, Jurges edged toward the outside corner, then beyond it, so Shawn twisted even more so he was facing the left field line. Roger put the ball right where Jurges called for it, perhaps four inches off the plate, and The Rake, guarding against strike three, against ending the eighth inning, against leaving the tying and go ahead runs on base, swung and made clean contact. The entire McMaster's bench inhaled when they saw the line drive screaming down the left field line, rising and slicing away from Shawn, toward what looked like acres and acres of soft green grass inside the left field line. Open, inviting, a perfect landing place.

Shawn was already leaning hard in that direction when contact was made, and when he saw the ball jump off the bat, he launched himself toward the left field line. He knew right where he had to go to make the catch. He had known for over ten years where this ball would land, and a zillion others that flew off the bat of left-handers, and sliced toward the corner of the field. He knew right where this ball would land.

And he knew he couldn't get to it. Oh, he would try, but each step he took further convinced him of this fact. It would be just out of his reach. He should have known this sooner and circled behind it, letting it fall in for a hit, still giving him the chance to keep that second run, the go-ahead run, from scoring. But he hadn't made that decision, instead, he was on a beeline to where this ball was going to bounce, and he imagined himself diving. Imagined himself missing. Imagined the ball skidding into the corner, Bobby chasing it down as both runs scored, as The Rake cruised into third base, clapping his hands, pointing into the dugout as his teammates pointed back.

His automatic mental calculation told him he would miss by an inch or two, which would drive the crowd nuts. They'll yelp when the ball disappears behind Shawn for a moment, thinking he caught it, then groan when they see it rolling toward the fence. And as Shawn lays in the grass, the front of his uniform and face getting wet from the forming dew, they'll look at each other knowing that McMaster's had given it their best shot, but the inevitable had happened.

Recalculating. Something felt funny. No, weird. No.... Good. He was gaining ground on the ball faster than he had anticipated. The ball started to fall, to drop back to earth, like gravity pulling a shoe down to the ground. There was no way it was going to be foul. Everybody in the McMaster's dugout, and most of the people in the bleachers above could see it. It was dropping fast, and would hit the ground a foot or two to the right of the left field foul line. Fair as fair could be. They all watched the ball drop, and they watched Shawn rush toward it, beginning to lean forward with each lightning-quick step.

He had a chance, somehow he was going to have a chance, he would have to dive, no doubt, and stretch all the way out, but the calculation was telling him he now had a chance to make the catch. Three more steps, then he would have to dive. All three steps had to be perfect, no missteps or slips, no loose turf under his shoe, hindering his take off. Three more steps toward the ball, then a leap.

Step one, clean and true. Recalculating, recalculating. Yes, still good.

Step two, solid and strong. Recalculating, recalculating. Yes, yes, yes.

Step three, firm, his cleat digging into the soft, green turf and pushing off, launching his body into the air. Shawn flew as if he were diving into a pool, his body parallel to the ground, his arms extended in front of him, the glove on his right hand wide open. There was nothing more to do other than catch the ball if he had the chance, if he had calculated correctly. He started to angle down toward the ground, hands and arms first, angling down like the ball, both rushing to reach the same spot, the same patch of soft green grass.

The crowd gasped, inhaled, silenced itself as the ball and Shawn fell toward the ground. Nobody could take a breath, could utter a sound until the ball touched.... Something. The grass. The pocket of Shawn's glove. Fans began to stand up, to lean forward, as if that would help, help Shawn catch the ball, or help the ball safely to the ground.

Shawn's glove was about a foot off the ground when the ball landed in it, and he squeezed it tight. His hand in the glove with the ball tightly gripped and his bare throwing hand hit the ground first, slipping on the soft, moist green grass. A perfect landing place. The rest of his body followed, chest, then stomach and legs. The impact jarred his entire body, slammed his pelvis into the ground, rattled his shoulders, slammed his jaws together.

Everybody on the benches and in the crowd was now standing. They couldn't find the ball. Did he catch it? Did he actually catch that? The home plate umpire charged out toward Shawn in left field. "Show me the ball! Show me the ball!"

Muldoon waved both runners home, "Score, dammit, score. He didn't catch that, no way he caught that!"

"Show it to me!" yelled the umpire.

Shawn rolled onto his right side, and opened his glove far enough for the umpire to see the smudge of white, with red laces, tucked safely in a bed of black leather. The umpire raised his arm with a fist to signify Out!

The crowd erupted. They hadn't seen too many catches that good, that amazing. And they had never seen one like that with so much on the line, so late in a game, in The Final Exam. They clapped, cheered, whistled, and called as Shawn jogged in toward the dugout. But Shawn barely heard any of it, hardly heard the roar of the crowd. He couldn't believe CeCe missed that catch. This game. Where the heck was she? He scanned the crowd again, she had to be there.

But his vision was obstructed by his teammates grabbing his arms, hugging him, slapping and rubbing his head. Al's players lumbered out to their positions with heavy legs, and McMaster's prepared to hit in the bottom of the eighth inning. They still had the lead, and could add to it, before trying to get the last three outs to win The Final Exam.

84

The top of the ninth took no time at all, a one-two-three inning for Al's. Shawn felt like his teammates seemed to feel, a two-one lead was good enough. Let's just get back out there and finish this thing. Some insurance runs would be great, but the waiting was too much to handle. The batters in the top of the ninth saw a total of five pitches. Two infield groundouts and a pop up to second base.

The McMaster's nine charged out to their positions for the bottom of the ninth, clinging to the smallest lead a team could have. One run. So many ways to produce one run. A walk, then a bunt, then a single. A walk, then a double. A single, then a walk, then an error. A solo home run. The possibilities were endless. Mac Green was due to hit fourth this inning, and if he made it to the plate at all, he would have to be, at the very least, the winning run. Shawn didn't even want to think about it. Leaving Mac in the on deck circle, watching him remove his helmet and slam in down in disgust as McMaster's ran in to celebrate would be simply delicious. But there was work to do first.

James Walton, Al's center fielder, led off the inning. He looked at strike one, then ball one, and hit a one hopper to Chuck at shortstop. An easy play, one out. Shawn looked at his shoes and the grass around them, at the shadows the lights made on both sides of his body. He didn't look into the crowd, and none of the teammates dared look in each other's eyes. They smoothed the dirt at their positions. They made sure their hats were on straight. They didn't breathe too deeply, or say "one down" too loudly, because it finally felt like they were going to win this damn thing.

John Kresge hopped into the batter's box next. The lefty-hitting second baseman got ahead in the count two and oh, then turned on Roger's inside fastball that found too much of the plate. The ball launched off the bat destined for the right field corner. But Jackson Miller reached across his body and stabbed it out of the air. The double disappeared into his first baseman's glove. Two outs.

Two outs! One out to go. Again, no eye contact. The McMaster's nine informed each other that there were two outs as if there were two outs in the top of the fourth inning of a game in late June. But the buzz from the crowd was undeniable. One way or another, something big was about to happen. Jim Bob Dayton, Al's right fielder and three-slot hitter, was their last chance. Shawn looked in at Roger, followed the pitches into the plate, never lifting the brim of his cap high enough to see the crowd. The blades of grass in left field painted water on the toes of his cleats. The two-two pitch was on its way.

Fly ball to left field, to Shawn in left. He looked up at it and headed toward the foul line, toward where the ball would land. Except it wouldn't hit the ground, right? It would find the pocket of his glove, and he would end the game. After all of this, coming out of hiding, reconnecting with his family, after losing his father. And CeCe, where was CeCe? She was in the crowd now, to watch this, right? She had to be. Shawn took his eyes off the ball, only for a second, just to peek into the crowd. CeCe would have to be there, bundled up next to his mother, ready to cheer when Shawn caught the ball. But Greta stood alone. Where was CeCe?

Shawn looked back up and relocated the ball. But it had moved off its path. Or he had, because something didn't feel right. The ball wasn't going to land where he thought it was. He must have drifted when he looked in the crowd. What the hell is wrong with me? Why wouldn't I catch it, then worry about CeCe? She was going to see it or not see, whether he saw her or not.

No problem, just back pedal, a few steps and make the catch. But the push off wasn't true. Shawn slipped as he reached back to catch the ball and it dropped in behind him. He lay on the ground, flailing his arms as if he were making a snow angel, trying to find the ball. Luckily, Chuck was sprinting out toward Shawn, presumably to hug him after he made The-Final-Exam-ending catch. Instead, he grabbed the ball and whipped it into Dusty holding Dayton to an improbable two-out single.

What the heck happened? The game should be over, but they were still playing. Shawn should have caught the fly ball, a fly ball that he had caught a million times in his life, a fly ball he could catch in his sleep. But he missed it. He lost focus, or misjudged it, or both. A game isn't over until it is over. Especially, The Final Exam. There was quiet from the McMaster crowd as Shawn walked back to his spot in left field. There was snickering from the Al's crowd. "You suck, McMaster."

Shawn thought about running. Turning and hopping the fence in left field and running. The eyes of the crowd were looking at him again. Where was CeCe? He promised to never run from her again, where was she? To make him keep his promise. A voice, calling to him from the direction of right field.

"Shawn! Hey, Shawny!" A man's voice. Benny Lopez's voice. "Step out, take a breath, ok?"

Shawn laughed. What else could he do? And he laughed louder as Mac Green stepped into the box, once again, burying his right foot. So loud, in fact, that Green stopped what he was doing and looked out to left field to see what was so damn funny. Shawn stopped laughing, and this time under his breath said, "hit the ball to me." And he repeated it over, and over, and over again, all the way to a full count. The tying run at first base would be off with the pitch. The winning run, casting a shadow larger than the entire right-handed batter's box, gripped the bat tight, and launched a long, high fly ball into deep left field. Shawn turned and sprinted to the fence, reaching out with his glove hand to find it. Dusty and Chuck saw this and in unison said, "oh shit!"

Shawn stood at the fence and waited. Eyes on the ball the entire time. No peeks into the crowd. Calculating and recalculating. His original calculation was off by a couple steps. To make the game ending catch, he would need to adjust. He took two giant steps in toward home plate and extended his glove into the air. The ball fell into it, and Shawn squeezed it tight with two hands, continuing to look up at the sky as he started to sprint in toward the rest of his team gathering on the infield.

All of the McMaster's players were hugging behind the mound, but then one by one, then two and three, and the rest all found Shawn and hugged him. He disappeared under a pile of McMaster's uniforms. They hooted and hollered, rubbed heads and tossed hats, hugged and cheered and cried. They had done it. They had beaten Al's Everything Shop. Shawn had beaten Al Muldoon.

Muldoon leaned on the wall of the dugout, watching the celebration while his team consoled each other, untied their cleats, and put away their bats and gloves. Shawn looked into the Al's dugout, to make eye contact with Muldoon, to take more joy from his pain. But Muldoon didn't pout, didn't cry or curse. Instead, he looked out at Shawn with the biggest of grins, and without moving his torso, pointed his chin out toward the bulldozer beyond the right field fence. He, then, reached into his jacket pocket, pulled out the key for the Winner's Locker Room, and hung it on the fence. Then, he picked up his things, and without saying a word to his team, left the dugout and walked into the darkness.

Shawn stepped away from his team, his team, which was still hugging, laughing and celebrating, and

337

looked out toward right field. Then he looked up at Greta, who was already looking at him, crying. The game had ended exactly how they wanted it to, except for one thing. It ended. The last game, the last Final Exam at McMaster Field. Ever. Shawn's teammates and the rest of the crowd somehow tapped into the feeling that the two McMasters were experiencing, and the noise shrunk, like somebody turned the volume dial on a radio from six down to one. The celebration changed from that of a wedding to that of a funeral.

Shawn walked over and grabbed the key to the winner's locker room. Then, he turned to walk up into the crowd to find his mother, but two opposing players blocked his path.

"That was the greatest catch I've ever seen, and in the most important game," said the Russian Rake, extending his hand toward Shawn. Shawn shook his hand and nodded his head in thanks.

"You play the game well, McMaster. Stick around this time, and keep playing it," said Mac Green, who slapped Shawn on the shoulder. The two smiled at Shawn, then disappeared into their dugout.

The rest of the McMaster's team was heading into the restaurant for a celebratory meal. Shawn jogged up the bleachers to find his mother waiting for him. They walked toward each other, right into a long embrace. "Daddy is very proud right now."

Shawn said nothing, just sobbed on his mother's shoulder. They stood there for minutes, the moment perfect except for one thing.

85

The team devoured burgers and fries, and meatloaf sandwiches with mashed potatoes. Not to mention tons of ice cream sundaes. Shawn had his share, but every few minutes, he would scan the restaurant, peek at the front door, glance into the parking lot to look for her. Nothing.

The crowd had gone, the staff was cleaning up the kitchen, and Greta flopped into the seat across from Shawn. She dried her dry hands on a towel, and Shawn spun the key to the Winner's Locker Room on his finger. "I have to go in there."

"Are you sure?" asked Greta.

"Definitely. The winner gets that locker room. And even if it is just for one night, McMaster's is the winner. And a McMaster will sit behind the coach's desk. Grandpa did it, and so did Dad. Now, I will too."

"I suppose."

"Darn right, you suppose," said Shawn, feigning anger. He drained the rest of his coffee, winked at his mother, kissed her on the cheek, and walked out of the restaurant.

The field lights were still on. Some of it leaked out of the bowl that was McMaster's Field, onto the front of the restaurant, into the parking lot, or beyond the outfield fences. But most of it stayed on the field, greening the grass, illuminating the dirt, glinting off the metal fences and the tops of the dugouts. Shawn put his hand on the power switch on the side of the building, but looked down at the field. This would be the last time these lights would be turned off. He took a deep breath, and pulled the switch down, darkening the field, but turning on the stars. Sometimes, things are right in front of your eyes, even if you can't see them. Shawn squinted. He could make out the field below, the infield dirt and the outfield grass. The outfield fence and the scoreboard. Something big, yellow, and ugly off in the distance.

He turned and walked around the side of the building, and unlocked the door to the locker room. It was pretty much as he remembered it, save a few minor changes Muldoon had made. Pictures of the past nine Final Exam winners framed and hung on the wall. Shawn glanced at them, walking past them, Muldoon in each one with that crap-tasting grin. Shawn dumped into the chair, and put his feet up on the desk, rocking himself back and forth, back and forth. He closed his eyes and thought of his father, and his father's father. He thought about the field and the restaurant, and their house. Most people were sad about the field and the restaurant. Shawn and Greta were too. But they were also losing their home. Shawn opened his eyes and found Muldoon in one of the pictures, grinning that grin. It pissed Shawn off, and he rocked faster and farther back, until he felt something tap him on the head.

It was a key. Hanging on the wall, a rather large key, on a large ring, like something you would see hanging in a jail in an old western. Shawn pulled it off the hook and held it in his hand. What could that be for?

Then it came to Shawn, all at once, and it whitened and opened his eyes wide; and it slammed his feet on the ground. He stood up and charged toward the door. "No, Larry," he said to the empty locker room, "not refuse the key. *Fuse*. Key. This is the key to the fuse box!"

86

October 1, 2013 - 8:49 am

October picked up where September left off, the sky an impossible blue, a crisp, clean backdrop for the changing leaves. The folks of Quail gathered at the McMaster property for the public auction. They were telling stories, not only from The Final Exam last night, but games from the recent past, and not so recent. Larry plodded down the bleachers, taking in McMaster Field from every elevation he could before finding a seat close to the bottom, two rows above the dugout on the first base side of the field.

District Justice Cahill wandered between foul and fair territory on the first base side, two or three steps out of the left-handed batter's box. The bleachers were filling up, but not as full as last night. In a few minutes, all eyes would be looking toward home plate. But unlike last night, everybody knew the how this would end.

Larry looked at his watch: eight-fifty-one. He still had nine minutes, or was it eight, to find what he had been looking for the past ten years. Once the clock struck nine, the McMaster property was no longer the McMaster property. Larry reached into his chest pocket and pulled out the laminated corner of paper that he had toted around with him, down to the field, up to the restaurant, even into town. 'Last of the third,' a phrase he had read, uttered, yelled, thought about, cried about, complained about so many times. What in the world did it mean? He knew Muldoon was about to sweep in and buy the property, but could he at least know what the four-word phrase meant? He would have to live with letting the McMasters down, with not granting the dying wish of his best friend, with not taking care of his family. But could he go to his grave at least knowing the answer to this riddle?

341

Just a few minutes before nine and the villain of the day pulled into the McMaster parking lot. Soon to be the Muldoon parking lot. He marched past everybody standing outside the restaurant, which was closed for the day. Past the folks looking at the plaques, the flag pole and electrical box for one last time. Down the steps, past all the people in the bleachers telling stories about games they had watched here, the meals they had eaten here, and time they had spent here with boyfriends, girlfriends, husbands, wives, children, and grandchildren. Muldoon sat in the front row, right in front of Cahill.

Seconds before nine, Cahill addressed the crowd. "Well, I suppose we can get started," he said, as if he were getting ready to show a movie to a crowd that had seen it hundreds of times before. The stories stopped, the laughter stopped, and the people of Quail became as still as the sky. Cahill opened his mouth to speak.

"Hold on just a second there, Justice Cahill," interrupted Shawn, arriving at the top of the bleachers. "I have something here that you need to see."

Larry watched Shawn walk down the steps holding what appeared to be most of a scorebook sheet. Larry blinked, then blinked again, then shook his head. Squeezed his eyes tight, then opened them... And when he did, Shawn was still holding that sheet.

Shawn stopped and looked at Larry. "Would you happen to have that ripped sheet of paper you carry around with you?"

"Of course I do, Shawn. Of course I do!" Larry walked up the bleachers toward Shawn, waving the laminated sheet. He handed it to Shawn, who held the two pieces of paper together, pieces that had been separated for ten years. Larry leaned on the railing at the top of the steps, trying to look relaxed, but mostly to keep from falling down, from passing out.

342

"Justice Cahill, may I read something to you before you, um, continue?" asked Shawn.

Relief washed over Cahill's face. "You bet."

Muldoon had stood up, facing Shawn, arms crossed, but the shit-eating grin had disappeared. Shawn raised his voice for all to hear, and read from the two sheets puzzled together, which now looked like this:

"The Last Will and Testament
            of Wilbur Ryan McMaster
      The third

                        My body is failing, but my mind is
fine
                        I hereby leave the McMaster property
and everything
                        on it and all the monies associated with
it to my son
                        Billy and/or his wife Greta and/or their
son Shawn."

Muldoon slumped back into his seat. Then his eyes got wide, and he started to say something to Cahill. But Cahill's beefy palm stopped him. "Shawn, is it signed?"

"Yessir. Lemme show you." Shawn paraded down the bleachers, gripping the reunited scoresheet tightly. He handed it to Cahill, who made a show of investigating the paperwork. But the enormous smile on his face told everybody that there would be no public auction today, or ever.

Cahill stepped up the bleachers as quickly as his legs could carry that body, and hugged Greta, who was standing at the top of the steps. He whispered something in her ear, then stepped aside.

"The restaurant is now open!" yelled Greta. "Everything is half price today," she said as she hustled toward the front door.

Shawn hopped up the bleachers toward Larry, taking two steps at a time. He stepped right up to the old man, grabbed him by the shoulders, and looked him dead in the eye, "Fuse. Key. Fuse box and key. Not refuse the key." Shawn pointed over to the flagpole.

"I don't understand," said Larry, his face looking slightly confused, but still mostly relieved and completely elated.

"I went into the winner's locker room last night and found a key. And as I held it in my hand, it just hit me. How many damn times have we all walked past that thing in the last ten years? I took the padlock off the electrical box and there it was; the ripped edge was right up against the side of the box. Grandpa must have stuffed it in there to hide it."

Larry smiled. "From Muldoon, I'm sure."

"Yeah, that makes sense. Grandpa probably wanted to hide the whole thing in there, but left some of it hanging out, so he ripped it off and gave it to you so you could find it."

And in that moment, Larry realized that while he didn't find the will, he looked into his best friend DJ's eyes and knew that he found something so much better.

87

October 5, 2013 - 8:57 am

Shawn was on his third cup of coffee when he slid his breakfast plates to the side, making room for her hands in front of him. She sat across from him and smiled. Just smiled.

"What is it, Mom?" Shawn asked, returning a smile of his own.

"Nothing, I suppose.... Just good to have a McMaster man around. Permanently."

Shawn pulled the dishtowel away from his mother and took both of her hands in his. "I'm here now," Shawn said, and he meant it. It was his plan to stick around, to play ball, to do the books, to rake the field and mow the grass, to wash some dishes, to play baseball. "And if I am going to live in the in-law-quarters, I am going to have to stock the refrigerator and the shelves with some stuff, don't you think?"

"I believe you're right. Did you get enough to eat?" Greta smirked at the two empty breakfast plates.

Shawn looked at his cell phone. "I'm good until eleven-fifteen, maybe even eleven-thirty, Mom." He let go of his mother's hands, rose from his chair, leaned across the table, and kissed her on the forehead. "I'm off to the supermarket." He walked quickly toward the door. Then stopped, turned to Greta and said, "I'll be back in an hour or two."

Greta dried her dry hands on a dishtowel. "I know you will."

The parking lot at the Eden Market in Quail was packed, as was typical for a Saturday morning... Mid-morning, the sun was rising through wispy layers of gray and white autumn clouds, stamped on the background of

345

blue. A familiar face was exiting as Shawn was ready to enter. "Sir Larry, what are you up to?"

"I needed milk, so I went to get milk. And now, I am carrying it to my car," Larry said with a wink.

"Indeed you are, Larry, indeed you are." The two separated, Shawn stepping toward the entrance, Larry toward the parking lot. "Have a good day, Larry Last."

"No promises, but I won't go down without a fight."

Shawn wiggled a shopping cart free from the nested queue inside the automatic doors. He sauntered toward the produce, taking note of the soreness in his quads and the middle of his back. Twenty-two certainly was not eighteen. But that post-game soreness always hurt so good, especially after a victory.

"My word," said a voice from across the way, "that strut.... Does he own this store?" It was Chuck.

"Own this store? My friend, this guy owns all of Quail after the other night's performance," said Dusty.

Then Chuck said, in a small print, end of commercial speed voice, "Technically, Shawn-only-owns-the-small-part-of-Quail-not-owned-by-Albert-Muldoon. But still, what I wouldn't do to, just once, borrow his toothbrush."

"Chuck," said Dusty, into his cell phone shaped microphone, "that notion is more disturbing than picture three-forty-one on your cell phone."

"Thank you for not bringing up four-ninety-six."

"Trying to keep this morning rated R."

Shawn turned a hard left against the will of the vibrating wheels of his shopping cart. He watched the left front wheel shimmy back and forth, chuckling at the sound it made. "The microphones really never shut off with you two, do they?"

"Not when we are in the presence of greatness," said Chuck.

The next words out of Shawn's mouth were going to be: Greatness that missed that fly ball in left and almost cost us the game? But instead, he said, "It was pretty cool to catch the fly ball for the last out."

Then Dusty asked through his nose, "Was it pretty cool to make the greatest catch in the history of McMaster Field? In the history of Quail County? Maybe even the history of extreme northern, south central Pennsylvania?"

"Yeah, I guess, but it hurt my boobs." Shawn massaged his own chest.

Chuck jumped back in, "This man most certainly does not have boobs, but if he did, they would have stayed tucked neatly in his bra, showing just the perfect amount of cleavage, even when diving through the air."

"Even after crash landing, Chuck?"

"Even after crash landing, Dusty."

Shawn shook his head, coaxed his cart back in the direction of the produce, and decided to ignore Chuck's commentary on his eastward-bound buttocks, flattering though they were.

Aisle by aisle, Shawn compared and chose, keeping some items, putting the others back. He spent several minutes in front of the various types of apples, testing their weights, sampling their scents, choosing the ones he would most like to eat. He immersed himself in the different styles and brands of pasta, whole wheat or regular, rotini or spaghetti. He chose a few different ones with which to stock his small pantry. Sauce also. Two marinara, one vodka.

He excused himself when he passed in front of other customers, and fought the urge to duck his head, and instead made eye contact when crossing paths with a stranger saying, "good morning," or "have a good day." He examined each aisle, reading the informational signs, finding everything he was looking for. But every so often, he would look up over an apple, look past a box of whole grain cereal, look through a bottle of translucent, yellow household cleaner, to see if there was anybody he knew walking by. Occasionally, he could pick out a feature, the texture of hair, the color of eyes, the muscle in an upper arm. But never all together, never all in one.

The carriage was full, bags and boxes, plastic and cardboard all the way up to the edges, and mounding even higher in the middle. Shawn heaved the cart around the final corner after picking up milk and orange juice, and carefully balancing them on Mount McMaster.

Darn, one thing he forgot, one of those shower puffy things to lather up with. He slowed the momentum of his cart and pulled it off to the side in front of the bakery, parking it like a trucker would an eighteen wheeler. He went down the toiletry aisle, past the facial scrubs, not quite to the shaving accessories, across from the shower gels. There were a few types of puffy things. The typical puffy things, in an assortment of colors, and a newer kind that had an abrasive side. That seemed excessive, so he picked up two of the normal, old-fashioned puffy things. One red, one blue, trying to decide the perfect color.

"Shower loofah," said a familiar, female voice from behind him. "Definitely female, knowwhatImean?"

Made in the USA
Charleston, SC
12 January 2017